REVIEWS OF OTHER CHUCK BARRETT BOOKS

"*The Savannah Project* signals the arrival of a new member to the thriller genre. Chuck Barrett. The tale contains all of the danger, treachery, and action a reader could wish for. The intrigue comes from all directions, slicing and stitching with precision. A worthy debut from an exciting talent."
—**Steve Berry**, *New York Times* bestselling author

"From the tree-lined streets of Savannah to the mossy stones of an ancient Irish castle, *The Savannah Project* weaves a fast moving tale of murder, mystery and suspense. Chuck Barrett has written a winner here. A must-read novel for thriller lovers."
—**William Rawlings**, bestselling author of *The Mile High Club*

"*The Toymaker* is a fun, fast moving thriller with plenty of gadgets and a lot of action."
—**Phillip Margolin**, *New York Times* bestselling author of *Capitol Murder*

"*The Savannah Project* is a bona fide suspense thriller. Rife with abundant mystery and intrigue, author Chuck Barrett's standout tale takes the reader on a tortuous path of all-engrossing action and adventure. A highly recommended instant classic."
—Apex Reviews

"*The Savannah Project* is an exciting thriller that will prove hard to put down."
—The Midwest Book Review

A taut, pulse-pounding thriller."
—*ForeWord* Clarion Reviews

"Chuck Barrett's *The Savannah Project* grabs your undivided attention from the very first sentence and does not let you truly exhale until the very last, chilling-to-the core line…"
—Olivera Baumgartner-Jackson/Reader Views

"*The Toymaker* provides everything a thriller reader would want. Characters that jump from the page, a deep plot that feels timely and current, and all the action you've come to expect from Mr. Barrett. I found the book a page-turner and as always, filled with tidbits and information that taught me things I did not know. Mr. Barrett's

exhausting research shows in every scene, and his pace and plot development held me enthralled from the first page to the last."
—**Richard Hale**, Author of *Near Death* and *Frozen Past*

"Having read and enjoyed *The Savannah Project*, Chuck Barrett's first novel, I was eager to read more. *The Toymaker* is great! I was captivated by the suspense, the characters, the fast pace, and the plot twists and surprises. I particularly marveled at Barrett's ability to explain and educate about real spy toys on the cutting edge of technology in a way that makes them understandable, without getting in the way of the driving story and thrilling tension."
—Artie Lynnworth—author of *Slice the Salami: Tips For Life and Leadership*

BREACH
OF
POWER

Also by Chuck Barrett

The Savannah Project
The Toymaker

BREACH
OF
POWER

CHUCK BARRETT

SWITCHBACK PRESS

Breach of Power is a work of fiction. Names, characters, places, and incidents are products of the author's imagination or are used fictitiously. Any resemblance to actual events, locales, or persons, living or dead, is coincidental.

Cover design by Mary Fisher Design, LLC, http://www.maryfisherdesign.com

FIRST EDITION

ISBN: 978-0-9885061-0-7
Library of Congress Control Number: **2012953611**

Barrett, Chuck.
    Breach of Power / Chuck Barrett
    FICTION: Thriller/Suspense/Mystery

Published by Switchback Press

www.switchbackpress.com

For Debi.

"Nearly all men can stand adversity. But if you want to test a man's character, give him power."

—*Abraham Lincoln*

PROLOGUE

Zugspitze, Germany
February 1946

When the Austrians came for him, he knew what they wanted.

The journal.

He could never let them have it. That would be his death sentence.

He ran down the corridor, grabbed a coat from the resort's coat closet, tucked the journal inside an interior pocket, and buttoned it tight. He slipped on his gloves and ventured out into the storm.

Howling wind buffeted against his body. Ice crystals ripped at his exposed flesh like tiny shards of glass. Snow crunched beneath his boots. With each laborious step, the deeper drifts swallowed his legs to his knees. Without goggles his eyes stung and his eyelashes froze. Ice clung to his brows. He wiped it away with the back of his glove.

The 1917 Waterbury watch his father gave him, his only possession other than the clothes on his back, read 1:00. His father had carried it during World War I. Now it was his only heirloom. The last evidence that he had a past.

The blizzard, already raging for two days, was forecast to pound the area for another thirty-six hours. It had shut down the recently commandeered Schneefernerhaus Hotel and Resort atop Zugspitze, Germany's highest mountain. The United States Army closed the resort hotel over 24 hours ago and all guests and non-essential personnel were sent down from the summit. Only a skeleton crew remained and were scattered throughout the resort. The only transportation from the mountaintop, a twenty-year-old cable car, was closed due to high winds, forcing him to escape on foot.

His first plan was to retreat across the sloping terrain of the Zugspitzplatt, a plateau below the summit of Zugspitze, and down through Reintal Valley to Garmisch. Ages ago, the Zugspitzplatt was carved by glaciers, which left in its wake a plateau with hundreds of limestone caves.

The Zugspitzplatt was a longer route, but its slopes offered a better alternative than the treacherous northeast face of Zugspitze. Even though he'd scaled that mountain face numerous times, it had been in warmer weather, and he'd never descended it. Under existing conditions, with gale force winds and icy rock faces, escape in that direction would be perilous, if not borderline suicidal.

In the howling snowstorm he trudged eastward through the crusty snowpack across the Zugspitzplatt when he spotted three Austrians fifty meters in front of him. Each man carried a rifle. He turned south, only to see more Austrians moving in his direction. He was trapped.

Like a loose cow on the prairie, he was being herded back to the hotel. Slowly. Deliberately.

He had two choices. Surrender, and surely die. Or take his chances descending the north face of Zugsptize in the raging blizzard, where he'd probably die anyway. He wouldn't give those bastards the satisfaction, he thought. There was a slim chance he could make it, and right now, that was better than no chance at all.

Most importantly, she wouldn't have the book.

He circumnavigated the hotel and fled for the summit.

He reached the vertex of Zugspitze exhausted, voices behind him barely audible over the wind whipping across the mountain's peak. He leaned into the wind and let the thought of keeping the journal from her drive his determination.

Descending the northeast face of Zugspitze offered no shelter from the squall. In fact, just the opposite, it kept him in the brunt of the storm's fury. The bitter cold wore on him with each passing minute. Each time he stopped to rest, he thought he heard voices above him mixed with the whirlpool of wind whipping and swirling through the jagged rocks. The threat forced him to keep moving, descending the treacherous decline toward the Höllentalferner glacier, where he knew he could make faster progress. But first, he still had to descend the *klettersteig*, or climbing path, a near vertical rock face outfitted with cables, ropes, stemples, and ladders. It was intended solely for climbing—not descending—and he knew it would be covered with ice.

When he reached the precipice, he looked down at the sheet of ice blanketing his path and knew the descent would be perilous.

And foolish.

He studied the path down the mountain and located each stemple, a wooden or iron peg wedged into the rock, and gauged how much ice had accumulated on the wall.

The next four hours were spent in a slow, meticulous descent. Grasping the frozen guide rope with one hand, he lowered himself to the next stemple, knocking it clear of ice with his boots before putting his full weight on it. His gloves, shredded against the jagged rocks, left little for protection and warmth. His fingers were numb. How he longed to return to the hot and humid South, where winters in his small hometown in northwestern South Carolina were mild in comparison to the brutal winters of Germany.

He'd long since forgotten about the men chasing him when it occurred to him that he hadn't heard their voices in over three hours. Maybe they gave up and turned back.

Fifty feet above the glacier he caught his first glimpse of the barren ice field through the raging snowstorm. Thirty more minutes, he thought, perhaps forty-five, to descend to the glacier. He stopped to catch his breath. His fingers throbbed from the cold so he cupped his hands and blew hot breath into them in a vain attempt to stimulate blood circulation to his fingertips.

Small rocks and ice pelted him from above, and he knew the woman and her Austrian thugs were still in pursuit. He tripled his efforts, traversing the steep decline faster, not taking the time to clean the ice from the stemples before each step.

Twenty feet above the glacier a wooden stemple broke. With one hand still clutching the guide rope, he swung away from the stemples and crashed against the icy rock face. A shot rang out and simultaneously a shock wave pounded his chest radiating upward through his shoulder and into his arm. Too painful for him to cling to the safety line, his hand slipped free and he plummeted toward the glacier, bouncing off a rock outcropping on the way down. A thick snowdrift next to the icy rock face cushioned his fall.

He grabbed at the searing pain. Underneath his heavy coat, he felt his warm blood spreading across his shirt.

He'd been shot.

He heard men yelling. He looked up and saw three faint silhouettes move across the snow-covered, icy crag. He pulled himself to his feet and sprinted across the glacial ice field. And away from his pursuers.

The man shouted again, then he heard the blast from a rifle. A patch of ice next to him exploded. He turned around to see where the shot came from but the snowstorm had swallowed the side of the mountain and the rock face was no longer visible.

Thank goodness he made it to the ice field. Although not level, it still allowed him to move much faster in the raging storm.

He was on the Höllentalferner glacier's accumulation zone, where each year's buildup of snow and ice fueled its downhill movement. The northeast facing notch in Zugspitze provided a perfect scoop to collect and add several feet of fresh snow and ice to the zone. The more the accumulation of snow, the easier it was to traverse the glacier's ice field. This blizzard alone would provide enough supply for several years' melt.

Without warning, the ice broke beneath his feet.

When he fell, his waist pounded against the lip on the opposite side of the crevasse, leaving his feet dangling in air. His fingers clawed at the snow and ice. He dug his fingernails in to keep from being swallowed by the mighty glacier. But he couldn't find a hold and he felt his body slide deeper into the crevasse, as if something was pulling him from below.

His fingertips gripped at the icy ledge, temporarily stopping his fall. Suddenly his grip broke free, and he was once again falling. He bounced off the cavern wall and caught a quick glimpse of the hard ice floor thirty feet below rushing up to meet him. He extended his arm to break his fall and felt is snap on impact.

Pain raked through his body.

He lay on his back trying to push through the daze. He couldn't move. At the bottom of the crevasse, deep inside the bowels of the Höllentalferner glacier, his body raked with pain. His brain raced through a self-diagnostic, interpreting every signal his body sent. The bullet felt like a hot ember burning inside his torso. With every heartbeat, every pulse of blood, his body screamed.

Minutes passed and his mind slowly cleared. When it did, panic moved in.

The Austrians.

Painfully, he rolled over. His first thought was that he couldn't let the woman and her men find him. He pulled himself as far under a ledge as he could to hide from the opening above him. With his right arm, he pushed himself into a seated position against the icy wall of the cavern. His left arm throbbed. Glancing down he noticed his elbow was twisted in the wrong direction.

He caught his breath, unbuttoned the top of the coat, and looked at his wound. The side of his shirt was soaked in blood. Fresh blood oozed from the gunshot wound.

As the minutes passed, he wondered what had happened to his pursuers.

At least he was still alive.

Focus.

He surveyed the cavern, searching for any sign of escape but the blue-green walls of ice fully encompassed him. For the first time since he'd plummeted to the ice floor, he felt the bitter cold overtaking him. Next to him lay a 6-foot pile of snow and broken ice, all that remained of the hidden ice bridge that collapsed under his weight. Although the dark sky above was unleashing its fury, the cavern was tranquil, and he came to the realization that his only escape was straight up.

He thought he heard voices yelling through the howl of the blizzard. He tensed but then the sounds subsided and he relaxed. The men with their rifles had been high on the ridge above him when he fell. Surely, the gale force winds and blowing snow had erased his tracks by now. The glacier was so expansive that, in this blizzard, it would be a fluke if they located where he fell. He couldn't take any chances. He knew, when the weather cleared, she would send the Austrians to find him and retrieve the book.

He pulled out the journal. His blood had stained its leather binding. A hole perforated its center, cover to cover, where the bullet passed through it and into his torso. Perhaps the only reason he was still alive. He understood why someone would kill for it; he just didn't think he would be the target.

He opened the journal and dug around for the pencil he kept tucked inside. Time for one final entry. Identify his killer and hide the book before his hunters found their quarry.

After several minutes he heard shouts followed by a rumble.

The glacier trembled. A sound he recognized.

The blizzard had dumped several feet of snow over the past two days and the vibrations from the rifle blast had loosened its grip on the mountain.

Now, gravity would do the rest.

No need to hide the book, he thought, the avalanche would soon do that for him. He tucked it back inside his coat, buttoned it up, closed his eyes, and waited.

At first it was only a trickle of snow and ice finding its way into the crevasse. Seconds later, a turbulent mass pounded on top of him like a hundred trucks had dumped their loads. The cavern filled with snow, packing it tighter around him. Instinctively he clutched his coat and felt for the book underneath.

His lover had betrayed him and his fate was sealed—all because of the journal.

He had one final thought.

At least she won't have it.

Major Don Adams smiled.

CHAPTER 1

August 11—Present Day
12:15 A. M.

Jake's first visit to the West Wing of the White House promised to be a memorable one. When he and Francesca Catanzaro arrived, a guard escorted them to the Executive Conference Room where their boss, Elmore Wiley, was already waiting.

While in the Navy, Jake had worked at the Pentagon under, then Admiral now CIA Director, Scott Bentley and found the Pentagon didn't live up to its menacing reputation. In and of it, the Pentagon was a small city with over 700,000 square feet and 24,000 military and civilian employees, most with over-inflated egos who always seemed in a rush to get somewhere.

The Situation Room in the White House was the opposite—intimidating. Created in 1961 by John F. Kennedy after the Bay of Pigs fiasco, the Situation Room was a 5000 square foot complex designed to address the nation's business, as well as the world's, on a real time basis.

He now sat in the same room where the President of the United States and the President's advisors met on a routine basis, the room where many of the most important decisions of the Presidency were made.

Command Central for the National Security Council.

Despite calming reassurances from Wiley, Jake felt like he did on a first date. Nervous yet excited knowing he and

Francesca were about to have a top-secret midnight meeting with the President of the United States.

Jake's first encounter with Francesca was in San Sebastian, Spain when she passed him vital information in his relentless pursuit of an al Qaeda cell handler. That operation ultimately led to his current employment as an emissary for the Greenbrier Fellowship under the direction of Elmore Wiley, a seventy-one year old man affectionately referred to as *The Toymaker*. He was a man who had spent his entire adult life supporting covert operations for every intelligence agency and Special Forces branch in this country, as well as many foreign nations. When asked, he claimed his business was radio frequency and microwave emission technology. What he really did was make "toys for spies." A go-to man for espionage gadgetry.

"Mr. Wiley, can you tell us what this is about?" Jake drummed his fingers on the conference table.

"I would if I knew, Jake." Elmore Wiley did his characteristic hair swipe. First the left hand followed by the right, front to back across his hair, and always in that order. Followed by pushing his metal-framed glasses higher on the bridge of his nose. "Problem is, I don't know any more than you do. I was asked by the President to be here by midnight and bring my two most trusted employees."

Francesca tossed her dark red hair over her shoulder and smiled at Jake. "That would be us."

The door to the conference room opened and instinctively the three of them stood. No coaching required. Whether you agreed with the current President's political views or not, it was a fundamental sign of courtesy and respect for the highest political office and the individual who held it.

And besides, who didn't like this President?

Jake was about to meet the only President in his lifetime to reduce deficit spending and squarely turn around the country's economy. Only three years into a first term and this President had actually cut the federal deficit by 30% simply by sticking to the platform outlined during the primary elections.

The country wanted a break from the same old political rhetoric of past administrations. This former Secretary of State, now President of the United States, gave the voters what was promised before the election—change. A positive shift in philosophy fostered by strong character and moral integrity. The President's *No-Bull* policies cut spending and government waste while finding creative avenues to raise revenues from previously untapped resources. Markets were up, unemployment down, consumer confidence and spending had increased, which had the economy booming again.

A President with balls.

The first person through the door was the President's Chief of Staff, Evan Makley. Makley was a 47 year-old career political assistant. A man at the apex of his career, he was tall and thin and his dark hair was streaked with wisps of gray at the temples. Tonight he seemed overdressed in his tailored Armani suit. His outwardly go-getter style and aggressive personality had helped him in political life, overcoming personal tragedies, and propelling him inexplicably toward retaining his Chief of Staff job with the President's almost certain reelection.

During his three years as Chief of Staff, Makley had endured a very messy and public divorce. The media sharks had a feeding frenzy over the divorce proceedings that left him virtually homeless, with minimal visitation rights with his two daughters, and on the brink of financial disaster. His rise to the top hadn't come without a price.

Four feet behind Makley walked the Commander In Chief, Rebecca Rudd, the first woman President of the United States. Tonight, the world's most powerful woman wasn't wearing her usual attire for public appearances. She was dressed in jeans, a long sleeve white collared shirt covered by a charcoal vest, and black flats. Even behind her casual appearance she presented herself as competent and polished, a woman of unwavering integrity and passion. Short in stature but admired and respected by most of the world's leaders. The press nicknamed her *No-Bull Becky*, which the public adored. So much so that she had held an impressive 85% approval rating for over two years.

She often quoted Abraham Lincoln to the press, her favorite quote was: *Be sure you put your feet in the right place, then stand firm.* And Rudd walked the talk.

She pushed past Makley toward Wiley and embraced him with a hug followed by a kiss on the cheek. "Good to see you again, Elmore."

Jake was surprised by the informal and intimate appearance of their relationship and wondered how long they'd known each other.

In her flat shoes she was shorter than she looked on TV; must have been the heels Jake concluded. She had graying blonde hair and sparkling blue eyes. She looked fit and toned and her voice, warm and friendly.

"Madam President," Wiley pointed across the table. "As you requested, my two most trusted emissaries. Jake Pendleton," he swept his arm to the left, "and Francesca Catanzaro."

"Mr. Wiley has spoken highly of both of you. Please excuse the lateness of the hour but it was unavoidable." Rudd leaned down and pressed a button on her console. Two flat-screen TV monitors rose from a cherry hardwood table at the end of the conference room. "I trust you understand this is strictly off-the-record and classified."

Jake and Francesca nodded.

"What you are about to see and hear carries with it issues so sensitive that not even my National Security Council is privy to it." Rudd placed her finger on another button. "Any questions before we get started?"

CHAPTER 2

Iron Staircase "Leiter"
Höllental Valley, Germany

Ashley Regan sat on a rock at the base of the Leiter, an iron peg staircase on a steep rock wall; the first real obstacle of her annual hike to the summit of Zugspitze. She pulled her climbing harness and helmet from her backpack and placed them down beside her. Her partner, Sam Connors, was still a hundred feet from the base.

"Come on, Connors." Regan shouted. "Get your ass in gear. We don't have all day."

"Yes we do." Connors yelled back. "And by my calculations, we're ahead of schedule."

Regan knew Connors was right; they were ahead of schedule by at least an hour over last year's hike to the summit.

She and Connors met two years ago at this very spot. Connors had been resting when Regan approached and started a conversation. The two hiked together that day to the summit and by nightfall, Regan knew their newfound friendship was destined to turn into a romantic involvement. Just like last year, they were celebrating the anniversary of their first meeting by scaling the same mountain on the same date.

When the two returned to the States after their first meeting, Connors, a work-from-home day-trader, moved from Atlanta to Charleston, South Carolina where Regan was a CPA with a prominent accounting firm. The physical attraction was strong between Regan and Connors. The 31-year old Regan had two inches and ten pounds on the younger 27-year old Connors. By most standards, Ashley Regan was considered tall for a woman, 5'9", tanned with shoulder length thick brown hair and hazel eyes. Sam Connors, her polar opposite, had short, dirty blond hair, fair skin, and a prominent nose. Both enjoyed hiking and rock climbing and stayed in excellent physical condition.

Initially Regan wasn't sure they'd get to hike to the summit since the forecast called for rain, but the couple geared up anyway and left the Höllental parking area at 5:00 a.m.—right on schedule. Regan was intent on sticking to a schedule. Something she valued in her profession as an accountant that spilled over into her personal life.

The first part of the hike through the Höllental Gorge was along an easy footpath to the base of Höllental Klamm. The early morning sky was still waking, so headlamps helped them navigate through the dark, narrow gorge. A light drizzle coated the rock and droplets spit down on her as she walked.

Connors was a fair weather hiker and wanted to turn back but Regan insisted they push forward or they would regret it when the weather broke.

As she predicted, by the time she reached the top of the gorge, the sky had cleared and Regan could see their destination in the far distance—the cross at the Zugspitze summit. Regan and Connors passed the hikers' hut at Höllentalanger without stopping. Many hikers wanted to get an early jump on the mountain and hiked to the hut the night before in order to shave a couple of hours and 600 meters vertical climb off their hiking day. The warning sign next to the hut said the Randkluft, the crevasse that formed between the ice of the glacier and the sun-warmed rock cliff, was very difficult and dangerous.

Regan hated that Connors was a wary climber and not the risk taker she was. But Connors was the cautious type, always gathering information before making a decision. At work and at play. Regan, on the other hand, jumped in headfirst and lived for the thrill. Risk taking and danger was what it was all about. Which made Connors the perfect compliment. Sam Connors kept her grounded. It seemed neither of their personalities matched their respective occupations—a conservative day-trader and a thrill-seeking accountant.

Connors caught up to Regan and sat down on the rock next to her. "I'm going to rest for a few minutes and psych myself up a bit."

Regan cinched her harness, picked up her helmet, and stood. "Just remember, as long as your harness is fastened to the cable, you can't fall."

"Yeah, yeah, I know." Connors slipped a leg into the harness. "It's just having nothing under me on the rock face except those small iron pegs bothers me. And you know I don't like heights."

Regan let out a short laugh and looked into Sam's blue eyes. "You're such a wimp."

† † †

White House Situation Room

Jake watched President Rebecca Rudd's facial expression change. Her furrowed brow and downturned frown spoke volumes of the gravity of her dilemma. She pressed another button on her console and the large monitor on the left flickered then started playing a video. The images were washed out, grainy, and in black and white. Or at least it looked black and white.

"Oops, almost forgot. Evan, get the lights, please." President Rudd paused the video while Makley dimmed the lights. "Before I begin I must warn you, this video is violent, sexual, and disturbing."

"We understand, Ms. President," Wiley pointed at Francesca then to Jake, "they can handle it."

The video resumed, it was color but poor quality and the bad lighting in the scene didn't help.

Rudd was right, the video was disturbing and Jake presumed it was filmed somewhere in Southeast Asia. On the large screen in front of him stood a man with his back to the camera; he was older with gray hair, slightly hunched, frail looking, and Caucasian. On her knees in front of him was a young Asian girl performing oral sex on him. By her size and features she couldn't have been more than twelve. They appeared to be in some sort of primitive structure, perhaps a thatch hut, and in the background, a mattress lay on the dirt floor.

"A village orphanage in Vietnam." Rudd said. "Kim Ly. She was thirteen."

"Was?" Jake asked.

"Keep watching."

Jake already felt the rage building inside him. What he was watching made him sick to his stomach. Repulsed by the actions of the old man. How could someone do that to a young girl? Sexual abuse was unforgivable, especially when it involved a child.

The girl pulled back and spoke something in a language Jake assumed was Vietnamese. The man yelled back at her in the same language then hit her on the side of the head. Kim Ly started crying. Her tone sounded as though she was begging. The old man yelled at her again then clutched her hair on both sides of her head and shoved her face into his crotch.

Jake looked at Francesca. She had her hand covering her mouth and a horrified look on her face. He saw a tear roll down her cheek.

Kim Ly pulled away two minutes later and the old man yelled again then hit her in the face. Jake saw the crimson blood trickle down the young girl's face.

"Oh, my God." Francesca grabbed Jake's hand and squeezed.

President Rudd had gone quiet. Jake didn't know if the video had upset her or if she didn't want to minimize the impact the video was having. He assumed the latter since without a doubt, she had seen it before.

Kim Ly clenched her tiny fist and swung, striking the man in the groin. He doubled over, grabbed the small girl, clamped his arthritis-deformed left hand over her throat, and shoved her to the ground. His right hand stretched outward and for the first time since the video began, Jake saw the cane. The man grabbed the cane and started beating the girl, bashing her face and head repeatedly with the hook of the cane.

Kim Ly struggled for fifteen seconds then her small frame went limp.

The man hunched over her for a few moments then, using the cane, pushed himself to his feet, grabbed a rag, and wiped the blood from his cane. The old man stared down at the young girl while he zipped his pants. He tossed the bloody rag on the floor next to Kim Ly's head and turned to leave.

Rudd paused the video.

Jake knew that face. He pulled his hand free from Francesca's grip and balled it into a fist. His own face felt hot and his blood pressure rose as full recognition of the decrepit old man on the screen hit him.

Senator Richard Boden.

Chairman of the Senate Committee of Homeland Security and Governmental Affairs.

The man who, less than a year ago, had ordered his former boss, Director of Central Intelligence Scott Bentley, to fire him from the CIA's Clandestine Service.

The man who had threatened to have Jake thrown in jail.

The same man whose life Jake had saved during a terrorist attack in New York City.

"Boden." Jake blurted. "That son of a bitch."

President Rudd turned around.

"I'm sorry, Ms President." Jake's tone apologetic. "The Senator and I...have—"

"Mr. Pendleton, I'm well aware of your history with Senator Boden," Rudd said, "that's one reason I requested you."

"Requested?" Jake looked at Wiley.

The old man gave nothing away.

"Who is this guy?" Francesca asked.

"That's the sensitive part, Ms Catanzaro." Rudd turned off the video and Makley raised the lights in the room. "Senator Richard Boden has two Purple Hearts from the Vietnam War, he's a decorated war hero, and a recipient of the Medal of Honor."

"Jeez." Francesca looked at Jake. "You know this creep?"

"And on top of all that." Rudd interrupted. "He's the most senior senator on Capitol Hill...and the most influential." Rudd drew a deep breath. "Acting on a tip, I covertly sent two agents to Vietnam to investigate and gather evidence about the allegations. For him or against him, I didn't care. I wanted it handled quickly and quietly. The tipster claimed Boden has been going to Vietnam for sex with young girls for decades. At the time it was taken, this was a live video feed but before my agents could get to the scene, Kim Ly was dead...and Boden was gone."

Wiley, who had been silent since the video started, spoke. "Madam President, how can I...we, be of service?" Wiley did the hair swipe. First the left hand, then the right hand.

"As you probably already guessed." Rudd, perhaps taking Wiley's hair swipe as a subliminal message, ran her fingers through her hair. "Kim Ly was an orphan. She had no family that we could locate. Senator Boden is a powerful man with powerful allies. Allies who paid authorities in Vietnam to look the other way." Rudd paused and drew another deep breath. "This presents me with a moral dilemma, the likes I have never before faced."

"What would you like done?" Wiley asked.

Before Rudd could answer Jake interrupted. "I'd like the chance to take this creep down." Jake thought he saw a suppressed smile flash across the President's face.

"Elmore, I've used your services in the past and I require them again now." Rudd picked up a folder from the conference table and handed it to Wiley. "As you know, the Summit meeting is in a few weeks and our relations in Southeast Asia is at a critical juncture. If this were to become public, it is the type of scandal that could set us back years. Their alliance with us at this time is very important.

"As I said earlier, this meeting is off the books. Only the five of us in this room and the two Secret Service agents know about this video or this incident." President Rebecca Rudd stood and motioned for Wiley, Jake, and Francesca to remain seated. "I won't mince words. I kept the CIA out of it for good reason—too many eyes and ears." She paused and took a deep breath. "I took an oath as leader of this country to uphold justice. Every day I struggle with decisions that are in America's best interest...even if it goes against my personal values. Dammit, I can't believe I'm asking you to do this."

Jake could tell she was struggling with a decision.

She continued. "What I'm about to suggest may seem morally wrong, perhaps a breach of power, but Senator Boden is an evil man. He's been doing this to these young orphan girls for decades. He's a liability to this country and must be stopped." She stepped to the doorway and opened the door. Makley moved behind her. She hesitated, and then turned toward them. "Elmore, there is no official order. It would be a shame though, if Senator Boden were to have an accident...or a fatal health issue."

† † †

Höllental Valley, Germany

Fifteen minutes after Ashley Regan left Sam Connors sitting on the rock at the bottom of the Leiter, she arrived at an almost vertical rock face with an iron cable secured across it called the Brett. When there was no path or ledge to walk on, iron bolts had been anchored into the rock face to serve as steps across the lateral passage. Regan gazed down the slope and saw Sam nearing the top of the Leiter.

"Do you need another rest?" Regan shouted down the iron staircase. "Or can we keep moving forward?"

"Go on, Ashley. I'm right behind you." Connors reached the top of the Leiter and was walking toward Regan. "I'll catch up to you at the glacier."

Regan attached her two umbilical cables from her harness to the iron cable and stepped out onto the first iron peg, moving skillfully across the rock face. She looked back and saw Sam attaching the umbilical to the cable.

She reached the end of the Brett, unhooked her umbilical, and pulled her hiking poles from her backpack. She had fleeting thoughts about waiting for Sam to catch up but knew it wouldn't be too long before they were together at the base of the Höllentalferner glacier. Besides, if the past two years were any indication, it would take Connors a painfully long time to cross the Brett, and Regan was not a patient woman. After the Brett, Regan knew, Sam would have no trouble with the remaining hike to the glacier. All that remained was to follow the trail over the meadows and scree-covered slopes leading to the glacier. Centuries ago the very same meadow was covered by the glacier. Now, recessional moraines deposited by the glacier marked the path from the Brett to the base of the glacier. There, they both could take a needed rest before donning the crampons to walk across the icy glacier to the Klettersteig. From the glacier, the remaining hike was nearly vertical and the most challenging.

Regan reached the base of the Höllentalferner glacier by 9:30 a.m. There were actually three glaciers at Zugspitze but this one, the Höllentalferner, was the only one with a glacial tongue. And at the base of the tongue was a small ice cave carved by the summer's heat. Water on the glacier's surface flowed down through crevasses and fractures in the glacial ice melting out channels called moulins. These moulins transported the water to the base of the glacier helping it slide across the ground beneath. Last year, and the year they met, the ice cave was too small to enter without belly crawling through the ice cold glacial melt. But this year had been a warm summer in the southern mountains of Germany and the glacial tongue revealed an ice cave with an opening five feet in diameter. Large enough to venture inside without getting soaked.

Regan searched down the mountain and located Connors, a tiny speck trudging up the slope. She figured another twenty to thirty minutes before Sam could reach the glacier.

Plenty of time to take a look inside.

Regan stuck her hiking poles into the ground next to the opening forming an X-shaped cross, a signal to Sam that she'd gone inside. She bent over, and crept into the ice cave. At first she wasn't sure how far inside she could go as the blue-green ice walls narrowed around her. At one point the passage constricted until she could go no further without removing her backpack, which she did, pulling it along behind her. She sidestepped through the confining divide, her chest and back both pressing against the ice walls. A large ice room opened in front of her. The temperature had been dropping the deeper she traveled into the cavern but once she entered the chamber, the temperature seemed to plunge. She pulled off her sunglasses and squinted at the glare from the ice. Her eyes soon adjusted and she pushed forward.

She reached the end of the rocky, earthen floor about fifty feet inside the ice cave. Her next steps would be on the ice. She grabbed her crampons from the side of her pack and attached them to her boots.

Ice crunched beneath her boots as she stepped across the solid ice. Ahead another twenty feet, she came to a blockage where the sides of the ice cave had collapsed, almost completely obstructing the path ahead. She considered turning back but her curious nature pushed her forward. She peered through a two-foot diameter hole and saw that the cave continued on as far as she could see. She stared at her watch and counted. She'd been inside seven minutes, which meant Sam was still at least fifteen minutes down the mountain. Five more minutes of exploring then back out with plenty of time to meet Sam at the base of the glacier.

Regan pushed her backpack through the small opening then squeezed through and into the next chamber. She walked forward another two and half minutes, crouching for the last two, when she spotted something sticking out of the ice wall twenty feet ahead. She shivered. Regan knew she needed to leave now to meet Sam but curiosity pushed her toward the brown object sticking out of the ice.

Her inquisitive nature had landed her in hot water on several occasions, both as a child and as an adult. Maybe it was her rebellious nature or her anti-authority attitude, it seemed she was never one to do the right thing and always the first to get in trouble.

Ten feet away she stopped. She rubbed her eyes in disbelief.

A human body.

She'd heard the stories of bodies from ancient times being unearthed by glaciers in this part of the world, but the closer she got the more she realized, this body wasn't that old. Decades, maybe a century, but no older. The clothing was too modern. She could tell the body was a man; the ice had preserved him well with his face still buried behind three inches of ice. He appeared to be sitting when he froze, knees tucked toward his chin, left arm dangling by his side. His right hand was clutching his chest, maybe a heart attack she thought. He was half in, half out of the ice wall. Legs and chest almost completely exposed.

Curiosity, not fear, fueled her excitement and pushed her forward. "What are you doing here?" Ashley said aloud…as if expecting a reply from the frozen man.

She looked at her watch. Sam would have to wait.

"The bigger question is." She said aloud again. "Who are you?"

She reached out and touched his chest. The fabric on the coat was stiff and unyielding and she could see his hand was clutching something underneath his coat. By the crease formed in the coat, she guessed it was a small box or book of some kind.

She pulled on his hand. "May I take a look?"

The ragged glove tore loose from his hand exposing his freeze-dried skin. She tugged again on his hand and it moved slightly away from the coat. She grabbed the top of his coat and tried to unbutton it. The fabric and the button were still frozen together, but pliable.

Most people she knew couldn't stand the thought of touching a dead body. Certainly Sam wouldn't have touched it, just gone in search of help and let someone else handle the situation. But she wasn't like Sam. She was fearless, open to adventure, and full of curiosity. Always in search of a thrill. Always pushing the limits and challenging boundaries. And mischief found her at every juncture. It was her way.

As a child, she was a tomboy and played with frogs, lizards, rat snakes, and garter snakes. To her mother's dismay, she would catch two small green lizards in her backyard in Charleston and let them bite her ear lobes and hang there. It didn't hurt, just pressure, and as long as she kept moving the lizards wouldn't let go. She'd run in the house and yell to her mother to come look at her new earrings. Her mother fell for it every time...or at least pretended to.

She worked the frozen fabric back and forth until she was able to free the top button. She started working on the second button when she heard a distant noise coming from the entrance to the ice cave.

"Ashley? Are you in there?" Sam's voice echoed through the cave.

Regan picked up her pace. She couldn't let Sam know what she was doing without having to listen to another morality lecture on doing the right thing.

"I'll be right out." Regan yelled back. The reverberations of her voice inside the small enclosure made her uncomfortable as small chips of ice fell around her. She wondered if this man crawled up in here and made some sort of noise only to cause the walls of the cave to crash down around him.

She feverishly worked the second button free. "Let's see what you have there." She reached her arm inside his coat. It was cold and damp and for the first time she realized she was touching death...or at least something dead. She let her fingers feel around, deeper inside his coat until they found the item. She felt the edges. Leather, cold and wet. It was a book. She grasped the top and tugged but it wouldn't budge.

"Come on, come on. Let go." She hit the man's chest and felt embarrassed.

Clutching the top of the book, she rocked it from side to side, slowly freeing it from the icy grip of the coat. With an upward pull, the book started moving. Rocking and pulling until she caught the first glimpse of her prize as a corner of the book exposed through the opened buttons near the collar.

"Ashley? What are you doing in here?" Sam Connors was getting closer.

Regan worked it carelessly upward through the coat until she could get a two-handed grip. She grasped each corner of the book and pulled upward with all her might. The book let loose and Regan tumbled backwards onto the ice—book in hand.

"Ashley."

"Dammit, Sam. I'm coming." She eagerly wanted to look inside the book but had no time. Connors would want her to put it back and then let the authorities have it. She found it, it was hers now. She unzipped her backpack, stuffed the book inside, and zipped her pack secure. Then she returned to button up the man's coat.

"Oh my God." Sam's voice was close. "What have you found?"

Ashley turned and saw Sam peering through the opening. "A frozen dead man."

"What are you doing to the body?" Sam Connors pointed to the body. "We should get out of here."

"I was checking for identification, but he's too frozen." She lied. She'd done it so many times. Sam was always trusting and gullible. Ashley gave Sam an impish smile, another trick she learned that always worked. "We'll report it when we get to the summit."

"Let's get out of here." The worry in Sam's tone wasn't lost on Regan. "This place is creepy. I can't believe you found a dead body."

Regan found it hard to contain her excitement, but she knew Sam would complain that the book didn't belong to them. Ashley didn't want to hear it. Finders—keepers. Sam would try to reason with her, say the book was evidence, perhaps it was, but Regan instinctively knew the book had an intriguing story behind it. Maybe it was just wishful thinking, but her meddlesome nature would never allow her to give it up.

Regan slipped her backpack over her shoulder. "Lead the way."

Connors turned and walked back toward the mouth of the cave.

Ashley Regan smiled. The book's existence would remain her secret.

CHAPTER 3

Pointe-à-Pitre, Guadeloupe

Abigail Love had been following Martin and Teresa Kingsley through the streets of Pointe-à-Pitre all morning. The wealthy New Hampshire couple arrived at their Pointe-à-Pitre condominium, one of the many homes they owned around the world, yesterday afternoon after a long layover at the San Juan Airport in Puerto Rico. Love knew because she was on the same flight. The couple, both in their mid-fifties, were here on business. Which is exactly why she was here.

Love was hired by the Kingsleys' competition, a successful businessman who didn't want outsiders taking his hard earned business away from him. Martin Kingsley and a local man from the nearby town of Morne Rouge had formed a partnership and planned to open a rum factory on Guadeloupe. Kingsley had recently sold a recording studio and planned to invest that capital into this new venture. Love was hired to ensure that never happened.

She found her appearance made it easy for her to get close to her targets, often to the point of befriending and socializing with them prior to the hit. She was attractive, physically fit, tanned, and heartless. *Lure them into my web like a spider and then attack* was her mantra. That's one reason she rented a condominium in the same complex as the Kingsleys.

The waterfront streets of Pointe-à-Pitre were lively early in the morning and the outdoor market crowded. A small cruise ship had deposited a few hundred visitors in town, which created a traffic jam in the narrow streets.

Love already knew the Kingsleys' schedule, Martin Kingsley's anyway, courtesy of her employer. He'd provided a package complete with all the details of the Kingsleys' itinerary. That's how she knew which flight they were on, which condominium they owned, and where Martin would be at any given time. Her employer had created a spreadsheet meticulously detailing her target's information. If only all her hits could be this easy. Many of her contacts left out vital information, which on occasion had put her in harm's way. She'd been tempted to pay those employers an unwelcome visit but the money was too good to jeopardize her reputation.

Her career was born out of violence. When she was twenty-two and in her final year of college, she began an affair with an older man. Although she didn't know it at the time, he turned out to be a drug dealer who had doubled crossed one buyer too many. One night, her jealous lover accused her of flirting with a young waiter. The quarrel turned into a shouting match until he hit her—a backhanded blow to her jaw that knocked her to the floor.

She touched her face and felt the warm blood spilling from her mouth. She stood and screamed. "You bastard!"

"Shut up, bitch." His next blow knocked her against the kitchen counter.

She felt her eye starting to swell. Blood trickled from her brow.

He walked up behind her, grabbed a handful of hair, and pulled her upright.

His hot breath next to her ear, "pack your shit, bitch, and get the Hell out of my house."

She spotted a meat cleaver on top of a carving board in front of her. She grabbed the handle, spun around, and slammed the blade into the side of his neck. A fountain of blood sprayed the kitchen as the man fell to the floor in disbelief. Blood gushed across the tile floor. Within a minute he grew still. The blood flow slowed. His face turned ashen. Another minute later, he was dead.

While serving two years in prison on a plea bargained Involuntary Manslaughter charge, she met another abused woman and a friendship evolved. Along with their friendship, an idea emerged for a new line of work. Now, almost seventeen years later, she owned her own business—all women. All trained to kill. *Love's Desperate Desire*. She called them *escorts*.

At 9:00 a.m., Kingsley answered his cell phone. Five minutes later a car pulled to the curb. Kingsley kissed his wife on the cheek and folded his six-foot three-inch frame into the compact car. Love knew Kingsley and his partner were driving to look at the property they planned to buy for their rum factory. She also knew they had plans to attend dinner parties tonight and tomorrow night and were scheduled to close the real estate deal the following day. A date he would never make.

Love followed Teresa Kingsley the short few blocks back to the condominium complex. Twin eight-story buildings standing only four feet apart. She was in the East Tower and the Kingsleys were in the West. A six-foot concrete wall surrounded the complex with security guards at the main entrance to the complex and again at the entrances to each building. Security cameras monitored the lobbies of each building as well as the front gate. Security was state of the art at this upscale complex. Although violent crime wasn't a problem in Pointe-à-Pitre, burglary and vandalism were. Peace of mind for the owners outweighed the added cost of good security.

Love stood behind Teresa Kingsley at the complex's main entrance and waited while Kingsley looked for her identification and room key to show to the guard.

Kingsley turned to Love with an embarrassed look on her face. "I'm sorry. My husband has my passport. This might take a while. Why don't you go ahead?"

Love smiled. "That's quite alright. I don't mind waiting. I'm just going to the pool anyway." One large pool with a bar and a grill served the twin towers. Her employer had provided her with a detailed layout of the complex.

"Ma'am." The guard motioned for Love to walk around Kingsley.

Love did as instructed, showed her identification and key, and was cleared into the complex.

"I'm so sorry." Kingsley said as Love walked around her.

"Good luck." Love nodded at the guard and walked to her building.

The typical assassin's creed was to strike your target and vanish without a trace. Abigail Love didn't see it that way. It was much more than just a job. She enjoyed playing with her unsuspecting prey. Luring her victims into a false sense of security. Luring them to their doom. All of this felt thrilling. Tantalizing. It made the kill almost orgasmic. Little did Teresa Kingsley know, she had less than two days left to live. Just the thought made Abigail Love shiver.

† † †

Belle Haven Country Club
Alexandria, Virginia

Jake had never worked with the carrot-topped man but the warning Francesca had given him was right; his cocky demeanor was annoying. The tall thin engineer, known to him only as Matt, had worked for Elmore Wiley going on two years and had only one job function, pilot Wiley's miniature spy drones.

Last year's drone was Wiley's electronic wasp equipped with an infrared video camera, microphone, and operated on three tiny watch batteries. Obsolete in comparison to Wiley's latest invention, which Matt called Skeeter, a spy drone the size and shape of a mosquito, also equipped with a video camera and microphone. The nanotechnology Wiley used allowed the mosquito replica to operate on a miniaturized single cell battery, which also served as the drone's torso. Although Skeeter didn't have infrared capability, it did have a needle capable of drawing a DNA sample, delivering a toxin, or injecting a micro RFID under the skin of its intended victim. The radio frequency identification device would allow the target to be tracked within a two-foot tolerance. Just like a real mosquito, Skeeter was propelled by flapping its silicone wings allowing it to hover, climb and descend, and travel at a speed of eight miles per hour in no-wind situations.

Matt opened his case and pulled out a small box similar in size and appearance to that found in a jewelry store. He opened it and held it out for Jake to see. "Pretty cool, huh?" Matt snapped it closed.

Earlier Jake had parked the black van belonging to Commonwealth Consultants in the back parking lot of the

Hampton Inn on Richmond Highway just north of the Belle Haven Country Club fence.

"Boden's tee time is in ten minutes, can you make it?"

"Just let me do the flying, Navy boy, and we'll be fine. Now hold out your palm."

Jake's initial urge was to punch the arrogant man in the face but he suppressed the feeling, knowing it would not sit well with Wiley. He held out his hand, palm up. Matt placed Skeeter on Jake's palm and turned to his command console.

Matt flipped three buttons and wrapped his hands around two joysticks. "Now watch and learn."

Skeeter's wings vibrated and the tiny drone lifted off Jake's palm. "Here we go," Matt said. The drone darted out the van's open side door.

Jake stared at Matt's monitor and watched the ground pass underneath. The video was clear but somewhat grainy, certainly good enough to qualify for the task at hand. The drone flew over a small tributary then lifted over a row of trees and across the expanse of fairways at the golf course. Within seconds, the clubhouse came into view in the distance. It surprised Jake that his aging target could even swing a golf club without falling over. But it was a routine the man only missed when the weather was inclement or he was out of town.

"Does this thing have a zoom?" Jake asked.

"I wish. I'll have to fly it up close and personal for positive identification. That's why you're here. If I pop the wrong target, then you're to blame." Matt laughed.

Francesca was right. Matt was a prick.

Jake held his tongue and continued to watch. The view on the screen showed the clubhouse getting closer, a row of golf carts lined up at the tee box. "Guess you'll have to check each one. Start with one closest to the tee." Jake instructed.

"Yeah, I think I got that much figured out."

Matt piloted the mosquito drone past the first two golf carts. Nothing but a bunch of old men he didn't recognize. As the drone passed in front of the third cart, Jake saw something. "There." He pointed to the screen. "Fourth cart. The man with a cane, check him out."

"Roger that," Matt replied.

Jake watched Matt maneuver the drone around the third golf cart and sweep in front of the fourth. "Can you give me a close up of the man in the passenger seat?"

"Of course." Matt's hands expertly tilted the joysticks from side to side as the view on the screen seemed to finesse the man's face into a full face image.

"That's him," Jake said. "Now what?"

"Now comes the tricky part." Matt explained. "I'll land Skeeter on his back collar for a moment." The view on the screen showed the camera sweeping around the target's head and when it was lined up with the back of the man's head, it landed on the back of a pale blue collar. "One limitation of Skeeter's camera is the inability to sweep. We can only see straight ahead. And unfortunately Skeeter weighs a little more than a real mosquito, so when I come off his collar and land on his neck, he'll feel something and try to swat it. I have to land, pull a sample, and get out of there before Skeeter gets squashed."

"Has that ever happened?"

"Once," Matt admitted. "Knocked Skeeter to the ground. I was able to locate him later though and retrieve the sample."

"What's next? Land on his neck?"

"No. That's how I got caught. I've found the best place to land is behind the earlobe."

"Behind the ear?" Jake asked. "Won't he hear it?"

"Possibly, but he won't hit himself in the ear. The tendency is to just wave a hand by the ear and then pull it away. When he pulls his hand away, I'll fly Skeeter out of there."

"Do it," Jake said.

"Extending the needle...and here we go." The monitor showed movement toward the man's right ear. The bottom of the ear lobe came into view then filled the screen. "Extracting a sample...retracting the needle, now wait. One thousand one, one thousand two, one thousand three. Now, let's get him out of there."

As the image pulled away, the target's hand was seen waving in front of the drone's camera. Then the image cleared the golf cart.

"Piece of cake," Matt said.

"Let me see his face again."

The image on the monitor rotated around and the target's face came into view as Matt maneuvered Skeeter in front of the golf cart.

Senator Richard Boden.

"Nicely done, Matt. Now get Skeeter out of there."

†††

Abigail Love lay on a beach towel by the pool, her mind running through her mental checklist of things she had to do to prepare for the hit on Martin and Teresa Kingsley. She was staying in a room on the fourth floor of the East Tower and Kingsley and his wife were on the seventh floor of the West Tower. Guests were only allowed access to the building they were staying in unless accompanied by an owner or guest of the adjacent tower. The only common areas were by the pool and at the grill. Logistically an issue, but one for which she had accounted.

She wore big tortoise shell sunglasses with UV lenses to protect her eyes from the harsh Caribbean sun. She studied the rooftops and balconies; they might be her only choice.

A shadow blocked the sun from her face and she turned her head to see who it was.

"Well, hello again," Teresa Kingsley said.

"I see they let you inside." Love pulled her glasses on top of her head and squinted at the bright sun. Kingsley was tall and thin. She wore a sheer white tunic revealing a black bikini underneath. Her long dark hair and brown eyes accentuated her good looks. For a woman of fifty-four, Love thought Teresa Kingsley looked spectacular.

"Yes. I had the guard call the manager, he vouched for me." She pointed at the chair next to Love. "Mind if I join you?"

"Not at all." Love smiled. "My pleasure."

"Thank you." Kingsley extended her hand. "Teresa Kingsley."

"Abigail Love." She grabbed Kingsley's hand. "My friends call me Abby."

"Abby, nice to meet you." Kingsley pulled her tunic over her head and spread the towel across the chair. Without the tunic, Teresa Kingsley looked even more spectacular than Love originally thought. Her French-cut bikini bottom accentuated her already long, tan legs.

Kingsley pulled a bottle of tanning oil out of her bag and squirted some on her legs and started rubbing it in. "How long have you owned here?"

"I don't own a unit here. A friend of mine is letting me stay here for a few days." Love pointed to the East Tower. "I'm over there."

"My husband, Martin, and I are up there." She pointed to the West Tower. "Is this your first time in Pointe-à-Pitre?"

Love couldn't help but smile. Not at what Teresa Kingsley said, but at how often this routine worked. A chance first meeting followed by a second. The woman had already let her guard down so now Love would just pour on the charm and in no time Teresa Kingsley would think she had met her new best friend. And her new best friend would prove to be the death of her.

They talked for an hour, ordered lunch from the grill, and then started drinking.

By 3:00 p.m. Love was getting a slight buzz and Teresa Kingsley was well beyond that point. Her speech was slurred and she had almost fallen out of her chair three times from laughing so hard.

"Abby, you are one of the funniest women I've ever met. Martin will love you." Kingsley sat up in her chair and turned to face Love. "I have to go with my husband to a business dinner tonight, will you go with me?"

Love hadn't expected this. She had too much to do tonight while Martin and Teresa Kingsley were at their dinner meeting. That might be her only opportunity to case the Kingsleys' condominium since the hit was planned for tomorrow night. "No, that wouldn't be right. But thank you for the generous offer."

"Please, Abby. All they're going to talk about is business. Blah. Blah. Blah. Real estate, rum factory, yada, yada, yada. I won't know anybody there. I'll be bored to death. It'll be so much more fun if you're there with me. I'll have someone to talk to for a change."

"No. Really." Love insisted. "It wouldn't be right."

"Come on, Abby. After dinner, we'll leave them to their business and go do something fun."

"I don't know." Love found this woman's pleas hard to resist.

"It won't cost you anything, Abby. My treat. Please? You'll have fun, I promise."

Love couldn't believe she was giving in, that was unlike her. Especially when it came to a hit. "Alright, Teresa. I'll go." She saw Teresa Kingsley's smile turn into a grin. *Enjoy it while you can my new friend…because my idea of fun is beyond your imagination.*

CHAPTER 4

August 17—1:00 P.M.
METech Laboratories
Leuven, Belgium

He extended his hand to greet Kyli as he walked into her lab.

She moved past his hands and wrapped herself around his chest in a full embrace, squeezing him tight. He liked the warmth and feel of her body molded to his.

Nearly a year had passed since Jake met Kyli Wullenweber, a scientist for METech in Belgium. The lavender smell of her hair filled his nostrils. She lifted her head and her soft amber eyes met his.

"Do I make you nervous?" Kyli asked.

Jake unwrapped her arms and held her hands at arm's length. "Sometimes." He wanted to say more but he knew he'd fumble it and besides, Francesca might walk in any second.

"Like now?"

"No." Jake wanted to look and act calm.

She didn't flinch when Jake spoke, just laughed. Her sexy, playful laugh. Kyli was tall, nearly as tall as him with an ivory complexion and thick chestnut hair. She had a splash of freckles across the bridge of her nose and her eyes sparkled every time she smiled. Even though he would never admit it, she excited him every time he was around her. She acted so cool. He knew she was taunting him.

"How long will you be here this time?" Kyli asked.

"Only as long as it takes you to make a DNA toxin."

"Is that all?"

"I'm afraid so, we're in the middle of an assignment."

"Careful Jake, Kyli will put her spell on you."

"Huh?" Jake turned and saw Francesca standing behind him. "How long have you been standing there?"

"Long enough," Francesca said.

"Busted." Kyli smiled.

Jake felt his face flush. He pointed his fingers to Francesca then back to Kyli. "You two have met, right?"

Both women laughed. "Of course we've met, Jake," Kyli said. "Franny's been here lots of times with Mr. Wiley."

"Franny?" Jake smiled at Francesca. She shrugged her shoulders and shook her head.

Kyli interrupted. "That's my nickname for her. Francesca sounds so...formal and exotic. Franny is cozy and friendly."

"Right. Tell that to her next victim." Jake laughed and shook his head. "We should be done in a few days then I have a couple of weeks off."

Kyli leaned close to Jake's ear and whispered.

He smiled. "Sounds like fun."

Kyli motioned with her head, like she was trying to be subtle. Jake followed her eyes and noticed the new plaque on the wall. "Is that it? Your doctorate diploma finally arrived?"

"Yep. Two days ago." Kyli pulled it off the wall. "Can you believe it took them nearly four months to get this little piece of paper to me?"

"The bastards."

"Shut-up." Kyli swatted Jake's chest. "Now you're just picking."

"A little." Jake reached into his coat pocket and pulled out a clear sealed bag. "Brought you something." Inside the bag was a tiny vial.

"What do we have here?" Kyli grabbed the bag and held it up to the light. "Ah, from Skeeter?"

"How'd you know?"

"I designed the DNA extractor for Wiley's mosquito drone." Kyli put one hand on her hip. "Whose is it?"

Jake glanced at Francesca then back to Kyli. "Can't tell you," he said.

"Is this a hit?" Kyli placed the bag on her workstation. "Don't answer that. How long do I have to work on this?"

Jake pulled up a metal stool and sat down next to Francesca. "Wiley said to make it your top priority."

He remembered the first day he met Kyli; Wiley dropped him off at the lab, leaving Kyli in charge of his orientation. They were in this laboratory when she explained her research with DNA. With the growing threat of DNA toxins by hostile governments and militias against the West, she explained, her research was based on the premise of learning how DNA assassination worked so it could be defended against.

In the months to follow, her research had reached new proportions and she'd perfected the toxins and antitoxins of DNA assassination. So much so that Elmore Wiley, at the mandate of the Greenbrier Fellowship, had authorized the first assassination utilizing a DNA toxin on a human subject. The toxin was delivered by one of Wiley's emissaries, a South Korean woman named Su Lee, who delivered the toxin to Kim Jon-il on a train in North Korea causing the ailing dictator to have a fatal heart attack.

"How long will you need?" Jake asked.

"At best? Three or four hours." Kyli reached into a box and pulled out two gloves. "Is Skeeter delivering the toxin? Because that hasn't been tested yet?"

"Nope." Francesca slid an open pack of Wrigley's peppermint gum across the desktop. "Chewing gum."

"Seriously? How can you be sure he'll chew it?"

"What makes you think it's a man? Could be a woman, you know. Women like chewing gum too." Jake smiled. "Right, Franny?"

Francesca sneered then nodded.

"You two aren't going to answer any of my questions, are you?" Kyli asked.

Jake shook his head.

"Very well. Any chance you have medical records?"

Jake opened his backpack, dug around and pulled out a large manila envelope with a metal fly clasp. "Latest blood work-up. Copy of physician's records."

"Seriously?" Jake heard the excitement in Kyli's voice. "How'd you pull that off?"

"Compliments of one of Wiley's hackers at the new office in Virginia. Sanitized, of course."

"But of course." Kyli slipped on a purple glove. "I would expect nothing less."

"Purple now, huh?" Jake pointed at the box of gloves. "What happened to the pink gloves?"

"Found out I'm allergic to latex." Kyli held up a glove. "These are nitrile rubber. Where can I find you?"

Jake pointed at Francesca. "We'll be in the conference room by the RF lab."

He stood, pushed his stool under the counter, and followed Francesca out of Kyli's lab. Jake and Francesca stopped at the elevator door as Francesca pushed the call button.

"What the hell was that?" Francesca asked.

"What?"

"That." She motioned back toward Kyli's lab. "Between you and Kyli. Are you banging the boss's granddaughter?"

"Banging?" Jake furrowed his brow. "Seriously?"

The elevator door opened, Jake followed Francesca inside, the door closed.

"So you're the one," Francesca said. She pushed the button for the RF lab.

"I'm the one...what?" Jake felt the elevator move.

"She would never give me a name, but her eyes would light up every time she talked about that *special guy* she'd been seeing. And I just saw that same sparkle when she talked to you...so now I know."

"I don't know what you're talking about. Kyli and I are just friends."

"Just friends, my ass. I should have known. It all makes sense now." Francesca grabbed Jake's arm. "Does the old man know?"

The elevator chimed and the door opened.

"Does the old man know what?" Elmore Wiley, Kyli's grandfather stepped into the elevator.

†††

August 17 7:30 A.M. CDT
Katzer Funeral Home
Nashville, Tennessee

Scott Katzer knew his suspicions were correct as soon as he unzipped the body bag. The transferring funeral home claimed to have effectually embalmed the kid's body even though the odds were stacked against it. The seventeen year old died from a drug overdose, his body undiscovered for nearly thirty-six hours. Decomposition and bloating had set in by the time the funeral director embalmed the young man. When Katzer unzipped the bag, the bloated face of the young man stared up at him, tongue protruding through swollen lips. The deceased had been discovered in his bed with his head hanging over the side, a pool of dried vomit on the floor.

The odor told Katzer that putrefaction had set in. Purge from the deceased had discharged from the mouth, nose, and ears. With modern advancements in embalming, it had been a number of years since he'd encountered remains in this bad of shape and decided as soon as he saw it that he was too old to deal with remains in this condition. It was time to let the younger embalmers handle the distasteful parts of the job. His gag reflex kicked in, the three-day cross-country drive from the Portland, Oregon funeral home to Nashville in the back of a van under the scorching August sun was too long for any dead body, much less this one.

"Oh, Hell no. Not today." Katzer turned his head and zipped up the body bag. Why couldn't the relatives just spend the extra money and fly their loved one home? Six hundred more dollars was all it would have taken yet they opted for a three-day van rental plus driver expenses versus a nine-hour plane ride. As soon as the driver had dropped off the body bag, Katzer thought he could detect the faint smell. Now the stench would remain in his nostrils for hours.

He burst into the break room and pointed at a junior embalmer and a summer intern from the Gupton-Jones College of Funeral Services in Decatur, Georgia. "You two handle Mr. Wilson's remains—he needs to be ready by noon." He looked at the young intern sitting at the table. "It'll be good experience for him. I need to call the family and try to cancel, or at least postpone, the family viewing."

"Yes, sir," The junior embalmer said.

Katzer started to leave, then turned to the young apprentice. "And you...try not to vomit on the deceased this time, please."

Katzer himself was a 1964 graduate of the John A. Gupton School of Mortuary Science when the school was located in Nashville. His courses seemed easy. An advantage he had since he'd worked in the funeral home for his mother and stepfather since he was ten. The Katzer Funeral Home was located on the opposite side of Lebanon Pike from the Mt. Olivet and Calgary Cemeteries. Although not his biological father, Matthew Katzer was the only father he'd ever known and had adopted him and his twin sister when they were two years old. Matthew Katzer died tragically and mysteriously in 1966 in an accident while working on a tractor in the Mt Olivet Cemetery. Scott and his mother had been running the funeral home ever since.

Katzer remembered the somber mood of preparing his stepfather's body while his petite mother stood silent and watched, her blue eyes swollen and bloodshot from the seemingly endless flow of tears. The next day they interred his remains in a small plot in the back of Mt. Olivet Cemetery. The young Katzer thought it odd his mother chose to bury her husband in such a parsimonious manner. It wasn't' like the family didn't have money. The funeral services business had proven lucrative for the Katzer family. Funerals were expensive and there was never a shortage of customers, especially now, as the baby-boomers were coming of age.

His mother was one of the most respected funeral directors in Nashville, handling funerals for some of the city's most prestigious residents including congressmen, senators, as well as several top country music artists. She had a soothing, empathetic voice. While the emotional duress of the situation made the grieving family vulnerable, his mother was an expert at influencing them to open their pocketbooks.

He flipped open his appointment book and dialed the number. A woman answered on the second ring. "Mrs. Wilson…"

A few minutes later Katzer placed the phone on the receiver after successfully convincing the family that a viewing was not a good idea due to the condition of the remains. He was surprised by the family's response. Initially, the Wilsons had been downright difficult to deal with and he dreaded making the call, but strangely enough, the family seemed to take this news in stride. Perhaps now they had accepted the painful truth behind the demise of their son. The drugs had alienated him from the rest of the family. In a strange way, Katzer sensed, the Wilsons were relieved the ordeal was over.

Death can cause a myriad of emotions.

He remembered a late November day in 1967 when a man was so distraught because the cosmetologist was unable to completely conceal a bruise on his deceased wife's forehead that he balled his fist and struck Katzer on the jaw in the viewing room. Katzer fell backward and crashed into a spray of flowers, shattering vases and ruining the display. He was shocked when he looked up and saw his mother holding a gun. She put a quick stop to the fracas and, after his mother explained the reason for the blemishes on his wife, the man apologized.

After business hours, Katzer sat with his mother and recounted the day. She explained to him that it wasn't the first time she had been forced to pull a gun in the funeral home. The first time she actually shot a man. Trying to deal with his loss with a bottle of whiskey, a man came to the funeral home drunk, began to rant, and throw things. He grabbed pictures from the walls and hurled them across the funeral parlor, busted a candle display against the piano, and threw an urn through a window. That's when she shot him in the leg. The police came, arrested the drunkard and never charged his mother with any wrongdoing.

That was also the day he found out that Matthew Katzer was not his real father.

And how he really died.

And why.

†††

Charleston, South Carolina

Ashley Regan unpacked her Eagle Creek luggage in a hurry to get to the book. She never got a chance to thoroughly examine it before she and Sam Connors left Europe to return home. Because of the cold and moisture of what she figured must have been decades in the ice, the book must be handled with special attention to avoid damage.

She had sealed the book in a plastic bag and then wrapped it with care inside some of her clothes before packing it in her checked luggage. She didn't want to risk the possibility of losing the book at security by carrying it onboard.

There were laws against what she was doing. International laws. She knew because one of her clients narrowly escaped jail time for removing an ancient artifact he discovered while vacationing in the ancient city of Istanbul, Turkey. Found guilty of violations of the UNESCO Convention on the Mean of Prohibiting the Illicit Import, Export, and Transfer of Ownership of Cultural Property, her client was lucky to walk away with nothing more than a hefty fine and forfeiture of the artifact. All because he thought the item would make a cool display on his mantle.

When Regan and Connors had reached the summit at Zugspitze, she'd reported finding the man's body. The authorities took her statement and dispatched a crew to recover the body from the ice. The couple's itinerary took them from Garmisch, Germany to Venice, Italy the next day, which suited Regan. She wanted to get as far away from the German mountain as possible in case someone raised concern over the body found frozen in the glacier. The last thing she wanted was to be called back and interrogated...or worse, have her belongings searched. There was no plausible explanation for her possession of the book and it would have been obvious where she found it. The German authorities would take it back and her troubles would just be starting.

The two days spent in Italy on pins and needles, wondering if she would be found out, were unnerving. She kept expecting authorities to discover the identity of the frozen man, come after her, and search her luggage for any missing artifacts. She searched the newspapers every day and found it odd that she never saw any news reports about the body she discovered.

The flight back to the United States was long but the exhilaration and mystery behind the book deprived her of sleep. All she could think about was the leather bound book and what might be written in it. The notion the book didn't contain any secrets never crossed her mind. Even more intriguing was what she found after she had a chance to examine it.

After she had returned to her room in Garmisch and unpacked the book, she'd noticed a hole in it, small but large enough to slip her finger through. Under the table lamp she noticed a discoloration resembling blood stains on the leather binder. Perhaps it was her imagination gone wild, but after closer inspection she deduced it could have been made from a bullet and that piqued her interest. The thought of opening the book and discovering its secrets caused her heart to race with curious anticipation.

She located the sweater that concealed the book and carefully unwrapped it. Moisture had coated the inside of the sealed plastic bag containing the book. She assumed the restorative drying process would have to be slow and tedious and she wanted to make sure she didn't damage the book so she decided not to open the sealed bag until she consulted an expert in document restoration. For added protection, she sealed it inside another bag and then the second bag inside a third. Overkill perhaps, but she didn't care.

Even though she was exhausted from traveling, the curiosity of her new found treasure fueled her. Her Internet searches for document restorers failed to provide any results near the Charleston area. She decided she'd call the university library to find an expert and then make up a story to get the information she needed.

While her mind wandered through the intricate details of her scheme, her fingers caressed the book through the plastic bags, feeling every detail. Her middle finger found the hole on the front. She held it in front of the light and saw the filtered glow through the hole in the journal.

"What is in here that is so important?" She whispered out loud. "And did someone have to die to protect it?"

CHAPTER 5

Senator Richard Boden was among the most prestigious of the nation's politicians. In addition to his war record, Boden was a founding member of the Inner Circle of the United States Senate. Known as *the yachtsmen,* although most members didn't even own a yacht, this Inner Circle had wrestled power from a handful of senior senators and changed the way the Senate chose committee chairmanships. In true Orwellian style, the Inner Circle believed not all 100 senators were created equal. They alone held the power. Aspiring new senators were molded—or destroyed—by these Inner Circle members.

Wiley wanted to make the senator's demise look like natural causes...and that's what Jake resolved to do.

Four computer monitors surrounded Jake and Francesca, each containing mission sensitive data about Boden, his residence, and his security system. The two had been sitting at the conference table next to the RF lab at METech for the past four and half hours without a break and had made very little progress determining how to handle suspicion from Boden's fellow Inner Circle members. The aging senator was part of the *good ol boy* system and had strong allies in Washington. They would insist on an investigation and an autopsy.

Jake stood, yawned, stretched his arms as far as he could, and said, "We're getting nowhere. I'm going to make a head run and get a soft drink. Want something?"

"Dr. Pepper would be nice. I could use the caffeine." Francesca covered her mouth while she yawned.

Jake smiled, yawns always seemed contagious, he thought. "You got it." He and Francesca had been paired on missions more times than they'd been on solo missions over the past year. With the exception of the scar on her left cheek, Francesca was a woman of flawless beauty. As a matter of fact, he felt the imperfection added to her Italian mystique. Working as a team had nurtured their friendship and added confidence in each other's abilities. Their strengths and weaknesses created the perfect balance and their skills complimented each other.

Wiley had created the perfect union.

He trusted her with his life, and he knew she reciprocated. He supposed that was why Wiley kept them paired. The old man was a matchmaker in the world of espionage. Their vows were simple—*From this day forward, I got your back.*

Jake turned toward the door as it opened. Kyli walked in with a smile on her face holding a pack of gum and a clipboard.

"Piece of cake." She handed the pack of gum to Francesca. "You're all set."

"That was fast." Francesca took the pack of gum from Kyli and placed it on the conference table.

"Should I ask how?" Jake asked.

"How...what?" Kyli asked. "How I finished in such a short amount of time or how the gum works?"

"Yes," Jake said.

"Start with how you finished so fast," Francesca said.

Kyli pointed to one of the computer monitors. "I know him. Isn't that the senator who—"

"You didn't see that." Jake leaned over the table and minimized the windows on the monitors. "This one's from the top."

"That explains why this was so simple." Kyli pulled up the clipboard. "Your *target* has high blood pressure, has had a serious stroke and a major heart attack. He takes nitroglycerin tablets for chest pain. It also looks like he's had several mini-strokes as well, which I'm willing to bet he doesn't even know he's had. So," Kyli picked up the pack of gum, "this is your lethal weapon. It will have a double whammy effect. Within a few minutes of ingestion, he'll have severe chest pains mimicking a heart attack and will grab his nitroglycerin pills and take them. But this formula is already packed with nitro, so he'll overdose but won't know it. Within seconds after ingesting the nitro, the other ingredients will kick in and he'll have a massive stroke that will render him unconscious. Total time from gum to loss of consciousness, four to five minutes. Total time to death, seven to eight."

"Wow. That fast?" Jake asked.

"He's no health club member. More like a walking time-bomb." Kyli pointed to the papers scattered on the table. "What'd he do to deserve this?"

Neither Jake nor Francesca answered her question.

"I know. I know. You can't tell me. And if you did, you'd have to kill me. Yeah. Yeah. Yeah." Kyli frowned. "Heard it all before."

"Is it traceable?" Francesca asked.

"Good question," Jake added. "Our target has some powerful friends who will no doubt want to know how he died. They will suspect foul play and will certainly request an autopsy. Will your formula show up?"

"Nope. All they'll find is nitro." Kyli checked her watch. "How much longer before you're done here? It's getting time to eat."

"Kyli, you'll have to eat without Jake tonight," said Francesca. "We still have some logistical issues to work out."

"She's right, we may be here quite a while," Jake said.

"Anything I can help with? Knock out the security system? Take out the guards? Blueprints for the house?" Kyli looked at Jake. "I was hoping we could spend a little time together before you leave."

"Blueprints and security system we've taken care of." Jake said. "His P. A. could be a problem. He always has her with him. Got an alchemy for that?"

"P. A.? As in personal assistant?"

"Yes."

"How old is she?" Kyli asked.

"Mid to late thirties," Francesca said.

"Know if she's had a hysterectomy?"

Francesca answered. "No, but I can get that information for you."

"That would be great. You know their schedule?"

Francesca grabbed a piece of paper from the table and handed to Kyli. "As a matter of fact, we do."

"Thanks, Franny." Kyli studied the schedule for two minutes and then smiled. "I might know just the thing."

Three hours later, Jake and Francesca completed the planning phase of their mission. An analyst at Wiley's new Virginia office researched the medical history on Boden's P.A. and found no record of a hysterectomy. Kyli had been a big help and offered a solution to their problem with removing Boden's personal assistant from the equation.

"It is convenient that Boden's P.A. is a woman," Francesca said. "Kyli's solution should work like a charm."

After he heard the plan he thought the same thing. He knew he and Francesca could control the situation, avoid detection, and administer the compound to Senator Richard Boden. In theory, anyway. And that was the only thing bothering Jake at the moment. If the hit wasn't timed with precision, they might get busted. This was a personal favor for the President of the United States from Wiley. And on a personal level, a chance for Jake to seek revenge for past transgressions.

"I think that's it." Jake looked at Francesca who was already gathering all the paperwork in one pile. "We're a go for tomorrow night."

"I don't know, Jake. This mission still bothers me." Francesca looked at her watch. "When it appears easy, something has been overlooked."

Jake knew about Francesca's failed first mission, an attempt to capture an assassin that resulted in the loss of two of her team members, and that she'd been overly cautious ever since. He knew she was reminded of her failure every time she looked in the mirror and saw her scar. That demon in her past would never leave.

He knew about demons.

He had a few of his own.

"Relax. We've covered every angle and besides." Jake paused. "I've got your back."

The Hotel Carpinus was a short drive from the lab, just across the canal to the small village of Herent. Jake had spent many nights there on his numerous trips to Belgium and was on a first name basis with most of the hotel and dining room staff.

Jake grabbed his room key from Jordy at the front desk. Same room as always, number 7. And, as was standard protocol for him at the Hotel Carpinus, he knew the light would be on, his bag would be in his room, bed turned down, and a chocolate on the pillow.

When he opened the door, he realized he was wrong.

The only light in the room came from several candles flickering on the dresser. His bag was tossed on the floor, clothes scattered all over. The bed was turned down, but instead of a chocolate on his pillow, it was something much more appetizing.

Kyli.

CHAPTER 6

Ashley Regan was an adrenaline junkie and her recent discovery kept her imagination stoked with possibilities. At first, her calls to the College of Charleston seemed a dead end but every junkie knows that persistence is the opposite of failure. She struck pay dirt with the third person she spoke to at the College. The librarian gave her the name of a local antiquary who not only collected antiquities, but also restored damaged documents in his home. The man had assisted several libraries and companies in Charleston with restoring documents and books water damaged as a result of Hurricane Hugo in 1989.

Regan took the man's name and number and made an appointment to bring the book for an evaluation and restoration estimate.

One step closer to her goal.

The contents of the book had become her idée fixe. She had to know what was written inside. Her mind thought of dozens of possibilities for a bullet hole to be in the leather-bound book.

She studied the book one last time...touching it through the plastic bags. She used a bright light and magnifying glass to study the water-stained leather cover. The leather-bound book measured roughly 6 inches wide by 8.25 inches tall and was a little over an inch thick. The leather appeared to be cowhide, possibly stained dark, with a pattern tooled on the front.

Two patterns actually, initials tooled near the top and a small emblem or pattern centered an inch from the bottom. The patterns were worn flat. With the discoloration of the leather, the patterns were impossible to decipher through the sealed plastic bags. Moisture had visibly collected on the inside of all three bags so she didn't dare remove the book.

She grabbed a blank sheet of copy paper and a pencil then smoothed the plastic bags as much as possible over the front cover. Placing the blank paper on the cover, she gently rubbed the pencil lead across the book. With each pass of the lead across the paper, the patterns from the leather cover slowly appeared. The initials revealed themselves a small portion at a time until they were clear—W. F. It meant nothing to her. But as the smaller pattern emerged that changed.

A crest.

With a swastika in the center.

Now the book had an approximate age dating back to World War II—Nazi Germany.

A valuable piece to the puzzle.

The region made sense. Technically she'd found the book on German soil. The identity of the man remained a mystery. Perhaps the protector of the book was a German soldier. Could explain the bullet hole, if that's even what it was. She knew the bloodstains, the hole, and the swastika might arouse suspicion and prompt some questions—questions she was preparing herself to answer. She'd already devised a story, now she just had to make some minor alterations and she had her perfect lie.

GPS was a wonderful invention she thought as she parked her car in front of Arthur DeLoach's three-story home in historic Charleston. It amazed her that with a compass and a map she could roam the wilderness and never get lost, but put her in the city and she'd get turned around almost every time. And to make matters worse, she'd grown up in Charleston. Now all she had to do was input the address and the electronic device guided her to his mailbox with voice commands. She grabbed her bag and walked to the doorstep. No doorbell to announce her arrival, only a brass knocker on the oversized wooden door. She reached for the knocker but before she could grab it the door opened. A middle-aged black woman stood in front of her, almost as if she had been waiting for her to arrive. Might have even been sizing her up as she walked to the front door.

"Hello. I'm Ashley Regan."

"Ms Regan, Mr. DeLoach is expecting you. May I take your bag, ma'am?"

"No, thank you. I'll keep it. It's carrying the item I brought for Mr. DeLoach."

The old house had a musty odor with twelve-foot ceilings, large oriental rugs in every room, and a long hallway extending from front to back in the center of the home. A stairway led upstairs in the middle of the main hallway. "How old is this house?" Regan asked.

"Over two hundred years. It was built in 1811." The woman explained. "Out back are the gardens and a carriage house. The carriage house was built in 1813."

Regan followed the woman down the long hallway to a closed door near the back of the home. Every inch of wall space, it seemed, was covered with paintings. Cabinets and display cases full of antiquities that appeared to have come from every corner of the world. Through the rear windows she could see the gardens full of assorted flowers, most in full bloom, and the old carriage house.

The woman knocked twice then opened the door and walked in.

"Mr. DeLoach, Ms. Regan is here to see you." The woman turned to her. "Go on in, honey, and talk loud, he's hard of hearing."

As Regan walked in, the woman closed the door behind her. The room was full of equipment some of it small, some not so small. She had no idea how any of it worked, nor did she really care. Next to a wall was a large table with different colored vials of what she assumed were chemicals, a large magnifying glass with a light mounted under the rim illuminating a book that lay across the center of the table, and standing at the table, an old man wearing jeweler's glasses and white gloves.

"Mr. DeLoach, I'm Ashley Regan. We spoke on the phone."

The old man held up his hand. "Shh. I'll be with you in a moment." He sounded angry and impatient. "Have a seat. And I'm not hard of hearing so you don't have to yell. Zula Mae tells everyone that so she can listen through the door."

She smiled at the thought of a nosy housekeeper, found a chair next to a window, and sat down.

Regan guessed Arthur DeLoach was in his seventies, perhaps as old as eighty. His gray hair was thin, long, and scraggly. His old hands showed signs of arthritis induced deformity but they seemed steady when he worked. His shoulders had a permanent hunch and he shuffled when he walked. She realized he wasn't angry or gruff, his voice just made him seem that way.

"So Ms Regan, what do you have for me?"

She was on. Time for the lies to begin.

"Mr. DeLoach, my Uncle William Franks, my mother's brother, died a couple of months ago, and since I was the only relative left, I was named executor of his estate. When I went to clean out his house I found this." She pulled out the book in the plastic bags. "It was frozen in the back of a freezer in his garage. Years of frost had accumulated on it. I know this sounds odd, but my uncle was an odd man. A bibliophile...his house is full of books. I don't know where I'm going to put all of them. As the frost melted, I suspected this might be his personal journal so I wrapped it up and put it back in my freezer until I could find someone to safely restore it. It has his initials on the binding and some sort of crest. Maybe a family crest, I don't know. My uncle grew up in Germany, Bavaria I think. Also there's a hole punched through it and some sort of stain...I don't know what happened to cause that."

There. Her story complete. Her lies told. She designed her story to cover all the bases and hopefully deflect any suspicion the old man might have.

"May I hold the book?" DeLoach held out his old arthritic hand.

She placed the book in his hand. He held it up to the light, pulled his jeweler's glasses down and studied the book.

"Why so many plastic bags?" He asked.

"I was afraid if it started to dry out, it might ruin it."

"I can dry it out with my vacuum drier, but I won't know the condition of the pages until I take a look to see how extensive the restoration will be...if I can restore it at all."

He raised the glasses and looked at her. His slate gray eyes looked worn and tired. He had dark circles, droopy cheeks and eyebrows a decade overdue for a trim.

"And how long do you think this will take?" She tried not to sound eager.

"If everything goes well, three or four days."

"And if it doesn't?" She asked.

"I only have one other project right now." He pointed to the book on the table. "So I can give this book a lot of attention. No more than a week, I'd say."

"And the cost?" Regan smiled.

"I'm old Ms Regan. I don't need the money. I do this because I enjoy it and want to stay busy. If I sat around here every day with my thumb up my ass, I'd probably die in a couple of months. Zula Mae..." DeLoach pointed to the door. "...Nosy woman but she takes good care of the house which leaves me time to do this. I'll only charge you what it costs me—basically chemicals, electricity, and supplies. To do this right, you're looking at around five or six hundred dollars, payable in cash, *before* you get the book back. Those are my terms and as you can probably guess, I'm quite inflexible. But rest assured, the restoration *will* be done properly."

"That sounds more than reasonable. Quite frankly, I expected to pay more." She smiled again at the old man. "I can't imagine why my uncle put this book in the freezer. He moved to the States in his twenties. I'm hoping it has my family history in it, which is something I'd like to know more about."

"I understand, Ms Regan." DeLoach paused.

"Please, call me Ashley." She tried to look calm. Had his suspicions already been raised? Was her story not convincing enough?

"Very well, Ashley, a word of caution. Family is important. Roots are important. But I have lived long enough to know that all families have secrets. Some with dark secrets. I hope your uncle's book does not alarm or disappoint you."

"My uncle was an eccentric old man. My parents thought he was crazy, but as a kid, I thought he was neat." She paused. "There's no telling what's in that book."

"As long as you're prepared."

"Nothing about my uncle or his life would surprise me." She shifted the subject back to the old man. "The librarian at the college told me you're an expert, how long have you been doing these types of restorations?"

"Over fifty years of document restoration and thirty years of genealogical studies."

"Genealogy?"

"Yes. I used to teach a course at the university," he paused, "until they decided I was too old."

"Nonsense. I can't believe they would waste your knowledge and experience."

DeLoach stared at Regan. "They wanted new blood. Someone younger, someone more in touch with the digital age, they said. I taught the old school methods of research in libraries and courthouses with a small amount of emphasis on the use of the Internet. They claimed they wanted it the other way around. I think they just wanted to pay a smaller salary."

DeLoach stood. "Call me in a couple of days and I'll give you a progress report."

DeLoach yelled. "Zula Mae, you can quit listening through the door now and show Ms Regan out, please?"

†††

Pointe-à-Pitre, Guadeloupe

Abigail Love stared down at the four-foot gap between the East Tower and the West Tower of the condominium complex then gazed out across the few remaining lights in the sleepy Caribbean town. She tossed her nylon rope across the chasm to the roof of the West Tower, stood on the two-foot high ledge and held her breath. She was on the rooftop of the eight-story East Tower and she knew the fall would be nearly a hundred feet. She'd practiced this jump several times in her room. Now was the moment of truth. She bent her knees slightly, flexed her muscles and pushed off with all her strength.

Love's small framed cleared the two-foot ledge on the West Tower and as her feet touched the rooftop, she tucked and rolled and then sprang back to her feet. Just like she'd practiced.

She grabbed her nylon rope, secured it to a vent pipe, and walked to the edge of the roof. Two floors below was the Kingsley's unit.

It was funny how things worked out, she thought; she had been so worried about when she would get to case the Kingsley's condominium but Teresa Kingsley had innocently made it all possible.

Dinner with the Kingsleys the previous night went so well that Martin insisted she join them again tonight. Teresa seemed excited but Abigail Love saw through Martin Kingsley's motives. He wanted Teresa out of his hair and Abigail was the perfect solution.

Teresa and Love spent the day touring the island on scooters rented from a vendor down by the waterfront. The women stopped for lunch at an island grill on the west side of the island where the specialty was conch fritters. The grill was located adjacent to a clothing-optional beach where, after several drinks at the grill's bar, Abigail and Teresa removed their tunics and bathing suit tops and spent a few hours sunbathing next to the emerald Caribbean waters.

At 3:00, they returned to the Towers where they each had another drink poolside before to returning to their suites to get ready for dinner.

When Love met the couple downstairs, it was obvious that Teresa was still tipsy. She wore a red sundress with flat sandals and Martin was in long khaki pants and a loose fitting tropical print shirt.

During dinner Teresa complained to her tall olive-skinned husband that all he and his partner ever did was talk business. After dessert, Teresa decided she and Love would walk the few blocks back to the condominium and have another drink.

The town's streets were eerily deserted after dark and the entire district took on a seedy atmosphere. The ten-minute walk took nearly twenty minutes while Love half-walked, half-carried the drunken Teresa Kingsley through the narrow streets. After arriving at the complex, Teresa invited Love to her unit in the West Tower for a nightcap. This time she didn't refuse.

Love leaned over the roof and looked down at the Kingsley's balcony, twenty-five feet she guessed. She mused at how easy Teresa Kingsley made it for her. Using the video feed from the camera she planted earlier, Love waited a full hour after Martin turned out the bedroom light before she made her move.

Earlier in the evening, after another drink, Teresa passed out on the sofa. Love seized the opportunity to case the layout of the condominium, disable the lock on the balcony door, and plant a miniature camera. When she was finished, she helped Teresa from the sofa and walked her to her bed where the woman passed out again. Love removed Kingsley's sundress and slipped her beneath the sheets wearing only her black thong. Love draped the sundress over the back of a chair, scanned the floor plan one last time and let herself out, locking the door behind her.

Most of her kills had been similar to this. Cozying up to her victims in order to deflect any suspicion and above all, to get them to let their guard down. She could have killed Teresa Kingsley earlier in the evening. She had the opportunity. But that wasn't her plan. There were probably other ways she could have gotten herself into the Kingsley's condo, but this was the plan she liked best. She thought about Teresa and how naïve and trusting the woman was. But that was how it always was, just when she was getting to like someone, she had to kill them. The ruse was always part of the scheme. Too bad for them that Teresa Kingsley was so stupid—or at a minimum, naïve.

She glanced down at the balcony again; Martin and Teresa Kingsley would not see another sunrise.

She methodically checked her equipment. She pulled out the silenced Sig Sauer SP Mosquito with the threaded barrel from her fanny pack. She was unfamiliar with the pistol but on this island, she would take what she could get. Her employer had arranged for the delivery of the weapon. It was an ideal weapon for a close range kill. The mosquito would fire a .22 caliber round into her victim's skull. Enough power to penetrate but not enough to exit leaving the bullet to ricochet inside the brain, stirring up the gray matter like a blender.

Next she tossed the nylon rope over the edge and clamped the rope with her gloved hands. She hoisted herself over the edge and lowered herself down the side of the West Tower. When she reached the Kingsley's balcony she leaned over and grabbed the metal railing and pulled herself to it. She slid over the balcony rail and secured the rope to it.

She had memorized the layout of the condo in her head and even counted the steps from the balcony to the kitchen to the bedroom. She slid open the balcony door and stepped inside using the curtains as cover—just in case Martin Kingsley got up to go to the bathroom or the kitchen in the middle of the night. She knew it wouldn't be Teresa; the alcohol should keep her out for much longer.

Love crept in the room, all quiet. She turned on her penlight with the red lens and made her way through the kitchen, and counted the steps to the bedroom. She heard Martin Kingsley snoring and followed the sound. She flashed the red light across the bed. He was sleeping on his back, his breathing labored. Teresa was underneath a jumble of covers and pillows. Love would handle her after Martin.

Suddenly Kingsley stopped breathing. Love extinguished the penlight and stepped away from the bed. Martin sat up in the bed and took a huge gasp of air. He sat upright for several seconds before falling back on his pillow. Sleep apnea, she thought. The older man she dated in college had it. Same symptoms. Now Martin Kingsley would meet the same fate.

When the man's snoring resumed, Love stepped forward and without hesitation fired two shots into Martin's head. The snoring stopped. She turned on the penlight—blood and brain matter cascaded from his skull, across the pillow, and onto the sheets—he was dead.

Love walked around the king-size bed and sat on the edge next to Teresa. The woman roused, shifted to her side, and fell back asleep.

Love removed her left glove and placed her hand on Teresa's head. She slowly stroked the sleeping woman's hair.

"That feels nice," Teresa muttered in a half sleep state.

Love removed her hand.

"Don't stop, Martin." Her speech still slurred from alcohol.

"It's not Martin," Love whispered.

"Oh Abby, you're still here. That's nice. I thought you were Martin."

Love could tell Kingsley wasn't really awake, just drifting in and out of a drunken slumber. She reached out and put her hand on Teresa's cheek letting the back of her fingers slide down the woman's neck and across her shoulders.

Kingsley moaned and arched her back. "Abby, you're the best friend I've ever had."

Abigail Love pulled her hand back and stood beside the bed. She slipped her glove back on her hand and smiled. "Goodbye, Teresa."

"Goodnight, Abby." Kingsley muttered with a slight giggle. "I'll see you in the morning."

Love raised the firearm and pointed it at Teresa Kingsley's head. "No, you won't." She fired the weapon twice in rapid succession putting two dime-sized holes in the woman's head.

CHAPTER 7

Francesca leaned across the car's center console as Jake logged into the secure website with his new, Wiley engineered iPad courtesy of METech, Wiley's Texas factory. Wiley's special design integrated the tablet and his miniature Bluetooth headset allowing for continuous encrypted video and audio communication to Wiley's new facility in Fairfax, Virginia. They were parked on a dark street behind Boden's residence on Ballantrae Farm Drive in McLean, Virginia.

Before Jake and Francesca left Belgium for Washington, DC, Wiley had informed him a new employee would be their handler for the hit on Boden. Jake followed the prompts and placed his thumbprint in the square on the screen to complete the authentication of the 24-digit password he'd just entered on the keyboard. After the scan the screen blinked and a familiar face appeared on the live feed.

"George?" The man on the screen was George Fontaine, a CIA analyst he'd worked with on a number of occasions. "How did you—"

"Just like old times, huh Jake?" Fontaine said.

"What are you doing at Commonwealth? Did Bentley loan you to Wiley for this op?" Jake knew the discord between him and Boden was no secret to Fontaine, but President Rebecca Rudd led him to believe the CIA wasn't involved in the hit.

Commonwealth was the name of Wiley's newest company in Fairfax. The four-story building bore no signs just letters stenciled on the entrance door, which read *Commonwealth Consultants*.

"Nope. Don't work for the Agency any more. I work at Commonwealth now...for Wiley."

"Wiley only goes after the best. Congratulations, George. Great to have you on board."

"Wiley made a convincing offer. I would have been a fool to turn it down. Nearly doubled my salary and the benefits are better. Plus I was already retirement eligible with the Federal Government so now I can double-dip." Fontaine paused. "Is Francesca with you?"

Jake turned the tablet toward Francesca. "Yeah, right here."

"Francesca, don't let Jake get you into trouble," Fontaine said. "He's been known to go rogue."

She laughed. "Don't worry, I can handle Jake."

"Okay, good." Fontaine said. "From here, I can handle most everything. I've already gained control of the security system. His doors will be locked," Fontaine paused, "Francesca, I hear you're pretty good at picking a lock."

"Inherited skill," she said, "my father was a locksmith. He taught me the tools of the trade."

Jake looked at her. "You never told me that."

"You never asked."

Fontaine continued. "If Boden sticks to his routine, then we'll have no problems." Jake watched Fontaine turn toward another computer monitor then back toward his video feed. "Boden is leaving the reception now. You have about fifteen minutes before the limo drops him off. He's alone. Kyli's solution for Boden's P.A. worked. She called a taxi and left in a hurry. We have confirmation that she is inside her Tyson's Corner residence."

"Good. One less thing to worry about," Jake said.

"Just curious," Fontaine said. "But what exactly was Kyli's solution to guarantee Boden's P.A. would leave and go home?"

Jake turned the iPad toward Francesca. "You want to handle this one?"

"One of Wiley's emissaries spiked her drink at the reception. The formula was supposed to induce severe menstrual cramps." Francesca explained. "And start her monthly flow."

"T.M.I. Francesca," Fontaine said. "T.M.I."

"You're a handler for an assassination," she said, "and this bothers you?"

"Men have boundaries, you know." Fontaine laughed. "I'll have the alarm offline by the time you two reach the house. I suggest you leave now."

"On our way," Jake said. "Nice having you along, George."

Jake first met Fontaine after CIA director Scott Bentley recruited Jake to assist in the capture of a former Irish Republican Army assassin who was involved in an arms deal with al Qaeda.

He again worked with Fontaine when he was part of a team who mounted a midnight raid to rescue a captured CIA operative in Yemen. That was the turning point in Jake's life, when he met Elmore Wiley. He didn't realize it at the time but Wiley had been grooming him as an operative for his own organization. Now, he was one of Wiley's most active emissaries.

An eight-foot high stone fence surrounded Senator Richard Boden's property with remote controlled iron gates guarding the circular driveway. Boden's pie shaped lot was at the end of a cul de sac in a prestigious neighborhood.

After Fontaine gave them the okay, Jake and Francesca scaled the stone fence, dropped into the spacious back yard, made their way past the oval shaped swimming pool, and to the glass French doors leading to the downstairs living room. Within seconds, Francesca picked the lock and Jake and Francesca entered Boden's residence.

He locked the door when they were inside. Jake spoke into his headset. "George, we're in."

Seconds later the security system rearmed.

Jake looked at Francesca and smiled. "Right on time." He pointed to the front door as headlights from a car illuminated the glass. "Let's get in position."

Beeping from Boden's security alarm announced the senator's arrival followed by keypad sounds of the deactivation code.

For the next five minutes Jake heard Boden rummaging around in the kitchen doing his usual routine of pouring himself a drink of water and sorting through his nighttime pillbox. The door to the study opened and Boden walked across the room using only the light from the foyer to guide him. Boden stood behind his desk and flipped on his desk lamp. He jumped backward at the sight of Jake sitting in the chair in front of his desk.

"You." At first Boden's voice quivered, then Jake noticed it became indignant. "What is the meaning of this? How did you get in here? Get out of here at once."

Boden turned toward the door as Francesca closed it.

"Who the hell are you?" He shouted.

"I'm with him." Francesca pointed at Jake.

"Sit down." Jake stood and walked toward the old man. "Sit down, now. We're going to talk."

"You don't intimidate me. Get the hell out of my house...and take her with you." Boden picked up the receiver to the phone, held it to his ear, then slammed it back down. "You cut the line to my phone?"

"Nope." Jake held up the end of the phone line. "Just unplugged it."

"I should have had you thrown in jail when you threatened me in New York." Boden shouted. "This time, you're going down."

Jake noticed the old man tremble. He couldn't tell if it was from fear or rage. "Missed opportunity, Senator. But I'm not here to make threats." Jake smiled. "It's a shame your P.A. couldn't join us. Probably for the best, though. I doubt you would want her to hear what we have to say." He was deliberately taunting the old man. Kyli told him to increase the old man's heart rate so the toxin would enter his bloodstream faster. "I hope she's feeling better."

"That was your doing?" Boden sat in his chair and propped his cane against the fireplace behind him. The lines on his face looked noticeably deeper.

"We had help," Francesca said.

Jake stepped up to the desk and picked up Boden's pack of gum.

He pulled out the top stick of gum, unwrapped it, and put it in his mouth. "Now I know why you like this, it's very good. Kind of relaxing." Jake placed the pack on Boden's desk and slid it toward the old man.

Boden stared at him. Jake knew he was a smart man. You don't make it to senior ranking senator without a certain level of intelligence and grit.

Boden waved his hand at the door. "I want you two out of here now."

"Not yet. First I want to talk to you about a little girl named Kim Ly." Jake noticed a twitch in Boden's face. "You knew her, didn't you? Thirteen-year-old orphan girl in Vietnam? Surely you can remember her."

Boden snatched open his desk drawer and pulled out a .38 caliber revolver. He pointed it at Jake. "You're a fool if you think for one second you can blackmail me. I have powerful friends. You can't get away with this."

Jake opened his left hand. Bullets.

Boden dropped the gun. "What do you want? Money?"

Jake gave Francesca a slight nod. She pulled her gun and aimed it at Boden. He leaned back in his chair. Jake saw the fear in his eyes.

"Are you going to kill me?" Boden's voice cracked.

"Try to relax, Senator," Jake said. "I'm not going to touch you. All I want to do is talk to you about a video."

Boden's hand trembled as he removed a stick of gum from the pack and slowly unwrapped it. He put it in his mouth and started chewing.

Francesca pushed her gun closer and aimed it at his head. "Ready to talk now, old man."

Boden unwrapped a second piece and stuffed it in his mouth.

"So predictable." Jake picked up the pack and held it out to Francesca. "Care for some?"

She shook her head. "Trying to quit."

"Please," Boden pleaded, "tell her to put the gun away."

Jake nodded and Francesca holstered her firearm. Boden had been chewing his gum with nervous intensity when he stopped abruptly.

Jake recognized the symptoms by the fretful expression that came across Boden's face. Kyli's formula was working. Time to turn up the heat, really get that heart racing. "You see, Senator, we watched this video the other day. Pretty disturbing, if you ask me."

"Sick is more like it," Francesca interrupted.

"I saw a 76-year-old man force a thirteen-year-old girl to perform oral sex on him." Jake leaned over Boden's desk. "Made me want to track him down and kill him. Give him a good bashing, just like he did to her."

Boden's face started sweating. He rubbed his left arm.

"Now, there's this video out there and I'm not sure I can stop it from going viral on the Internet. And the thing is…you can see the man's face clear as day."

The old man clutched his chest, squeezing his shirt tighter on his body.

"What do you think I should do about it?" Jake saw the man shaking.

"Heart. Attack. Call. 9-1-1." Boden cried out. His shaky hand reached for a bottle on his desk. "I…need…my…nitro pills."

Jake picked up the bottle. "These?"

Boden nodded. "Yes. Please. Give them here." The old man stretched out his trembling hand.

Francesca walked up and stood next to Jake while he opened the bottle and dumped the contents on the desk. Boden's hands scooped at them as a wave of nausea caused him to double over. He managed to pick up a few and put one in his mouth.

"By now, I can only imagine the pain coursing through your body." Jake said. "You see, Senator. I didn't lie. I told you I wasn't going to touch you." Jake looked at Francesca. "I guess this mission is over."

Francesca glared at the old man. "This one's for Kim Ly."

Jake watched the old man convulse.

Senator Richard Boden's eyes rolled back and he collapsed in his chair, still clutching his chest.

CHAPTER 8

Four days later Ashley Regan and Sam Connors lay in bed after making love. It wasn't their normal Saturday morning romp. The steamy sex stimulated their appetite for each other until their naked bodies were drenched in sweat. Connors had fallen back to sleep. Regan was almost asleep when she heard her cell phone vibrate on the nightstand.

Arthur DeLoach.

She grabbed her phone and padded naked across the room. She grabbed her robe and quietly closed the bedroom door behind her.

"Mr. DeLoach, what a pleasant surprise." Regan was good at turning on the charm when she needed to and this was one of those occasions. She walked into the kitchen and turned on her Keurig coffee maker.

"Your book is ready. Be here at 9:45 precisely. Six hundred fifty dollars, cash. As agreed?"

"Yes sir. I'll be—"

DeLoach hung up on her. What a grumpy old bastard.

She looked at the clock. 8:42. She had one hour to get ready, swing by the bank to get the cash, and drive to DeLoach's house.

Regan walked back to her bedroom and opened the door. Connors was awake.

"Ashley, why did you get up?" Connors asked.

"Turn on the coffee pot. I gotta get moving. I'm burning daylight."

"Come back to bed." Connors lifted the sheets. "We can go for round two."

"Not now, I have errands that can't wait." Regan slipped on her jeans and a t-shirt. "You wouldn't want me interrupting you during trading hours, would you? No. So respect my need to do things too."

"It's Saturday. It's not a trading day," Connors said.

"That's right. And since I can't get anything done during the week because of *my* job, I have to do it all on Saturday."

"You're right," Connors said. "You don't have to be get snippy about it. You've been edgy ever since we got back from Europe."

"I know, Sam. I'm sorry. I just feel…unsettled. Like I can't get back in the groove." She looked into Sam's eyes. "Does that make any sense?"

"I know just what you need to fix that." Sam said. "How about a 'wine and dine' tonight?"

Regan's lip curled into a faint smile. Today was the day she'd anticipated since she returned from Europe with the book. She wasn't about to let anything spoil her day. "That would be nice, Sam. It's a date."

Regan pulled in front of Arthur DeLoach's house with a minute to spare. She used the brass knocker to announce her arrival. Within seconds she heard DeLoach shuffling down the long hallway.

DeLoach opened the door and gestured her in with his arm. "Come in. Let's talk about your book."

"Good morning, Mr. DeLoach." Regan was determined not to let her discord with Sam Connors this morning ruin her enthusiasm about the book. "Did you have any trouble with it?"

"Not really, no. The pages are a bit stiff and fragile, so you'll need to exercise extreme care." DeLoach motioned for her to follow him. "The leather binding restored remarkably well considering where your uncle had it stored."

Ashley Regan noticed a strong smell of chemicals in the workroom, much stronger than her first visit. Her book was lying open on the table. It looked significantly different than the soggy book she'd found. The leather was supple and soft with a rich new color and the pages were lighter, the writing easier to read.

"I hope you can read German, Ms. Regan, because most of what is written inside is in German. As far as I can tell the book dates back to World War II. Of course, I'm basing some of that on the swastika branded on the front cover. If I had to guess, I'd say your uncle got this journal during the reign of the Third Reich. This could be a valuable find for you. As family heirlooms go, its contents could reveal volumes about your family history." He picked up the book and ran his hand gently across the cover, hesitating at the hole in the book. "I have no idea what caused this perforation, but it went through clean. I'm afraid these stains are set and won't come out. Looks like blood as best as I can tell. Kind of adds character and mystery to it, wouldn't you say, Ms. Regan?"

"It certainly has sparked my interest." Regan opened her purse and pulled out the cash. "Six hundred fifty dollars, just as you said."

"Ms Regan, the format of what's written inside doesn't look much like normal journal entries. It could be a family genealogy, which would explain the format. Family is important and so are roots. I've traced my family line back almost three hundred years. Beyond that, records become scarce and in many cases nonexistent." He took the cash and started to hand her the book. "Wear gloves or wash your hands well before handling the book. The oils from your fingers can damage the fragile pages."

"I will, Mr. DeLoach." She gently removed the book from his hands, her curiosity to learn the contents almost irresistible. "I promise to be careful with it."

Ashley drove all the way home thinking of nothing but the contents of the book. At last she would discover why the dead man was clasping the book. The thought of learning its secrets was delicious and she already savored it with anticipation. She parked her car in the driveway and grabbed the book from the seat next to her. She held it to her nose and took a deep breath. She expected the musty smell of leather and old pages, but all she smelled were the organic chemicals DeLoach used to restore it. She delicately pushed the leather binder into her purse, got out of the car, and walked toward her front door.

†††

Ashley Regan and Christa Barnett had grown up together in Charleston. Friends of their parents called them Frick and Frack. They did everything together. Went to school together. Studied together. Partied together. Got in trouble with the law together. But during college they drifted apart and lost contact with each other. Regan went to accounting school at the University of Georgia. Christa, graphic design at University of Florida. Christa was short in stature, barely reaching five feet. Her feisty personality matched her long dyed black hair. Christa was the only person Regan knew, and trusted, who could speak German. Who better to decipher the book?

Regan hated lying to Sam again but she needed an excuse to get away. Christa was her ticket to translating the book and Sam could never know of its existence. Sam knew Christa was Ashley's best friend so during their 'wine and dine' date, Regan told Sam that Christa was going through a rough breakup and she was going to stay with her for a few days.

At first Connors protested, but Regan resorted to the oldest trick in the book, sex. When they got home from their date, Ashley seduced Sam in an interlude that made their morning adventure pale in comparison. It was almost stereotypical. For Sam Connors, sex was the ultimate show of love. And after that romp, Regan knew, Sam would be content for a long time to come.

It took Christa a day and a half to translate all the entries in the mysterious book while Ashley Regan impatiently watched her work. Like a small child on Christmas morning waiting to run out and see what Santa brought, the anticipation was unbearable and intensified with each "oh my God" and "this is too weird" comment that Christa made.

Finally Christa held up the book. "Sister, this is un-freaking-believable."

"Don't keep me in suspense. What is it?" Regan nearly shouted.

"Here." Christa handed Regan the translated copy. "Read and be amazed."

She studied the translation and realized her work had just begun and, that to truly understand the significance of what she read, extensive research would be required.

Christa was the first to break the silence. "We can do this," she said. "It'll be like the old days."

"You know what this means, right? You'll have to take time off work."

"So what. I'll get someone to cover for me."

"We'll be breaking the law," Regan said. "If we get caught we lose our jobs for sure. And maybe even go to jail."

"Ashley. We can do this. Sure, it'll be risky, but that's part of the fun. Right?" Christa smiled. "And you know what the best part is?"

"What?"

"We get rich while we're having fun."

It did sound like fun, Regan thought. And Christa was right. They could get rich. Very rich. And what was the real danger after all? Getting caught and being arrested? They had been arrested before—misdemeanors in high school—but arrested nonetheless. It wasn't like anyone would get hurt. No one's life would be in jeopardy. It wasn't dangerous, just illegal.

"Well, Ashley? What do you say?" Christa egged her on. "You up for another adventure of a lifetime?"

"We need to do some research." Regan closed the book. She was already envisioning her forthcoming adventures with Christa, although somewhat remorseful that they wouldn't include Sam Connors.

"Something else."

"What's that?" Regan's thoughts were clouded by her good fortune in the ice tunnel in Germany.

"Buy a map." Christa smiled.

CHAPTER 9

Scott Katzer opened the doors to the Katzer Funeral Home at precisely 8:00 a.m. so the McClaine family could start making funeral arrangements for Mr. McClaine's 86-year old father who passed during the night after a prolonged battle with prostate cancer. Katzer gave McClaine an orientation package and tour of the facility including a breakdown of the fees associated with each portion of the post-mortem care for his departed father.

Katzer excelled at developing the calm, reassuring demeanor and sympathetic voice that was crucial for a funeral director. Clients who entered the door were usually grieving and vulnerable which, as his mother had reinforced repeatedly over the years, made them spend more to ensure their departed loved one rested in comfort for eternity.

Maybe it was a result of the years of his mother's sardonic influence, but the whole idea seemed ludicrous to begin with, Katzer thought, that families would spend several thousands of dollars to bury the dead. In reality, the money wasn't spent on their dead loved one—it was spent to make them feel better. If they could think logically about death, they would realize it didn't make any difference to the dead whether they were laid to rest in a solid mahogany casket with velvet lined interior or a simple wooden box or, for that matter, cremated. Grief, and perhaps guilt, overshadowed their judgment, which his mother claimed was good for business.

Katzer systematically maneuvered McClaine into the casket room, the money room in the funeral home business according to his mother, where the price markup on a casket could be as high as 250 %. In some cases, the profit margin alone on particular high-end models could amount to a few thousand dollars. His mother trained him to always give the illusion he cared and to try to comfort and console the grieving family while convincing them that their dead loved one was worth the price they were spending. But at the end of the day when he locked the doors, she said it was all about the money. And the Katzers had made plenty with their lucrative business.

McClaine's father had been a respected businessman in Nashville for several decades and the wealth of the family was well known—including their lavish lifestyle. Katzer guided McClaine to the newest model casket in the showroom, the Mercedes. The casket was a 32-ounce solid bronze sealer with brushed natural bronze rails, a beige velvet interior, and full glass inner seal. Basically, a casket within a casket. Double protection. Katzer noticed McClaine's instant attraction to the gleam from the casket. Lighting around the casket had been meticulously placed to enhance its luster and shine—his mother's idea. A cheap trick but it worked. With a price tag of just under $12,000, the Mercedes was a moneymaker. A splendid choice for a man who would want a grand display for hundreds of the area's upper echelon guaranteed to be in attendance at his ceremony.

As Katzer explained the merits of the double seal protection, an associate director interrupted.

"Excuse me, Mr. Katzer?"

"What?" Katzer heard the annoyance in his own voice too late. He was on the verge of making the sale and the interruption could give the wealthy McClaine son time to reconsider his choice.

"I'm sorry." She looked at McClaine then back to Katzer. "Mrs. Katzer requests you come to the office immediately."

"Tell her I'll be there in a few minutes."

"I'm sorry, sir, but she was quite insistent that I take over so you can go to the office at once."

"Very well." Katzer looked at McClaine and smiled. "I am very sorry for the interruption, Mr. McClaine, but it seems I must attend to an urgent matter. This is Heather Anderson. She is one of our Associate Directors. She's been with us for five years so you're in good hands." He turned to Heather. "I was just explaining the advantages of the double seal protection on the Mercedes to Mr. McClaine."

Katzer stepped away and motioned to the casket to draw McClaine's attention back to the casket. "If you'll excuse me please while I check with Mrs. Katzer. Heather will answer any questions you may have."

Scott walked into his office to find his mother, Heidi Katzer, waiting. She had an ambivalent look on her face, he thought, a mix between concern and relief depending on how the light from the window played across her pasty white skin.

"What's so important, Mother, that couldn't wait until I finished with Mr. McClaine? I was about to cinch a sale on the Mercedes."

She looked at him with her blue eyes, still resilient at her advanced age. "Did you read the newspaper this morning, Scott?"

"Just a quick glance. Looked like the same partisan mudslinging that's been dominating the news for months. Politicians are all crooked anyway." His mother's stern look gave him pause then he thought about what he had said. "Almost all."

He could tell something was troubling her. "What was in the paper?"

She turned the paper facing him and pointed her finger at a small sidebar article no more than three inches tall. "This could be it." She said.

"It?" He gave an inquisitive look and slipped on his reading glasses.

"Just read."

> **Germany: Hikers find human remains inside glacier.**
> *Garmisch| A German news agency has reported that two American hikers have found the well-preserved remains of a man inside the Höllentalferner glacier below the summit of Zugspitze, Germany's highest peak.*
> *Police told the German Press Agency the hikers located the corpse of the frozen man while exploring an ice cavern carved out by the summer's glacial melt. The hikers were scaling the famed mountain located on the German/Austrian border when they discovered the remains.*
> *No identification was found on the dead man but experts say they believe the body dates back to World War II. Authorities conducted an extensive search of the ice cavern but found no clues as to the man's identity or how he got there.*

"Wow." Scott Katzer removed his glasses and set them on top of the newspaper. "And you think this is him? After all these years."

"I never knew if Don was still alive or dead." She struggled to stand. "I need you...to go find out."

"You want me to fly to Germany?"

"Yes, I do." She hobbled toward the door. "Find out about the book. I don't want to know how you do it...I don't care how you do it. Just find out whether it's him or not. And if it is him, find out what happened to my journal."

"I can't leave right now, we have three services scheduled over the next two days. And that's provided the phone doesn't ring again." He was protesting her order more than making a solid argument. "You can't handle this by yourself."

"Yes I can. I might be old, but I'm not helpless. Give your mother some credit. Besides, I have Heather."

"But—"

"No, Scott. I need you. I expect you on a plane this afternoon. Tonight at the latest." She stood in the doorway without speaking for almost a minute. Then she spoke without facing him. "Don't come back unless you know for sure about the book."

Heidi Katzer walked out without another word.

† † †

The mission was called Task Force Christman in honor of Private William Christman, a Civil War soldier who was the first soldier buried at Arlington National Cemetery. Troops from Delta Company of the 1st Battalion of the 3rd Infantry Regiment were tasked with the execution of the mission. They were known as the Old Guard, the Army's official ceremonial unit, which provided escorts to the President and helped conduct military funerals.

Sergeant Blaine Roberts wasn't dressed in uniform but rather blue jeans, a t-shirt, and flip-flops—all approved attire for this mission. The mission was to photograph the more than 219,000 grave markers and more than 43,000 cremated remains markers at Arlington National Cemetery. The army's task, as mandated by Congress, was to visually account for every grave, update the cemetery database, and digitize the cemetery's maps. In order to accomplish this without disrupting funerals, therefore this portion of the mission was conducted at night after the cemetery was closed to the public.

Roberts had been doing it all summer, walking through the graveyard and taking pictures with an iPhone. The photos taken by him and the rest of his Company were compared and matched with other records in order to identify any discrepancies that needed to be corrected. Congress tasked them with this mission due to the scandal over mismanagement at the nation's most famous cemetery. But the hours were getting to him. All summer he'd been walking the graveyard. Night after night, the same routine, sleep during the day, walk the cemetery all night.

At 3:20 a.m., Roberts wasn't at the top of his game.

His routine had been simple, walk down a row of headstones, stop and take pictures, and log the headstone information on his clipboard. After snapping the photo, penlight between his teeth, he walked to the next marker while writing on his clipboard. Combining the tasks expedited his mission. He'd done it all summer so now it was a mindless rote habit.

Tonight was warm and muggy. His clothes clung to his sweaty body. Earlier in the day thunderstorms drenched the cemetery leaving the ground saturated and the nighttime air hot and sticky. Roberts had just finished a row and rounded the last marker to make his next sweep in the opposite direction. Preoccupied by logging in the last marker, his foot caught on a pile of wet dirt.

Then, he fell.

His clipboard flew from his hands knocking the penlight from between his teeth.

He tumbled against a moist earthen excavation pile, rolled down, and crashed onto something hard at the bottom of the pit.

A casket.

A sharp pain shot through his right shoulder from the impact. Dirt and mud caked his face and clothes. He spit the grit from between his teeth. Musty damp earth filled his nostrils.

How could he have been so careless?

But the bigger question stirring around in his mind was why a grave was left open? Even with the heavy rains, the pit should have been covered. No casket should be left in an open gravesite. And no open gravesite should be left without, as a minimum, flagging to prevent what had just happened.

The casket rocked back and forth while he climbed from the pit. He looked for his penlight and clipboard and found both in the wet grass. He didn't remember seeing any notices of interments among his assigned markers, so why was this one open?

Sergeant Blaine Roberts flashed the beam of light down into the grave.

"Holy crap."

CHAPTER 10

Scott Katzer almost missed his connecting flight to Germany because of a weather reroute around thunderstorms in the D.C. area. His flight from Nashville left on time, but with the last minute booking, his layover time at JFK was short. The en route weather delay left him with only twenty minutes to change planes. And at JFK, that meant changing concourses as well.

He arrived in Munich on time, but his luggage didn't. The airline informed him it would be the next day before his checked bag would arrive. Fortunately, Katzer carried the bare essentials in his carry-on. Enough to get him by until the airline delivered his bag to him in Garmisch-Partenkirchen. What he didn't have, he would buy.

Garmisch, in the west, and Partenkirchen, in the east, were separate towns for centuries until 1935 when Adolph Hitler forced the two respective mayors to combine the two towns in anticipation of the 1936 Winter Olympic Games. Even though the two towns maintain separate identities, the twin townships are generally lumped together and referred to simply as Garmisch.

Katzer didn't want to spend the time required for the long train ride from Munich to Garmisch, so he paid too much to rent an automobile to make the 120-kilometer drive. At least this gave him some mobility after he arrived at his destination. Upon arriving in Munich, Katzer received a text message from his mother; she had booked him for three nights at the Hotel Bavaria in Garmisch.

His fluent German paid off after he arrived at the Garmisch Polizeistation—police station—since the only English-speaking officers had gone home for the day. He inquired about the man recovered from the glacier and was informed the body was being kept frozen at the Klinikum Garmisch-Partenkirchen, the clinical center in Garmisch. Further query revealed the officer in charge of the case was the only person that could approve a viewing and even then only when accompanied by him.

Katzer arrived at the police station early the next morning and was met by Gerhardt Zeilnhofer, officer in charge of the investigation of the man found inside the Höllentalferner glacier. Zeilnhofer was a short man, maybe 5'6" with an athletic build, close-cropped blond hair, and a defined swagger when he walked.

"Mr. Katzer, how may I be of assistance?" Zeilnhofer asked.

"The man you found inside the glacier last week, have you identified him yet?"

"No, his identity remains a mystery to us, but we are still in the infancy of our investigation. The only thing we have determined is he appears to have fallen into the glacier sometime in the mid-1940s. Probably around the end of the war."

"Did he have any belongings on him, perhaps a book of some sort?" Katzer knew his lack of tact would draw suspicion, but he already had a cover story—the truth—with some selective omissions.

Zeilnhofer was silent for a few seconds. "A rather pointed...and somewhat odd question wouldn't you say, Mr.

Katzer? Perhaps you have something you would like to share."

"So he did have something on him," Katzer said.

"No, Mr. Katzer, he did not." Zeilnhofer pointed to a chair. "Have a seat. Please, explain yourself and your questions. I insist."

Katzer spent the next ten minutes explaining that his mother, who was from the small Austrian village of Ehrwald, fell in love with a United States soldier who went AWOL while serving his post at Zugspitze in 1946. She met the man after his father died in the war. The only thing missing other than the man was her diary. If the man they found had the diary, then that would provide positive identification.

Zeilnhofer rubbed his chin. "And you think this Major Don Adams could be this man?"

"I don't know," Katzer said, "but my aging mother does. Enough to send me here to find out so she can have closure. She could never accept the thought that he abandoned her. She was convinced their love was eternal. To know he died in that glacier might lift the burden of the painful memories she's carried with her nearly 70 years."

Zeilnhofer didn't speak at first. He reached into his desk drawer and pulled out a file folder. Using his finger as a guide, he scanned down a handwritten list of names stopping halfway. "Major Don Adams is on the list of possible identities…but so are 30 other names. I can assure you this man's body had nothing on it but an old watch, which we could not trace back to anyone, and a Schweizer Offiziersmesser."

"A what?" Katzer asked.

"Swiss Army Knife, I believe you Americans call it."

"And that was it?"

"I assure you, Mr. Katzer, there was nothing else on him."

"Did you search the cave?"

"I had my men conduct an exhaustive search of the ice cave. There was nothing else in there but ice."

"Tell me about the watch."

"The watch?" Zelinhofer asked.

Katzer nodded.

"The watch was an old 1917 Waterbury, the kind the U. S. Government issued to soldiers in World War I, which is why we originally thought the remains were much older...the knife changed that. It was crafted in 1945."

Katzer stood and pointed to Zeilnhofer's file. "How many names are on that list?"

"Originally, thirty-three."

"Have you ruled any of them out at all?" Katzer asked.

"Actually we have," Zeilnhofer continued, "we have ruled out thirteen. Either confirmed dead or alive and living elsewhere."

"Which still leaves twenty unaccounted for," Katzer said.

"Precisely," Zeilnhofer said, "and Major Don Adams is one of them. As a matter of fact, all of the remaining names on the list are U. S. soldiers who disappeared during World War II."

Katzer walked around the room then turned to the police officer. "This might seem an odd request, but I'd like to have something definitive to tell my mother. Is there any chance I could see the body and maybe even take a look at that file?"

Zeilnhofer was silent. He seemed to be studying the taller, older Katzer. "I guess I don't see the harm." Zeilnhofer walked to his office door and pulled it open. "Meet me at the clinic in thirty minutes."

Exactly thirty minutes later, Katzer and Zeilnhofer walked into the basement morgue of the Klinikum Garmisch-

Partenkirchen. The room was cold—both in temperature and appearance—a stainless steel personality. Stainless tables, chairs, stools, and freezer compartments for the cadavers.

Zeilnhofer walked to one compartment, opened the door, and slid out a smaller table with a corpse covered with a sheet. The police officer pulled back the sheet revealing the torso and arms of the naked man.

"What happened to his clothes?" Katzer asked.

"Removed for autopsy." Zeilnhofer pointed to a bag on the floor. "I can assure you we have searched them diligently looking for any indication as to his identity. Because of the length of time in the ice, there was nothing we could use."

The man's skin was dark brown and stretched tight around his skull, limbs, and torso, yet remarkably preserved for a man dead nearly 70 years. Katzer noticed the twist in the man's arm. "Looks like he must have fallen into the glacier."

The police officer stared at Katzer. "What makes you say that?"

"I'm a mortician by trade." Katzer pointed to the man's arm. "The way the arm snapped, typical when someone tries to break a fall. And here." Katzer pointed to the man's abdomen. "Is that a gunshot wound?"

"The medical examiner said it appeared to be by the nature of the wound, but he indicated the bullet must have been traveling at a relatively slow speed when it hit him. Perhaps a long distance shot." The officer handed Katzer the file. "Is there anything else you can see from a mortician's point of view?"

"Too long in the ice to detect bruising or lacerations, however, it looks like his clavicle fractured when he fell." Katzer rifled through the police file until he found what he was looking for. The police officer took good notes but didn't seem to follow up on any leads. Or, at least what Katzer viewed as leads, anyway. "I guess this was a wasted trip. My mother will go to her grave still wondering what happened to her American soldier."

Katzer closed the file and handed it back to Zeilnhofer.

"Will you be leaving now?" Zeilnhofer asked.

"Not immediately, no. I have relatives in nearby villages that I haven't seen in many years. I planned on paying them a visit." Katzer reached into his coat pocket and withdrew a business card. "If you discover this man's identity, I would appreciate a call or an email. Regardless of whether it is Adams or not, I'd like to be able to put my mother's mind to rest."

The police officer took the card. "Enjoy the rest of your stay, Mr. Katzer."

"Thank you. I will." Katzer turned and walked out of the morgue. Not only did he have what he wanted but he'd confirmed the man's identity as well. The body on the slab in the morgue was indeed that of Major Don Adams. The watch and the knife were good evidence...but the gunshot wound in the abdomen cinched it. Now, time to return to the United States and track down the person listed in the police file as the one who reported finding the body.

Ashley Regan of Charleston, South Carolina.

CHAPTER 11

Maldive Islands
Indian Ocean

The 21-meter luxury yacht—a two-masted schooner—sliced quietly through the water toward the resort's pier, still an easy kilometer away. The long pier was lined with tiki lanterns pointing toward the shoreline. From this distance, Jake thought, it looked like the schooner was lining up with a runway.

Whether he was fishing in a mountain stream or sitting on the deck of a boat, Jake loved the water and its calming appeal. He looked at Kyli, with her hair tucked behind her ears in an attempt to keep it out of her face as the warm ocean air washed across them, and smiled. The light from the full moon played across her face. Even in the moonlight, her eyes seemed to sparkle.

It felt like it was so long ago, but it had only been eighteen months since his life had changed so drastically. His psyche seemed tranquil now compared to the tumultuous feeling of the old days—before Wiley. Back then he thought he had it all with Beth, his then fiancée, and felt he could never live without her.

And then he had to.

Life *was* better now. His self-confidence rose to a higher level than ever before. He had perfected his tradecraft skills. His keen insight was sharpened and enhanced. He had become an effective emissary doing the bidding of Elmore

Wiley and the Greenbrier Fellowship, a worldwide organization made up of some of the most influential persons the world had to offer. A group who met once a year at the Greenbrier Resort in West Virginia to discuss the world's greatest threats. Although never in an official capacity, the Fellowship made recommendations on how to deal with those threats. Recommendations that typically sent Wiley's emissaries into action.

That was where Jake came in.

He wasn't chosen by accident, he knew that now, he was chosen because of his innate ability to assess, analyze, and act quickly to resolve issues on a real-time basis. And as Wiley had repeated to him on numerous occasions, "meet the objective, the how doesn't matter." That maxim didn't mean to proceed with reckless abandon either, as all objectives, he learned, included discretion and secrecy. And, at his disposal to accomplish those tasks, were some of the greatest minds money could buy. Analysts like Fontaine, engineers like Matt, and scientists like Kyli, made up his support team including the master of radio frequency and microwave technology himself—Elmore Wiley—the Toymaker.

The cruise was relaxing and he could tell Kyli was pleased with her choice of vacation destinations. The schooner slowed as it neared the pier, Jake watched resort employees take their positions to catch the lines to secure the yacht. He also noticed the shadowy silhouette of a woman standing back from the edge of the dock several meters. And even though it was just a shadow he knew it belonged to Francesca Catanzaro. He also knew her presence signaled the end of his vacation with Kyli.

"This can't be good." He mumbled to himself.

Jake and Francesca sat on the edge of the infinity pool while Kyli was in the bedroom crying. Her big plans for a two-week romantic get away with Jake had just been dashed by Francesca's news that Jake had to leave and return to the United States immediately. Jake had never seen Kyli this upset, not even after the explosion in Paris that had injured her and her girlfriend.

He was disappointed too, but knew broken personal plans came with the job.

Kyli walked out and sat down next to Jake, dangling her feet in the water. Her eyes were red and puffy. Jake put his arm around her.

"I know I'm being selfish but this was our first real trip together." Kyli put her hand in her lap after wiping her eyes with a tissue. "I just wanted everything to be perfect."

"I know you did." Jake used as much of a consoling voice as he could. "And everything was perfect…it just got cut short this time."

"Will it always be like this? Never being able to make plans because my grandfather has some other secret mission where he whisks you away at a moment's notice."

"Absolutely not. We'll have plenty of time for more trips, uninterrupted ones too." Jake wished he could honestly say that were true, but he knew that wasn't the case. And never would be.

"Kyli," Francesca said, "your grandfather wouldn't have sent me after Jake if it weren't important. He knows how much effort you put into planning this trip and how much you were looking forward to it. If there was any other way, he would have found it."

"How long before we have to leave?" Kyli asked Francesca.

"Mr. Wiley wants all of us out of here tonight." Francesca explained. "I have a boat waiting to take us to the airport and I came in Wiley's personal jet."

"Kyli's going with us?" Jake asked.

"As far as Brussels. Then you and I are flying to D.C."

Jake looked at Kyli then back to Francesca. "Blowback from the last op?"

"I didn't get that impression from Wiley." Francesca stood. "I'll be waiting at the boat while you two pack your things. We leave in 30 minutes."

CHAPTER 12

Evan Makley stared at the document attached to the email in disbelief. If it were authentic, the President's career was about to crash and burn—and his with it. Whether true or false, these were the types of allegations that ruined a politician's career. Even one as popular as Rebecca Rudd. He kept staring, afraid to blink, hoping and praying this was some sort of sick joke but somewhere deep inside, he knew it wasn't. Maybe it was a case of mistaken identity, he rationalized. That was the only hope he had. Still, the tone of confidence and authority in the words caused his heart to sink.

Another thing troubling him was the fact that the attached file slipped past White House screening. Most worrisome of all was that the sender used an alternating combination of his and the President's social security numbers as the document's password. Information protected by a number of safety measures put in place by the Secret Service.

He'd worked too hard and too long to reach his position as Chief of Staff of the White House. At forty-seven a scandal of this magnitude would destroy any chance for post-White House employment. In politics, he would be the fall guy. His job was to keep these kinds of things from happening and he'd failed. He knew there was still time for damage control. His job was to protect the President.

Covering his own ass at the same time was a welcome side effect.

He opened his computer's web browser and typed in *www.lovesdesperatedesire.com*. The page loaded fast and was simple with only three drop down menus. He clicked the first menu and chose his unique yet discrete user name—*First Mate*, chosen for his love of sailing. And even today, it seemed appropriate for his professional standing. The second drop down indicated coded locations. He chose *JM* for Jefferson Memorial, his usual spot. The last drop down menu was an appointment list in fifteen-minute increments starting at the closest next quarter-hour mark. If a time was grayed out, it wasn't available. He looked at this watch, 9:17 a.m., and clicked 10:00 a.m. He submitted his request, closed his browser, and started reviewing the President's schedule for the afternoon.

Within one minute he received a text:

JM0945.

He stood and hustled to the door, told his secretary he had to run a quick errand and headed to his car. The President would be locked in her meeting for another hour so he would have time to make the meeting and return—no one the wiser.

†††

Abigail Love had done business with the man on several occasions, but not since he'd become Chief of Staff. Dealing with public figures hadn't worked out for her in the past but because of some sense of customer loyalty, she would hear him out. Besides, he was a very good-looking man. One with whom she would like to spend a couple of hours alone behind closed doors.

From the shady park bench, a hundred yards east of the Jefferson Memorial, she gazed across the tidal basin, through the dogwoods, past the National Mall, beside the Washington Monument, and over the Ellipse at the White House. From where she sat she knew the distance was just over a mile.

She'd all but written Evan Makley out of her customer database since he'd risen to his current heights working for the only politician she'd ever admired. Rebecca Rudd had aggressively moved up the political ladder with a style and grace that reflected well on women. Her *No-Bull* platform seemed ambitious yet she was able to achieve most of her campaign promises within the first two years of office. Rudd was the model for women nationwide. The first female President of the United States. Even Love, a woman who spent most of her life on the wrong side of the law, appreciated the job Rebecca Rudd had done.

Slightly to her right and across the tidal basin, dozens of paddleboats were tied to the dock, waiting to be rented. The shore lined with cherry trees, which in springtime would be covered in blossoms. She wondered what business Makley could have with her. Special care must be taken this time, no slip-ups.

In her peripheral vision she saw someone moving on her left—Makley. She looked at her watch, 9:45. Right on time. Makley sat down on the bench at the opposite end from Love. Neither said anything for several minutes.

"Evan, I must say I was surprised to get your submission." She looked straight ahead, never turning to face him. Nor would he toward her. Love was very strict about that rule. "How might Love's Desperate Desires be of assistance?"

Makley reached into his jacket and pulled out a letter-sized envelope and placed it between them on the bench. "I have a problem."

"You wouldn't be here if you didn't." She put her hands together and interlocked her fingers making a steeple with her index fingers. "My rates have gone up. Inflation is making it harder to keep up with the Joneses."

"How much?"

"Double." Love knew if Makley or the President were in trouble, he'd readily pay her price.

"You can't be serious. That's outrageous." Makley protested.

"Take it or leave it Evan. I agreed to this as a favor for you as a repeat customer."

Makley was silent for a few seconds. "Same arrangements as before?"

"Only the rate changed. Procedure is still the same. Half now. The rest at consummation."

"No screw ups, okay? Too much at stake."

She ignored his remark. "Any special instructions?"

"To start with, identify the source with a full background check." Makley pushed the envelope toward the center of the bench. "I'll let you know what I need after that."

"Anything else?"

Makley didn't speak at first. "Can you make this a priority?"

"It'll cost you another 25%."

"Agreed." Makley stood and walked off.

Love opened the envelope and started skimming the contents. Her face felt flush with anger like the raging torrent of a flooding river. Whoever was doing this had to be stopped. She could never allow this to surface and ruin Rebecca Rudd.

Unless.

She smiled. Sometimes Evan Makley could be so naïve. Knowledge of this, especially if she found it to be true, was more dangerous in her hands than Makley might realize.

This could be her proverbial *ace in the hole.*

A very real 'get out of jail' card.

For life.

CHAPTER 13

It was the second late-night clandestine visit to the White House in as many weeks. Jake found himself sitting in the same seat in the Executive Conference Room in the West Wing of the White House. Francesca sat next to him. This time they were alone, Elmore Wiley was at his factory in El Paso and couldn't attend the meeting.

President Rebecca Rudd opened the door and whisked into the room, motioning for Jake and Francesca to remain seated. Evan Makley followed, closing the door behind him. He had two manila folders in his hand.

"Mr. Pendleton, Ms. Catanzaro. Thank you for coming on such short notice. I hope I didn't take you away from anything."

Jake and Francesca looked at each other. "No ma'am. Not at all." Francesca said.

Jake felt the President knew she'd interrupted his vacation with Kyli but assumed she wouldn't have done it without a good reason.

"The reason I summoned you two here is because a situation has developed that needs to be handled delicately and discretely." Rudd paused. "By the way, I appreciate the manner in which you two handled my previous favor. I owe you a debt I can never acknowledge."

"Yes, ma'am. It's our honor to serve you," Jake said.

"This problem has the potential to create a scathing crisis. Minority and equal rights issues have always been important to me. It's something I want to continue to protect in the same manner with which I've approached it since the election. The only way to completely eliminate discrimination is to disallow it at every level." Rudd pulled out a chair and sat down. "Regardless of heritage, race, religious affiliation, or gender, nobody...I repeat nobody, gets preferential treatment. I will not tolerate it on any level."

"Yes, ma'am. I'm aware of the progress you've made developing a clear non-discrimination policy," Jake said. "With all due respect, I don't see how a discrimination issue should involve us."

"I'm getting to that." Rudd motioned to Makley. "Evan will you start the slideshow, please?"

"Yes, ma'am." Makley started flipping switches on the same console that the President used in the previous meeting.

"Another thing I won't tolerate is hate crimes." She pointed to the ceiling. "Evan, the lights please."

Makley dimmed the lights and started the slideshow. Pictures of a disturbed gravesite flashed across the screen.

"This is Arlington National Cemetery. These pictures were taken by the Old Guard last week. After the investigation, the contents of this grave were restored to original condition and the remains reinterred. Next group please, Evan."

More of the same type of pictures but of a different cemetery.

"This is Andersonville National Cemetery in Georgia. This happened two days ago." Rudd pointed to the pictures. "Both grave sites have several things in common. First, both soldiers died in combat. Both graves were disturbed but nothing appears to have been taken. It was as if someone was looking for something but didn't find what they wanted. Both soldiers died in World War II in Germany, 1944 and 1945, respectively. But the most disturbing thing is both soldiers were black."

"And you think this is some sort of hate crime?" Francesca asked.

"Honestly, I don't know if it is or it isn't, but the media would have a field day with it and make it look like hate crimes. For now I have this under wraps so I want you two to get to the bottom of it. Evan will give you access to all the information we've accumulated thus far. I've already spoken to Elmore, he assured me this would be your only assignment until it is resolved."

Evan Makley handed Jake and Francesca each a folder. "The information in the folders is identical. Please note your contact information at both Arlington and Andersonville. They are expecting you and have been told to assist you in any way they can. Basically, they're at your disposal," Makley said.

President Rebecca Rudd stood abruptly obliging Jake and Francesca to do the same. "Mr. Pendleton, Ms. Catanzaro, call Evan with daily updates please. His direct line is in your package."

"Yes, ma'am." They both said in unison.

The President left the room followed by Evan Makley.

Jake turned to Francesca. "I hope you like cemeteries because it looks we'll be hanging out in them for awhile."

"I hate them. Cemeteries give me the creeps." She lowered her voice. "Just like Evan Makley."

CHAPTER 14

Jake assessed the young soldier sitting at the table when he and Francesca arrived at Arlington National Cemetery. It was early and Jake had already read the file on Sergeant Blaine Roberts over breakfast. The young soldier had dark hair, brown eyes, Jake's size, 5' 10", 190 pounds and young. Jake thought he looked early twenties even though the file said nineteen.

Evan Mackley had made arrangements for a private meeting at the end of Roberts shift. The graveyard shift, literally, Jake thought. The young soldier was dressed in blue jeans, New Balance running shoes, and a green t-shirt with "Go Army" printed on front.

Roberts jumped to attention when they entered. "Sir. Ma'am."

"At ease, Sergeant," Jake said. "We're civilians, no need for military protocol here."

"Sir." Roberts faced forward still at attention. "I was told you were a Naval Officer and served under Admiral Scott Bentley at the Pentagon and that I was to extend proper courtesy, Sir."

"Sergeant, that was a long time ago. I'm on my third employer since the Navy."

"Yes sir. All impressive, sir."

"Very well, Sergeant." Jake pointed to two chairs. He and Francesca sat down. "Please sit down now Sergeant or this will take a very long time. We will dispense with the formalities and protocol for the purpose of this interview. Is that understood?"

Roberts sat down. "Understood, sir."

"This is Francesca Catanzaro. She and I are partners on this investigation. I don't know how much you've been briefed but this incident garnered the attention of some major movers and shakers in D.C. I know you've been up all night so we'll try to keep this brief."

"I'm fine, sir."

Jake opened his folder and pulled out a notepad and placed it on the table in front of him. He reached into his pocket and pulled out a pen. He pointed to a briefing sheet from the folder. "It says here you're assigned to a mission called Task Force Christman. I'm not familiar with the mission, can you brief us on it?"

The next ten minutes were spent in a question and answer about the purpose of the mission mandated by Congress to validate each plot in the cemetery. Jake could tell the young soldier was nervous in the beginning but the more he spoke about his job the more at ease he became.

"Before each shift," Francesca asked, "do you get some sort of briefing?"

"Yes, ma'am." Roberts said. "We have a mission brief at 2100 hours every night which lasts about thirty minutes. Our assignments are made then."

"If there is a funeral scheduled for the next morning, wouldn't the grave be dug the day before?" She asked.

"Yes, ma'am. At the beginning of each shift when our survey areas are assigned, we're each given a call sheet. The call sheet indicates where any open graves are located, which I verify visually. The call sheet also indicates any graves that are recently covered. New interments alert me to soft earth so I avoid walking directly on top of the grave."

"Has anything like this happened to you before?" Jake asked.

"No, sir. I've run into rabbits, foxes, and even deer but this was the first time I'd come across an open grave that wasn't marked and flagged off."

"Flagged off?" Francesca asked.

"Yes, ma'am. Every open grave for next day ceremonies are covered by an open tent in case of rain and a yellow flagging tape is wrapped around it to serve as a warning so no one would accidentally fall in."

"Like you did," she said.

"Yes, ma'am. Like I did." Roberts smiled for the first time since the interview began. "But this grave wasn't listed on the call sheet, nor was it covered or flagged."

"And as we now know," Francesca said, "was vandalized."

"Which brings me to my next question," Jake asked, "how often does this happen? I mean, obviously there has been vandalism from time to time at Arlington, right?'

"Yes sir. Over the years we've had markers disappear, graves disturbed, markers defaced or broken. The cemetery has had instances of flowers being moved from one grave to another. We've even had a few instances of things being placed on graves in the middle of the night."

"What about grave robbers?" Francesca asked. "Just the other day I read an article about organ harvesting in Europe. They were stealing corpses right out of the morgue. Bodies that weren't embalmed were dug up the same night they were buried."

Roberts' smile disappeared. "There have been some instances in the past, but until the other night, it had been many years. And technically, this one wasn't a robbery. It's officially classified as a grave disturbance. Nothing appeared to have been taken. All his remains and personal effects were still inside the casket. I can tell you the family was pretty upset but the dead man's wife vouched for everything in the casket. The man died in an explosion and was mutilated so the ceremony was closed casket."

"When was that?" Francesca asked.

"He died in 1945 and was originally interred here at Arlington in 1946. His remains were moved thirty or so years later to their current location."

"Are remains moved often?" Jake asked.

"Not anymore. Reasons do come up that predicate moving remains from one plot to another. I imagine there will be quite a number of moves in the near future as Task Force Christman reveals more mistakes."

"How many mismarked graves have you found?" Francesca closed her folder, a signal to Jake that she had no more questions.

"Personally, only one. Collectively the Old Guard has found a couple of dozen. Not bad considering there are nearly 300,000 grave markers dating all the way back to the Civil War."

Jake noticed the sergeant's bloodshot eyes. He'd been awake all night walking through the graveyard verifying markers and was visibly tired and ready for some rest. But the young soldier had not complained. Jake thought he might have seen the man suppress a yawn once or twice but he maintained a professional attitude throughout the entire interview. "One final question."

"Go ahead, sir."

"What do you personally think happened to this grave?"

"I think it was kids, sir. Maybe some sort of prank, like a fraternity initiation or something."

"Thank you, Sergeant. You're dismissed," Jake said.

After the young soldier left the room Jake turned to Francesca. "I don't think I buy the fraternity prank theory."

"Doesn't ring true to me either." Francesca tucked her hair behind her ears.

"How's this for a theory?" Jake said. "What if the corpse is not the target?"

"Come on, Jake, that's ridiculous. If the remains aren't the target then how do you explain that all the caskets belong to black men?"

"Maybe to throw us off track." Jake smiled.

"Off track of what?" Francesca held up her finger. "Face it, Jake. This really could be a hate crime."

CHAPTER 15

Scott Katzer sat in a white unmarked funeral home van in front of the house in Charleston, South Carolina for over two hours before he saw any sign of life. A woman walked out to the mailbox, placed an envelope inside, raised the flag, and returned inside the home. He'd done his research since he left Germany. Ashley Regan was the name listed on the police report in Garmisch who had discovered the body inside the cavern in the glacier. It also matched the name on the mailbox.

Katzer checked the time—8:00 a.m. His hands trembled. He'd never done anything like this before but his mother had instilled a sense of urgency in him to protect the family. If Ashley Regan had the book, he needed to get it from her. There was too much at stake.

Even though he didn't tell Officer Zeilnhofer, he had indeed confirmed the man's identity, his mother's intuition had been correct. The fact that neither Adams nor his body ever turned up after decades of being missing, could only mean he didn't survive the avalanche. From the stories his mother told, it was only by the grace of God that she survived. If it weren't for the rock overhang she hid under when the avalanche began, she would have met the same fate as the Austrian men who were with her. They were swept up by the torrent of snow and catapulted to their deaths on the glacier below. Their dead, broken, frozen bodies were found

three days later when the storm broke. She seemed certain
that Adams was killed also even though no body was ever
recovered.

Katzer started the van, pulled forward, and then backed
into the driveway stopping only inches from the garage door.
He'd gathered all the chemicals he thought he'd need before
he left Nashville and made the nine and a half hour drive to
Charleston. His mother was resolute that if he couldn't find
the book, he was to bring the woman back to Nashville so
she could conduct the interrogation herself. If he found the
book his orders were to kill her if he had to and return with
the book.

He had never harmed another human. He had witnessed
a lot of death in his business but never was he a violent
person. As distasteful as the act of killing seemed, his mother
was right. He had to protect the family.

Katzer pulled the latex gloves over his hands, opened a
bottle and soaked a rag. It was an antiquated method but still
effective. Besides, he had plenty of other options available if
he needed them, this one was more convenient.

He walked to the door and knocked.

The door opened. "May I help y—"

Before she could finish her sentence Katzer pounced.
Her size no match for him. He smothered the woman's face
with the rag while he wrestled her to the floor. He kicked the
door closed with his foot. Sitting on top of her, his long arms
kept his face away from her claws as she kicked and
squirmed.

He'd now crossed the line.

Something he could never undo.

After several seconds of thrashing, the woman stopped
moving. He removed the rag and sat there. The rush of
overpowering the woman was a thrill he hadn't anticipated. A

feeling of power and dominance. At his age and in his profession, he didn't see much excitement. But now, he had to admit, he was aroused.

Without warning, a fist rammed into his stomach, knocking the breath out of him. She had tricked him by pretending to be overcome by the chloroform. He couldn't believe he'd been sucker punched.

With all the strength he could muster he slammed his fist into her jaw. Her jawbone cracked, blood splattered across the hardwood floor. His wrist felt like he'd hit a brick wall. She was alive, but unconscious. Katzer placed the rag over her nose and left it there while he searched for towels to wipe down the floor.

After he was certain the woman was unconscious, he searched the small home. Every drawer, cabinet, and shelf emptied. No book. The contents from every closet pulled to the floor. No book. Mattresses overturned. Every possible hiding place searched. Nothing. Katzer was convinced the book was not in the home. He leaned over, grabbed the woman, threw her over his shoulder, and carried her into the garage. He raised the garage door then grabbed the remote control attached to the visor of the car and put her in the back of the van. He used tie wraps and duct tape to secure her arms and legs and placed a strip of tape over her mouth to keep her silent after she woke up. He opened the lid to the casket in the back of the van and placed her inside. Prior to leaving Nashville, he'd rigged a special casket to allow for the circulation of air. Or sleeping gas if he needed it.

He closed the garage door, tossed the remote on the floor of the van, and pulled out for the long drive to Nashville. The best way to transport a body—dead or alive.

What should have been a nine-hour drive turned into a thirteen-hour drive due to a six-car pileup on Interstate 40 at the North Carolina/Tennessee state line. Katzer's van sat motionless for over two hours while rescue helicopters flew in to triage, stabilize, and fly out the critically injured. He knew from his experience that the rescue vehicles were transporting those bodies that were laying in the median covered with sheets to the morgue. When the wreckers finally cleared the debris from the mountain interstate, traffic crept along for nearly thirty miles before reaching speed limits.

He arrived in Nashville shortly after 11:00 p.m., pulled the van into the loading area, and crawled through the back to open the rear van door when it suddenly opened.

"It's about time," Heidi Katzer said.

"Give me a break, Mother. I called and told you about the traffic backup. I got here as fast as I could without risking being pulled over by the cops."

"Let's get her inside. Is she awake?"

"No," Scott explained. "She started making noise around Knoxville so I gassed her again. She should wake up within an hour or so."

Scott Katzer looked at the embalming table when he heard the woman groan. He'd tethered her arms and legs to the table with makeshifts bindings, duct tape still strapped on her mouth. He walked across the room and pressed the intercom call button, "Mother, she's coming to."

The newly remodeled embalming room was equipped with all the latest mortuary features. One wall was lined with stainless steel cabinets and sinks. Three white-porcelain embalming tables lined up side-by-side along the white tile floor. A drain in the floor near the middle of the room made wash down quick and easy. The white ceramic tile floor and walls gave the room a sterile look and feel. Above each table hung new H/Vac ventilation fans supported by articulating arms. The previous embalming room was dark and the rancid smell from decades of embalming had permeated the wooden cabinets and old equipment. Katzer's investment in the new embalming room was worth the money, he thought. His mother had initially objected to the expenditure but with some subtle advertisement, Katzer Funeral Home's new facilities had taken enough business away from its competitors to pay for the upgrade. And, as much as the grieving families would never realize, competition in the funeral home business could be ruthless at times.

Heidi Katzer opened the door. "How cognizant is she?"

"Still groggy but she'll be lucid soon enough," Scott replied.

"Turn on the heat spatula and melt some wax," Heidi instructed. "Just in case."

Obviously realizing her predicament, the horrified woman snapped her head from side to side as she struggled against her restraints. Muffled yells behind the tape strapped over her mouth grew louder.

Heidi stood next to the woman, held her head down, and ripped off the tape.

"What the hell is this all about?" The woman yelled. "Let me loose."

"Your fate depends on you, young lady," Heidi said. "First you're going to answer some questions. If I like your answers, you will be set free."

His mother's voice was too pleasant, Scott thought, given the fact that the young woman had just been abducted.

The woman jerked again against her restraints. "Where am I?"

Scott saw the woman's head lift, her eyes taking in her new surroundings.

"What the hell is this place?"

"None of that matters, my dear," The old woman reassured. "All that matters is that you cooperate." She paused. "Or the consequences will be quite severe."

The woman looked at Scott. "What's she talking about?"

"Just do as she asks," Scott said, "and you won't get hurt."

"Get hurt? What do you mean 'get hurt?' Let me go," she yelled.

Heidi leaned close to the woman's face. "Where is the book?"

"Book? What book? What are you talking about?"

"Let me refresh your memory," Heidi said. "A few weeks ago you climbed Zugspitze, correct?"

"Yes. What's that got to do with anything?"

"You found a corpse inside a glacier, correct?"

"Yes, but—"

"On that man's body was a book. A leather journal that belonged to me before he took it from me. I want it back," Heidi continued, "so tell me...where is my book?"

"There was no book. I promise" The young woman pleaded. "Now please, let me go."

Heidi stepped back. "Last chance. Tell me where you hid the book."

"I don't know what you're talking about. There is no book."

Heidi motioned to Scott then pointed to the table. "Stuff that rag in her mouth."

"But Mother, she doesn't know—"

"Do it now, Scott," Heidi ordered. "Do not question my judgment. I will get her to answer...one way or another."

The tone in his mother's voice frightened him. How could a woman only five feet tall be so intimidating? Scott obeyed her like a robot. He grabbed a cloth rag, walked over and clenched his hand around the young woman's throat. When she opened her mouth, he stuffed the rag inside, and then looked at his mother. "What are you going to do?"

"Offer her some incentive to talk."

Heidi grabbed an apparatus that looked like a wood-burning iron with a duckbill shaped attachment. He'd used the tool many times to reshape or reconstruct bodies disfigured by injury. The tool, called a heat spatula, allowed the embalmers to smooth wax across the deceased skin to remove blemishes.

"Is this really necessary?" He asked.

"Not another word, Scott." The old woman turned the dial on the tool. "Now my dear, you *will* tell me where my book is."

His mother poured the hot wax on the young woman's left arm. Hot enough to scald but not blister the skin. The woman bucked on the table and screamed into the rag. Tears rolled down both cheeks. After the wax cooled and the woman calmed down, his mother placed the heat spatula on the woman's arm.

Scott Katzer watched as his mother repeatedly burned the woman's arm with the heat spatula. When the hot duckbill attachment melted through the wax and touched the woman's skin, he could hear the sizzle of burning flesh followed by a wisp of smoke rising from the wound. The pungent smell of singed flesh filled his nostrils.

He always knew his mother could be callous. Her lack of empathy to their clients always bothered Katzer. But what he was witnessing now was torture and should be making him sick to his stomach.

It wasn't.

On the contrary, he was filled with a desire to torture the woman himself. Take control of the situation. Dominate. Get even for sucker punching him in the stomach in Charleston. He knew his mother would never relinquish control so he sat back and watched. The whole time imagining he was doing the torturing.

His mother worked the apparatus from the woman's elbow and slowly burned a small patch at a time along her upper arm until she reached the woman's shoulder. With each scald the woman jumped, her eyes bulged and more tears ran down her already tear-stained cheeks. Her mascara left black lines streaking from her eyes down the sides of her face.

Finally, his mother stopped.

She put down the heat spatula. "Remove the rag," she ordered.

The woman's moans filled the room. Impulsively, Scott grabbed the woman's jaw and held the scalding device inches from her face. "Stop your wailing, bitch, or you'll get more of this."

The woman took short gasps of air, sobbing uncontrollably.

His mother stared at him. He could only imagine what she was thinking. Finally she looked back at the woman and spoke. "Now Ms. Regan, I'll ask you one more time before we start on your face. Where is my book?"

"Ms. Regan?" The young woman panted in broken speech. "I'm not Ashley Regan. I'm Samantha Connors."

CHAPTER 16

Jake and Francesca arrived at the park office in the Andersonville National Cemetery at 8:30 a.m. with instructions from Evan Mackley to meet with a man named Adam Marshall. The Andersonville National Historic Site consisted of not just the cemetery but also the National Prisoner of War Museum and the associated Civil War prison site.

Camp Sumter, as it was originally known, was built in early 1864 and was one of the largest Confederate military prisons of the Civil War. The prison pen covered 26 ½ acres and was manned by guards who stood watch in sentry boxes spaced at thirty-yard intervals. These Confederate soldiers in the *pigeon roosts,* as the prisoners called them, monitored an area referred to as the *deadline,* a nineteen-foot sterile area between the stockade fence and the prisoner containment area. Any prisoner crossing the *deadline* was shot—dead.

The Andersonville Confederate Prison was in operation for only fourteen months and closed in May 1865. In July of the same year, Clara Barton, along with a detachment of laborers, soldiers, and a former prisoner named Dorence Atwater, came to Andersonville Cemetery to identify and mark the graves of the dead Union soldiers.

When the Citation 750 landed at Souther Field in Americus, Georgia, Jake's reserved rental car was waiting, a black Dodge Charger R/T equipped with a 5.7 liter HEMI V-

8, all of which appealed to Jake's hot rod mentality. The 8-mile drive down the barren country road from the airport to the park office took him just under six minutes. He'd grown up in Georgia and was at home on the Peach State's back roads. His father had brought him to Andersonville on occasion when Jake was younger, usually in conjunction with their father-son fishing trips to Lake Blackshear.

Jake noticed the heavy dew on the grass left by the cool September morning. While he and Francesca walked across the parking lot toward the office, Jake noticed a motorcade and a hearse parked across the cemetery lawn. As a former Naval officer, he recognized the sailors in U. S. Navy Dress Blues standing at attention under the Rostrum while family and friends mourned the loss of another of America's heroes.

Adam Marshall greeted Jake and Francesca in the office lobby. He was Jake's size except more of his chest had given way to gravity and moved to his waistline. He had short dark hair and wire-rimmed glasses and wore a uniform.

"You must be Jake Pendleton and Francesca..." Marshall paused. "I won't try your last name, I'm sure I'd butcher it."

"Catanzaro." She extended her hand as a greeting.

Jake and Marshall shook hands. "What is your job function at Andersonville?" Jake asked.

"Chief of Resource Management," Marshall said. "Most people see the uniform and just assume I'm a Park Ranger. After all, this historic site is part of the National Park Service and most people have been to a national park so they've seen the uniform."

"I take it you've already been briefed on the purpose of our visit?" Jake asked.

"I received an email from the Director of Park Services in D.C," Marshall explained. "He said I was to give you full access to the file of the deceased and the police report. He indicated there had been other instances similar to this." It was more a question than a statement. "I can show you the pictures but the grave is actually still open if you'd like to take a look for yourself. It had been scheduled for covering and repairs this morning but after the email, I postponed it until after your visit. Figured you might want a first-hand look."

"That would be great." Jake looked at Francesca. "Let's take a look."

Marshall picked up a folder from the receptionist desk. "If you'll wait out front," he pointed to the door, "I'll pick you up in the groundskeeper's cart. The grave is in the northeastern corner of the cemetery in Section P. No need to walk when we can ride."

Five minutes later the cart pulled up to an open grave surrounded in yellow warning tape. A canopy covered the site. The casket hung suspended in midair by straps attached to a lowering device.

"Looks like the exact same casket from Arlington," Francesca said.

"There's a reason for that, Ms. Catanzaro," Marshall said.

"Francesca," she corrected.

"Okay, Francesca it is." Marshall continued. "The Springfield Metallic Casket Company, now defunct, made thousands of these for the United States Government to ship back remains from World War II. Armco ingot iron, lead coated, glass sealed in patented cement. Each casket was packed in a wooden crate and stuffed with a wood curl packing material then transported by ship to a receiving station in the States. From there, the crates were transported as freight in rail cars to a depot nearest their destination, usually the soldier's home or national cemetery."

Marshall pointed to the open grave. "As you can see, this casket was buried in the ground. Sometimes caskets were buried in brick or concrete vaults with a concrete cap. Some even had a steel vault placed over the casket before it was covered. The casket is preserved better inside a vault, especially when there is no water intrusion."

"Are all of your World War II soldiers buried here?" Jake swept his arm across the landscape.

"Absolutely not. And that's probably why this is such a big deal." Marshall pointed to an old section of the cemetery where small white headstones were lined tightly next to each other. "Until this soldier, the only colored soldiers buried at Andersonville were those who died during the Civil War. They are buried in trenches like all the rest that died here during the war prison days."

"You buried them in trenches?" Francesca asked.

"Yes, ma'am. During the Civil War, 45,000 prisoners were sent to Andersonville. Almost 13,000 died here. The casualty rate was so high they decided it was easier to dig long trenches and inter the soldiers side by side. Even in the mid-1940s, no section plot had been set aside for colored soldiers from World War II, or World War I for that matter, until this man's family made the request for him to be buried here."

"It seems barbaric that black and white soldiers couldn't be buried next to one another," Francesca said. "They died equally, they should be buried equally."

"Keep in mind," Marshall continued, "this is the Deep South, and in the mid-1940s, racial prejudice ruled the day. The superintendent of the cemetery at Andersonville didn't want to make the decision so he kicked it up the food chain. Even in his letter you can detect a hint of a prejudicial mindset. Fortunately the decision came down from the Quartermaster General of the U. S. Army that all persons who served in the armed forces of the United States and honorably separated are entitled to burial in a national cemetery without regard to race or religion."

"I guess it goes without saying," Jake rifled through the folder Marshall had given him, "that if they died in the line of duty, the same privilege is extended as well?"

"Correct." Marshall rubbed his chin. "Shall I open the casket so you can see first hand?"

"I'll pass." Francesca stepped back.

"Jake?" Marshall asked.

"Was there any damage to the inside?"

"None the police or the park service could detect. That glass was still sealed and the clamps had not been tampered with. There was substantial decay and the top liner had fallen loose. The log roll cap was rusted as well."

"Is that unusual?" Jake asked.

"For a casket that had been placed directly in the ground over 65 years ago...I'd say no, not really, that wouldn't be odd. Matter of fact, I expected much worse. This casket held up remarkably well over the years."

"The casket at Arlington had the same thing. The top liner was loose in the pictures."

"It happens," Marshall said. "Not very often, but it does happen. And I wouldn't say it would be too unusual for both caskets to have similarities. They are the same model, by the same company around the same year. Was the Arlington soldier buried in the ground like this one, or in a vault?"

Jake opened his folder and studied the pictures. "I don't know. How do you tell?"

"May I look?" Marshall asked. Jake handed Marshall the photos. "He was buried in the ground. See here in this picture?" Marshall pointed to the photo of the grave with the casket at the bottom. "It's all earth and casket, no vault of any kind. Below the glass, the casket is sealed tight with clamps.

The lower portion of the casket is an airtight barrier to better preserve the remains. Not so above the glass. Moisture can work its way in over the years and liners decay and rot. I wouldn't even call it a coincidence. I'd say it should be expected."

"Better go ahead and open it." Jake looked at Francesca. "Sure you don't want to look?"

"I'm sure."

Marshall opened the casket. The glass had clouded over the years but Jake could still see the partial remains of the dead soldier.

Marshall pointed to the edges of the glass. "You see these clamps pull the glass against a rubber seal underneath. The only way inside is to remove these clamps and lift out the glass."

"Or break it," Jake said.

"This glass is pretty thick." Marshall rapped on it with his knuckles. "You'd need a sledgehammer and a strong arm to break it."

Marshall pointed to the headliner on the casket lid. "Notice how the mold and mildew has grown in here?"

Jake nodded.

"It adds to the decay of the material. All caskets this old will show some degree of decay. It varies, of course, with ground conditions. Dry, arid climates like the western states would show less sign of decay. Hot, humid, and rainy conditions like we find here in the South, the decay is much faster. Below the sealed glass, where the remains are contained, there is very little decay in comparison to above the glass."

"I've seen enough," Jake said. "Francesca, got anything else?"

"No." She looked at Marshall. "Adam, you've been a tremendous help. This has been very informative, as well as interesting."

"No problem. This is my interest. I have a master's degree in history. It's one reason I wanted to work here."

Adam Marshall dropped Jake and Francesca off in the parking lot.

The two slipped inside the hot Charger.

"Whoa. It's hot as hell in here," Francesca said, "turn on the A. C."

Jake started the engine and turned the air conditioner on high. It was amazing how stifling the inside of a car could get in such a short time, especially in the South in September. Beads of sweat rolled down his forehead in a matter of seconds.

Jake turned to face Francesca. "Did you notice the similarities?"

"You mean how the liner came loose from the same corner and was neatly folded back in the same two-fold pattern?"

"Yeah. You know what that means, don't you?"

"Someone was looking for something," Francesca said, "and it is the same someone."

"Which means there will be more." Jake's eyes lit up. "Or have been more."

CHAPTER 17

The car's engine was idling but Jake hadn't put it in gear.

"Jake, what are you thinking?" Francesca asked.

He unbuckled his seat belt and opened his car door. "Get out."

"What?"

"Get out of the car, Francesca. You're driving."

The two exchanged places in the black Charger and buckled their seat belts. Jake grabbed his iPad from the back seat with an outstretched arm. "Drive back to the airport while I give George a call."

"What about?" Francesca had a puzzled look on her face. "Jake, what about?"

Jake didn't respond, just punched away on his iPad, logging in to the secure network of Commonwealth Consultants. Within seconds, George Fontaine's face appeared on the tablet's screen.

"Jake." Fontaine acted somewhat surprised he'd logged in. "How can I serve you today, oh Master?"

"Funny." Jake dismissed Fontaine's attempt at humor and got down to business. "I need you to look something up for me."

"All work and no play makes Jake a dull boy." Fontaine paused. "What's going on?"

"Is there any way you can search for other instances in the area for disturbances of graves of soldiers who died in

World War II?" Jake looked at Francesca. She made a 'what's up' gesture with her hands on the steering wheel. "I'm thinking that the Arlington and Andersonville disturbances might not be isolated incidences."

"If you'll give me a minute," Fontaine said, "I'll log into the NCIS LInX server first."

"Linx? What is that?" Francesca asked.

"Law Enforcement Information Exchange. LInX, for short," Fontaine said. "It is what it sounds like. The Naval Criminal Investigative Service built it but they don't own it or control it. It's a tool to log information into, perform searches…basically it's just a database. Not *intelligence* gathering, *information* gathering."

Jake waited while Fontaine typed and Francesca drove. As the car pulled into Souther Field airport, Fontaine smiled.

"What do we have here?" Fontaine said. "Jake, I got some hits. Three actually. Two in Georgia and one in Florida."

"Recent break-ins?" Jake asked.

"All within the past few days."

Jake felt his stomach tighten. He thought it was too much of a coincidence and it seems he was right. "Where in Georgia?"

Fontaine looked into the camera. "Mt. Hope Cemetery in Dahlonega and Osborn Cemetery in Hiawassee. Also Bosque Bello Cemetery in Fernandina Beach, Florida."

She must have seen him smile. "Mean anything to you?" She asked.

"I know all three places. I looked at property in both Dahlonega and Hiawassee before I bought my cabin in Ellijay. And Beth…" Jake paused, memories of his fiancée and her death flashed through his mind. "Beth and I vacationed on Amelia Island a couple of times. Fernandina Beach is a quaint little town."

"Francesca, tell the pilots we're going to Gainesville, Georgia. I'll turn in the car." Jake waited until Francesca was out of the car. "George, would you mind getting someone to reserve us a car in Gainesville for the day with a late turn-in. It'll be a long day for Francesca and me. Also have them reserve two rooms at the Hampton Inn in downtown Fernandina Beach. Not on the waterfront side either. I don't want to listen to trains all night."

"Sure Jake. Anything else?"

"Is there any way we can search for more of these instances without arousing suspicion?"

"*We*, can't." Fontaine paused. "But *I*, can. I'll also program notifications so if any similar incident reports get filed, I'll be alerted."

"You can do that?"

"I might not slip out nights killing bad guys like you two, but I can do a lot with technology. Without me, you would be in the dark." Fontaine playfully rebuked. "Is that all?"

"One more thing." Jake looked across the tarmac. The pilots were starting a preflight inspection in preparation for departure. Francesca looked impatient standing at the top of the air stairs on the Citation. "Ask Wiley to schedule us a meeting with POTUS for tomorrow night."

† † †

From wheels up to wheels down, the flight from Americus to Gainesville lasted 33 minutes. It was nice having one of Wiley's jets at his disposal. As a team, Jake and Francesca had traveled from mission to mission primarily using the same jet. Twice they had flown on commercial airlines posing as a couple and once when the jet wasn't available for travel to Wiley's electronics factory outside of El

Paso. Usually they flew on the Citation to El Paso and landed on the strip at Wrangler's Steakhouse, where they were escorted to the factory floor beneath the restaurant. The same place Jake first met Wiley a year and a half ago when his then boss, CIA Director Scott Bentley, left him with Wiley because of Jake's bungled mission in Australia the week before. A move Bentley had to make because of pressure being applied by Senator Richard Boden.

Jake briefed Francesca on his follow-up conversation with Fontaine. "I also asked him to have Wiley hook us up again with President Rudd. We should probably tell her what we know."

"*We* don't know anything yet, Jake." Francesca argued. "What will we tell her, somebody just wanted to take a peek to satisfy their own morbid curiosity?"

"We'll know something by then," Jake said. "There are three more cemetery invasions to investigate. By the time we put the five together, we'll have some hard facts. I guarantee it."

"Evidence doesn't always provide clear motive, Jake. We need to be cautious or we'll look inept in front of the President of the United States. There's more, Wiley's reputation is at stake as well."

"Don't you think I'm aware of that?"

"Sometimes I wonder, Jake. Sometimes I wonder."

Jake gathered his backpack as the airplane's turbines spooled down. "We're burning daylight, let's go."

The rental car was waiting for them when they arrived, Jake took the keys and they drove off. Forty minutes later he stopped in the alpine resort town of Helen, Georgia for lunch. One hour after that they met the Towns County Sheriff at the Osborn Cemetery on the east side of Hiawassee.

The sheriff was young, maybe thirty, tall and skinny with short dark hair. Jake wondered if the young man could even hold his own in a scuffle. He doubted it.

Jake had been to Hiawassee several times when he was scouting for a mountain cabin. The vistas far surpassed any other place in North Georgia. The backdrop of mountains surrounding Lake Chatuge provided breathtaking views year round.

When he heard Fontaine mention Hiawassee, he figured the odds were in his favor that the grave invasion was not a black man's grave—not in Hiawassee. Minorities in Hiawassee accounted for only a small fraction of the overall population.

The sheriff led them to the recently covered grave of Arthur Chastain. "Mr. Chastain's body was shipped here in November of 1945. The family never opened the casket because he was disfigured from an explosion in World War II."

Having been away for so long, Jake had forgotten about the accents in North Georgia. The long drawn out syllables conjured memories of his grandmother when he was a child. She always seemed to be busy cooking something special in the kitchen at her home in Blairsville, Georgia. She was born in that home. It was sad that her mind was ravished by dementia by the time she turned seventy.

"You took pictures, correct?" Jake asked.

The man pulled out a folder. "Right here."

He took the pictures out of the folder and flipped through them one at a time, passing them to Francesca as he finished.

"I imagine it was just some kids having fun." The sheriff said. "We have vandalism like this from time to time. Not a lot for kids to do around these parts. Basically harmless. Just causes us to spend a few taxpayer dollars to clean up. Chastain's grandkids didn't seem too upset that the casket was busted open. They're the last living relatives, far as I know."

"Was Chastain Caucasian or African American?" Jake asked.

"The Chastains are white folk." The sheriff looked puzzled. "Is that important?"

"Not really, no. Just wondering."

"Did you investigate this crime at all?" Francesca asked. Jake noticed how sarcastic she sounded. "I mean you did have presence of mind to at lease log it into LInX."

"The incident report said this occurred night before last. Who discovered it?" Asked Jake.

"Alabama man named Darrell Blanton. Came out to visit a relative's plot early yesterday morning and saw the mess. Called it in, so I sent a deputy out to have a look. He took the pictures, said he thought it was kids just messing around. I told our County Manager, Smiley Lee, to buy a new casket and put Chastain back in the ground."

"You didn't get a funeral home to do it?" Francesca asked.

"No. Cheaper if the county did it. Just scooped everything out of the old casket and stuffed it in the new one. Didn't need a PhD. to figure it out."

Jake and Francesca walked around the perimeter of the cemetery looking for anything that might be of interest in their investigation but nothing was obvious. Any evidence left by the culprit had long since been destroyed by county vehicles and workers.

"We're done here." Jake motioned toward the car. "Let's go to Dahlonega. If we get there early, maybe we can get finished early and won't be so late getting to Florida."

An hour and fifteen minutes later Jake pulled into the entrance of the Mt. Hope Cemetery in Dahlonega, Georgia. The older part of the cemetery was built on a hill that overlooked the historic town and campus of North Georgia College and State University. It soon became apparent that Dahlonega law enforcement had treated this incident as a serious crime, protecting the scene with the same care and diligence as Arlington and Andersonville. Jake pulled the car to a stop near the yellow flagging tape that cordoned off the scene. Jake noticed a man in uniform walking in his direction. He was mid-thirties with dark hair cut in a flattop and a physique like a linebacker.

"May I help you?" The man called out as Jake and Francesca got out of the car.

"I'm Jake Pendleton. This is Francesca Catanzaro." Jake motioned her direction. "We're looking for Sheriff Klicker."

"I'm Klicker." He looked at his watch. "I wasn't expecting you so soon but earlier is better than later."

This sheriff had a professional, calm demeanor and seemed the polar opposite of the sheriff in Hiawassee.

"You two come on." The sheriff motioned by swinging his whole arm. "I'll give you a full briefing."

Klicker led them to an old section of the cemetery where a wrought iron fence was attached to the top of a small two-foot high concrete wall outlining a large family burial plot of at least a dozen headstones. "This is the Elliot family plot. Roy Elliot Sr. was a pillar in the community back in the 30s and 40s. And this..." Klicker pointed to a destroyed brick vault. The vault was half above and half below the ground. The concrete vault cap had been busted and moved to the side. "...is Roy Elliot Jr.'s grave. Or what's left of it."

"When did this happen?" Jake asked.

"Three nights ago. One of my officers was patrolling and saw a car up here. Figured it was teenagers making out. Been known to happen from time to time. He followed the access road this way." His finger outlined the deputy's route following the road. "Then the car sped away from here and out the exit over there." He pointed toward the main gate. "He used his spotlight to scan the area, noticed the broken capstone, and called it in."

"Did he get the license plate?" Francesca asked.

"No, I'm afraid not. He couldn't identify the make and model in the dark either. Just headlights and taillights."

Jake walked closer to the grave. The casket was covered with a tarp. "Elliot still in there?"

"Haven't moved a thing, it's exactly like we found it. The perpetrator broke into the sealed part of the casket and moved the remains."

"You think it was kids. Practical joke, maybe?" Jake asked.

"Not many practical jokers would go to this much trouble. They had to have brought along a hell of a big sledgehammer to break that glass, it's pretty thick. And there are some other peculiar things about it as well."

"Such as?" Francesca had deliberately stood back but now she walked over to the grave, lifted the tarp and looked in.

"Let me show you." Klicker pointed to small circular areas that had been marked to keep people out. "We had two people digging." He pointed to the footprints inside the marked off areas. "We took impressions. I have one of my officers searching a database to match the tread to the brand of shoe. Notice anything substantial?"

Jake looked at the footprints. "Two people with small feet. Could be kids."

"Or women," Francesca interrupted. "I recognize this tread. The multi-directional raised tread pattern is characteristic of hiking shoes. Looks a lot like the tread on my Keen hiking boots. Not a lot of kids wear hiking boots"

"That's what we ascertained as well," Sheriff Klicker said. "I'll have my deputy run down the Keen tread."

"What about fingerprints?" Jake asked. "Did you lift any from the scene?"

"Unfortunately, no."

"Gloves or wiped down?" Francesca asked.

"Gloves, for sure. Even then, with these surfaces, prints would have been difficult to lift. But we gave it the old college try." Klicker rubbed his chin. "I was surprised to get a response on my LInX report so fast. What else is going on?"

"Similar case in Hiawassee." Jake leaned down next to Francesca and lifted the tarp. Broken glass littered the bottom of the casket, Elliot's mangled remains covered in shards of glass. His mind was racing with questions. Not for the sheriff, but about who would be raiding World War II caskets after nearly seventy years and why? It was the 'why' that troubled him the most. "Except the sheriff in Hiawassee had already re-interred the remains. At least he had sense enough to take pictures. That's all we got to go on." Jake paused. "Was Elliot white or black?"

"Is that relative?" Klicker asked.

"We also had disturbed graves down at Andersonville and at Arlington."

"Mr. Elliot was Caucasian."

Jake stood and Francesca followed suit. "Sheriff, we need a copy of everything you have so far and we'll get out of your hair."

Sheriff Klicker handed Francesca his folder. "This was for you anyway. I have another copy at the station. One question though if you don't mind me asking?"

"Not at all," Jake said.

"Are you guys Feds or something? I got a call from the governor's office telling me to cooperate fully and assist any way I can."

"We're not Feds so I guess that put us in the *something* category. Our assignment came through different channels." Jake looked at Francesca then back at the sheriff.

"The governor said it came from the top. Does that mean what I think it means?"

Jake lowered his head momentarily and smiled at the sheriff's question. He gathered himself and said. "All I'll say is this. Two World War II soldiers' remains were disturbed at different United States national cemeteries within a three-day period. You take it from there."

CHAPTER 18

Jake and Francesca made it to the airport hours ahead of schedule. Fifteen minutes later the Citation lifted off from Gainesville, Georgia destined for the Fernandina Beach Municipal Airport on Amelia Island, Florida. The club seat arrangement allowed Jake and Francesca to sit across from each other with a small table between them.

"Ever been to Amelia Island?" Jake asked.

"No. My only trip to Florida was last year when we were on assignment in Jacksonville." Francesca said. "Not one of our better moments. The lab blew up before we got there."

"I remember. We were lucky. We'll be north of Jacksonville this time. Fernandina Beach is on Amelia Island in Florida's northeastern corner. I think you'll like it. Throughout history it has flown under eight national flags. And at one point it was a haven for pirates. We'll be staying in the historic district, a couple of miles from the cemetery."

"What about food?" Francesca asked. "I'm getting hungry. Any good places to eat there?"

"Plenty of good restaurants. Afterwards we'll go by the fudge shop then relax with a drink at the Palace Saloon." Jake paused, then pointed to the folder. "What do you think?"

"I don't know, Jake. Just when I think we can draw a connection, new evidence raises more questions."

"Like what?"

"For instance, why were there no footprints anywhere but Dahlonega? Why was the glass broken on two caskets and left untouched on two?"

"The graves at Arlington and Andersonville were out in grassy plots. Whoever dug up those graves was careful not to step on anything but grass. No footprint evidence to lift. No telling what evidence was destroyed in Hiawassee. That investigation by the locals was a fiasco. The sheriff is either incompetent or just didn't care. In Dahlonega, the cops surprised the looters and they didn't have time to cover their tracks." Jake pulled out four photos, one from each cemetery. He laid them side-by-side on a table between the jet's club seats. He spun each photo around for Francesca to view. "Notice. Both Arlington and Andersonville have guards patrolling the grounds all night." He pointed to two photos. "These don't."

"Which seems to be another coincidence," she said. "Two black. Two white. Two broken. Two intact. Do you still think it's the same people or perhaps random acts of vandalism that are not connected at all?"

"I don't' know. But my patience is wearing thin." He knew Francesca was right; it could be four unrelated incidents. But, Jake reasoned, more likely two. He was convinced the grave disturbances at Arlington and Andersonville were interconnected. He wasn't so sure the incidents in Hiawassee and Dahlonega were related to each other or to the national cemetery break-ins.

At Arlington, and again at Andersonville, the top liners in the caskets had fallen, or were pulled, from the same corner and folded underneath when the casket lid was closed. Too much of a coincidence not be connected. He didn't buy the story about the liners coming loose due to the caskets being buried in the ground and not in a vault. He didn't know much about caskets and decay or what years underground would do to the interior of the casket, but he did know that the lid had been opened because the liner was creased and folded back. That could only have happened if the lid was opened and then closed with the liner hanging down. What puzzled him was nothing appeared to have been removed from any of the caskets. The glass seals were never breached. So why would someone go to the trouble and risk going to jail if they weren't robbing the grave. What was he missing?

Jake opened the folder to review the crime reports again but within seconds his mind had wandered. He reminisced about Beth and the fun vacations they'd shared together in Fernandina Beach. Thinking about the casino cruises, picnics at Fort Clinch State Park, and the long romantic walks on the beach made him smile. He loved Beth. Her tragic death a year and a half ago left him feeling guilty and with an overwhelming emptiness inside. He never thought he could feel happiness again.

Then he met Kyli.

He wished Kyli was with him now. He felt cheated out of his time with her. He had put a wall around his emotions after Beth died, vowing never to let anyone in. Never to take down the wall. Was it too soon to let go of his feelings for Beth?

Kyli was different in so many ways. She made him feel alive. And it felt so damn good. Beth had been dependent on him, even needy at times, but he overlooked it because they always had good times together. Kyli was the polar opposite. Independent, light hearted, and a practical joker. A little on the wild side. Her tears at the Maldives resort was the first time he'd seen Kyli cry. Was it possible to fall in love with Kyli while he was still holding on to his feelings for Beth?

Their vacation cut short for this—investigating grave robberies. Not even robberies. Disturbances. Vandalisms. Never had anything been identified as stolen. He understood the President wanting to avoid a racial issue with the national cemeteries but why involve Wiley? Why couldn't Rudd's people handle this issue? It didn't add up.

The buzzer on the flight phone interrupted his thoughts. He picked up the receiver. "Yeah Mike?"

"We're starting our descent now, sir. We'll be on the ground in ten minutes."

Jake hung up the flight phone and looked at Francesca. "We'll be on the ground in ten so let's pack up this stuff." He paused. "You like seafood?"

"I'm from the southern tip of Italy. What do you think?"

✝ ✝ ✝

By the time Jake checked into the hotel and met Francesca in the lobby, the sun was disappearing in the western sky. The last of the day's burnt orange rays skipped across the waters of Fernandina Harbor. Shadows of sailboats moored in the harbor dotted the sparkling waters. Harbor sounds filled the air. Halyards clanged as sailboats rocked from the wake of a passing motorboat on the Amelia River. Its tiny engine hummed as it drove by. Screeching seagulls flocked behind an incoming shrimp boat, begging fishermen to throw scraps overboard.

Jake and Francesca walked down the sidewalk past the Palace Saloon, one of the town's feature landmarks.

"This is the place you wanted to come for drinks after we eat?" Francesca asked.

"Yeah."

"I'll pass. Smells too much like cigarette smoke."

"We'll just have drinks at Brett's Waterway Café." He pointed toward the sun. "If there is a breeze the gnats won't be bad and we can sit outside on the patio."

"I like that idea better."

They walked past a bookstore. An author sat at a table on the sidewalk signing his latest thriller novel. The setting sun glistened across beads of sweat on the author's bald head. Florida heat in early September was referred to as the dog days. And with 90% humidity, it felt like a sauna. Hot, sticky, and muggy.

The patrons sitting outside on the patio looked miserable, constantly wiping the sweat from their faces with their napkins. They opted to dine inside the cool air-conditioned restaurant.

"I'm sorry about your vacation with Kyli. She was really looking forward to it. I'm sure you were as well." Francesca brushed her hair behind her ear and smiled. "She had a big surprise in store for your second week."

"What was it?"

"Sorry. Not telling. She may still surprise you with it."

Jake ordered his second Margarita while Francesca drank white wine. While they waited for their drinks they sat silent, like an old married couple who had been together many years.

"Jake?" Francesca's voice went softer. "She's in love with you, you know?"

"We have feelings for each other but let's not get carried away. What makes you think that anyway?"

Francesca was about to speak when the waitress brought their drinks. Jake stirred his Margarita with his straw.

"Look, Jake. A woman can tell these things. I could see it in her eyes when she was telling me about the things she had planned for you two."

"I think she was just excited about the trip. Kyli wanted it to be an adventure."

"Wake up, Jake." Francesca's voice changed again. "Kyli is head over heels in love with you and you better start thinking about how you feel about her and how you're going to handle this when it comes up." She raised her finger. "And it will come up. Probably sooner than later."

"I'm a big boy. I can handle it."

"Well, keep one thing in mind." Francesca shook her finger at him. "Kyli is your boss's granddaughter and if it comes down to it, he'll pick her over you any day."

"I already know that." Jake took a long draw from the straw and swallowed. "He made that point perfectly clear last year on Ios Island."

"Then don't you dare break her heart." Francesca picked up her glass and took a sip of wine. "Or I swear to God I'll shoot you myself."

✝ ✝ ✝

The doorbell caught him by surprise, especially at this late hour. Evan Makley glanced at his watch and strode toward the door, pausing only long enough to check his appearance in the foyer mirror. His still had on his slacks from earlier in the day; his starched dress shirt untucked but still holding its press. He was barefoot, but it was his apartment after all.

The box above the door chimed again and again in rapid succession. Whoever it was, wasn't very patient. He stuck his eye to the peephole and saw a familiar woman's figure standing in front of the fisheye lens, Abigail Love. A flood of worrisome thoughts made him shudder.

Makley jerked the door open. "Abigail, what are you doing here?" He leaned out of the doorway and craned his head left and right. "Did anyone see you come in the building?"

Love pushed him to the side and walked in his apartment. "For crying out loud, Evan, give me a break. I'm not an amateur."

"Of course, of course. I'm sorry. I didn't mean to imply."

"Shut up and close the door."

Makley turned around and closed the door. She was wearing a long black trench coat with black leather boots that disappeared mid-calf behind the fabric. Her hair was pulled back in a ponytail and her brilliant green eyes bore in to him. "Do you have any news?"

"Not yet." She tossed her bag on his couch. "What about you and the President? Anything new happening that could be of use to me?"

"No. Rudd is worried about a few graves being disturbed in a couple of national cemeteries, that's about it." Makley let his eyes run up and down her torso. Her trench coat was cinched snug at the waist accentuating her figure. "If you don't have any news, why are you here?"

"A couple of reasons actually."

"I'm listening."

Love stepped closer to him. "I heard about your wife leaving, Evan, and taking your girls with her. You know, I can take care of her if you want me to...but it'll cost you."

"No. As tempting as it sounds, I'll pass. The girls need their mother, besides they're older now. One's even driving so I get to see them more often. The divorce really wasn't unexpected either. We hadn't been together as husband and wife in over a year before we split."

"Over a year? Damn. You are a frustrated man." Love removed the tie around her ponytail and let her hair fall to her shoulders. She shook her head to give her hair an unkempt look. She stepped close to him. "Which brings me to the other reason I'm here."

She was close enough he could smell her perfume. She put her hands on his chest, palms flat, and gently worked them in small circles. An instant twinge of excitement

"You know, Love's Desperate Desire can help with that too. And for you, Evan, it's on the house."

"What about your rule against getting involved with clients?"

"That's the good thing about being the boss, I can change the rules whenever I want."

"But—"

Love put her finger over his lips. He watched her systematically unbutton his shirt exposing his modestly hairy chest. She stroked her hands from side to side, top to bottom. By now his slacks showed visible signs of his arousal, but he didn't care. He'd already dreamed about a moment like this with the beautiful Abigail Love. Despite her line of work, despite the fact that she was a cold-blooded killer, he wanted her. He longed for her.

"Bedroom," she said.

More like a command.

He pointed to a door.

She grabbed his hand and led him across the room.

When they entered his bedroom, Love pulled him in front of her and slipped his shirt off his shoulders and then let it fall to the carpet. She turned him around and backed him toward his bed.

Love took two steps back and slowly loosened the belt on her coat. This was really going to happen, he thought. She let the coat hang open for a few seconds as if deliberately taunting him. He took it all in. From what he could see, she wasn't dressed underneath. Not in clothes anyway. She pulled her hands back, shrugged her shoulders, and let the coat fall to the floor.

Abigail Love had the best body he'd ever seen. Totally unblemished. From head to toe. Perfect in every way. She wore only a black lace bra and matching thong. Her boots, the ones that disappeared behind her coat, rose above her knees.

She stepped close to him again. He started to speak but she gave him the look. He knew to stay quiet. He wanted to get involved. He wanted to grab her and throw her on the bed, but he resisted. She ran her hands across his waist, working them forward until she came to his belt. He closed his eyes and felt her unlatch his belt and pull it through the belt loops. He heard it land on the floor. He felt her unbuttoned his pants and slowly unzip them. She pushed him backwards onto the bed.

She climbed on top of him. He opened his eyes when she kissed him. Her lips were wet, and warm, and sweet. Better than he ever imagined.

She pulled back and started kissing his neck, swirling her tongue below his ear.

She whispered. "Now, tell me more about these graves."

CHAPTER 19

The temperature dropped enough during the night to blanket the island in fog. After they checked out of the hotel, Jake drove the rental car east on Centre Street, the main road in Fernandina Beach's historic district, until it turned into Atlantic Avenue. Following the directions from the nighttime desk clerk, he turned north on 14th Street and drove the *mile or so* until he reached his destination.

He pulled into the Bosque Bello Cemetery. A police cruiser was waiting for them. After introductions, Jake and Francesca followed the officer to the scene of the crime.

Jake scanned the misty copse of live oaks whose canopy hung over the back section of the graveyard. Sunlight struggled to break through the thick fog. Droplets of moisture danced across the broken beams of light. In the distance, crime scene tape marked off an open grave. The air was still and sticky and the few patches of grass were covered in the morning's dew. It reminded Jake of a scene from an old horror film. Ironically that story took place in a small coastal town, much like this one, and involved a strange glowing fog that rolled in from the ocean.

He and Francesca were two paces behind the officer. "Was the glass in the casket broken?" Jake asked.

"No. Looks like all they did was dig up the casket. Can't tell if it was even opened." The officer stopped and turned around. "To be honest, if we hadn't received a call so soon after we found it, we would have just stuck him back in the ground." The officer pointed to the hole in the ground. "But we were instructed to do a thorough crime scene investigation."

"Fingerprints?" Jake asked.

"None."

"Shoe impressions?" Francesca asked.

"None." The officer walked to the side of the grave and pointed to the ground slowly moving his finger toward the grass line in the cemetery. "Actually, whoever did this was careful enough to cover his tracks all the way to the grass so we couldn't get any usable impressions. He knew what he was doing."

"Or she." Francesca asserted.

"Yes ma'am. I guess that's possible. Or she." The officer pointed to two piles of dirt. "One other thing about the perp, could be left-handed." He moved to a spot next to the grave. "He...or she, stood here and dug, tossing the dirt here." He pointed to the pile next to him. Then he pointed to a depression on the other side of the grave and the pile of dirt. "And stood there and tossed the dirt to that pile."

"Could've been two diggers working in synchrony." Jake said.

The officer pushed his hand under his hat and scratched his scalp. "Could be. We never considered two diggers, but it's possible."

Jake pointed to a corner of the lower section of the casket. "Was the top liner pulled loose there and folded underneath?"

The officer looked astonished. "How could you know that? You haven't even seen the pictures yet."

"Bet our soldier was black." Francesca said.

"That's right. But—"

"We've seen the same thing at other cemeteries." Jake looked at Francesca.

Jake's cell phone rang. He looked at the Caller-ID, Fontaine. "Excuse me, I have to take this." Jake turned and walked away leaving Francesca to wrap things up with the officer.

Jake answered the call. "George, what's up?"

"Jake, your meeting tonight with President Rudd has been moved up to 10:00 p.m."

"No problem. We're almost finished here then we'll be on our way."

"Sorry, Jake. Project Resurrection is growing."

"Project Resurrection?"

"Yep. Project Resurrection. Don't blame me, Wiley and Rudd came up with the name." Fontaine explained. "Apparently an older usage of the term *resurrect* was used the same as *exhume* or *disinter* is today."

"Sounds biblical."

"It does. Anyway, there have been two more reports. One in Savannah and one in Charleston. Wiley wants you to check them both out before coming back to D.C."

"Has any of this leaked to the press? We don't need any copy cats."

"No leaks that I know of, just more problems." George interrupted. "The grave in Savannah belongs to a black man."

"The one here was a black man as well and it's the same M. O. as the ones in Arlington and Andersonville."

"What do you think that means?" Fontaine asked.

"I don't know, George. But I intend to find out."

† † †

His mother had been so upset he had abducted the wrong person that she didn't speak to him the entire day. How was he to know that Sam Connors was Samantha Connors? It only made sense that the woman at the house was Ashley. He'd never even considered that she had a roommate.

His mother's silence was actually a welcome relief, he thought, because two nights ago when she found out Samantha Connors wasn't Ashley Regan, her reaction was insane.

He watched as his mother grabbed a large needle and plunged it deep into the woman's neck. Blood spewed onto the stainless steel table in spurts flowing down toward the woman's feet and into a drain at the lower end of the table.

"No." He yelled. "You can't do this."

She glared at him. He saw pure evil in her eyes. His greatest fear realized. "We have to do this. We have to protect this family. The whole family. Not just you and me, but this business as well. And your twin."

"But this woman had no part."

"Scott, if you hadn't kidnapped the wrong woman, we wouldn't be in this predicament in the first place. I'm cleaning up your mess. No loose ends." Heidi turned her attention back to the woman. "It'll be over soon, honey...it'll be over soon."

His mother stroked the young woman's hair like a loving mother comforting a sick child. Samantha's face grew ashen. He'd dealt with the dead for many decades but he'd never watched anyone die. The woman's eyes closed for the last time and blood stopped flowing from the needle. Samantha Connors, a victim of mistaken identity, was dead.

Heidi looked at Scott. "Prepare the crematorium. We need to destroy anything and everything that could link us to this woman. She's small, set the retort for 90 minutes. That should be more than enough."

He turned to leave, then glanced back. His mother was stroking the dead woman's hair again. The woman who gave birth to him, whom he loved, had gone mad…or had she always been insane? And he was helpless to do anything about it because in the eyes of the law, he knew he was just as guilty as she was. His mother was right about one thing; they did have to protect the family. All of it.

Katzer tried to compose himself and looked at his daily calendar, a family consultation and two funerals. The family consultation was scheduled in ten minutes. He thought he had time for another cup of coffee and then get back to business as if nothing had ever happened until the receptionist buzzed his office informing him that his consultation had arrived early. His palms were sticky. He went to the restroom and splashed water on his face. The man in the mirror looked haggard. He dried off, slipped on his dress coat and headed to meet the family.

Katzer joined the family in the conference room where he usually held all consultations. He'd known the family for years. The man in front of him had been in the Nashville Rotary Club with him for years. He'd socialized with the man and his wife and now, at 65, she was dead.

He began with the usual formalities of gathering information for the death certificate. It usually helped to get the difficult process started. After that he moved to the obituary. Katzer knew this was the part where he had to drag information out with a series of questions. Grieving family members seemed to have difficulty thinking of obituary wording, so Katzer did it for them. On rare occasions someone would walk in the door with an obituary already written. This was not one of those times. Excluding the obvious, Katzer asked the man about his wife's relatives, living and dead, schools attended, occupation or occupations in this case, church, social activities, and involvement in charity work. Something he knew the man's wife had been heavily involved in.

He asked about the type of service and where it would be held. The man had little trouble with this. As an active member of the largest Episcopal Church in Nashville, there was little doubt about selecting a church or priest for the ceremony. The man had little trouble in the casket room either. He seemed to know the casket his wife would have preferred as soon as he entered the room. Which was quite unusual because Katzer Funeral Home's casket room offered a very large selection of caskets. Several times larger than his closest competitor.

Katzer left the man in the conference room and told him he would return shortly with an itemized cost sheet. He handed the receptionist his notes. "Sylvia, will you prepare Mr. Parker's estimate?"

"Certainly, Mr. Katzer. Mike is waiting for you in your office again."

"Did he say what he wanted?"

"No, sir. Just that he needed to talk to you."

Katzer turned and headed for his office. If the cemetery manager was in his office it usually meant he would have to spend money. Sometimes, a lot of money. Something got damaged or a piece of equipment broke. It was never good news, only bad.

The cemetery manager stood when Katzer walked in. He'd been cemetery manager at Mt Olivet for over fifteen years. Katzer had personally recommended him. His appearance then was neatly groomed with short hair, average height, and very slim. No, skinny was a better description. The man he was looking at now had changed over the years. An easy forty pounds overweight, his now thinning gray hair was long and oily and pulled back into a ponytail. The top went bald years ago and the man kept it covered with a baseball cap. His hands were always grimy, clothes crumpled, and worst of all, he smelled. When his wife left him seven years ago, so it seemed, did his personal hygiene. Katzer sat on the corner of his desk.

"Mike, what do you need?" Katzer's tone was rather matter of fact. Not rude, but down to business.

"We had a break-in last night in Section 2."

"A break-in? What kind of break-in?"

"The Beckel crypt. Found the door busted in about ten minutes ago."

Katzer's heart skipped a beat. "Which casket?" He already knew the answer but he needed to hear it.

"Looks like they started with Andrew. The kid who died in the war. But all of them were broken into."

"How could you tell who they started with?"

"His casket was in the middle of the crypt, busted and torn to pieces. The parents' and grandparents' caskets were pulled down on top of his."

He knew too well what that meant. His mother told him about the Beckel crypt when she revealed everything else to him. About his stepfather. About his real father. This meant only one thing. Ashley Regan has the book and has been here. Only one day after his mother killed the woman's roommate. He could visualize his mother's reaction to the news. Her eyes ice cold, filled with anger. She would give him that sharp, penetrating stare, like she was measuring his value to her, then she would lash out at him again for abducting the wrong woman.

"Mr. Katzer? Excuse me. Should I call the cops?"

The question actually startled him. He'd just expected the cemetery manager had already made that call. "How much damage?"

"Quite a lot. Jimmied the door, broke the lock, and took a sledgehammer to the marble vault. Then they pulled the casket into the middle of the crypt and busted it open."

"Let's wait a bit to call the police, Mike. I don't want to alarm our customers." Katzer stood. "Anyone else know about the break-in?"

"No, I came straight here after I saw it. Haven't even finished my rounds yet. You want me to have someone from the maintenance shop go up and fix the door?"

"No, Mike." Katzer said. "Don't' tell anyone else just yet. Fix the door yourself. I want to read over our insurance policy again before I file a police report. I might try to handle this one under the table with the Beckel family. If I remember correctly, they seemed easy to deal with, so maybe I can work out an arrangement. Avoid negative publicity. I'd rather the media not get a hold of it."

"I understand." The man stood and walked toward the door.

"Thanks, Mike." Katzer called out.

The man didn't stop, just a raised a hand in acknowledgement.

He was wrong about his mother's reaction. Heidi Katzer sat in his office and seemed to take the news in stride. She actually seemed happy about it. He figured she was just having a good day. At her age the chasms in her moods swings were massive and, it seemed, dependent on how she felt that day. When she felt good, she was almost giddy.

When she felt bad, she was a bear. The night she tortured and killed the woman had been a bad day, he thought.

"This is good news," she said.

"Good news?" Scott said. "How the hell is this good news?"

"Don't you see? If someone wanted to see inside Andrew Beckel's grave that proves the book has been found. And it means that Ashley Regan has the book." She smiled a devilish grin. "Imagine her surprise when she found it empty."

"It was probably not the first one she's hit." Scott said.

"That makes it even better."

"I don't understand. Why would that make it better?"

"Because it being empty was unexpected. It'll knock her off kilter." Heidi grabbed a small bottle from her purse and rubbed lotion over her wrinkled hands. "And if she's off kilter, she may make a mistake. When that happens, we got her...and my journal."

CHAPTER 20

After the tenth ring Ashley Regan hung up. Sam Connors still wasn't answering the phone. It had been two weeks since their argument on the phone. She tried to explain her need to stay longer with her distraught friend Christa, but Sam pitched one of her hissy fits. Apparently Sam couldn't understand why Ashley would take so much time off work over a friend's relationship problems. In a way, Sam had a point, but when Sam hung up on her, Ashley didn't call her back right away.

She assumed by now Sam would be over her temperamental refusal to communicate. It had always been how she handled discord between them. She'd get mad, storm off, and refuse to speak. On the phone or face-to-face. Although a bit immature, she still was a caring, loving partner. Flaws and all.

Christa was driving the rental car, a Chevy Impala they'd paid cash in advance for a one-week rental. Their next stop was a small family plot in Butler, Tennessee. If the journal was accurate, that's where they would hit the jackpot. But the journal had been wrong in Nashville. The casket in the marble crypt did not contain the item listed in the journal. None of the caskets in the crypt contained it either. And for the first time since their adventure began, Regan and Christa came away empty handed.

The turn of bad luck began in Dahlonega when a cop making his nightly rounds spotted their car in the cemetery. She and Christa ducked when they saw headlights coming down the street and panicked when the cruiser pulled into the cemetery. They grabbed their gear, tossed it in the car, and fled the cemetery while the cop car was on the adjacent part of the circular drive. Fortunately for them, he didn't pursue.

Their first mistake. Regan was determined that was their last. She'd been careful to ensure their movements were untraceable. She didn't want to be 'on the grid' as they say. Everything paid for in cash. No credit cards to track their movements. They changed rental cars after each cemetery. And now that Christa had scored them fake driver's licenses, Regan felt untouchable.

She wanted to start with the local Charleston graveyard but resisted the temptation. The small out-of-town cemeteries were less of a risk so she opted to practice on cemeteries with very little traffic reducing their chance of getting caught. She had never dug up anything the size of a casket before and wanted to make a test run to determine what unexpected problems might be encountered. She was convinced that trial and error practice would help them gain the skills they needed to get in, retrieve the secreted item, and get out without being detected…or caught.

Their first attempt was a bust. They were unprepared. After more planning, Regan and Christa developed an equipment list and made another trip to an out-of-town hardware store to acquire the tools necessary to accomplish the task. Next, a dry run on a cemetery not listed in the journal. That rehearsal proved helpful and warranted another trip to a different hardware store. Now, the two women knew they were ready.

She was nervous when they finally hit the Charleston cemetery, the same cemetery her parents were buried in. Her hands shook with anticipation of what they would discover. She kept expecting the unexpected to happen any minute. It didn't. Regan and Christa were in and out of the graveyard in record time, prize in hand.

Nestled on Watauga Lake in the northeastern corner of Tennessee, Butler was a long drive from Charleston. Regan and Christa made a stop in Banner Elk, North Carolina for the night. The hotel was a cheap imitation log cabin lodge with ten rooms. While she was checking in she noticed the neon sign hanging over the entrance change from "VACANCY" to "NO VACANCY." The manager seemed to appreciate the cash she presented at check-in and asked no questions.

When they got to their room, Regan tossed her bag on the floor. "I guess this is their idea of 'rustic charm.' I have another description for it."

Christa Barnett flipped on the bathroom light. "Looks clean in here." She walked over to a bed and pulled down the sheets. "Beds are clean. Linen's been changed. So it ain't the Hilton, big deal. It's only for a couple of nights."

"Thieves can't be choosey, right?" Regan laughed.

"Let's go eat, I'm starving." Christa walked toward the door.

She pulled out her cell phone. "Let me try calling Sam again, then we'll go." She dialed the number and let it ring. When Connors voice mail answered, she hung up.

"Guess she's still pissed, huh?" Christa said. "She's acting kind of childish, don't you think?"

"I guess so. It's not like her to give me the silent treatment for this long." Ashley Regan couldn't imagine why

Sam still wouldn't answer. They'd had spats in the past but none had ever lasted more than a day or two.

†††

Jake pushed the backpack strap higher on his right shoulder while he waited for Francesca to authenticate her identity to gain entrance into the Commonwealth Consultants building from the subterranean parking garage. After she entered, it was his turn. Only one at a time was allowed through the door. Those were Wiley's security rules and the guards, all former Special Forces, got upset if the rules weren't obeyed.

The seven-story, all-glass building in Fairfax, Virginia was deceptive in appearance since the only windows in the entire building were in the top-floor penthouse suite. Behind the exterior glass veneer were two steel-reinforced solid concrete walls. Between each wall a two-inch lead lining. No signals got in. No signals got out. Even the penthouse had lead-lined walls and lead infused glass windows. If anyone knew how to shield a building, it was Elmore Wiley.

Jake entered the same 24-character password into the keypad followed by a thumbprint on the scanner. The door clicked and he entered the lobby through an enhanced body-screening unit. The unit didn't screen for weapons, since weapons weren't unusual at Commonwealth. Its technology was more sophisticated. The unit sniffed for explosives and scanned for electronic eavesdropping devices on everyone and everything that entered the building.

The lobby was a small fifteen-foot square room with three armed guards. Mounted on the wall next to the steel door was a retina scan unit. After passing the retina scan, Wiley's facial recognition software confirmed his identity and allowed Jake passage into the operations center where he found Francesca waiting. He wondered if all the security measures weren't overkill but, he figured, in Wiley's line of business there was no such thing as being too careful. One security breach and his business could evaporate overnight.

They took the elevator to the fourth floor and repeated the same drill without the guards and scanner. Required here was the same 24-digit password and thumbprint—opposite thumb than before—an added layer of security for this most sensitive area of Wiley's business. Inside George Fontaine monitored video feeds from Iran, Yemen, and Syria.

"Looks like Commonwealth might get involved in the Middle East. The Fellowship wants to topple a couple of governments but doesn't want us to send any assets. Too volatile, the Council said." Fontaine never looked away from the screens. "Jake, Mr. Wiley is in the penthouse. Said he's going to the meeting with you tonight."

"George, I need access to the mainframe for a couple of hours. Can you plug me in?" Jake pulled off the backpack, unzipped the top. "There has to be a common denominator with all these incidents and I really need to find something before the meeting tonight."

"Those arrangements have already been made." Fontaine said. "Wiley had me route an access terminal to the penthouse. He wants you and Francesca up there at eight o'clock."

"At eight? That's less than ten minutes from now."

"Yup." Fontaine shrugged his shoulders. "Take it up with the old man. I'm just the messenger."

"I'll let him know we're here." Francesca walked to the far wall and picked up the phone.

"How about doing me a favor while I'm up there?" Jake asked.

"I'll do it if you tell me your secret."

"What are you talking about?"

Fontaine lowered his voice and whispered to Jake. "I want to know how you always end up with good looking women around you. First Kyli. And now Francesca."

"Francesca's my partner." Jake leaned down next to Fontaine's ear. "How the hell did you know about Kyli?"

"Common knowledge around here. The boss's granddaughter dating an emissary is water cooler gossip." Fontaine explained. "News travels fast. Just keep in mind the consequences."

"What consequences?"

Francesca walked up next to Jake. "Wiley wants us upstairs now."

"Some guys have all the luck." Fontaine quipped.

"What's he talking about?" Francesca asked.

"Nothing." Jake scribbled something on a piece of paper. "Here's the address of the cemetery in Charleston. The traffic signal at the entrance has surveillance cameras. Since there's only one way in and out of the graveyard after hours, I thought we might get lucky and find our intruder."

"*If* I can hack into Charleston's traffic control center," Fontaine turned to face Jake. He took the paper. "Then I'll let you know what I find before you leave."

Two minutes later Jake and Francesca entered the penthouse and found Wiley waiting for them on the couch watching CNN and Fox on a split screen TV.

"Good, you're here." Wiley stood, pushed up his glasses, and made his trademark hair swipe. He walked over and shook Francesca's hand followed by Jake's. He pointed to a small office with a computer terminal on the desk. "Jake, you can get to work while I talk to Francesca."

The next ninety minutes passed by faster than he expected. He thought he heard the elevator a couple of times but was so entrenched in his work that he never turned around. After he was finished, he printed two copies of his report and logged off the computer.

Jake found Wiley sitting alone with a folder in his hand. "Where's Francesca?"

"I gave her another assignment. You won't need her on this one." Wiley raised the folder in the air. "George brought this up here for you. He said you'd know what to do with it."

Jake took the folder and scanned its contents. Good news and bad news. Which seemed to be the way this entire puzzle had been. Two steps forward, one step back. Jake looked at his watch. "Sir. We should get going."

"Something has come up that I must personally attend to. You'll be meeting with the President alone in the Oval Office." Wiley paused. It was apparent to Jake the Old Man was letting his news reach full impact. "Welcome to the big leagues, Jake. Only a handful of people ever get that opportunity."

CHAPTER 21

Jake cleared the front gate of the White House and followed the Secret Service agent to the Oval Office. The agent opened the door and followed Jake inside instructing him where to sit down. The room was more elaborate than he'd envisioned. A large rug with the sunburst pattern emanating from the Presidential Seal in the center dominated the room. There were three large south facing windows behind the President's desk and a fireplace on the north wall. Each President decorated the Oval Office to suit his, or now, her taste. President Rebecca Rudd, being the first female President in history, adorned the walls with portraits of famous women. Mother Theresa and Rosa Parks were the first to catch his eye.

He didn't have to wait long before President Rebecca Rudd walked into the room and dismissed the agent. He was expecting Chief of Staff, Evan Makley, to accompany her but he was wrong. When Wiley said he was meeting with the President alone, he meant *alone*. She walked straight to him and shook his hand, cupping her left hand over the top. He felt the warmth in her hands. Her face reflected the stress of the job. Dark circles and puffiness around her eyes a result of long hours laboring over endless mounds of paperwork. The office took its toll on every President, aging them years beyond their time.

She moved over to her desk and motioned for Jake to take the chair next to the desk. "Do you know the history of this desk?" She asked.

"Yes, ma'am. That is if National Treasure got it right."

Rudd laughed. "They got it right. Mr. Wiley left me a message saying Ms. Catanzaro couldn't make it. I was looking forward to seeing her again. She has a passion for ethical and moral justice."

"Yes, ma'am, she does. Unfortunately she was called out at the last minute."

"That's a shame. You two make a good team." Rudd held out an open palm. "What have you come up with on Project Resurrection?"

"I'm afraid not much. A lot of information that doesn't seem to lead anywhere." Jake opened his backpack and pulled a copy of his report and handed it to the President. "I've been trying to draw a nexus between all the grave disturbances, but just when I think the evidence starts to connect, new evidence comes along that invalidates my theories."

"For instance?" Rudd asked.

"To start with." Jake spread out the reports of four cemetery intrusions on the President's desk. "All these, which include Arlington and Andersonville were black soldiers killed in Germany during World War II. None of the bodies were disturbed. In fact, the glass seals were never broken. Whoever did this was very careful to not leave behind any evidence at all. No fingerprints, footprints, tire tracks. Nothing. On the surface, it looks like all they did was open the casket out of morbid curiosity."

"And below the surface?"

"If you don't mind, ma'am, I'd like to come back to that later."

"I don't mind." Rudd scribbled something on a notepad.

"The other three we investigated are a different story. The caskets were opened, the seals broken, and the body disturbed, but nothing was taken. All of these caskets belonged to white males." The President looked at him when he said this. "The sheriff in Hiawassee chalked it up to a teenage prank and had the body reinterred before we got there. Any evidence to suggest who might have done it was inadvertently destroyed."

Jake pointed to the next report. "The sheriff in Dahlonega conducted a thorough investigation. The entire scene was marked off and sealed. A deputy on night patrol saw a car in the cemetery and went in to investigate. The car sped off. The deputy assumed he'd just interrupted some teenagers making out in the car and didn't pursue them. When he saw the damage to the grave, it was too late to catch whomever was in the car."

Jake gingerly pushed some photos in front of Rudd. "Apparently the deputy startled our grave robbers and we got our first real piece of evidence. Footprints. And what we found is that we have two perpetrators. The footprints appear to be those of women."

Rudd looked up. "Women? Interesting."

"After Charleston, I realized we had a pattern. Only white soldiers' remains were being disturbed. I have no idea yet what that means. It just seems to be the pattern. At the Charleston cemetery, the glass seal on the casket was busted with something like a sledgehammer and the body moved. But, as with every incident, nothing seems to have been taken from any casket."

"So, what's the point?" Rudd asked. "Seems like a lot of trouble for nothing."

"I've heard that before." Jake pushed a picture of a license plate in front of the President.

"What's this?"

"My first real lead...or at least what I thought was a lead." Jake paused. "When Francesca and I went to the cemetery earlier today, I noticed a traffic cam mounted on the signal at the entrance to the cemetery. We accessed the video from the night of the break-in and this is the only vehicle that entered all night. It was in the cemetery for almost thirty minutes and then left."

"Excuse me," Rudd interrupted, "but where is this location?"

"Charleston. Not sure if this is relative, but the car belongs to a rental car company and was rented to a local woman named Ashley Regan. We are trying to track down her car now without alerting law enforcement. But the rental car being in the cemetery may not mean anything."

"Why do you say that?"

"Because Ashley Regan's parents are buried in that cemetery. Which gives her a legitimate reason to be there. The questions needing answers are why the late hour visit and why the rental car?"

"Maybe you should have a talk with this woman just in case."

"Yes, ma'am. I plan to pay her a visit very soon."

Rudd tapped her finger on the scribble she made earlier. "So, if this is not racially motivated," Rudd gave him a stern look, "what is your gut feeling?"

Jake took a deep breath. He remembered what Wiley told him earlier and tried to choose his words carefully. "The evidence doesn't point toward anything racial. So far we have four black and three white World War II soldiers' caskets that have been broken into. I don't see why the Army can't take over from here."

"But you think there is something else, don't you? Maybe something bigger."

"I haven't had enough time to thoroughly analyze all the data but I did find some things in common with all the break-ins." He waited for her to acknowledge him to continue which she did with a nod of the head. "First, all were soldiers who died in World War II in Germany. So far all the casualties were from 1944 or 1945. Second, every soldier's body was mutilated and in each instance the ceremony was closed casket. Third, they were all buried in the same model casket by the same company. The Springfield Metallic Casket Company, which went out of business in 1974. Fourth and probably the most significant is that every soldier whose casket had been disturbed was packed, crated, and shipped straight through to their destination by the same person. Major Don Adams of the United States Army."

"Interesting." Rudd paused. "Where is Major Adams now?"

"Don't know." Jake noticed the puzzled look on the President's face. "According to Army records, Major Adams disappeared during a blizzard in 1946. He was stationed at the commandeered resort at the summit of Zugspitze on the Austrian/German border."

Rudd was silent for an awkwardly long few seconds. "Do you have any hunches?"

"Only guesses. Just a hypothesis at this point."

"I'd really like to hear your thoughts. Please, share."

Jake paused. The intensity of President Rudd's blue-eyed stare made him nervous. He was sitting in the Oval Office, face to face with the most powerful person in the world. And she had asked him for his advice. "I think Major Adams put something in these caskets and shipped them here and now someone is finally getting around to retrieving them."

Rudd leaned back in her chair for the first time. "Sounds a little far-fetched." She steepled her hands beneath her chin. "But, let's suppose for a minute that you are correct. How old would Major Adams be now?"

"In his nineties."

"A little old to be running around robbing graves, don't you think?" Her tone sounded maternal and somewhat condescending. Both of which struck a slight blow to his ego. "And, if he were still alive, why would he wait until now to retrieve whatever he secreted away?"

"Like I said, ma'am, it's only a hypothesis. I have nothing to back it up."

Rudd smiled. "I want you to find the woman in Charleston and rule her involvement in or out. Wiley has bragged about your intuition. How long do you need to thoroughly analyze what you know so far?"

"At this point, I'm not sure. A few days. Maybe as long as a week."

"Jake, always bear in mind that your own resolution to succeed is more important than any other."

"Yes, ma'am. I believe Lincoln once said something like that."

Rudd smiled. "He said *exactly* that."

Rudd opened her desk and pulled out a plain white business card.

She turned the card over and wrote a phone number on the back. She held it out toward him. "Jake, this is my personal cell phone number. Only a handful of people have this number. Now you do too. It goes without saying that you are not to share it with anyone. Is that understood?"

"Yes, ma'am." He took the card from her. In raised gold letters centered in the middle of the card it read:

Rebecca K. Rudd
President of the United States

He flipped it over, and read the number. He quickly handed it back to her. "I won't need to keep the card."

She asked and he repeated the number verbatim.

"Jake, Elmore told me, that if I needed it, you were at my disposal. I want you on this as my personal...what's the term Mr. Wiley uses...?"

"Emissary?"

"Yes, Jake. Emissary. For the foreseeable future anyway, I'll need your services. But most of all, I need your allegiance." Rudd placed everything Jake had given her in a folder and stood. "Check in with me personally every night at 2300 hours Eastern time with a progress report. Is that understood?"

"Yes, ma'am."

Rudd pressed a button and the Secret Service agent opened the door. "Max will escort you to the gate."

†††

President Rebecca Rudd watched the young man leave the Oval Office. As her Secret Service agent closed the door, the door behind her opened and an elderly man walked in.

"Do you think he knows I'm sending him into a den of lions?" Rudd never took her eyes off the door where Jake Pendleton exited.

"No, Rebecca, he doesn't."

She looked at the wise old man. Her first encounter with him was when she was Secretary of State for her predecessor. She found him and his organization to be a resource she could call on to accomplish certain agendas that could not be handled through diplomatic channels. On more than one occasion she had covered the previous President's ass by utilizing the services of the man in front of her.

"I'm not sure I understand why you couldn't have been in here while Mr. Pendleton gave me his briefing," Rudd said.

He paused. "Call it an employee evaluation," he finally said. "If you and I are going to enter into a future arrangement, then I need to be sure Jake is going to meet my lofty expectations at this level."

"And?" Rudd asked. "Are you satisfied?"

"As usual, Mr. Pendleton exceeded my expectations."

"Do you think it's fair of me to put Mr. Pendleton in such a potentially uncompromising position?" She asked.

"Jake adapts quickly to change. He'll be fine."

"Ultimately he'll be faced with a dilemma. Can I trust him to make the right decision?"

"Jake is as loyal as they come." The old man pushed up his wire rim glasses. He swiped his hands through his gray hair. "You can trust Jake with your life. Just as I have with mine…and my granddaughter's."

CHAPTER 22

Evan Makley met Abigail Love at the same spot as the last meeting. They sat on the same park bench at the Jefferson Memorial. This time there were no paddleboats or sun glistening on the water. The weather had turned for the worst overnight, leaving the September morning rainy, dreary, and cool.

Love was waiting for him when he arrived. She wore an olive green raincoat that came below her knees and held a black umbrella over her head while she typed on her smart phone. At first glance his mind filled with pleasurable thoughts of their sexual encounter. It was the type of male fantasy written about in *Penthouse Forum*. Only this one was real. And it had happened to him.

Again, he sat down on the opposite end of the bench. She insisted it be done this way.

Makley was the first to speak. "Well? Did you find who sent the email?"

"No, Evan. I didn't. I'm go—"

"Why the hell not?" Makley raised his voice. "What am I paying you so much for if you can't trace a simple email?"

Love crossed her legs away from Makley signaling him to remain silent while a pedestrian walked past. It was a signal they had used numerous times on previous occasions.

A tall, thin woman with long red hair came into view. Under her umbrella she carried a small dog. The woman walked fast, never slowing or taking her attention away from her dog. When the woman was out of sight, Love uncrossed her legs.

"First of all, there were fourteen different email addresses being forwarded ahead of that one email you got. Ultimately they traced back to nothing."

"So, what? It's a dead end?"

"I didn't say that." Love unexpectedly turned to face him. "I was able to trace the ISP to Charleston, South Carolina. But that's as far as I can get without this." She held up a flash drive.

"What's that?" Makley asked.

"I have a tracer program on this drive. Stick it in any USB port on your computer and reply to his original email. Just ask him some questions."

"What do I ask him?"

"I don't know, Evan. You didn't get where you are by relying on someone to make decisions for you. Figure it out."

She was right. He hadn't climbed to the Chief of Staff position by relying on others. He used others to get him where he wanted, and then he discarded them like trash. Until the email, he thought he'd discarded Abigail Love. But some people prove more useful than others.

"How does it work?"

"When you reply, it embeds a tracking code in the email. As soon as your blackmailer opens the email, the tracking code installs a tracer on the hard drive so I can track the computer no matter where it goes. Once the computer accesses the Internet, we'll have him."

"You said you traced his Internet Service Provider to Charleston? That's coincidental."

"Why is that?"

"This morning Rudd briefed me on that grave robbing case and they have a lead in Charleston. A grave of a soldier killed in World War II was broken into in Charleston. Just more of what I told you the other night except now it's happened enough times to cause her concern. She's tasked someone to handle the investigation. She calls it Project Resurrection. The national cemetery here at Arlington was the first. She originally thought it was racially motivated because the first two break-ins were graves of black soldiers."

"Someone is stealing bodies from graves?"

"No. That's the strange part. Nothing appears to have been taken from any graves."

"Tell me more about this lead, Evan"

"It appears a woman drove a rental car into a cemetery in Charleston in the middle of the night, stayed for thirty minutes or so, and then left. That same night a soldier's grave was unearthed at the cemetery. Her parents are buried there also. No one else was seen entering or leaving the cemetery all night. Just her."

"Could be a coincidence, probably is, Charleston isn't a very large town." She paused. "Too much at stake not to check it out, though. I mean what are the odds that Charleston would come up twice like this?" She pointed to the flash drive. "You do your part and I'll check out Charleston. You remember the woman's name?"

"Ashley something," Makley said. "Ashley...Ashley. I can't remember. I'll have to send it to you."

He let his eyes scan up and down her torso recalling what was beneath the raincoat. The last time they'd met on the park bench she was wearing a spandex jogging suit so revealing that he could see every curve of her pleasing shape. Now that he had seen her uncovered, he had to admit she was too much woman for any man to resist. She had dark hair, dark tanned skin, and vivid green eyes.

Such a striking contrast.

"What is the chance for an encore performance?" He asked.

Love stared at him. "Perhaps. When I think it's safe, I'll come to you."

As she spoke, he remembered the woman's name. "Reagan. Ashley Reagan. No. No, wait. Regan. That's it. Ashley Regan."

"Are you sure?"

"Yes, I'm positive. Ashley Regan is the woman's name in Charleston."

Abigail Love stood. "I'll be in touch."

He watched her walk away while his mind relived that night.

†††

Francesca Catanzaro put the puppy back in the pet carrier, pulled the micro digital memory card from the handle of the umbrella and inserted it into her phone.

†††

Thirty seconds later, George Fontaine received the encrypted photos and processed them through Commonwealth's facial recognition software then transmitted the results.

†††

Less than a minute later, President Rebecca Rudd was looking at the photos with Elmore Wiley. Five minutes later she was looking at an FBI file on Abigail Love.

"Oh, Evan, what have you done?" She lowered her head and shook it. "Elmore, I'm open to suggestions."

"Rebecca, there are no circumstances where Evan Makley's association with Abigail Love, even if it is only as lovers, can be condoned by this administration. The mere fact he has met with this woman at all and that this picture even exists warrant, in my opinion, some sort of preemptive action on your part."

Rudd felt gastric acid churning in her stomach like molten lava. She reached into her desk, grabbed two Tums from a container, and popped them into her mouth. "I don't know what to say, Elmore."

"Rebecca, I'll handle this. The best thing for you to do or say...is nothing at all."

CHAPTER 23

Jake had time to study the traffic cam videos on the flight from D.C. to Charleston. Fontaine emailed the two videos to Jake after he dropped off the information packet at the Commonwealth penthouse. The entrance to the cemetery, as he was now aware, was never locked leaving access to the graveyard 24/7. The perimeter, a 6-foot high stone, masonry wall, along with several locked gates allowed for only a single point of entry and exit after regular hours. And, whether by design or not, was monitored by a traffic camera mounted at the entrance.

The City of Charleston had installed the cameras nearly three years ago when they installed the traffic signal at the entrance because of the heavy amount of traffic on the major artery leading in and out of town.

The camera didn't catch a shot of the driver as she entered the cemetery, only the vehicle and a clear shot of the tag. According to the time stamp, Ashley Regan's rented Chevy Impala entered the cemetery at 1:43 a.m. and exited at 2:29 a.m.

Forty-six minutes. Longer than he had originally thought.

It seemed to add an extra element of peculiarity to the event. First of all, who visits a relative's grave during those hours of the morning? He'd visited his own relatives' graves before and couldn't imagine staying for 46 minutes regardless of the time of day…or night. On the other hand, 46 minutes didn't seem like enough time to dig up a casket either.

Another oddity, he thought, was the fact that as she left the cemetery, the camera clearly showed two occupants in the front seat of the Impala. Two faces looking directly at the camera, eyes glowing green in the infrared picture. Both women.

Jake opened up the file Fontaine had prepared for him. Inside, a full background on Ashley Regan. He stared at the photo of her face. Then he looked at the still frame infrared shot of the two faces that the traffic cam captured through the Impala's windshield while the car was stopped at the cemetery exit traffic signal. No doubt about it, the driver of the Impala was Ashley Regan.

He flipped through the file and found Regan's address, pulled a handheld GPS unit from his backpack and loaded the address. He pulled out his Glock and a spare magazine and placed each item on the seat next to him. He slipped the GPS into his shirt pocket, stuffed the file along with his iPad inside his pack and zipped it closed.

He'd only gotten four hours of sleep, barely enough to keep him going. The last few days had kept him sleep deprived and that burning sensation in his eyes reminded him of it. He pushed himself out of the plush leather chair and walked to the galley as he heard the pilot of the Citation 750 say over the cabin speaker, "Fifteen minutes until touchdown, Mr. Pendleton."

How many times does he have to tell that man to call him Jake? He felt embarrassed to have the man, clearly twenty years his senior, call him "sir" or "Mr. Pendleton." He poured himself a cup of coffee. No sugar. No creamer. Black and bold, just the way he liked it. On rare occasions, if it was available, a dollop of honey might find its way into his cup. And over the past few days, he'd consumed many cups to keep him going.

Jake returned to the leather seat, still warm from his body heat, and sipped on the hot coffee. Wisps of steam spread the aroma throughout the cabin. Just the aroma of fresh brewed coffee helped him relax. He thought about his next move. He'd already been to the cemetery with Francesca. He'd seen all he needed. Time to pay Ashley Regan a visit at her residence and get to the bottom of her midnight visit to her parents' graves.

As it turned out the pilot was wrong. According to the co-pilot, the weather at Charleston had dropped below landing minimums and they would have to circle in a holding pattern for a few minutes.

The weather hold was brief. They commenced an instrument approach to the Charleston airport after only 30 minutes in a holding pattern. Jake didn't care. It allowed him a few minutes to close his eyes and let his mind run through everything that had happened since he was unexpectedly and literally plucked from Kyli's arms in the Maldives.

After landing, Jake hailed a taxi, climbed in the back seat, and gave the address to the Indian driver. The Charleston airport was considered Zone 4 and the minimum ride into downtown was $35. By the time the taxi pulled in front of Ashley Regan's house, the meter had already rung up $51. Jake asked the driver to wait only to be informed that the first five minutes were free and a dollar a minute after that. Jake agreed to the terms and got out of the taxi.

He walked up the driveway of an older red brick home. It was a single story, one of only two on the block, with a two-car attached garage on his right as he faced the house. There was no walkway to the front door leaving his choices across the wet grass or up the driveway and across the front porch.

When Jake reached the garage, he looked in through the glass panes that extended across the top of the garage door. One car parked inside. Not Regan's car according to Fontaine's report. And not the rented Impala.

He walked across the front porch, peering through the plate glass windows as he stepped. Someone had ransacked the living room. Jake pulled out his Glock, stepped to the side of the front door, and tried the doorknob. Locked. He took one step back and kicked open the front door just below the knob. The aging wood on the doorjamb broke free and splintered pieces of wood scattered across the old hardwood floor.

Jake stepped inside the house with his gun aimed straight ahead. He heard an engine roar. He turned to see his taxi speed off, leaving him without a ride back to the airport.

He scanned the room. Lamps lay broken on the floor. Bookcases emptied, piles of books strewn in all directions. From where he stood he could tell someone had emptied the cabinets in the kitchen as well. He cautiously went from room to room. Each room in the house was ransacked. In the bedrooms, mattresses were upturned and box springs slashed open. Someone was looking for something and there was a strong possibility they hadn't found what they came looking for since every room was ravaged.

Even the garage had been pillaged. Jake holstered his gun, pulled out his cell phone, and dialed George Fontaine. He explained what he'd found. "Whatever Ms. Regan is up to, she's pissed someone off. And, by the looks of her house, she could be in danger."

"I can try to track her cell phone," Fontaine said. "Good chance she won't think to disable it."

"Do that, George. And run facial recognition on the passenger too." Jake paused. "Also, can you track all the cemeteries that Major Adams shipped remains to?"

"What are you thinking?"

"That if Ashley Regan is the one looting these graves, then she knows something we don't. And now it looks like somebody else has come to this party uninvited. If we can figure out where she's going next, we can catch her. And if she is in danger, perhaps even save her life."

"And," Fontaine said, "we can answer the bigger question...why?"

Jake didn't reply.

"I'll check on the Army records. The question is whether or not they've scanned those archives into a searchable database. Remember, that was the mid 1940s." Fontaine chuckled. "I just got a hit on Regan's cell phone. Northeast of Johnson City, Tennessee."

He said nothing.

"Jake? Did you hear me?"

Nothing.

"Jake?" Fontaine's voice now blaring through his phone.

"Oh hell. This can't be good."

"Jake? What is it?"

"Sirens."

"Maybe it's not what you think."

Jake looked out the garage door window. "No, George. It's exactly what I was afraid of. Three cop cars just pulled up." Jake walked back into the house. "George, I don't have much time. Find out what you can about Regan's whereabouts. Keep tracking her. See if you can match any of Major Adams shipments to the area. After I take care of the cops, I'll call you back."

"Will do, Jake. Be careful."

"Always am." Jake turned off his phone as three policemen burst through the front door pointing their guns in his direction. He held up his hands.

The darts hit him in the chest.

His legs collapsed. Arms wouldn't respond. Head pounded.

Cuffs tightened around his wrists.

CHAPTER 24

Abigail Love watched the man kick in the front door. When the taxi sped off she couldn't help but smile. Perfect. She didn't know who the man was that entered Ashley Regan's house but he couldn't have been more obvious.

She had been watching the house, about to make her move, when the taxi pulled to the curb. Interesting, she thought. She hadn't made it as far as she had by acting hastily or overreacting. She knew when to resist the temptation to act on impulse. The situation warranted closer scrutiny. She had parked several houses down and on the opposite side of the street under a large live oak with a low hanging canopy.

Through the zoomed lens of her digital SLR camera, she had an unobstructed view of the house and the man entering it. He was average height, she guessed, had a muscular build, and carried himself with confidence. He was a good-looking man in his early thirties. She snapped pictures of his every move. As she sized him up she could tell he was alarmed by something he saw in the window. The drawing of the gun was her first clue. Her second clue was when he kicked in the front door. Clearly the man knew what he was doing. She inspected her camera; she'd taken 57 photos of the man since he'd arrived.

Who was this man and what was he doing at Ashley Regan's house? He didn't look like a cop. At least no cop she'd ever met. He approached the house in a tactical military style, disciplined and decisive. She recognized his gun—a Glock. What was this man's connection to Regan? More important, does he know about the blackmail attempt on the President?

Then she remembered that Evan Makley told her President Rudd was sending someone to Charleston. Maybe this was that man.

She'd found two good photos of the man's face and emailed them to Evan Makley along with a short message. After the man had been inside for ten minutes she started getting curious. Was he questioning Regan? If he was, then she stood to lose a lot of money. Evan Makley's money. She reached under her seat and pulled out her Smith and Wesson M & P .40 caliber Shield subcompact pistol. It was lightweight with a smaller grip than its Glock counterpart. She double-checked her pistol to ensure a round was chambered and tucked it in the small of her back. Time to see what the man inside was up to.

Just as she cracked open her car door she heard the sirens. Flashing lights from police cruisers rounded the street corners. Two in front, one from behind, all stopping in front of Regan's house.

One armor-vested cop from each car ran toward the house while the other cops stood behind car doors pointing their weapons at the residence.

Love closed the car door and melted into the leather seat. She removed the gun from her waist and slipped it back under the seat. This was an unfortunate turn of events. She could only assume the taxi driver called the cops. In less than a minute, the police brought out the blond haired man shackled in handcuffs, pushed him into the backseat of one of the cruisers, and drove off. He was out of the picture, for now, but it left her with a conundrum. Follow the cruiser to the police station or wait and try to gain access to the house after the police left.

From the nonchalant posture of the Charleston Police she reasoned they had no intention of leaving the scene anytime soon. Which meant an investigative team was on the way. The house would be sealed off and guarded for quite a while and her only lead was just hauled away in the cruiser.

She chose to follow the cruiser. She started her black BMW 750 Li, pulled away from the curb avoiding a van parked next to the curb, and accelerated around the corner in pursuit of the police car.

† † †

He watched the commotion in front of him with amusement. When the man entered the home, Scott Katzer called 9-1-1 and reported seeing the break-in. The police hauled the man from the house in handcuffs and all three officers that went in came back outside leaving no explanation other than Ashley Regan wasn't at home. No way would they have left her alone. Alive or dead.

The young man was evidently in search of one of two things, Ashley Regan or the book. Perhaps both. Something they shared in common. Now Katzer had a lead. All he had to do was follow and wait. Sooner or later the man would be released from jail. It wouldn't take long before the cops figured out that the man hadn't had time to ransack the house between the 9-1-1 call and the time they arrived at the scene.

Katzer was familiar with police procedure. Over the course of his forty years in the funeral home business, he'd been summoned on numerous occasions to crime scenes to remove dead bodies. Not so often anymore. Crime scene procedures were more sophisticated these days with an ever-increasing emphasis on forensics.

As soon as he saw the taxi let the man out, Katzer knew another party must be interested in the book. He'd already ascertained that Regan had the book and kept it a secret from her roommate. Mistaken identity had cost her her life. Needlessly, in his opinion. His mother had acted irrationally. The woman didn't need to be killed. And in the end, it was all for naught. He was no closer to obtaining the book now than he was before. Maybe even further, as Samantha Connors could've been used as a bargaining chip to get the book from Regan. That chip was gone.

Connors admitted that Regan was staying with a friend, but his mother had been too hasty trying to extract the information and the woman died before revealing the identity. Which is what brought him back to her house. He wanted to go through Regan's belongings to find something that might suggest who her friend might be. Now, with the presence of the Charleston Police, that wasn't going to happen either.

He put the van in gear and started to pull out to follow the police cruiser when the black BMW parked behind him pulled out cutting him off. He slammed on the brakes to avoid a collision. After the BMW passed him, he pulled into the street and proceeded to stay far enough behind the police cruiser to avoid being detected.

Two blocks before the police station, Katzer realized something odd, the other car was still in front of him. At the police station, the cruiser pulled into the secured lot. The black BMW parked in front of the station.

Keeping several parked cars between them, he parked the van close enough to allow optimal viewing of the police station and the mystery car and hopefully far enough away not to be noticed. Now he knew there were at least two other parties interested in the book, the man in the police station and whoever was in the BMW. He also knew he had to get to it first.

CHAPTER 25

J ake hated *riding the bull.* That's what they called being hit by a Taser at The Farm, the CIA's tradecraft training facility. A mandatory part of every agent's training. Thank goodness Wiley didn't require it of his emissaries. There was nothing fun about it.

His solitary cell was small, eight feet by eight feet, three windowless concrete walls and the fourth all bars with a door. Fluorescent lights outside the bars droned a continuous hum. He hadn't been questioned, just tossed in the cell, and told to wait. He guessed he'd been in there thirty minutes but he didn't know for sure. They stripped him of all his personal belongings, his belt, and his shoes.

The Charleston police never let him talk. And when he tried to offer an explanation, he got a truncheon to the ribs. His repeated demands for a phone call landed on deaf ears. The longer he was stuck in this cell, the further ahead Ashley Regan got. And perhaps, closer to danger. He needed to call Wiley and let the old man do what he does best, pull some strings to get him the hell out of there.

He heard a metal door clang and footsteps walking down the hall. Two linebacker-sized uniforms stood at the door to his cell, one holding a Taser, the other a pair of handcuffs.

"Turn around, hands behind your back." The man holding the handcuffs said.

Jake did as the man said. No sense in making things worse. Cooperation was likely the quickest way out of jail.

"Now back up to the bars."

Jake stepped backwards and felt the handcuffs clamp around his wrists.

"Forward five steps." The man ordered.

Jake did as instructed and the cell door opened. Each linebacker grabbed an arm and escorted him to a room he knew to be an interrogation room. Finally, he thought, he was making progress. He was pushed into a chair and cuffed to the table. Leg cuffs were clamped around his ankles and secured to anchors in the floor. The uniforms stood by his sides, batons in hand. *Who the hell did they think he was?*

The answer came when a man appeared in a coat and tie. He was a tall man who looked to be in his mid-fifties with a full head of salt and pepper hair. The man placed Jake's pistol, screw-on sound suppressor, pocketknife, and iPhone on the table in front of him. From his pocket he pulled Jake's wallet and flipped it open.

"Are you Jake Pendleton?" The man asked.

"You're looking at my driver's license, you can read." Jake realized his mistake as the words crossed his lips.

"Special Agent Donald Corbin, FBI." He pulled out a badge and ID from his jacket pocket, showed it to Jake, then put it back.

"FBI?" Jake asked. "Were you watching the house? Is that why I got picked up?"

"No. Until today the FBI had no interest in that house or Ashley Regan. You got picked up," Corbin put extra emphasis on his last word, "because a concerned citizen saw you kick in the front door and enter with a gun in your hand. They were concerned about Ms Regan's welfare and called 9-1-1."

"That doesn't explain you. Why the FBI and not a detective?"

Corbin picked up the sound suppressor and held it in front of Jake. "Suppressor, illegal. Glock 37 Gen4 .45 caliber special military issue." He slid the gun across the table then he picked up Jake's knife and phone. "Benchmade spring-assisted knife, and this," Corbin put the knife down and pointed to Jake's phone, "this is like nothing like I've ever seen before. What kind of iPhone is this anyway?"

"Custom made."

"Mr. Pendleton, who do you work for and what do you do?"

"Commonwealth Consultants, Fairfax, Virginia." Jake looked Corbin in the eyes. "Check it out."

Corbin stared back at Jake, raised his hand, and snapped his fingers. "Check it out." He sat back in his chair.

"I can straighten this out with one phone call, I'm entitled to that."

"Are you aware that under the Patriot Act I can hold you for a very long time without allowing you to make a phone call or retain legal counsel?"

"So, you think I'm a terrorist?"

Corbin waved his hand across the table. "Look at this stuff. These aren't your typical private investigator accessories, more like mercenary gear. On this table I have enough cause to hold you indefinitely, so I'll ask you again. What do you do?"

"Special Agent Corbin?" A voice from an overhead speaker. "Can you come in here, please?"

Corbin stood and smiled at Jake. "Don't go anywhere."

Jake turned his wrists up and pulled the cuffs against the restraints. "Funny."

Corbin left the room only to return five minutes later. He looked at the guards. "Unshackle him and leave us." He turned to the mirror behind him. "Video and audio off. Someone go get the rest of Mr. Pendleton's belongings."

Corbin sat down. "CIA? NSA?"

"Neither."

"Mr. Pendleton, what happened in that house?"

"I don't know. That's what I was trying to find out. When I walked by the window, I saw the house had been ransacked so I kicked in the door. I made a quick sweep of the house to make sure no one was inside and then the cops showed up." Jake leaned over the table. "And if someone had given me a chance to speak, this never would have gotten this far."

"The house belongs to Ashley Regan. She has a roommate named Samantha Connors." Corbin said. "What do you know about them?"

"Nothing."

"You're lying."

"Nope. Not lying."

"Mr. Pendleton, you're not leaving until I know what you were doing in that house. We've tried contacting both women with no luck. Ms. Connors works from her home and Ms. Regan is taking personal days from the accounting firm where she works. Who was it you came to see?"

This had gone far enough. Jake needed to get out of here and get the FBI off his back. "How about that phone call?"

"I'm not letting you make a phone call until I get some answers." Corbin said.

Jake stood. Corbin followed suit. "I don't want to make a phone call." Jake said. "You want answers, you make the phone call."

"I beg your pardon?" Corbin sounded surprised.

"You to make the call."

Corbin stared at Jake for several seconds without speaking. "Alright. But my patience has worn thin." Corbin pulled out his phone. "What's the number?"

Jake recited the number from memory then sat back down and listened to the one-sided conversation.

Corbin's eyes widened and he looked at Jake. "Special Agent Donald Corbin, FBI...yes ma'am...yes ma'am" Corbin wrote something in his notepad. "Yes ma'am, I'll do that right away, ma'am."

Corbin hung up the phone and looked at Jake. "Is this some kind of joke?"

"Call your field office, give them that authorization code, and see what they have to say." Jake said.

Corbin placed the call. His face looked like he'd seen a ghost. "Why didn't you tell me sooner?"

"Because, Special Agent Corbin, I'm not at liberty to discuss this with anyone...and that includes the FBI." Jake stood. "Now if you'll have Charleston's finest bring my stuff, I'll be on my way."

Jake checked his watch as he walked down the front steps of the Charleston Police Department. It had been over three hours since the taxi dropped him off in front of Ashley Regan's house. He pulled out his iPhone, punched in the special 24-digit password, scanned his left thumb, and unlocked the phone. Five missed calls from George Fontaine.

Jake stepped to the curb and hailed a taxi instructing the driver where to take him at the airport. He called George Fontaine.

"Jake. What the hell happened?"

"They hauled my ass off to jail, that's what happened. But not until after some young hotshot popped me with a Taser."

"How'd you enjoy riding the bull?"

"I didn't."

"Is it as bad as they say?" Fontaine asked.

"I still have a headache if that tells you anything. If I ever come back to Charleston, remind me to track down that officer and shoot him in the balls with one of Wiley's Tasers." Jake paused. "Got something for me?"

"Yeah, got your iPad with you?"

"No, it's on the plane. I'm headed that way now."

"When you get there, read what I sent. You'll find it more than a little interesting. Tell your pilots to take you to Tri Cities Airport in Tennessee. I've arranged a rental for a few days. You're on your own for lodging."

"What can you tell me now?"

"Jake, I ran facial recognition on the cemetery infrared photo and nothing turned up. So I hacked into Ashley Regan's facebook account and ran a facial comparison with all her photos and I found our mystery woman. Her name is Christa Barnett and she and Regan grew up a few houses apart. Best friends since childhood. According to their high school records, the two of them were in trouble on more than one occasion. Mostly harmless pranks but it got them suspended on the third incident. I'm running a background check on her now."

"What about Adams? Did you find anything there?" Jake asked.

"We got lucky again. The Army has moved into the digital world by progressively scanning and cataloging war casualty records. Adams shipped remains to several towns in Tennessee. Memphis, Nashville, Knoxville, and Butler."

"Butler? Never heard of it." Jake prided himself on knowing his way around the southern Appalachian Mountains, but this one was new to him.

"I'm almost a hundred percent sure Regan is going to hit Butler. Everything you need to know is in the file I sent. After you read it, call me back so we can discuss it."

"Sure thing, George. We're pulling up to the airport now."

"And Jake?"

"What?"

"Wiley was here a few minutes ago asking about all the details. Seems he got a phone call from President Rudd about your run-in with some FBI agent."

"Was he pissed?"

"Didn't seem that way. Concerned mostly. He told Rudd where you're headed."

"How'd he know that? You tell him?"

"I did. Hope you don't mind."

"Nope. Saves me the trouble of making the call myself." Jake paused. "I've got a hunch Ashley Regan and Samantha Connors aren't the only missing pieces in this puzzle."

CHAPTER 26

Jake climbed into the cabin of the Citation 750 and gave the pilots his new destination. He grabbed a sandwich and two miniature cans of Mountain Dew from the galley and sat down in his usual spot. He needed food and a good caffeine jolt. He devoured the sandwich and guzzled the first can of soda while the jet taxied. Better already. Low blood sugar always made him grumpy. His morning had gotten off to a rotten start and he despised playing catch-up. He felt a twinge of déjà vu as he readied himself to track down Ashley Regan. It had been nearly a year since his hound dog pursuit of a terrorist who threatened to blow up a museum in New York City. And as with that search, Jake always seemed to be one step behind.

With the surge of the jet's engine as the aircraft accelerated down the runway, he instinctively checked his seatbelt. After wheels up, he retrieved his iPad from his backpack, unlocked the tablet computer, retrieved his messages, and downloaded the encrypted files Fontaine sent him. Some of the information was a repeat from the phone call. Fontaine had sent volumes of data; enough to keep him busy at least an hour reading through all the detailed reports. Then he still had to analyze the data and formulate a new course of action.

Jake was a top analyst when he was with Naval Intelligence; to such a degree he was assigned to work directly

with the Chairman of the Joint Chiefs. He'd proven his worth
on numerous occasions during his brief stint with the CIA.
But regardless of how good his analytical intuition was, he
wouldn't be nearly as effective if it weren't for Fontaine's IT
skills. A perfect complement for his tradecraft.

The three hundred mile flight from rainy Charleston to
the sunshine of Northeastern Tennessee was estimated to
take forty-five minutes so Jake scanned through the
documents and reports as quickly as he could, trying to
absorb only the important details. As he soon realized, it was
all-important. With fifteen minutes of flight time remaining,
he logged in to the Commonwealth server with his encrypted
iPad.

Fontaine's face appeared on the new enhanced screen. In
fact, his face filled the screen. Top to bottom, left to right.
Always smiling, head full of silver hair, and his crooked nose
shifted to one side. Fontaine's left, Jake's right. A feature he
thought fit the jovial man's demeanor. "Hi, Jake. We're
burning daylight, ready to start?"

"Ready, George. Let's do this."

"As you're aware from the history on Butler—"

"I didn't really read that file, just a quick glance.
Something about TVA and a flooded town. I figured I'd get
to it later."

"You'll need to read it to get a good understanding of
what's about to transpire. And more than likely you'll come to
the same conclusion I have." Fontaine said.

"And you're not going to tell me right away, are you?"
Jake knew Fontaine's style was to fill him full of facts and
then disclose the remaining piece of the puzzle at the last
minute. A flare for sensationalism. It was a game Fontaine
played, a test of sorts, to see if Jake could figure out the
puzzle without the final piece. Most times he could.

Fontaine shook his head.

"Go ahead then."

"At first I figured the women would just see what had happened in Butler and keep on going but it looks like they're sticking around, which is good news for us because it will take them a couple of days to get what they came for."

"Not a simple smash and run this time, huh?"

"As you'll read, Adams shipped the remains to Butler in January of 1946, one month before he disappeared. Much has changed in Butler since then and Regan and Barnett will be in for quite a surprise when they get there."

"What makes you think they're going to stick around?" Jake had asked Fontaine to track Regan's cell phone before he left Charleston. "New developments?"

"Oh yeah. I pinpointed four stops with Regan's phone. First, the Butler Museum. Which was strange because according to the website the museum was closed. From there, she stopped at a bait shop in Butler for about fifteen minutes and then drove to two different scuba diving shops. One in Kingsport and the other in Johnson City. Which tells me Butler is definitely the target."

"Where is she now?" Jake asked.

"Let's see." Jake could hear Fontaine typing on his computer. The familiar sound of fingertips striking a keyboard. "Right now she's back in Butler. Looks like at one of the marinas on the lake."

"What about Adams? Anything new?"

"Nothing specifically on Adams but I did come across something I think you'll find enlightening."

"I'm listening."

"I decided to track Ashley Regan's passport and you'll never believe what popped up."

"To use your words, enlighten me." Jake saw Fontaine smile.

"In August, Ashley Regan and Samantha Connors made a hiking trip to Germany. Third year in a row, same time period. Each year they hiked from the base to the summit of Zugspitze. Same mountain Adams disappeared on in 1946."

"That is interesting," Jake said, "but how does that relate to now?"

"Patience, young Jedi." Fontaine, a Star Wars geek had used that line on him on more than one occasion. "As it turns out, this year Regan found the frozen remains of a body inside an ice cave in the Höllentalferner glacier, which is on the north face of Zugspitze."

"No kidding," Jake said, "was it Adams?"

"Don't know," Fontaine explained. "The remains have yet to be identified. All I could find out is that it was a man and the time period is about the same. To this day there are still an awful lot of missing and unaccounted for soldiers from the World War II era."

Jake was silent. His brain cells went into overdrive as he rolled through the possible alternatives. Too coincidental for the body in the glacier to be anyone but Adams.

"Jake? You still with me?" Fontaine asked.

"She's not vandalizing caskets," Jake said. "She's robbing graves. She must have found something on the frozen body and kept it. That had to be Adams' body. I'll bet he'd been shipping something to the States in those caskets and had it all written down in something, maybe a journal or ledger of some sort. And Ashley Regan found it and kept it for herself. Which means whoever ransacked Ashley Regan's home, was looking for it too."

"And she solicited her best friend to help her out." Fontaine injected. "Who also took four semesters of German in college *and* is a certified scuba diver."

"Interesting." Jake smiled. "I need to find Regan and Barnett and get my hands on that book."

"I already gave Wiley my suspicions, you want me to brief Rudd as well?"

"Not yet, George," Jake said. "Not until I have something definitive. Even though we know the truth, it's only conjecture. We need proof. We need the book."

"No personal items have been taken from the caskets, so what do you think is hidden inside?"

"I have a pretty good idea," Jake said. "George, here's what I need you to find out."

Jake gave Fontaine specific instructions and logged out. He thought about everything he'd just learned and smiled. He needed to personally give President Rebecca Rudd an update after all.

✝✝✝

Abigail Love plugged Butler, Tennessee into the in-dash GPS unit in her black BMW. Three hundred fifty miles. Six hours.

That was one hour ago.

While she was waiting for the man to come out of the Charleston police station, she had received a text message from Evan Makley in reply to the photos she took of the man earlier. It simply stated:

Butler, TN. More to follow.

She took an exit in Spartanburg, South Carolina for the triple purposes of refueling the BMW, getting something to eat, and going to the bathroom. Seventy-five dollars and fifteen minutes later she pulled back onto Interstate 26 with a full tank of gas, a bag of fast food, and an empty bladder. She rummaged around in her food bag and pulled out some French fries. Why did something so bad for you, smell so enticing and taste so good?

Her cell phone rang, Evan Makley, she recognized the number on caller-id.

"Hello, Evan."

"The woman has a book. A journal of some sort. That man you saw arrested in Charleston is working for Rudd. He could be a problem. Whatever is in that book is no doubt what she's using to blackmail me...and the President. Abigail, I need that book. Do you understand?"

"Yes, Evan. I'm not an idiot." Now she remembered what she didn't like about Evan Makley from before. It was his condescending tone whenever he was upset or nervous. "I'll take care of the woman."

"There are two of them."

"Two of them, what? Women?"

"Yes. Two women. Ashley Regan and Christa Barnett. Get the book and kill them both."

"What about the man? What if he interferes?"

"His name is Jake Pendleton. If he gets in the way, kill him too."

† † †

Francesca Catanzaro turned off the recorder when Evan Makley disconnected his call with Abigail Love. Her palms became clammy as the feeling of anxious apprehension grew inside. The Chief of Staff just ordered a known assassin to kill two women and Jake Pendleton.

The President's suspicions about Makley had been correct. He was in over his head. Whatever he was trying to do, for whatever reason, was illegal and now Jake's life was at stake. Jake was her partner. There was no way she would sit idly by and let Evan Makley get away with ordering a hit on him. The Chief of Staff just made a critical mistake. A fatal mistake.

She thought about her options for a moment and realized that Chief of Staff Evan Makley was a bigger liability to President Rebecca Rudd's administration than Senator Richard Boden had been. When Wiley split Jake and her up, he tasked her only to observe and gather intelligence on Makley but that time had now passed. Now was the time to take action.

Swift and decisive action.

She picked up the phone and dialed Elmore Wiley.

CHAPTER 27

A breeze slid down the mountain and across the small town of Butler, Tennessee. It was everything Ashley Regan had expected. She gazed across Watauga Lake and saw fishing boats and water skiers slicing through the calm waters. A serene lake where parents took their families on all-day outings, anchoring in a shady cove along the 106-mile shoreline and letting the kids swim while mom and dad enjoyed a cool drink on deck. Or perhaps, camping on one of the many islands inside the peaceful lake.

At one end stood the Watauga Dam, 318 feet tall and over 900 feet wide. Watauga Lake extended eighteen miles from the dam before the shoreline doubled back. At the base of the dam the water was 280 feet deep at the lake's fullest stage. But this year had seen a severe drought, the second year in a row, and the lake was nineteen feet below full stage.

This information was important to her after she spent the morning scanning the history records at the Butler Museum and talking to the old man at the Butler Country Store and Bait Shop. Five hours ago, when she and Christa Barnett drove from Banner Elk, North Carolina to Butler, it would have seemed like useless information. Now, it was worth over two million dollars.

At nine o'clock this morning when the two women arrived, Regan set out to do what they had done everywhere else, case the area to determine the location of the cemetery and grave. They also scouted the primary and alternate access points along with all highways and roads leading in and out of Butler. Careful preparation and planning were necessary to achieve her goal. What she found when the two of them arrived in Butler was totally unforeseen.

There was no grave for Norman Albert Reese, Jr. in the Butler Cemetery. As a matter of fact, the only Reese graves in the cemetery belonged to his parents, Norman, Sr. and Sarah Hawkins Reese, both who died over fifty years after their son was killed in the war. She scoured through the archives of the museum and found only one entry about Norman Jr.'s burial. According to the records, his family refused a military funeral and buried him on the family homestead where he grew up. She could find no further mention of Norman, Jr. or the Reese homestead.

The cemetery was a dead end, Regan pulled into a Butler Country Store and Bait Shop to get gas for the rental car. It had a rustic overhang and a single gas pump. Hanging on the screen door was a long, flat, plastic bag filled with water. She walked in and noticed an old man with a cane rearranging cigarette packs in the rack behind the counter. Two aisles were stocked with fishing gear—rods, reels, tackle, nets, paddles, life jackets, and more. The old building was musty. She heard a gurgling sound coming from a tank in the back of the store. Minnows in the tank with an aerator, crickets in a cage making annoying chirping sounds next to the tank, and a box of black dirt lined the back wall. The handwritten sign above the box read *Worms.*

She grabbed two soft drinks and two bags of chips and took them to the counter. She looked at the screen door. "What's with the bag of water?" She motioned toward the door.

"Keeps the flies out." The old man never looked up.

"How's that?"

"When the flies get near it, they see their reflection. The bag makes their reflection look like a much larger bug so they fly away."

"Does that really work?" It sounded like country hocus-pocus to her.

"It wouldn't be hanging there if it didn't." He looked up at her for the first time. "Will this be all?"

She nodded and slid the items across the counter. While the old man took her cash she noticed several old wartime photos on the wall behind him.

She pointed to one on the wall. "Is that you in those pictures?" She asked.

"Eh?" He cupped his hand around his ear. "Speak up missy."

"The pictures." She raised her voice. "Is that you in the pictures?"

He turned around and looked. "That's me and my friend in all these pictures." He limped with his cane and pulled one off the wall, blew several years worth of dust off of it, and placed it on the counter in front of her. It was a picture of two men in uniform, barely old enough to be considered men. He tapped on the picture. "He's dead now."

"I'm sorry," Regan said. "How long ago did he die?"

The man grew silent. He rubbed his arthritic hands across the glass covering the photo. "One month after this picture was taken. We went off to war together." He paused. "I came home in a cast. He came home in a box."

"I'm so sorry to hear that." Regan genuinely felt sorry for the old man. She knew what it was like to lose someone close. Her parents died while she was attending college. During her freshman year, her mother got sick and battled breast cancer. While she was undergoing chemo, her father was diagnosed with Stage 4 prostate cancer and died two months later. Six months after his death, her mother died from an infection contracted during her treatment. "Which war was that, Korea?"

He didn't answer at first. She could tell his thoughts had drifted elsewhere. She guessed back to the war.

"World War II," he said. "We took a mortar round in our bunker. Landed five feet from Norm. Blew him to pieces. I was further away, but shrapnel still tore up my leg. Almost lost it."

Did he say Norm? Could she be so lucky? "Norm? Was that your friend's name?"

"Yep. Norman Reese. Died one month shy of his twentieth birthday."

At first, she thought the odds of running into the one man who could help her locate Norman Reese Jr. were staggering. Then she remembered the sign said population 3977 and realized in this small southern town, the odds were probably pretty good if she talked to the elderly. People in this part of the country don't leave like they do in larger cities. Families had been here for many decades. Some, even longer.

In retrospect, this is exactly how she should have started her inquiries. This man knew more about the town than she could ever hope to find in the Butler Museum.

"That's horrible. He was so young. Is he buried in the cemetery here in town?" She knew he wasn't but it was a good leading question without tipping her interest in the man.

"Naw. His parents buried him on their old property. Had fifty acres on a bluff on the Watauga River. They buried Norm on a knoll overlooking the river and Old Butler. It was Norm's favorite fishing spot. He used to have an old tire swing hanging from an oak tree. We'd swing over the river and drop in. He was actually born under that tree." The old man went quiet again.

"It sounds like a very pretty place. Do his parents still own it?"

The old man looked at her without speaking. She felt like he was looking right through her, knowing that it was all a ruse. She had a rush of anxiety but covered it with a smile. The same smile she always gave Samantha whenever she wanted her to do something. Thinking of Sam Connors made her feel guilty. It had been two weeks and Sam still wasn't accepting her calls. She missed Sam and vowed to go back home and patch things up with her. And with any luck at all, going home a lot richer.

"Nope. They're dead."

"Are all of them are buried on the property?"

"You sure ask a lot of questions, young lady."

"Oh, I'm so sorry. I didn't mean to sound nosy. You're such a nice man and your friend obviously meant a lot to you. I meant no disrespect." She stuffed her wallet back in her purse and turned toward the door.

"No, no. It's just that I haven't talked about Norm in such a long time. Brings back so many memories. Norm's parents died after the TVA flooded the valley, so they're in the cemetery down the street."

"TVA?" She turned around and walked back to the counter.

"Tennessee Valley Authority. You see, Watauga River used to flood a lot back in the day, and after the big flood of 1940, they decided to construct a dam and flood the entire valley. They started building it and then along came World War II, which put a big stop to that project along with all other domestic work projects, and the government's focus shifted to support the war. After the war was over though, the TVA came back in and started working on the dam. They tried to move Norm's body several times but old man Reese wouldn't let 'em. Every time they'd show up, he'd run 'em off with his shotgun. I think he might of shot one of 'em."

"So what happened to Norm's body?"

"Still in the ground on that knoll, far as I know." The old man picked up the picture, grabbed a dirty rag, wiped the rest of the dust from the top of the frame, and hung it back on the wall.

"Well if they flooded the valley, where is this knoll you're talking about?" Regan had gotten lucky. Extraordinarily lucky.

"Like everything else in Old Butler that wasn't torn down or relocated to New Butler, it's underwater. Been that way since 1948 except that one time they drained the lake to repair the dam." The old man reached below the counter and pulled out a map of Watauga Lake. He grabbed a marker and circled a small area on the map. "The old Reese place was somewhere around here. Under about sixty feet of water."

That was three hours ago and now she was sitting in the car staring at the map while Christa drove them back to Butler. She and Christa had just purchased scuba diving equipment from two different dive shops in the Tri Cities area. One in Kingsport and one in Johnson City. She had just spent over three thousand dollars to fully equip both of them with dive computers, buoyancy compensator vests, regulators, masks, fins, tanks, and dry suits. She figured three thousand dollars was a small price to pay compared to the cache she was about to extract from the grave of Norman Albert Reese, Jr.

CHAPTER 28

"There must be some mistake," Jake said to the man behind the rental car kiosk. "I don't think my vehicle is supposed to come with a boat."

"Yes sir, Mr. Pendleton. That order is correct. I took the reservation myself. I've never had a special request quite like this one before so it isn't something I'd forget." He typed something into his computer terminal. "It says here the order was placed on your behalf by George Fontaine...and paid for by Commonwealth Consultants of Fairfax, Virginia. Does that sound right?"

"Yeah, that's right," Jake said. "I just don't understand the boat."

"There's an envelope on the front seat with instructions from Mr. Fontaine," the man said. "Maybe that will clear it up."

"I hope so." Jake thanked the man and walked across the lot to the rental, a white Chevrolet Tahoe with a nineteen foot Bass Tracker. A 90-horsepower Mercury outboard hung from the transom.

The big surprise was what he found in the back of the Tahoe—a full complement of fishing tackle, a dive bag of scuba gear, and tanks. Lying on the front passenger seat was an envelope with a note and a State of Tennessee Non-Resident fishing license. He unfolded the note. It read: 'Enjoy your fishing trip, call me when you're underway.'

Nothing more.

Jake folded the note, slipped it and the fishing license back into the envelope, tossed his backpack on the floorboard, climbed inside the Tahoe, and sat in the plush leather seat. Jake paired his Bluetooth headset to his phone then slipped it around his ear, started the SUV, and pulled away from the Tri Cities Airport.

The dash-mounted GPS screen lit up automatically displaying the distance and route to Butler. The woman's electronic voice called out, "Please drive the highlighted route." *Son of a bitch thinks of everything.*

Jake followed the voice's directions and pulled onto Bristol Highway, hit speed dial, and waited.

Two rings later Fontaine answered. "Been expecting your call. Hope you found everything satisfactory."

"What's the punch line?" Jake asked.

"About the scuba gear?"

"Nope. Got that figured out. Don't know that I quite understand the fishing gear unless it's to use as a ruse to get into a particular area. In case I'm stopped or something."

"A little more complicated than that, Jake. It is your cover to be there because there is a bass fishing tournament on the lake for the next two days. Keep that fishing license on you and play the part. In the bow of the boat you'll find compartments large enough to conceal the scuba gear—tanks and all."

"It's been a long time since I dove, George. I'm out of practice."

"Gee, Jake. According to your file, you were certified as a Search and Rescue diver in the Navy as well as certified to operate underwater communications equipment."

"I was, but it's been probably ten years since I strapped on a tank."

"Eleven years, five months, and twenty-one days according to your Navy records. Still, it's like riding a bike, right?"

"You hacked my Navy records? What else did you hack? Wait. Don't tell me. Do you know where I'll be diving?"

"I pulled the pre-flood land survey records from the TVA from October of 1946 when they recommenced construction on the dam. The grave of Norman Albert Reese Jr. is depicted on the survey. The family refused to let the TVA or any authorities move their son's body. Old man Reese even knew the valley was going to be flooded before he buried his son there so he had a concrete vault installed with a metal lid bolted onto it. He didn't want his son floating up after the flood. He also put a large marker in the ground at the head of the vault. That's what you'll be looking for."

"How deep is it?" Jake asked.

"As best as I can figure from the topographic and water table charts, should be around sixty feet. Give or take a few feet. Also the water temperature could be as low as the upper 40's. Research indicates the visibility can range anywhere from fifteen to twenty-five feet so that is in your favor. Another thing, according to the topo charts, the knoll where Reese is buried is only about fifty feet from the shoreline so you might be able to shore dive."

"How much of this intel do you think Regan and her friend have?"

"I can't say for sure, but I think it's unlikely they have anything very precise. I think they'll have to search for the grave. It could take them a while to find it."

"What about lodging, are they staying someplace in Butler?"

"Again, don't know for sure. According to the hotel in Banner Elk, the room was booked for two nights. Paid in advance. In cash. I'll keep a tracker on her cell phone. See if they stay in Butler or return to Banner Elk. You know, if the coast is clear, you might want to consider diving tonight."

Jake turned the Tahoe onto Interstate 26 toward Johnson City. He was already thinking the same thing as Fontaine. If he could find the grave first then he would be a step ahead of Regan and her friend. It would also give him something far more important.

Control.

There was another option, he could always follow and locate Regan before she had a chance to make a dive. Confront her on dry land, expose her illegal activities, hopefully acquire whatever she found in the glacier, and then determine what she was retrieving from the graves. But a public confrontation carried with it the possibility of law enforcement involvement, which had to be avoided at all costs—for President Rudd's sake. He'd already had a run-in with the Charleston Police Department and the FBI, fortunately it was handled without consequence to the President. Until he knew what he was involved in, he needed to avoid any volatile situations. Confronting Regan and her friend in public could turn volatile fast.

"Tell you what, George. Unless Regan decides to go after it tonight, I'll be doing just that." Jake paused. "There wouldn't by chance be a dive light in that bag, would there?"

"Not one dive light, two of them. Along with one replacement battery."

"Looks like you thought of everything. Any thing else I should know before I let you go?"

"Couple of things, Jake." Fontaine said. "From what I've found on the Internet, most of the divers have reported a rather heavy layer of silt near the bottom of the lake. Up to

eight feet deep in some places so stay away from the lake bed
or you'll lose your visibility."

"What else?"

"I sent you some information on possible lodging in the
Butler area. I hope it helps."

"Thanks, George. I'll take all the help I can get."

In Johnson City, Roxanne, the name he gave the woman's
electronic voice from the GPS unit, instructed him to turn on
U. S. Highway 321 to Elizabethton where he pulled over at a
truck stop to take advantage of good cell phone reception. He
wasn't sure how good the service would be in Butler.

He pulled his iPad from his backpack and downloaded
the information Fontaine had sent him. He'd been thinking
about lodging and decided to rule out campgrounds and B &
B's because his comings and goings would be too noticeable.
What he needed was a private place, preferably on the lake
where he had quick access to the boat. A quick Google search
under   his   favorite   websites,   VRBO.com   and
HomeAway.com, revealed nothing useful. Another search for
fish camps, even though not as desirable, also turned up
nothing. A third search under 'Butler, Tennessee lodging' hit
pay dirt. Several sites he'd never heard of showed up but only
one proved useful. He found several lakefront cabins but only
one that wasn't booked. He figured it was because of the
price, $450 a night. Most families weren't going to pay that
price, especially this time of year during the middle of the
week.

He called the number and secured the cabin from the
owner for three nights using his Commonwealth Consultants
credit card.

He plugged the cabin's address into his iPad and was
pleased when he saw the cabin was just across Watauga Lake
from the location Fontaine had identified as the site where

Norman Reese was buried. Using his distance-measuring tool he realized the straight-line distance across the water was less than a mile. By road it was nearly fourteen miles from the cabin to the point where Reese was buried and another four miles to Butler itself. He needed to mull over the geographical logistics of his predicament. A visual of the area would help so he put the Tahoe in gear and pulled back on the highway toward Butler.

At the intersection of U. S. 321 and Tennessee State Road 67, Roxanne told him to turn left on SR 67, cross Watauga lake, and into Butler. The map on the iPad showed both the cabin and the grave site on the east side of the lake.

Jake wanted eyes on Regan and her friend first. The only way he could do that was with Fontaine's help. He pulled to the side of the road and called Fontaine.

Fontaine answered.

"Is Regan still in Butler?" Jake asked.

"According to her cell phone, she's at the *Pizza Place* and has been for the past fifteen minutes."

†††

The waitress placed the pizza on the table and asked if she could get them anything else. Regan shook her head and thanked her. She pulled two pieces of pizza from the platter and placed them on her plate and did the same on Christa Barnett's plate.

She sprinkled pepper seeds and Parmesan cheese on her pizza then looked at Barnett. "When should we do this?"

"It'll have to wait until tomorrow. I can't do it by myself and I don't want to throw your ass in the water until we've had a chance to go through all the equipment. And I'm certainly not taking you down at night. Not on your first dive."

"Oh hell no. I'm not going underwater at night period." Regan paused. "Maybe we should just skip this one. I was excited at first but now...I don't know. I'm kind of scared. What do we do if something goes wrong?"

"Relax, Ashley. It'll be okay, I promise. Nothing will go wrong. We bought the very best equipment. The full-face mask will allow you to breathe normal and the communications system will allow us to talk when we need to. I'll be right there by your side. Besides, it'll be fun."

"Should we put the stuff on and get in the pool tonight? Maybe that would help."

"Might draw unwanted attention," Barnett said. "The last thing we want is for someone to remember us."

"No, no. Of course you're right." The room lit up when the front door opened. Rays of sunshine blasted across the floor then disappeared as the door closed. Regan noticed Barnett wasn't paying attention. "Christa. You're not listening."

"Check this guy out. He is H-O-T."

Regan looked. A man with dirty blond hair, jeans and a long sleeve button down shirt walked behind Barnett toward the counter. His sleeves were rolled to his elbows and he had a five o'clock shadow on his face. "Not interested."

"Are you kidding? He looks like Chris Pine. Makes for nice eye candy, right?"

"He's handsome, I guess. Hard to tell anymore. I haven't been on that side of the fence for a long time."

"Yeah, yeah, Ashley. Maybe it's time you gave men another try." Christa turned her head and watched the man while he placed his order at the counter. "Now that you and Sam are on the fritz, might be a good time to experiment."

As if she wasn't worried enough about scuba diving,
Christa's remark certainly didn't help any. She was already
concerned that Sam hadn't answered her phone in over two
weeks. What if she'd moved out? Maybe back to Atlanta.
Regan resolved that as soon as they were finished in Butler,
she would go straight to Charleston or wherever Samantha
Connors was, apologize, and try to reconcile with her.

✝ ✝ ✝

Jake recognized both women from the photos. They were
sitting together at a table sharing a pizza. The taller one,
Ashley Regan, had long, thick brown hair pulled back into a
ponytail, which was stuffed through the opening in the back
of an Atlanta Braves baseball cap. Fontaine's report indicated
she was 5' 7" tall but he couldn't judge her height while she
was seated. She was very attractive but didn't fit the image he
had in his mind.

Christa Barnett's long black hair that didn't look natural
compared with the rest of her facial features. He'd seen the
photos Fontaine had sent him. Barnett was born a blonde, so
the dark hair didn't compliment her tanned face. According
to her file, she was an even five feet and barely topped a
hundred pounds.

They were both wearing blue jeans and t-shirts.

Regan looked stressed, frown lines visible on her face
from across the dining room. Barnett seemed to be reassuring
her of something. He'd strategically selected his table and
chair so he would be able to observe them while he ate. He
noticed Barnett glance his direction several times and smile.
Regan looked his way once and smiled, but it looked feigned.

His food came and he inconspicuously analyzed the two women while he ate. It was the visual threat assessment he needed to evaluate what he was up against and what, if any, element of danger the women might present.

The women finished eating first, paid the waitress, and left. Jake didn't move. He knew Fontaine would track their movements.

He made his decision.

Tonight, after he checked in with President Rebecca Rudd, he would make a dive to locate the grave of Norman Reese, Jr.

CHAPTER 29

Evan Makley pushed the *End* button on his phone. He didn't know how to decipher the tone in President Rudd's voice. He discerned something different in her authoritative command. A sharp edge in her tone he wasn't accustomed to hearing. He glanced at his phone, 8:30 p. m. She didn't have anything on the schedule for the evening, and he would certainly know if she did, so something must have come up after he left the White House at 7:00.

He summoned his waiter, asked for a to-go box, and the bill. He'd eat the rest later, after he finished with Rudd. Her message was clear, "Drop whatever you're doing and get back to the Oval Office immediately." Personal time was a luxury he rarely enjoyed as the rigorous demands of Chief of Staff continuously encroached on his personal life. There always seemed to be some crisis situation that required her White House staff to leave their families for the good of the nation. Situations they would likely never be able to discuss.

His waiter insisted on boxing his meal for him. Chicken Lo Mein, his favorite. He slipped the box and some fresh chopsticks in a bag and thanked him in advance for the generous tip the Chief of Staff always left. Makley grabbed the bag, left $30 on the table for his $15 meal, walked outside, and hailed a taxi.

Since his wife left him, took the kids, and filed for divorce, he'd been living in the city. Initially he lived in a suite in Georgetown but after his wife was granted full custody of their two daughters, sole ownership of the marital home, and the majority of his bank account, he was forced to find a cheaper apartment in the city.

That was a long time ago. It was tough in the beginning but he'd grown accustomed to his new budget. Rudd had been patient with him, always allowing him time to attend his divorce hearings and mediation. His oldest daughter was driving now, which allowed him to see both his daughters more often. The hardest part, Makley thought, was the loneliness. At night, when he returned to his apartment, he was alone. For some reason, all his prospects for dates had shied away from him. Probably the result of his much-publicized divorce.

His last face-to-face contact with Abigail Love at the Jefferson Memorial reminded him of the night she showed up at his front door. For a brief moment, his mind replayed the adventure.

He pushed the thoughts from his head and focused on the matter at hand. What prompted Rudd to call him in? He scanned the CNN and Fox News websites with his smart phone for answers, but found nothing that warranted his return to the White House. However, he concluded, Rudd's call-in was likely preemptory in nature, which meant the news outlets wouldn't have wind of it yet. That was a good sign. It meant he was being called in for damage control.

The taxi dropped him off at the corner of Pennsylvania Avenue and 17th Street NW. He cleared the first security checkpoint and walked the remainder of the way to the White House enjoying the cool September night air. Another security checkpoint at the West Wing entrance and he was on his way through the corridors toward the Oval Office. He was greeted outside by the Executive Secretary to the

President of the United States who informed him that *they* were inside waiting. Rudd hadn't said anything to him about *they*. This must be big if she'd called in the entire White House Staff.

When he entered the Oval Office, he realized he had misinterpreted Rudd's tone and intent for the call-in. There were no other White House Staff, only the old man Elmore Wiley, one of his emissaries, the lovely Francesca Catanzaro with the scar visible on her left cheek, and President Rebecca Rudd. And from the look on Rudd's face, she was not pleased to see him.

"Evan, come in and sit down." She pointed to the couch opposite the coffee table from Wiley and Catanzaro.

"What's this about?" Makley looked at the President then back at Wiley. "More news on the grave robberies?"

Rudd said nothing. She pushed herself up from behind the Resolute Desk. He noticed she looked like she carried the weight of the nation on her shoulders. She walked around to the front of her desk, pushed her pen set out of the way, and did a half sit-half lean against it while looking him in the eyes.

"Let me get right to the point, Evan." Rudd looked at Wiley seated on the sofa. The old man placed some pictures on the antique coffee table in front of him. "What's your involvement with Abigail Love?"

If it weren't such a cliché, he would think this was that defining moment in his life when he was about to hit rock bottom. His mind raced through his past foibles, all of which he'd somehow talked his way out of and come away unscathed. He knew this one was different. He couldn't tell Rudd the truth, not yet.

"As you know, I just took a bath going through that ugly divorce." Evan Makley had prepared a speech for a moment like this if it were to arise. He'd always been a smooth talker, weaseling his way out of trouble on numerous occasions. This was no exception. "For the sake of our friendship, I have remained on the straight and narrow. I haven't dated, gone to nightclubs, or done anything that would tarnish this administration. I remained abstinent for two years. But even I have needs."

He scrutinized their expressionless faces, looking for any sign of empathy, but found none. "Someone gave me the name of Love's Desperate Desire. Told me that discretion was her forte. So I gave her a call. I guess I screwed up. We've only been together once. I swear, I'll terminate my involvement with Abigail Love's service immediately." He didn't lie, technically. More like selective omission.

Rudd lowered her head and shook it from side to side. "Evan, when Mr. Wiley told me what was going on, I didn't want to believe it. I gave you a chance to come clean, yet you chose to lie."

"Madam President, with all due respect, it's only been the one time with Abigail Love."

"Dammit, Evan. I don't give a damn *who* you screw. I'm talking about you betraying me and this country."

Rudd knew something else and maybe he'd spoken prematurely about Abigail Love. "Ma'am, what are you talking about?"

Rudd nodded at Wiley again. Francesca Catanzaro pulled out a micro recorder and pressed play. It was his own voice he heard on the recorder. *His name is Jake Pendleton. If he gets in the way, kill him too.*

He was beaten and he knew it. There was no explanation for that comment. And no way to bullshit his way out of it. A moment of indiscretion had cost him his career. It could even cost him his freedom. He'd thought about it before, if he had to play the blackmail card, he would.

"Evan, what is this all about?" Rudd asked.

His mind went into the survival mode when out of the blue an idea came to him. "May I speak to Mr. Wiley alone for a few minutes. I have information that I can't share with you. I was trying to handle this on my own but I guess I'm in over my head."

"Evan, I'm the President of the United States for God's sake, there is nothing you can't tell me."

Rudd's change in pitch startled him. A vein on her forehead and another in her neck bulged. He noticed red splotches forming on her chest under her necklace. He'd never seen her lose control of her emotions in all the years he'd known her. He stared at Wiley, pleading with his eyes. "Five minutes. That's all I need. Anything I've ever done was in a manner to lend you plausible deniability. Let me tell Mr. Wiley first, let him decide."

Finally the old man spoke up. "Rebecca, with all due respect, you're upset. Let me hear what the man has to say. Maybe it has merit, although I find it difficult to believe."

Rudd was silent for an uncomfortable amount of time. Finally, she nodded. "Five minutes. Then I want to be briefed."

Wiley turned to Francesca. "Please accompany the President while I talk with Mr. Makley."

Rudd and Catanzaro left the two men alone in the Oval Office. Wiley looked at him, ran his fingers through his hair, and pushed his glasses higher on the bridge of his nose.

"Before you begin," said Wiley. "There is nothing you can say that will justify ordering Abigail Love to kill one of my employees. Nothing. Do I make myself clear?"

"Yes, sir." Makley was a star at diplomacy and he needed to shine now. "I'll retract the order with Love immediately, I promise."

Wiley pointed to his watch. "You've got four minutes now. This better be good."

With a minute to spare, Makley had given Wiley the abbreviated briefing.

"You understand I'm going to require verification." Wiley said.

"No problem. I'll give you full access." Makley made a head nod toward the door. "I can show you everything when we're finished here."

The Oval Office door opened and President Rebecca Rudd and Francesca Catanzaro walked in. Rudd gave Wiley an apprehensive look. "Well? What do you think?"

Wiley hesitated for a moment. The old man looked at him then back at Rudd. "If what Mr. Makley says is true, and I will verify it," Wiley pushed up his glasses again and swiped his hair, "then, in my opinion, this isn't something you should know about until all the facts have been checked out."

"Elmore. That is ridiculous. I am the President, for crying out loud."

"Rebecca, you've known me a long time. I would never mislead you or try to deceive you. You must trust me." The old man said. "If this is a hoax, then I'll tell you. If this is true, we'll deal with it at the appropriate time. In the meantime, your prior knowledge of it without verification of its authenticity could very well affect and potentially alter your decision-making. You have a very important summit meeting to attend and you don't need any distractions. It is my opinion that it is in the best interest of all parties involved and this nation that you, as the leader of this country, not have this information disclosed to you at this time."

Makley forced back a smile. He'd done it again. He'd talked his way out of immediate peril. He had won a temporary reprieve, or as a minimum, bought himself a little extra time. Time to regroup and devise a plan to keep him from becoming the inevitable fall guy. Something Rudd would eventually need.

"Francesca," Wiley said, "go with Mr. Makley. Get a full briefing and meet me back in Fairfax." The old man turned his attention to him. "And you…" He paused, an attempt to intimidate him no doubt. "Your number one priority is correcting that matter we discussed. Is that understood?"

With some planning, maybe he can turn this around. Maybe he can even make Elmore Wiley the fall guy. After all, he just gave the old man full disclosure.

Makley nodded and followed Francesca out of the Oval Office.

††††

"Well, what do you think?" Rudd asked.

"I think Evan Makley tried to do a good thing in the beginning. Not necessarily the right thing, but perhaps, with honorable intentions. I think he genuinely believed he was trying to protect you, keep you out of trouble. He let greed take over and now is trying to capitalize on something that might or might not be true."

"What do you think I should do with him?" asked Rudd. "I can't leave him on as Chief of Staff. He's untrustworthy."

"Take him out of the circle, especially about the book." Wiley pulled out his phone. "I need to talk to Jake. Let him know what's going on."

"Not until you tell me what Evan said to you in private."

"Rebecca." Wiley walked over to the President and kissed her forehead. "I meant what I said. This one, you can't know anything about. Not right now anyway."

CHAPTER 30

Francesca Catanzaro followed Evan Makley down the White House corridors to a corner office. The Chief of Staff's office was better furnished, in many ways than the President's. Her furnishings were traditional whereas Makley's were more modern with state of the art equipment. He had a large conference table where the staff gathered for meetings. Francesca figured he justified the extra expense since his position oversaw the actions of the White House staff, managed the President's schedule, and had the power to decide who was allowed to meet with the President.

On his mahogany desk next to a desktop American flag was a picture of two teenage girls, both blonde, both wearing dresses and smiling for the camera. She picked it up. "Your daughters?" She asked.

"Yeah," he paused, "back then I only got to see them one Saturday a month, one week during the summer, and rotated holidays every other year. Divorce sucks. Even with the President's hectic schedule, when I was married I saw them almost every night."

"How old are they?"

"This one was twelve when this picture was taken." He pointed to the smaller girl then moved his finger to the other. "And this one fourteen. She just got her driver's license."

"They're very pretty. I know you're proud."

"I am. And they were just getting interesting when..." His voice trailed off.

In a way, she felt sorry for the man. He seemed to show genuine remorse for losing custody in the divorce that she, along with the rest of the country, witnessed on the six o'clock news. But he had a darker side that made her despise him. He was betraying the President and the country. And worst of all, he had ordered her partner killed.

She and Jake had been partners for almost a year and were such a good union that somehow, instinctively, they knew what the other was thinking. One of the many things Wiley excelled at was pairing his emissaries. They were an effective team, probably the best Commonwealth Consultants and the Greenbrier Fellowship had ever had. She trusted Jake with her life and knew he reciprocated.

Elmore Wiley had recruited her as an emissary for the Greenbrier Fellowship nearly two years ago while she was an operative for Italy's External Intelligence and Security Agency. Apparently impressed by her reputation for successful missions, he tendered the job offer one week after their first encounter.

Her training was intensive—six months tradecraft followed by six months field training. Even though her first assignment was a failure, the old man's persistent efforts molded her into an emissary with exceptional talent and skill.

In the beginning, she was reluctant about being partnered with Jake. Her first impression was that he was impulsive and audacious. Soon, she realized Wiley knew what he was doing.

She put the picture back on Makley's desk. "Let's get down to business, Mr. Makley. Show me what you have."

She spent the next thirty minutes scouring through the data Makley had given her. She read the lengthy email three times looking for any indication of where the email originated. "You know, this could be a hoax." She had moved a chair next to his while he walked her through the collected data.

"I don't think so," he reasoned. "It's written with a very clear message. Whoever wrote this knows something we don't."

"I disagree. The only thing I can ascertain from the writing is that whoever sent it is not young...or at least is trying hard not to sound that way."

"Now you see why I felt I needed to call Abigail Love. I needed a tight-lipped investigation. I couldn't let the President find out. Therefore, I couldn't call the Secret Service or FBI. I had to handle this myself...in case it had validity."

Francesca stood. "No. Abigail Love is an assassin. You should have gotten the authorities involved. If this is true, then there is nothing you or anybody else can do to protect the President."

Makley stood next to her. "I won't let anything happen to President Rudd. It's my job to protect her and this country."

Francesca balled up her fist and punched Makley in the face splitting his lip open. The Chief of Staff fell back into his chair and covered his bloody lip with his hand. The look in his eyes showed a combination of confusion and anger, but she didn't care. She grabbed the arms of the chair and leaned close to his face. "You ordered Abigail Love to kill my partner. You better hope like Hell she receives your retraction because if anything happens to him, I'll personally see to it you never make it to the inside of a jail cell."

She stood back, letting her words sink in.

Makley pulled a handkerchief from his pocket and wiped the blood from his lip.

"You said you'd do anything to protect the President, well, I'll do anything to protect my partner. And if that means killing a treasonous bastard like you, then so be it." She pointed to a chair against a far wall. "Get up and sit over there while I let an expert track down this email."

While he sat, Francesca logged into the Commonwealth Consultants secure portal, entered her 24-digit password, and waited. Her cell phone rang. "Voice activation authorization India, Tango, Alpha, Lima, Yankee, Five, Echo, Whiskey." She selected her own code for voice recognition. Letters spelling her home country—Italy, she was the fifth emissary, and her employer's initials, Elmore Wiley. She thought it was a clever selection. *I-T-A-L-Y-5-E-W.* She waited until a familiar voice picked up. "Hi, George."

She explained the situation to Fontaine and then an authorization box appeared on Makley's computer screen. She clicked on the box and sat back. She watched the cursor move as Fontaine took control of Makley's computer.

"What's going on?" Makley leaned forward, obviously trying to get a look at the monitor. "What is he doing to my computer?"

"I don't know. Way over my head." She looked at Makley. The man was the highest ranking employee in the White House yet he looked like a schoolboy who had been put in time-out.

Twenty minutes later the monitor flickered and her cell phone rang. She answered the call, "Go."

"Give Mr. Mackley his computer back," Fontaine said, "I've got all I need. He can't do anything without us knowing about it, and the same goes for Abigail Love. I found her tracer and located her server. It was embedded in the code she had him install. It sends all his received emails to her server. From there they run a—"

"George."

"What?" Fontaine said.

"I don't care. All that I.T. stuff, I don't need to know how it works. I don't want to know how it works. Just find who sent the email and let me know. Okay?"

"Heard anything from Jake?" Fontaine asked.

"Nothing since Wiley split us up."

"He's not in any kind of danger, is he?"

She glared at Makley and spoke loud enough for him to hear. "He better not be in any danger or President Rudd will be looking for a new Chief of Staff."

† † †

Abigail Love had been following the man since she saw him at the *Pizza Place* near the marina. He was driving a white Tahoe. After he left the diner, he met an elderly woman at the Butler Museum. Love strategically parked where she would be able to see him come out without being noticed.

She figured if she followed the man, whom she now knew was named Jake Pendleton, he would lead her to the woman. The woman would lead her to the book.

After Pendleton had been in the museum almost an hour, she received a puzzling message from Evan Makley.

CANCEL KILL ON JAKE PENDLETON

In her past experiences with Evan Makley she learned he was not a man who often had a change of heart. Usually when he made a decision—good or bad—he stuck to it. Maybe something had happened. Something she should know about. If that was the case, then he should have sent a

9-1-1 through the lovesdesperatedesire.com website. She tried
to log on with her cell phone. Nothing. Her server was down.

Her Gmail account was Makley's backup. She told him
never to send an email from the account, only edit the one in
the *DRAFTS* folder. She gave him the username and
password along with detailed instructions for its use in the
event normal channels of communication were unavailable or
imperiled. She logged into the Gmail account and located the
message.

> **We have been compromised and you have been identified.
> Your server has been shut down and your assets
> confiscated. DO NOT RETURN TO D.C.**

Damn you, Makley. Her first reaction was to abort the
mission. She hated failure. She mulled over her options and
came to the conclusion that obtaining the book and keeping
it for herself was her best plan. If anyone got in her way after
she had acquired the book, she would kill them. And that
included the handsome Jake Pendleton.

Makley's use of the word 'We' infuriated her. He was the
one that compromised her. The son of a bitch was stupid and
had become a liability. One she needed to deal with. Nothing
would give her more pleasure, she mused, than to show up at
his apartment under the pretense of her first visit, something
the horny bastard would no doubt relish, put him in a
sexually compromising position, and then kill him.

Not a quick, painless death, but a slow and agonizing one.
She envisioned cuffing him to the bedposts again, gagging
him, and then taking her razor sharp knife to his genitals.
After he had suffered enough, she would put a round in his
head with her Smith & Wesson.

One round.

Right between the eyes.

As much as she'd like to handle this one herself, she was 400 miles away and there was no time to waste. She opened her phone and searched through her contacts until she located the number for her best *escort*. She placed the call.

As soon as she hung up, Pendleton and the old woman came out of the museum. The woman locked the door to the museum and Pendleton walked her to her car, shook her hand, and waited until she drove off. Then he climbed inside the Tahoe and drove off.

Love pulled out, keeping a safe distance. There was still a lot of traffic on these backcountry roads at night, which worked to her advantage. She stayed back letting the occasional car or truck pull between them. She checked her GPS, which showed she had followed him all the way around to the other side of the lake from the town of Butler.

She saw the Tahoe's left blinker flash and the SUV turned off the main road at a mailbox. She slowed but kept driving noting that he pulled into a cabin with a short driveway. She saw lights reflecting across the water behind the house. She logged the location on her GPS, turned around a half a mile down the road at the next driveway, and drove back toward town.

She didn't understand why the Charleston Police Department had released Pendleton so quickly; she assumed it must be his connection to President Rebecca Rudd. One thing seemed clear to her, he was reckless.

She smiled.

And reckless people have accidents.

† † †

Scott Katzer followed the same black car he'd followed for the past eight hours. He noticed the man from Charleston at the *Pizza Place* and again at the museum. He was pushing seventy years old and growing tired of this game of cat and mouse. He was following the woman who was following the man who was trying to find Ashley Regan. That's all he knew about either one of them. But the woman seemed to have an inside source for her information. There was no other explanation for it. She pulled away from the police station in Charleston, jumped on Interstate 26, and drove to Butler, Tennessee.

With both the man and the woman in Butler, he had to presume that Regan and the book were nearby. Acquiring the book was all he cared about. He'd never seen it, only heard a narrative description from his mother. She had recounted its contents to him several times over the years, always expressing her concern that if the book ever became public, the aftermath of what was written in the book would be devastating to their family. The gain from the fortunes, if there were any, would be no consolation compared to the blow the Katzer name would receive.

She referred to it as a journal. A leather bound book filled with blank pages that was given to his real father on his birthday by the fuehrer.

A gift from Adolf Hitler.

The father he never knew.

Wolfgang Fleischer.

Katzer learned volumes when he researched Wolfgang Fleischer on the Internet. His father had been commandant of Dachau prison and crematorium in Germany during the Third Reich. It seemed an odd coincidence that he too, like his father, was charged with the disposal of dead bodies. Katzer's was a more civilized and accepted practice.

During the fall of the Third Reich, his father fled south into Austria where he was captured. He was tried as a war criminal in a fast-tracked post war justice system—tried, convicted, and executed. By then, Fleischer's lover, Heidi Scheller, was already impregnated with twins.

According to his mother, she and Wolfgang had been secret lovers for three years while he was commandant. The long-term affair started when Fleischer stayed at Schneefernerhaus Hotel for the first time. He was walking across the grounds when he slipped on a patch of ice and twisted his ankle. Heidi, a resort nurse, attended to his injury. The passionate feeling of attraction started during his treatment. While wrapping his ankle, Wolfgang grabbed his mother's arm and pulled her toward him. The kiss ignited their lust for each other. Their affair was a secret he took to the grave.

After the journal was lost, Heidi Scheller moved to Nashville, Tennessee, where she met and married Matthew Katzer, the man Scott thought was his father until he was fifty years old.

Katzer had learned to be a patient man and he knew if he waited in the shadows, the journal would reappear. And when it did, he would reclaim his family's property. As much as he initially abhorred his mother's brutality, he knew he would eventually have blood on his hands too in order to protect the family.

CHAPTER 31

Jake picked up the tails right away.

As soon as he left the Butler Museum, he noticed both vehicles were parked in a way deliberately chosen *not* to draw suspicion. Which was exactly why he noticed them. At The Farm he was trained to observe his surroundings in survival situations, assess what he saw for threats, and determine his best course of action. A process drilled into him until it became second nature.

It was the same black BMW 750 Li with Virginia plates and the same white van that were parked across the street from Ashley Regan's house in Charleston.

After he thanked the museum director for opening up after hours, something else prearranged by Fontaine, he pulled out of the parking lot and verified the front license plate on the BMW was from the State of Virginia. What were the odds that identical models—both with Virginia plates—would be in Butler, Tennessee the same day he saw one staking out Regan's house in Charleston? He knew it was a stake out in Charleston when he noticed the silhouette of a woman through the tinted windows holding a camera with a long-range lens.

After the Charleston police arrested him and hauled him in for questioning, he'd noticed both the BMW and the van when he got out of the police car at headquarters. He didn't think anything more about it until now, when he noticed both vehicles outside the museum in Butler, Tennessee.

He ran the math in his head and knew both vehicles could have driven the distance from Charleston to Butler with little time to spare. The question looming in his mind was whether or not they were working together. It didn't appear that way, but after the events of the day, anything was possible. He knew there was only one person in the BMW, but couldn't tell how many were in the van. One thing was certain, he was outnumbered.

The fact that both vehicles were in Charleston, South Carolina this morning and have shown up 300 miles away in Butler meant one thing.

There was a leak.

Someone on the inside had informed them where he was going. Doubtful the leak came from within Commonwealth, Elmore Wiley's vetting procedures were unsurpassed by anyone. The more likely probability was the leak came from the White House, which pointed to only one person—Evan Makley.

Jake drove a steady speed toward the cabin he'd rented, always keeping track in his rear view mirror of the two vehicles following him. Cars pulled between them periodically, but eventually it was just the three vehicles on the lonely stretch of road.

Jake hit the familiar speed dial on his cell phone. "George, I need you to run a plate." He gave Fontaine the license plate number he'd captured in Charleston when the taxi pulled away from the police station. "Couldn't verify the numbers now, but I could tell it was a Virginia plate."

"Got it." Fontaine blurted after a few keystrokes. "Black BMW?

"Yep. 750 Li."

"Belongs to a Deborah Layne of Leesburg, Virginia. Mean anything?"

"No. Mean anything to you?" Jake heard Fontaine pecking at his keyboard.

"Oh, shit."

"That doesn't sound good." Jake looked in his mirror. Both vehicles were still there. The BMW was maybe a half a mile behind him. The van, slightly farther. "What did you find, George?"

"Facial recognition matched Deborah Layne as Abigail Love. Love is on both the FBI and Interpol's most wanted lists. This lady is bad, Jake, she's an assassin. I'm sending a photo. And Jake?"

"What?"

"According to an entry from Francesca, Evan Makley instructed Abigail Love to get the book and kill anyone who got in her way...your name was specifically mentioned in his communiqué to her."

Jake was quiet for a few seconds. "Guess I'll have to take care of that weasel when I get back to D.C."

"That is if Francesca doesn't beat you to the punch."

He checked his mirror when Roxanne, his GPS voice, announced the distance to his destination as one mile ahead on the left. The BMW was in sight but no van. Within seconds the van appeared from around the curve. He reached behind him to the small of his back and pulled out his Glock, cocked and locked, just the way he was trained. Professionals always kept a round chambered with either the mental or mechanical safety engaged. And on a Glock, that meant the mental safety. Chambering a round made noise, which could alert your opponent.

"Bring Wiley up to speed. Let him know Love is here in Butler. I gotta go." Jake disconnected the call before Fontaine could respond. He pulled into the drive and watched through the rear-view mirror as the BMW passed the driveway. Within seconds the van did the same.

Gun in hand, Jake jumped from the Tahoe, ran to the hedges lining the street using them as cover, and searched for the BMW. In the distance he saw the BMW's brake lights. The BMW made a k-turn, and then he watched as the headlights returned. The van kept going. He lay on his belly, peering through the base of the hedges as the BMW slowed. He readied his grip on the Glock. The BMW cruised past the driveway then accelerated. A minute later the BMW rounded the bend in the road and disappeared from sight. Jake panned back in the opposite direction. The van had turned around and was accelerating. It blew past the driveway, down the road, and out of sight around the curve.

Jake couldn't tell if the van was tailing him or the BMW. Either way, the situation just got a lot worse.

Earlier in the afternoon, Jake had launched the boat and motored it to the dock behind the cabin. He checked and loaded his equipment in the boat for tonight's dive. He needed his truck and since it was still at the boat ramp, he talked a nearby neighbor into driving him the fourteen miles back to the marina to pick up the Tahoe, keeping the conversation focused on the fishing tournament. When the old man dropped him off, he told Jake there was another boat ramp closer to the cabin, less than a half a mile down the highway. Jake thanked him and promised to use the closer ramp when he got ready to trailer the boat.

With the BMW and the van out of sight, he let himself into the cabin and set safety traps on the doors and windows. Traps too small and nondescript for anyone but him to notice unless they knew what to look for. More tradecraft skills he'd learned at The Farm. It was precaution. When he returned from the dive, Jake needed to know if anyone had been snooping around in the cabin. One last check of his messages revealed an urgent message from Elmore Wiley advising him there was a problem, which would delay the arrival of his backup. He was ordered to sit tight and wait for their arrival. Wiley's timetable wouldn't get backup to Butler until almost noon tomorrow. That was unacceptable. He hated to defy Wiley's orders, but too much could happen in the meantime and he couldn't chance the possibility Ashley Regan and her friend would get to the casket and disappear again.

He deleted the message from Wiley, turned off the lights, set the final door trap, and made his way in the darkness to the dock fifty feet below and one hundred feet behind the cabin. The steep steps reminded him of his own cabin in North Georgia. His retreat on Mountaintown Creek in Ellijay was over three hundred vertical feet above the creek. *It* had a lot of steps. This was nothing in comparison.

A full moon in a cloudless sky highlighted the shoreline guiding him as he motored the boat away from the dock. The vast contrast between the glittering water and land made it easy to navigate through the waters. The small outboard hummed like a sewing machine as the boat sliced through the calm waters of Watauga Lake.

Jake followed his programmed handheld GPS. The unit, customized by Wiley's lab, was precise to within two lateral feet. If Fontaine's coordinates were accurate, he should descend on top of the grave marker of Norman Albert Reese, Jr.

When his GPS beeped, he flipped the windlass switch, which automatically plunged the anchor toward the bottom of the lake while he kept the boat centered over the coordinates. A few seconds later, the anchor line went slack indicating it had hit bottom. He set the anchor so the boat wouldn't drift off while he was underwater, shut off the engine, and waited.

He didn't move for fifteen minutes. Driving a boat in the dark without running lights was illegal and, for the most part stupid. But tonight, stealth was necessary. He had to ensure no one saw or heard him, got curious, and came to investigate. While he waited, he slipped into his polar shell under-suit and then into a dry-suit sealing each with meticulous care.

In the Navy, he'd learned the difference between a dry-suit and a wetsuit. Although both were designed to keep the diver warm, a wetsuit allowed water inside. The water formed a layer between the neoprene suit and the diver's skin. Heat from the diver's body warmed the water inside the suit. A wetsuit was good for cool and moderately cold water only.

A dry-suit, on the other hand, was just that—dry. Gaskets at the neck, legs, and arms were designed to keep the water out and the diver's body dry. When used in conjunction with a polar-shell insulated under-suit, the diver could safely dive in extremely cold waters for long durations.

The water wasn't too cold on the surface, but according to Fontaine, at sixty feet it could be around fifty degrees and upper 40's near the bottom. And that *was* cold. He knew about hypothermia from his Navy dive training and, most recently, when he had to abandon a sinking vessel off the northern coast of Spain and swim nine miles to shore in the cold waters of the Cantabrian Sea.

That was ten months ago. And it was still fresh in his memory.

Jake lifted the hatch on the bow compartment and retrieved the rest of his dive gear, checked its working condition, geared up, and eased into the cold lake water. He used the low side rails of the boat to pull himself along the

side of the boat until he reached the anchor line. He pulled
his mask over his face, made a final equipment check, put the
regulator in his mouth. With one hand on the anchor line, he
deflated his buoyancy compensator and sank into the dark
lake.

CHAPTER 32

Jake descended in the water using the anchor line and felt the water temperature dropping fast. He was nervous and the cold, dark abyss didn't help. It had been a long time since he had been scuba diving. He felt his chest tighten and his respiration increase. He held his lighted computer closer to his face, 27 feet below the surface. He tightened his grip on the anchor line and stopped his descent. He was sucking air from his tank. He needed to calm down and get his breathing under control. Mind over matter discipline was what the Navy had taught him. The power to control and influence his body with his mind. He closed his eyes and let his mind go someplace calm.

It took him to the infinity pool in the Maldives tree villa with Kyli. He envisioned her smile. Her eyes sparkled. The gentle ocean breeze blowing through her hair. Just the thought of her image seemed tranquil.

His pulse slowed, returning to normal. Breathing slowed.

His tense muscles relaxed, his respiration under control. He was no longer nervous. He relaxed his grip on the anchor line and once again descended toward the bottom. At 35 feet below the surface, he turned on his dive light. The high beam was designed to put out 400 lumens of light for nearly fourteen hours. Much longer than he'd need it, but he had a backup in the boat just in case.

He flashed the beam downward, from side to side and saw nothing. Fontaine had indicated the visibility varied between 15 and 25 feet year round. Not great, but not bad either. At 50 feet below the surface his light beam found a cut off tree trunk. He followed it down with his light. The trunk was brown and blended into the brown mud bottom. Finding the marker might be harder than he had anticipated.

At 62 feet, he hit the muddy bottom, stirring up a slight plume of silt with his fins. It wasn't level. It sloped rapidly to one side of the tree and rose on the other. He'd carried with him a guide rope with one end attached to his weight belt and the other to a carabiner. He slipped the oval-shaped straight gate carabiner onto the anchor line, let out 20 feet of guideline and started making tethered, partial circle search passes to try and locate the marker, a search and rescue technique he learned in the Navy. Essentially the bottom was barren except for the occasional tree stump, which he had to circumnavigate so the tether wouldn't tangle.

On the 40-foot pass, at 56 feet below the surface, the bottom leveled out. He scanned the area with his dive light. Moments later the beam found the marker. It looked like what it was, a concrete monument, brown from decades of exposure to the mud and turbidity of Watauga Lake. It stuck out of what could be considered a knoll on the side of a hill now flooded with water. Jake swam toward the marker spraying the beam to find the capstone. Not an easy task when everything looked the same. A desert of brown mud.

As soon as his light found the metal plate capstone, it happened. Something rose from the gravesite and moved at him in slow motion. Like the apparition of Norman Albert Reese Jr. rising from the depths in protest of being disturbed. It was as big as he was, maybe bigger. Then it sped up, moving straight for him. His heart pounded, he inhaled rapidly through his regulator. It was almost on him. At the last second, Jake jerked to the side to avoid the collision. Something powerful struck his left arm causing him to drop the tether and the light. The impact knocked him fins over mask. The dive light struck bottom and tumbled toward the depths of the lake. He watched the beam bounce like a lopsided ball off the sloping bottom. It grew dim and stopped. He could barely see the beam shining on the bottom of the lake. He knew he had enough tether so he headed deeper to retrieve his light. He'd been careless not to secure the wrist strap.

On his way to the bottom he thought about what he'd seen. He'd heard the stories and had just assumed they were just that, fish stories. As he replayed it in his mind, he knew he'd spooked a giant catfish. A catfish with a mouth almost big enough to swallow him whole.

As he descended, the light got brighter. He reached the light and checked his dive computer. 127 feet. *Shit.* Now he was in the decompression mode instead of merely a safety stop. He grabbed his light, secured it to his wrist with the bungee strap, and started his slow ascent. At 60 feet, his dive computer signaled a decompression stop. He waited while the computer counted down. Ignoring the computer warning to stop could bring with it dire consequences. He had a buddy in the Navy who got the bends and had to spend a lot of time in a hyperbaric chamber recovering. His buddy still walked with a limp.

At 56 feet, he relocated the grave marker with his dive light and found the metal capstone. He waved his hand over the metal plate to clear the silt and read the inscription. He now understood why Reese was buried here and not relocated.

Norman Albert Reese Jr.
Born January 14, 1925
Died December 14, 1944
World War II took our beloved son.
Born here, under this tree.
May he rest for eternity.

Jake studied the capstone; eight bolts secured the metal slab to the vault. Regan and the other woman would need a large wrench to remove the capstone and he doubted that either one of them would be able to free the bolts from the vault. Even if they did, could they remove the steel capstone itself? It probably weighed over a hundred pounds alone. No easy task underwater where leverage wasn't the same.

He'd seen all he needed to see. Jake pulled himself back to the anchor line and slowly ascended. At 30 feet, his dive computer signaled another deco stop. He checked his pressure gauge. He was in the red and had no idea how long he had been there. At 15 feet, the computer signaled a 5-minute safety stop. He doubted he'd make it without running out of air.

CHAPTER 33

Her cell phone alarm beeped—4:30 a.m.

Startled out of a deep sleep, it took her a few seconds to wake up. She rolled over and picked the sleepy crust from her eyes. Ashley Regan and Christa Barnett hadn't gotten to bed until midnight and for a woman who needs at least eight hours sleep, Regan thought she did good just to hear the alarm. She pushed herself to a sitting position on the edge of the bed and tried to clear the cobwebs from her head.

"Christa." She shook the bed next to hers. "Christa. Time to get up."

"I've been up." The bathroom light came on behind her. "Been checking emails and stuff for the last thirty minutes."

"Have trouble sleeping?" Regan asked.

"No. I slept fine. I'm just used to getting up early."

"I'm having trouble waking up." Regan used the bed to push herself to her feet.

"When you get dressed we'll go get coffee and breakfast," Christa said. "A good breakfast before a day of diving is a must."

Now she was glad they had loaded everything in the car the night before. At least Christa had the forethought to suggest doing it to make the morning a little easier. But that's the way she'd always been. Even as teenagers, when everyone else was stumbling around wondering what to do next, Christa had already planned every detail. They spent several hours the night before reviewing the scuba equipment, its function, and how to use it. Christa had made sure Regan knew what to do. Christa had drilled scuba diving procedures with her until she felt comfortable she knew what to do. At breakfast, the drill continued.

The drive from Banner Elk, North Carolina to the marina in Butler, Tennessee was exactly 42 miles and took 59 minutes, which put them at the marina at 6:05 a.m. The sky was clear and starting to brighten in the east. To the west, the full moon had slipped behind a mountain creating a bright halo around its summit.

She expected the marina to be quiet at this hour, but she was wrong, very wrong. Two pickups were launching boats side by side while eight other vehicles were waiting their turn in line. Fortunately she had rented a boat from the marina, which was waiting for her in the slip marked *15*. It took the two women fifteen minutes and two solo trips apiece in the predawn light to move the dive gear and supplies to the 20-foot Bayliner cuddy cabin rental boat. The third trip they took together to move the heaviest piece—a filtered air compressor.

Within minutes of placing the compressor on the rear deck, Christa had the boat underway. Regan, an expert in navigation acquired from years of extensive hiking, studied the map and, coupled with the use of the onboard GPS, guided Christa toward the spot the old man had circled on the map, a notch in the shoreline on the western bank at the mouth of where the Watauga and Elk Rivers meet the rest of Watauga Lake. According to the old man in the bait store, Old Butler was located at the confluence of the Watauga River and Roan Creek. The Reese property was on the southern bluff, overlooking the old town.

Twenty minutes later they had traveled the four miles from the marina to the bluff. Regan had rented the expensive boat because it came with a GPS linked, bottom-mapping depth sounder and a swim platform, both of which would simplify their diving. She set up a grid pattern and tracked it in a northwest/southeast manner until she located what appeared to be the knoll the old man described. Then she signaled Christa to drop anchor.

Christa wasted no time slipping her dry suit on over her polar shell under suit. After it was sealed tight, she strapped on her Buoyancy Compensator with a full tank attached and pulled it snug. She walked onto the swim platform and sat down. She slipped into her twin jet fins, pulled on her hood, and donned her full-face mask. After a quick equipment function check, she grabbed a buoy bag and stepped off the platform feet first into the water while keeping one hand on her mask.

Regan scanned the area. A red and white striped bass boat she recognized from the boat ramp whizzed across the middle of the lake sending a small wake toward her boat. Dawn had brightened the morning sky but the sun still hid behind the mountains to the east; the glow from the full moon had long disappeared due to the brightened sky. A small metal bass boat driven by a younger man motored into the cove and anchored nearby. He wore khaki colored pants, a long sleeved shirt, and wide-rim safari hat. The man promptly cast his fishing line in the water. She inspected the water and wondered if the man could see Christa's bubbles rising from below.

For the next few minutes, boats of all shapes and sizes went by. Mostly fishing boats, it seemed, but she saw two houseboats and, across the lake, a group of kayakers. Watauga Lake was a popular place. She checked her watch; 35 minutes had elapsed since Christa slipped out of sight beneath the boat. She knew from the safety drills she had gotten from her friend that she couldn't stay down too long. She leaned over to check for bubbles just as Christa's head broke the surface.

"Found it." Christa pointed toward shore.

Regan looked up and saw an inflatable marker buoy bobbing in the wake of a passing boat. "How long's that been there?"

"Six or seven minutes, maybe. I made a five minutes safety stop on the way up. I'll need to off-gas for at least an hour before I go back down." She threw her mask and fins on the swim platform. "This is going to be a lot of work. Metal plate bolted down. Looks real heavy." She was taking short choppy breaths. "Glad I brought those tools. Looks like we're going to need them."

"We got company." Regan pointed with a nod of the head. "Been here about thirty minutes."

"Fishing the whole time?"

"Yeah. He's already caught three or four that I've seen. Threw 'em all back in though."

"We'll raise the dive flag before we go down. That way he won't hook one of us."

Regan laughed. "That'd make for one hell of a fish story, wouldn't it?"

✝✝✝

Jake admired Regan's choice of boats, a Bayliner 192 cuddy cabin inboard/outboard with canvas Bimini top and full swim platform. A much more suitable boat for scuba diving than his metal-hull bass boat that didn't have a swim ladder. The name written in bold green script across the transom was *Miss Debi*. He checked his watch when he pulled into the cove where the grave of Norman Reese was located, 7:00 a.m. He hadn't anticipated the women would arrive this early. There was only one woman on board the boat now, Ashley Regan, so he assumed her friend was already underwater trying to locate the grave.

He anchored 150 feet away near a tree that had fallen into the water. He cast two lines, one on each side of the tree, letting one sink to the bottom while he used a top-water plug with the other. He'd noticed Regan was watchful until he caught his first fish. Then her interest in him seemed to wane.

Jake smiled; he'd used the same ruse off the northern coast of Spain last year in the Cantabrian Sea while he was chasing a terrorist. The terrorist was lulled into the same false sense of security when Jake and two CIA agents caught their first fish.

A slight breeze worked in his favor and weathervaned his boat so he had clear vantage point of the Bayliner without having to turn his head.

The second and third fish strike came in rapid succession. By the time he had reeled in his top-water plug which had a large mouth bass, his bottom fishing rod had doubled over. All the excitement caused him to divert his attention away from the Bayliner. When he looked back up, an inflatable marker had surfaced. Shortly after that a diver climbed onto the swim platform. He knew by the location of the marker they'd found Reese's grave.

A few hours prior he hadn't even surfaced when he ran out of air. Fifteen feet below the surface with less than a minute left on his safety stop, he exhaled and when he tried to take a breath, there was nothing left in the tank. He had expected it and surfaced anyway. He knew he'd have plenty of time to rid any excess nitrogen from his blood before he was forced to dive again and knew he was well within Navy safety margins.

When he had returned to the cabin after the dive, none of his safety traps had been sprung. He checked his email. He found a photo of Abigail Love from Fontaine and a terse message from Wiley about waiting for backup.

He knew he couldn't wait on Wiley to send reinforcements. There wasn't time. This might be his only chance to find out what Regan was doing and what she possessed that had morphed her from accountant to grave robber.

At 8:30, both women put on their dry suits. He knew it was time. He noticed a deck boat driven by a woman pull into the open cove. She was alone. Jake used his miniature spyglass to get a better look. He recognized her immediately and lowered his head blocking his face with the rim of his hat.

He knew she could jeopardize the entire mission.

He also knew that Abigail Love could recognize him.

CHAPTER 34

George Fontaine sat down at his desk when the alerts flashed across two of his four big screen wall-mounted monitors.

The tracker program Evan Makley had installed on his computer courtesy of Abigail Love did more than she'd advertised. In a sense it was a Trojan virus with specific non-malicious tracking capability. Every email he sent had the virus attached, even the ones to himself allowing him to work from his home computer. And each recipient's computer was now accessible by Love's servers.

That meant Love's servers could have had access to every bit of data stored on over fifty national security computers, most in the D.C. area.

Could have had being key if Fontaine hadn't hacked the virus code and rerouted the pathway to the Commonwealth Consultants servers. Now, Love's servers saw nothing. Taking her out of the loop was his number one national security priority. Fontaine developed algorithms that not only allowed him to reroute the pathway from Love's virus but also installed a similar track back virus of his own construct, revealing her IP routing.

The first alert on his screen pinpointed the exact physical location of Love's servers. Within the hour, Wiley's team would take down the servers, remove the hard drives, and destroy the complex.

The second alert listed every IP address Makley sent emails to. Computers that now had Fontaine's tracking virus attached. The virus enabled him to see and download everything on each of those computers. He scrolled through the list until he located the server he needed. Now the back trace began.

After hacking through the firewalls of 27 anonymous servers around the globe, Fontaine located the server that sent the blackmail message to Makley. To his good fortune, the computer was still online and within a few seconds he had captured the physical address of the computer, a Starbucks. Moments later he commenced a download of the contents of its hard drive.

Only minutes into the transfer, the download stopped. Fontaine smiled. He already knew two important things about the blackmailer, she or he was using a portable device and it wouldn't be long before the computer came back online.

Half an hour later he was alerted the computer was back online. The physical trace revealed the computer accessed the Internet from a Cadillac dealership less than a mile from the Starbucks. Wiley's assets were a minimum of two hours away. He needed the computer online in a single location when they arrived. He knew this wasn't going to be it.

Thirty minutes later, the download stopped again. Fontaine partitioned what he had obtained on his computer and started sorting through the bytes of information. He was amazed at the lack of precaution this person had taken to protect the information on the computer. No encryption. No hidden files. It seemed the only precaution was the use of several anonymous servers and email clients.

Almost everything on the computer was standard and straightforward. The person's identity revealed, Fontaine started a background check while he combed the remainder of the data.

Midway through the data, he found something that shocked him. Jake's guess had been correct. After a background search, another name popped up.

The threat against the President was real.

"Holy Crap." Fontaine reached for the phone. "Mr. Wiley, I think you need to see this."

Wiley entered through the secure complex two minutes later. "What is it, George?"

Fontaine showed Wiley what he had uncovered when he processed the hard drive's contents. Now they knew the reason why caskets had been broken into and what was in them. "Where should we go from here?" Fontaine asked.

"Get a hold of Jake. Tell him what he's looking for. His number one priority is to acquire that book. I want Regan and the other woman alive." Wiley turned to leave, then stopped. "Inform Jake to consider Abigail Love a preemptive sanction. And bring Francesca up to speed. She might need to cover his back."

"Yes, sir."

Wiley stared at Fontaine without saying anything.

"Sir? Something wrong?"

"Wrong? No. Nothing wrong. Just thinking." He paused. "Tell Jake to be discreet. I don't want all of northeastern Tennessee in turmoil because of a shootout on that lake. And, no repeats of Charleston." Wiley opened the door to leave.

"Sir?" Fontaine asked. "In case I run across anything else, where can I find you?"

Wiley looked at his watch. "I'll be in the building for a few more hours, then I'm going to Nashville."

†††

Abigail Love idled the deck boat as she pulled into the cove on Watauga Lake.

She made a quick situation assessment. On the far side of the cove was a man fishing in a bass boat, just one of the dozens she'd seen so far. Not expected, but not unusual, especially in light of the fishing tournament. She could deal with him if need be. The Bayliner cuddy cabin with two women onboard was the only thing of interest to her. She saw a short woman with dark hair lower the antenna, attached a dive flag, and raised it back up again.

Moments later a second woman appeared from the cabin—Ashley Regan. She recognized her from the photos Makley had emailed her. *Game on.*

She pulled the bow of the boat closer to shore, about seventy-five feet from Regan's Bayliner, walked through the split windshield and let out the anchor line. She walked to the helm, put the boat in reverse and backed up about thirty feet then threw out a stern anchor. She cinched them both snug and shut off the engine.

She stripped off her clothes, revealing her bikini bathing suit underneath, hopped over the transom onto the swim platform and dipped a foot into the water. She scanned the cove. The fisherman was on the other side, maybe a hundred yards distance, looking in the opposite direction. Regan and her friend kept glancing her way.

The morning sun had cleared the mountains and its rays penetrated her skin. She felt its warmth on her dark tanned skin. Beads of sweat lined her forearms. It was already hot and would only get hotter as the day wore on. She glanced at Regan and saw her putting on a dry suit and could only imagine how hot she must be. Love dove into the water and swam out twenty feet and then back.

The water was much colder than she expected. She pulled herself back on the swim platform. Goose bumps covered her from head to toe.

Her ruse had worked. The women were now ignoring her, which is what she was counting on.

† † †

Jake didn't like what he saw unfolding in front of him.

Ashley Regan and her friend were gearing up to make a dive to the bottom. They took turns zipping up and sealing each other's dry suit. The smaller woman, Christa Barnett, hoisted the tank and BCD combination onto Regan's back, helping her secure it, then escorted her to the swim platform. Barnett slipped her arms into her own BCD and stood. Within seconds, both women were sitting on the swim platform slipping on their fins. Each pulled on their full-face masks and fell forward into the water.

In the meantime, Abigail Love had shed her clothes down to her bathing suit, took a quick dip in the lake, and had lathered herself with sunscreen. She spread a towel on the bow cushion of the deck boat and lay on her stomach. Jake noticed Love had positioned herself for a vantage point to watch Reagan's boat. And his. No way he could dive with her watching without raising her suspicions.

He started weighing his options when his phone vibrated. Fontaine.

He slipped his Bluetooth earpiece in and answered the phone while he continued fishing. "Go George."

"It's confirmed, Regan does have a book, a journal of some sort that she found inside the glacier. Perhaps on the corpse itself. You were right…again. I read Wiley in on everything I've found so far. He's not pleased. Looks like the communicated threat to the President is real."

"My instructions?"

"Priority one is the book. Find it and secure it."

"Regan and her friend?" Jake had another strike on the fishing line.

"Wiley wants them both alive." Fontaine paused. "Seen Abigail Love?"

"Looking right at her." Jake watched the deck boat. Love was moving toward the stern with towel in hand. "She hasn't made me. What about her?"

"Expendable civilian target."

"Seriously?" Jake pulled another large mouth bass to the side of the boat.

"Jake, this woman is an assassin. And as a reminder, with instructions to kill you if you get in the way. Wiley's exact words were for you to consider her a "preemptive sanction.'"

"Anything else?" Jake had heard all he needed to hear.

"He said to be discreet. I know that's hard for you."

"You're a regular comedian, you know that, George?"

"I know. Sounded important to Wiley, and I think Rudd as well. He was adamant there was to be no blowback from this at all. Can you do that?"

"Tell Wiley not to worry. I'll sanitize the target area. Where is he now?"

"Said something about going to Nashville. He didn't say why, but if I was a betting man—"

"Spill it, George. I'm sure it's related to my overall mission."

Jake got the abbreviated version from Fontaine and understood the renewed urgency of the situation. He hung up and started connecting the pieces to the puzzle when he heard the ignition of a boat motor.

He turned and saw Abigail Love and the deck boat accelerate away from the cove. He pulled out his mini spyglass and scanned the boat when something caught his eye. The swim platform on Regan's Bayliner was wet and neither Regan nor Barnett had come back onboard.

Which left only one explanation.

Abigail Love had been on Regan's boat.

CHAPTER 35

"Christa, what just happened?" Regan noticed the large drop in water temperature.

"Stay calm, Ashley. Nothing happened. Everything is fine."

"No. Why did the temperature drop so fast?" As soon as she submerged Regan noticed how different it was breathing underwater. It wasn't difficult just different. Uncomfortably different. The underwater communication system allowed them to speak to each other, which was helpful, but at times it was troublesome to understand what Christa was saying.

"It's called a thermocline. It's where the water temperature drops faster below the line than above it."

"Is that normal?"

"Yes, perfectly fine. Just means it's going to get a lot colder before we get to the bottom. The good news is we should only have to deal with one thermocline. There might be another one deeper in the lake."

She looked at Christa who was descending down the line attached to the grave marker below. Attached to Christa's BCD was a five-pound mallet. Regan carried the adjustable wrench.

Regan had never been exposed to the underwater world, at least not in a lake. She and Sam Connors had snorkeled in the Keys a few times and once on a reef in Jamaica when they went to the Sandals Resort in Ocho Rios. She'd never been farther than a breath underwater. She was never a strong swimmer, and although adventurous on land, she was skittish in the water.

She kept descending, keeping the same distance above Christa. Every few feet, she cleared her ears as the water pressure built against her eardrums.

Last night Christa showed her several techniques to equalize the pressure in her ears while underwater. She suggested she try flexing her jaw first. If that didn't work then try either the Valsalva or Toynbee methods—pinch and blow or pinch and swallow—Christa's tried and true methods. Or she could simply tilt her head back while looking up. That was the method Regan preferred.

She looked up and noticed the bottom of the boat bobbing in the water against another boat's wake. The world above her seemed so bright in contrast to the darkness below.

A tree appeared a few feet from where the rope attached to the marker, its limbs cut short and trunk covered in a brown muck. She imagined it was the same tree the old man described with the rope swing attached when he was young.

Seconds later, she hit bottom.

Christa removed the mallet and placed it on the metal capstone. With her gloved hand she waved the silt from the plate. "Ashley, hand me the wrench and let's get to work."

Regan stared at the grave. A metal capstone bolted to a concrete vault. The muddy bottom had receded over time revealing the top six inches of the vault. "These bolts haven't been touched for a long time. Metal to metal, in the water, they're probably fused together. We might be able to loosen the grip by banging on the bolts first with the mallet."

"Let me try my luck with the wrench first." Christa insisted.

"Remember, I'm the one who knows how to work on cars. I think you're just being stubborn." Regan said. "But go ahead, knock yourself out."

Regan snickered as she watched Christa fumble with the adjustable plumbers wrench. "You may have to take your gloves off to tighten it." Regan said.

Christa struggled with the wrench for a few more seconds then looked up at Regan. "Alright, Ashley, you win. You do it."

Regan started at one corner and worked her way clockwise around the metal plate attempting to loosen the bond between the metal bolts and the steel plate. Each strike of the mallet sent shock waves through her fingers and up her arm. The sound thundered in her ears.

"Did you know sound waves travel 4.3 times faster in water than in air?" Said Christa. "It's something crazy like 3300 miles per hour."

"Next time the subject comes up I'll try to remember."

She methodically moved from bolt to bolt giving each one ten sharp raps. "Let's give it a try." Regan pointed to one of the bolts.

Christa slipped the wrench over the bolt, ensuring the clamp was snug and gave it a tug.

Nothing.

"Maybe we should use the mallet," said Christa.

"Flip the wrench over then."

"What for?"

"If you hit the wrench in the opposite direction from the open end, you'll just knock the wrench off. Always strike toward the opening." Regan explained.

"And you know this how?"

"From busting my knuckles more than once when a wrench popped off a stubborn bolt." Regan put out her hand. "Let me show you."

After her demonstration of what not to do, she showed Christa how to keep the wrench from coming off the bolt. Regan pounded the mallet against the wrench until her arms ached.

"Is it moving at all?" Christa asked.

Regan shook her head. "Hard to tell, maybe a quarter of a turn."

"It'll get easier, right?"

"Normally I'd say yes. But this has been underwater for almost sixty years. It might be like this until it's out. Every bolt, too."

"This is going to take a lot longer than we figured, isn't it?" Christa asked.

"At this rate we'll be lucky to remove two bolts on each dive. After that we still have to contend with moving that heavy piece of steel."

She swapped with Christa, letting her friend take a turn. The bolt had turned one full revolution when Christa stopped. She looked at her computer then her air gauge. "My air is under 500 pounds. We need to go up now. How's your air holding up?"

"Look like about 450. Is that okay?"

"That's good. Let's go."

"Can we leave the tools here?"

"Well, I'm sure as Hell not hauling them up and down each time. Just leave them on top of the plate, they'll be here when we get back."

Regan followed Christa up the same line they came down. At twenty feet, they did a precautionary five-minute safety stop to allow extra time for absorbed nitrogen from the compressed air to be released by their bodies. After the five minute interval, they headed for the surface. Her mask broke the surface. The woman and her deck boat were gone. She was startled by what she saw next. The fisherman who had been next to them in the cove was sitting on the deck of their Bayliner, his bass boat anchored next to hers.

She swam over to the platform and the man extended his arm in assistance. "Who the hell are you?"

"Hey, you're the guy from the *Pizza Place* last night." Christa shouted.

"That's right. My name is Jake Pendleton."

"Well, Jake Pendleton, what the hell are you doing on my boat?" Regan shouted.

After Christa said it, Regan recognized the man from the restaurant. She looked up at the man, early to mid thirties, dirty blond hair, well built, and handsome. He had captivating blue eyes and gentleman's demeanor. She extended her arm and allowed him to help her onboard.

"Ms. Regan, Ms. Barnett, we need to talk."

CHAPTER 36

Jake helped Ashley Regan out of the water and extended an arm to Christa Barnett. "Why don't you take those dry suits off before we talk?" He noticed Regan give him a funny look. "Or don't. But I guarantee you'll overheat."

"Why are you here?" She demanded. "And how do you know our names?"

He helped Barnett onboard and walked from the swim platform to the deck. "Your lives are in danger."

"What the hell are you talking about, mister?" Barnett was almost yelling. "No one's trying to kill us...except maybe you. What are you, some kind of stalker? Have you been following us since last night?"

"You saw the woman on the deck boat earlier?"

"The one who went swimming?" Regan said. "What about her?"

"She and I are here for the same reason. The big difference is I won't kill you to get it."

"Won't kill me to get what?"

"The book."

Regan felt dizzy when he mentioned the book. How could anyone possibly know about it? "What book?" She asked.

"The book you found in the glacier." Jake noticed Barnett move.

The small woman charged at Jake with a boat hook. "Get him, Ashley." She yelled.

He sidestepped her approach, grabbed the boat hook with one hand and threw her overboard with the other. He looked back at Regan. "Don't even try it," he warned. He pointed his finger at Barnett while she swam back to the swim platform. "You can come back onboard if you can behave yourself, otherwise stay in the water." He turned back to Regan and pointed to a deck chair. "Take that suit off and sit down."

She did as he instructed. Barnett crawled back on the swim platform and pulled off her dry suit. She took a seat beside Regan.

"While you two were in the water, that woman swam over here and rummaged through your boat." He studied Regan's face as he spoke. Not a flinch. A good poker face, he thought. "So if the book was on this boat, it isn't anymore."

Still nothing.

"Where is the book, Ms. Regan?"

"I don't know what you're talking about," she insisted.

"Okay. We can play this game all day but that won't get you any closer to Norman Reese Jr.'s casket. Eight bolts holding a steel plate to a cement vault." He noticed Regan look at him. "Yeah, I know. I've already checked it out and I know why you're here and what you're after."

"We don't know what you're talking about. Do we, Ashley?" Barnett said.

Jake pointed his finger at Barnett. "Tell you what. You don't say another word unless you want to go swimming again." He turned to Regan and put out his hand. "The book."

Nothing.

"Ms. Regan, let me tell you how much trouble you're already in with the law." He glanced at Barnett. "This goes for you as well. Numerous counts of felonious grave robbery, theft, willful destruction of private property, and that's just for starters. The list goes on. But if you turn over the book, no charges will be filed and this ends here. Shall I continue?"

"Are you a cop?" Barnett asked.

"No. If I were a cop, you two would be in handcuffs and I'd be hauling your asses off to jail."

"If you're not a cop," Regan finally spoke, "then who do you work for?"

"I handle special assignments as inconspicuously as possible."

"What? Are you like some kind of spy or something?" Barnett asked.

"No. I'm not a spy. But, I do work for a company who gets its contracts from the government. I have access to the highest levels of intelligence. Here's what I know. And keep in mind that I'm one of the good guys. Ms. Regan, you and your roommate Samantha Connors were hiking in Southern Germany when you found the remains of a soldier from World War II inside an ice cavern in a glacier. You also found a book he had with him when he disappeared in 1946. I'll spare you the details of the contents of the book, you already know because your friend here is well versed in German and translated it for you."

The two women looked at each other.

"After you robbed the cemetery in your home town of Charleston, we captured you on a traffic cam video, including the license plate of your rented Impala and two perfect infrared mug shots. I went to Charleston, to your house, but someone had already been there. Someone who was obviously looking for something and didn't find it. Your house was ransacked. No sign of Ashley Regan or Samantha Connors."

"My house was broken into?"

Jake nodded.

"Sam?"

Jake recognized the concern. "You don't know where she is?"

Nothing.

"Dammit. This is no time for games. These people play for keeps. Her life might already be in jeopardy."

Regan started crying.

"Where is the book? Did the woman get it?"

Regan shook her head then held her palms to her face.

"Is it at the Crooked Moose Lodge in Banner Elk?"

She looked up at him. He saw the surprise in her eyes. "No," she said, "it's safe."

"Tell me where it is. I can protect you." He looked at Barnett. "Both of you."

She wiped the tears from her eyes and pulled her shoulders back. "No. Not until Christa and I get what we came for," Regan said. "Help us get into this casket, and I'll give you the book."

"No deal. Give me the book so I can get both of you out of here and into protective custody."

"You help us open the casket and you can have the book." Her tone indicated her desire to negotiate. "No criminal charges. We get to keep what's inside. And you leave us alone."

"Something you need to know about the woman who was here. She's a hired assassin. I don't know where she went, but you can bet if she doesn't have the book she's coming back." Jake explained. "When she does, she will kill you." He paused to let his words sink in. "She might not be alone either."

"More the reason we need your help. We can't get the bolts loose. You're stronger. You can do it faster." Regan said. "With your help, we can open the casket, get what we came for, and be out of here before she gets back."

"And if she shows up?" Jake questioned. "With reinforcements?"

Regan shrugged her shoulders but said nothing.

"We're all dead. That's what happens. And she'll have your treasure...and the book."

"Then you can't let that happen, can you?" Regain said. "We need to get back down there now and get back to work."

He studied the two women for a *tell*. Anything that might giveaway the location of the book. A pat of the hand or a glance of the eyes. A shrug or a slight nod. Anything. But neither woman gave anything away. Their poker faces were on.

Together, Regan and Barnett's resolve was strong. He knew he could haul them in and try to force them to talk, but that was another delay. A delay his gut told him he couldn't afford. Instinctively he knew there were larger, more important issues at stake than just Ashley Regan and the contents of Norman Reese's grave. Issues that affected President Rebecca Rudd.

Jake knew what was in the casket and so did Regan. Neither Wiley nor Rudd wanted criminal charges filed against the women, and probably could care less about what happened to the casket's contents, as long as Jake contained the situation.

"I don't like it. I think we're putting ourselves in unnecessary danger, but I'll do it your way. However, you don't get what's in the casket until the book is in my possession. Understood?"

"Deal."

CHAPTER 37

Maybe it was all the Clive Cussler books he'd read over the past twenty years, but the whole idea of a hidden treasure submerged under sixty feet of water was intriguing. Too intriguing to pass up. Even though it meant disturbing another grave, Jake yearned to see it with his own eyes. An excitement he wasn't sure he could describe in words, not unlike the thrill he had as a child when he ran out on Christmas morning to see what Santa Claus left him under the tree. The allure of treasure was overwhelming even if he already knew what it was.

Jake made the women wait an hour to off-gas and rehydrate. While he waited he wondered when Abigail Love would return. It wasn't a matter of if, but when.

He was always amazed how spending so much time *in* the water would deplete your body *of* water. He pulled his dive equipment from the bow hatch on his bass boat and geared up while the women did the same. After he checked and double-checked his dive gear, he slipped into the water and waited on the women.

He sent Barnett down the line first, followed by Regan. That way he could keep them both in sight during the descent. He wasn't sure whether or not he could trust Regan; she could be setting him up for a double-cross. He knew he didn't trust Barnett. Proceeding under that line of reasoning kept him on his guard.

Two things were different than when he was down here last night. One, he could see the brown environment without his dive light. He could make out the slope of the bottom. Just above the metal grave capstone was the upright stone marker the line was tied to. Slightly up from it was the cut off tree. And second, he rotated his head from side to side, the monster catfish was gone.

Barnett secured Regan's BCD to a five-foot umbilical she'd evidently used on their previous dive. With Regan's lack of underwater experience, Jake thought it was a good idea to keep the woman as relaxed as possible in the unfamiliar environment.

He looked at Regan and Barnett and could tell they were talking to him. He motioned to his ears and watched the epiphany flash across their faces as they realized he couldn't hear them talking. Lying on top of the metal plate were three tools, a crowbar, a large adjustable plumber's wrench, and a mallet. He looked at the bolts and could see the fresh scarring on the bolt heads from the wrench.

He released the remaining air from his BCD and descended to the bottom, he would need all the weight he could get for leverage. He grabbed the wrench, slipped it over the first bolt, tightened its jaws around the hexagonal bolt head, and tugged.

Nothing.

Without hesitation, he grabbed the mallet and pounded it against the wrench. As it impacted the handle of the wrench, he saw the bolt turn. It turned noticeably with each additional smack. He glanced at Regan, her eyes told him she was smiling. It was slow progress but after five minutes, the first bolt was loose enough for Jake to remove using only the wrench.

He removed two more bolts and checked his computer and air gauge. Using hand signals, he motioned with a balled fist thumb sticking up followed by cupping his hands together. "Go up to the boat," was the signal. Barnett led the way, followed by Regan and Jake.

Back on board after the safety stop, Jake fired up the air compressor and refilled the tanks. He grabbed a double tank harness and rigged his regulator for a two-tank dive.

† † †

Like most men, he figured, he had his routines. Unless White House duties hindered, which they often did, every weekday, rain, snow, or shine, Evan Makley went to the Starbucks on the corner of K Street and 16th Street NW to grab a bite to eat from the bakery and a large cup of House Blend coffee. It was a short three-block stroll through Lafayette Park and up 16th Street. He enjoyed the daily respite from his White House office.

Now, more than ever.

After Elmore Wiley's team uncovered his clandestine meetings with Abigail Love, Rudd had all but formally removed him from White House business. The Executive Secretary to the President had assumed most of his job functions.

President Rebecca Rudd had given him 48 hours to tender his resignation—a timeline that was drawing near. He'd done everything he could think of to warrant a reprieve, but nothing seemed to work. He had fully disclosed every detail about his involvement with Abigail Love. He'd called off the hit on Jake Pendleton. But first he'd warned Love on her Gmail account.

All this trouble because he was trying to save President Rebecca Rudd from a scandal that would certainly oust her from office. In a sense, he was the Good Samaritan. He didn't deserve everything that was happening to him. Rudd was going to make him a scapegoat.

Rudd had scheduled a one-on-one meeting with him for this afternoon. It might be his last chance to salvage his career. The past three years had been, without a doubt, the worst of his life. He was kicked out of his home, lost his wife, custody of his children, and most of his money and possessions. His face had been plastered over all the national media outlets. He was disgraced on television, the news, in the papers, magazines, and even Talk Radio.

Rudd stood by him during all that.

Why not now?

Makley cleared the security gate on Pennsylvania Avenue, crossed the barricaded street, and entered Lafayette Park when the answer occurred to him. He would use what he knew to blackmail the President if he had to. He'd tell her the truth, how her days as President were over unless she withdrew her demands for his resignation and gave him another chance. He could regain her trust.

As he approached the equestrian statue of Andrew Jackson in the middle of the park, he noticed several children playing tag. *Oh, to be young and innocent again.*

Suddenly he felt a crushing blow to the chest followed by the sound of a firecracker. His legs faltered like someone had stripped the bones out of them. He fell to his seat but remained upright. He heard faint sounds of kids screaming. His eyes lost focus as everything blurred and the sounds faded. Something was sucking the life out of him. Was this what a heart attack felt like? His chin fell. He looked at his chest; his pressed blue dress shirt was red. *What was happening?*

Movement caught his eyes. He glanced up and saw mothers and fathers running toward their children, scooping them in their arms, and carrying them away.

Another blow to the chest.

Another firecracker.

Evan Makley fell over and watched as a river of blood flowed across the sidewalk in front of his eyes.

The bright, sunny day grew dimmer.

His mouth filled with blood.

He spit and gasped for air.

Nothing came.

† † †

Abigail Love swore she would never do this again, but she saw no other way. She put the regulator in her mouth and slipped in the water.

Three years ago while deep reef diving in the Turks and Caicos Islands, her regulator separated from her mouthpiece as she exhaled at a depth of sixty feet. She kept her mouth closed so saltwater wouldn't fill her mouth. With no air in her lungs and no way to breath, she panicked. In her terror, she'd forgotten about her integrated backup regulator until the arm of her dive buddy reached out and shoved it in her mouth. She was still shaking when she surfaced ten minutes later. She called off the rest of her dives that trip and vowed never to scuba dive again.

Until now.

When she arrived this morning at the cove, the women were in their boat donning their scuba equipment while a man was in the distance fishing in his small bass boat. She observed both boats under the pretense of sunbathing. It worked. The women paid her no attention and continued their dive preparations without interruptions. She did get a kick out of the fisherman stealing glances after she removed her tunic revealing her bikini. Typical male, she thought, always thinking of one thing. Or maybe two—tits and ass.

After the two women had been underwater for ten minutes, she swam to their boat and rummaged though the cabin, under every cushion, in every cubby and storage, and through the women's personal belongings. No book. She heard the faint echo of banging under the water and felt the vibration through the boat's hull. She made the decision to return and eliminate the friend and capture Ashley Regan. She would torture her until she relinquished the book.

It took her almost two hours to find suitable dive equipment in the small town of Butler, but she managed, as she always did. A lesson she learned long ago, anything could be bought if the price was right.

When she returned, she anchored her boat on the opposite side of a point separating the cove from the main section of the lake, which meant an underwater swim of three hundred yards. She was in excellent physical shape and knew it would not be a problem after she descended in the water.

She kicked to the edge of the point and watched as the two women dove into the water. There was something more troubling though; the fisherman had joined them. She noticed the small bass boat was anchored next to the larger boat and realized the fisherman must be the man from Charleston, Jake Pendleton.

This was unexpected. Despite what Makley ordered, Pendleton would die along with Regan's friend.

After the three submerged, Love pulled out her dive computer with an integrated compass and took a bearing to the spot where they dove. 160 degrees. While she descended toward the bottom, she set her timer and tracked the bearing toward the spot. If her calculations were correct, a hard kick at 2 MPH should get her close in five minutes.

She tracked the same bearing and followed the sound on the metal banging. Even though direction of sound was difficult to gauge underwater, volume and vibration wasn't. She could tell she was getting closer.

Visibility was worse than she anticipated but she realized that also offered her an advantage. If it was harder for her to see them, then it was harder for them to see her. She was coming in silent and unexpected. They, on the other hand, were making a lot of noise, which gave her the upper hand.

When the three of them came into view it looked like an underwater construction site. The two women were holding dive lights on something while the man was turning a wrench. Each turn made a grinding sound painful to her ears.

When the man, whom she presumed was Jake Pendleton, stopped, they all seemed to show some sign of happiness with high fives and fist bumps. Then Pendleton grabbed a crowbar and started prying off something that looked like the top of a concrete box. It appeared to be a large metal plate loosely anchored at one corner. He slowly rotated it until it was clear of an open space in the center of the concrete box.

The women looked at each other. Both women wore matching black dry suits and identical scuba gear. With both of them crouching over the metal plate, she couldn't distinguish one woman from the other in the murky waters.

Pendleton reached into the concrete box and pulled up on something, which appeared hinged on one side. She couldn't discern what it was from her position, but an object rose from the box and floated to the surface. He picked up the crowbar and smashed it down into the box. More debris floated out of the box.

He buried his arms down into the box to his elbows. Both women leaned over with the dive lights. He rose up and she saw small bright objects glistening under the bright dive lights as they slipped through his gloved fingers.

Something shiny.

Something gold.

She readied her spear gun and made her move.

CHAPTER 38

He didn't know which was harder, loosening the bolts or rotating the heavy metal plate covering the concrete vault to the side. Jake left one bolt in place so he didn't have to lift the metal plate. He used Regan's crowbar to wedge the plate away from the concrete vault then, using it as a lever, rotated the metal plate away from the opening.

Inside was the casket.

The same make and model as all the others.

He hesitated. Did he really want to disturb Norman Reese's grave? He didn't, but his orders were to acquire the book and stop any further marauding of WWII graves. Regan had offered him a deal and he took it.

He was a man of his word.

When the deal was consummated and the book in his hands, the grave robbing would stop. If President Rudd wanted to pursue what happened to the contents of the graves, she could do that through other means. His objective was to retrieve the book. He thought about Wiley's words to him last year when he was pursuing a terrorist, *Meet the objective, the how doesn't matter.*

Jake reached into the concrete vault and lifted both lids to the casket. Pieces of Welkin Twill, braided cords, and tassels floated out with a few escaping air bubbles. Beneath the glass he saw more air bubbles and remnants of a tattered uniform. He lifted the crowbar and slammed it into the glass seal.

Thud.

The glass didn't break, but it did crack. He watched the cracks move from the impact point outward toward the edges. He raised the crowbar again but before he could take a swing the glass seal exploded. Pieces of glass peppered his dry suit, none compromising its integrity. He looked at the women, Regan was fist-bumping Barnett. Debris spiraled upward toward the surface. He recognized pieces of uniform mixed with decayed liner.

The casket was empty—nothing inside.

No corpse.

No bones.

Nothing.

He looked at Regan who motioned for him to lift the bottom. It made no sense but he did it anyway and soon realized the casket had a false base. He ripped out the remaining liner and removed the base. Fontaine had not prepared him for what he saw under the dive lights.

Built into the base of the casket was a grid of compartments, two widthwise, six lengthwise. Each compartment contained a leather pouch with a leather drawstring top. He lifted a pouch and emptied its contents into the compartment.

Gold ingot bars. Each with an inscription. He picked one up and rubbed his thumb across the engraving.

DEUTSHE REICHBANK
1 Kilo
Feingold
999.9

At the bottom of each one was inscribed a serial number. Each different from the next. There were dozens of ingots, glistening in the light. He grabbed another pouch.

Silver Reichsmark coins.

With the playfulness of a child, he emptied each one in the compartment it came from. Amazed at the dazzling display of gold and silver. Under the bright lights it reminded him of a pirate's treasure. In a sense, it was. This time the pirate was Major Don Adams.

All total, he emptied one bag of Silver Reichsmarks, three of gold ingots, two of gold English Sovereigns, one of gold Napoleons, one of U. S. $20 gold coins, and four of gold Swiss Francs.

He cupped his hands, scooped out Swiss Francs, and held them up into the light. He let the coins slip through his fingers as he watched in amazement at the brilliance of the metallic gold reflection under the dive lights. He didn't know how much the cache was worth, but in today's commodities market, he figured it was well into the millions of dollars. No wonder Regan wanted to negotiate for the book.

Barnett motioned to get his attention. He looked and saw her unzip an outside pocket on her dry suit. She pulled out a clear dry bag and extended it in his direction. He recognized it immediately.

The journal.

Suddenly a glint of light, a flash of metal reflected by a dive light, and then the book fell to the muddy bottom. A shadow moved behind Barnett. A torrent of bubbles escaped from behind her head. Her air hoses had been severed. Her eyes bulged and she streaked upward. Her dive light fell from her hand and started rolling down toward the bottom of the lake. He tried to grab her fins but was too late.

He turned to Ashley Regan. An ever-expanding halo of red encompassed her body. Blood oozed from the hole in her dry suit. A metal spear tip protruded from the center of her chest. The grimace on her face said it all; there was nothing he could do for her now. He recognized the look in her eyes.

Ashley Regan was already dead.

Her body floated upward until it reached the end of the tether.

A shadow moved toward him, gobbling the book from the muddy bottom. He blocked the dive knife with his right forearm as the shadow swam past him, over the grave and the gold, and down toward the deep bottom of the lake. The same direction his dive light fell last night. He should have anticipated it, but he didn't and now Regan was dead. At the hands of the assassin Abigail Love.

He looked upward as Christa Barnett's silhouette ascended toward the surface. She was on her own now. Love had the book and was swimming away. She was his number one priority. With the low visibility in the lake, he couldn't let her get out of sight or he might never find her or the book again.

With every passing second, Abigail Love's shadow grew fainter in the murky depths of Watauga Lake. He propelled himself off the lip of the concrete vault and kicked furiously over the muddy mound that was once the dry knoll where Norman Reese was born. The deeper they dove, the dimmer the ambient light and the fainter her image appeared.

She was a strong swimmer and he began to think he was chasing a mermaid. He wasn't losing ground but he wasn't gaining either. She was faster than he'd anticipated and his extra tank was slowing him down. As they approached the bottom, he knew she could use the silt as a cover. He kicked harder hoping his Navy endurance training would give him an edge. He'd stayed in good shape, but his Navy days were a long time ago.

The lakebed flattened out, as he knew it would, and Love's fins stirred up silt further restricting his visibility. He ascended a few feet to get out of her wake and could barely discriminate her fins kicking fifteen feet in front and below him. He kicked harder.

Jake knew he had an advantage over Love, several of them actually. Even though she was still swimming at a fast pace, she was tiring and had slowed. He knew he still had plenty of kick left in him. And with only one tank at a depth of 115 feet and, at this furious pace, she would soon run out of air. He had two tanks, which gave him a longer bottom time. More time to recover the book, and still make his decompression stops with air to spare.

Out of nowhere a four-foot stone wall appeared on the bottom outlining a raised foundation. Halfway down the wall he saw five wide steps leading down to what he assumed was an old street. They had stumbled on Old Butler. The old town that was relocated prior to the flooding of the valley.

Love doglegged around the felled skeleton of a large tree and doubled back leaving him no alternative but to circumnavigate the tree as well. He closed the gap to ten feet when Love turned again. His leg muscles burned. He felt like he had run a marathon but he refused to slow his pace. Now it was an underwater race—winner takes the prize—only in this race, the stakes were much higher.

Her gray figure stayed the same distance in front of him. No closer. No farther. Every few seconds she would make a slight course change. Each time turning her head to see where he was.

She swam past a large concrete support structure and her shadow almost disappeared in a shadow from the structure above. He glanced up. The remnants of an old metal bridge loomed overhead.

Love turned hard around the concrete support footing and disappeared in the murky waters. Jake followed her around the concrete structure but she was gone.

Nothing.

Vanished like a ghost in the murky waters.

Jake relied on his Navy training. A trick he'd learned to locate his dive buddy after being separated was to stop scanning the bottom and look higher—for bubbles. Within thirty seconds, he'd picked up Love's bubbles and feverishly kicked in her direction. Another thirty seconds later, he reestablished a visual on Abigail Love.

Jake checked his air pressure. Between the two tanks, he had over 2500 pounds. That meant Love probably had less than 1000. Her air was running out. And so was her time.

She slowed and now Jake had a clear view of her when a small stone and cement building appeared, becoming distinctly visible as he approached. Built with the same type stone as the wall he'd just seen, the building sat alone on the barren muddy bottom. Love swam inside a large window opening. He guessed the small building was only about fifteen feet wide. He slowed as he followed her inside only to discover she was already exiting out of a rear opening. *She has to be getting tired.*

He'd lost precious ground and needed to move faster in order to catch her. The structure had no roof so he swam up between the few trusses that had remained intact from years of decay and looked in the direction Love turned. She had stopped and was wielding her knife. She was prepared to attack as soon as he followed her through the door.

His sudden appearance above caught her off guard and she swam away, but not before Jake closed the gap to less than ten feet. Once again the sprint was on.

He checked his gauges, 1750 pounds. Love was getting dangerously low on air. No way could she have enough for proper decompression stops. A critical mistake.

Two minutes later another structure from the flooded town of Old Butler appeared—a covered concrete building with walls on three sides and windows in the rear. Love was heading for one of the two openings on the front. She was slowing. The gap closed to five feet and when he extended his long arms, he felt the wake of her kick. With his outreached hand, he could almost touch her fins.

This race was almost over. She swam into the structure as Jake closed in. When he entered behind her, he knew the chase had ended.

She was trapped.

Bars.

The building appeared to have been an old jail. There were bars on the windows and no way out except the way they came in. Behind him. She stopped suddenly and he crashed into her. She spun around wielding the dive knife.

Her right arm thrust down toward him with a powerful slash. He blocked it with his left forearm then jabbed the butt of his palm into her abdomen. Her BCD absorbed most of the blow but the impact knocked her against the concrete wall.

He kicked backwards and motioned for her to stop but she came at him again.

She slashed her knife from side to side. He countered each swipe with a deflection until the blade tore across the arm of his dry suit. At first he felt the trickle of cold water soaking his arm. He hesitated, and it cost him the upper hand. She whipped the blade left and right at his midsection like a Samurai with a sword. He jerked back but not before the blade made contact and sliced a ten-inch cleft in his dry suit.

The gash gaped open and his dry suit swallowed the cold lake water.

Jake grabbed Love's knife hand as it passed through his suit pulling her arm. The cold water washed down his legs and across his chest. Concentration on the battle with Love was being countermanded by the shock of the cold water to his body.

He had to end this now.

He never got the chance.

He squeezed her hand until she dropped the knife. He held her mask-to-mask and saw terror in her eyes. At that moment they both started tumbling as their legs were swept from beneath them. He caught a glimpse of the culprit. Another monster catfish. Or perhaps the same one from last night. Their underwater battle had spooked him from his hiding place. His sheer size and strength upended them both.

He lost his grip on Love and, for a split second, had forgotten about the cold water licking its way around the inside of his dry suit. She broke free and swam toward the opening. He reached out with one hand and grabbed her fin. She kicked him with her other fin. He tried to hang on, but she kicked his hand free and swam out of the old stone jail. He followed her and watched as she made a beeline for the surface. He made two kicks to follow then stopped.

Looking up, he saw her break the surface and start swimming. He followed her from below, slowly ascending until his dive computer signaled a deco stop at 60 feet. He stayed at that depth and continued following.

The shivering started within a couple of minutes, but he couldn't surface. Not yet. He held his depth as he tracked her from below. He knew the water would warm as he ascended above the thermocline. His only chance against the cold. At this temperature, hypothermia wasn't far away.

She swam toward the hull of a boat and disappeared from the water. Moments later he saw the anchor being hoisted and simultaneously felt and heard the vibration of the boat's engine. Within seconds, the boat was gone.

And so was the book.

He ascended to 30 feet, his next deco stop, waited, then ascended to 15 feet, his safety stop depth, and waited again. His shivering was almost uncontrollable but he kept on. His Navy training had taught him several techniques to prolong his time to hypothermia—he used them all. When he surfaced he was on the outside of the cove. The water on the surface was much warmer than below.

His bass boat was anchored alone in the cove and Barnett had taken Regan's boat.

Ashley Regan.

In the frenzy, he'd forgotten about her.

CHAPTER 39

After today's events, Abigail Love swore she'd never get in the water again. Not even a swimming pool. And scuba dive? She'd rather jump off a cliff than strap on another tank. The last twenty minutes had been the most harrowing of her life. The fear of being eaten alive by the monster fish had overwhelmed her. In her fifteen years as a hired gun, she'd never had an emotional jolt like she'd experienced today at the bottom of Watauga lake.

The knife fight she could handle but the monster at the bottom of the lake with the long barbell whiskers hanging from its lower lip, no way. She saw it as soon as she entered the second small building on the bottom of the lake. But when she stopped, Pendleton slammed into her from behind. All she wanted to do was get the hell out of there, but he kept blocking her path.

He left her no choice but to come at him with the knife to get him away from the exit. She grabbed her titanium dive knife in case she needed it to fend off the fish. The monster fish made its move right after Pendleton knocked the knife from her hand. The knife fell on top of the fish, spooking him. She saw the monster's muscles contract on alternate sides as it whipped its mighty tail back and forth. The fish charged the exit and didn't seem to care that it was blocked. It wanted out, and so did she.

They could have both been killed. What was Pendleton thinking? And why didn't he follow her to the surface? She saw his bubbles following her and expected him to come after her but every time she looked down through her mask, the idiot was far below. What was he doing?

She feared he would surface before she could make her escape but she never saw him again. His bubbles were still under her boat when she raised the anchor and sped off. She couldn't help but smile at her good fortune. She had gotten away from Pendleton *and* she had the book. Now to get as far away from Tennessee as she could.

She flexed her knees and shoulders, feeling the soreness from all the exertion of the chase and the fight with Pendleton. She had run marathons when she was younger and never felt this sore. Age was simply not just a state of mind. It also took its toll on the body.

She had rented a fast boat and was pleased she'd spent the extra money. The quicker she got back to the dock the better. Her skin began to itch and she realized she still had on her dry suit. No wonder she was so hot. She peeled it off a little at a time while she drove toward the marina. After she removed her polar under suit, she sat in the captain's seat and fatigue hit her. She was exhausted. She grabbed a bottle of water from the cooler and some painkillers from her bag, maybe that would help stave off the headache she felt coming on.

It was getting time to change her line of work, or at the very least, her level of active involvement. At 39, this type of contract work was for her younger *escorts*. She rubbed her arms to stave off a chill then slipped on her tunic. It was time for a change of pace.

The afternoon sun had moved past its apex and westward toward the mountaintops casting tiny shadows along the western shoreline of Watauga Lake. She missed the turn to take her to the marina twice, which just pissed her off. *Come on, get it together.*

She had Makley's precious book, one he'll never see if her escort did her job. Now, she'll use it as leverage to get herself out of the country and someplace outside the long arms of the United States authorities. Even if they had taken down her complex like Makley indicated, she had enough cash reserves tucked away to live comfortably for several years. Maybe she'd set up shop someplace else. Australia, perhaps...or maybe New Zealand. Contracts might be few and far between, but that could ease her into retirement.

She pulled into the slip at the marina, cut the engine, and tried to stand. Her legs were wobbly like she'd had too much to drink. She caught herself by grabbing the console, shook it off within a few seconds, and gathered her bag and personal belongings. The rest of the stuff could just stay; someone would claim it sooner or later.

She felt an itch and scratched her ear with her slender fingers. Definitely *not* getting in the water again. In the afternoon sunlight she thought her tanned skin looked strange but dismissed it as fatigue. It had been a long, tiring day.

She looked for her car and spotted it just beyond a white van where an older gentleman was threading a fishing line through a rod. She walked past him and gave him a faint smile.

Two seconds later she was being pulled backward.

She tried to resist.

†††

Francesca dialed Jake's cell phone for the fourteenth time in the past three hours. She'd been waiting in Butler trying to locate Jake so she could assist him with the mission. But the woman's arrival at the marina changed that. Now she was calling him to leave a message to let him know what had just happened. On the third ring Jake answered.

"Jake. Damn you. Where the hell have you been?"

"Last hour or so? Underwater. What's going on?"

"Abigail Love showed up here at the marina."

"Good, go after her. She's got the book and we need to get it back."

"I'm following her now. You all right?"

"I'm fine. Stay on Love. I have everything under control here. Besides, she'll need your help very soon."

"She needs my help now." Francesca memorized the license plate in front of her. "She was just abducted while walking to her car, thrown in the back of a van, and now they're heading out of town. I'm already in pursuit."

"What color van?" Jake said. "White?"

"Yes. How'd you know?"

"Same van was in Charleston yesterday morning then again here in Butler last night. The van was tailing Love."

"Now they have her. Jake, all hell is breaking loose and I'm afraid President Rudd is about to be caught in the middle of a maelstrom as you would say."

"I know. I think I've already figured that out."

"So you know about Evan Makley?"

"Makley? What about Makley?"

"He was shot and killed across the street from the White House. In Lafayette Park. He died on the pavement under the statue of Andrew Jackson's horse."

"You think it was us?" Jake paused. "Or Rudd?"

"Us? What makes you think it might be us?"

"I found out there are a few things Wiley deliberately didn't bother to tell us."

"It's not like Wiley to keep information from us about a mission. If he did, I'll bet President Rudd withheld information from us too." Francesca slowed down as the van pulled off the road. "How did Love get the book from you?"

"I never had the book. She killed Ashley Regan, grabbed the book, and then took off. I chased her for a long time underwater, but..." Jake paused. "She got away."

"What now?"

"Don't let Love out of your sight. She needs medical attention."

"Looks to me like she's in need of a rescue. What kind of medical attention?"

"I'm pretty sure she's going to get the bends."

"The bends?"

"Decompression sickness. Keep following the van. Don't let her get away. If you get the chance, get the book and then get her to a hospital. And in that order too. I've got a few janitorial duties to take care of here first, then I'll meet you and Wiley in Nashville."

"Nashville? What makes you think this van is going to Nashville?"

"Because that's where Wiley is going."

He hung up on her without another word. It was a bad habit of his. At first it bothered her that he would never acknowledge the end of a call, all the time thinking maybe she said something to upset him. Now she understood Jake's business-like attitude and propensity to forgo pleasantries, like ending a conversation.

The van pulled off the road forcing her to pass it, which made it very difficult to follow someone especially when they were behind you. Just outside of town, she pulled into a gas station and pretended to fill her car with gas. If the person in the van was indeed taking Abigail Love to Nashville, then the entire mission had taken a turn for the worst.

When the van passed by, she returned to her running vehicle and pulled back onto the highway.

A safe distance to follow, she thought, four cars back.

†††

Jake allowed a minimum amount of time to off-gas before plunging back into the cold water. He'd done a field repair on his dry suit using Wiley's special brand of duct tape. The same type of tape he'd once used on a mission to mend a damaged glider in Yemen.

He grabbed the spare tank from the front compartment, rigged his gear, grabbed his dive light, and hoped like hell his patch job worked.

He followed the guide rope down to the grave marker of Norman Albert Reese, Junior. Everything was the same as when he left it an hour and a half ago. All the tools and gold and silver were still where he'd left them, ironically, still guarded by the dead body of treasure hunter Ashley Regan who was still fastened to her umbilical.

He put the gold and silver back in the leather pouches. He wished now he hadn't been so exuberant about displaying the trove of wealth from the casket. He couldn't afford another trip to the bottom of the lake so he had to get everything ready to haul to the surface in one trip. He grabbed three mesh utility bags and stuffed them with leather pouches of gold and silver and with the tools and Regan's scuba gear.

He knew Regan's dead body would be hard to explain to authorities without revealing everything that had transpired—something President Rudd and Wiley were adamant about keeping under wraps. He removed Regan's tank and fins and, as unsettling as it was, stuffed her dead body inside Reese's casket. He closed the lid to the casket sealing her inside.

After he rotated the metal plate back on top of the vault, he reinserted the bolts and gave each a few turns to keep the plate intact on top of the concrete vault. One final sweep of the knoll to ensure no indication remained of his presence. Only another draining of Watauga Lake and close inspection of Reese's grave would uncover any tampering. By then, it would be just another one of history's mysteries that could never be solved.

Jake released the mooring ball from the bottom, letting it drift freely toward the middle of the lake, grabbed the ropes that he'd secured to the utility bags, and ascended to his first deco stop.

Once onboard his bass boat, he noticed the afternoon sun was setting lower in the western sky. He still had a lot to do and he was running low on time. He hoisted each utility bag to the surface, placed them inside his boat, started the outboard engine, and headed back to the lakefront cabin.

The cooler air cleared his head while he thought about what had transpired so far and began to wonder about the fate of President Rebecca Rudd. The secrets he now possessed about Rudd made him wonder if perhaps she had known all along. But if she didn't know, how would she handle the inexplicable threat to her presidency? She was a savvy politician and one of the most beloved in recent history. There were no scandals. No skeletons in her closet—until now.

Christa Barnett potentially knew the truth about Rudd. She'd translated the journal for Regan, so, as unlikely as it seemed, with some research she could have made the connection. Even though in the short time he'd been exposed to her, neither she nor Regan had said anything that suggested they had any interest other than the hidden treasures. Eventually, he'd have to find Barnett and let Wiley debrief her. In exchange for her silence, no criminal charges would be filed. She'd be convinced that it was necessary for national security. She could return to her life as a graphic designer and never discuss her adventures with Ashley Regan again. Or the journal.

Abigail Love, on the other hand, was a problem. A big problem. He knew Evan Makley had hired her to get the journal. In the beginning his motives may have been altruistic, but greed clouded his judgment. Or perhaps it was an overwhelming desire for self-preservation. He had commissioned Love to obtain the book at any cost, which she had done.

Now, it seemed, Abigail Love was a target. According to Francesca, she was nabbed as soon as she returned to her car. It wouldn't be long before she realized her panicked dash from the lakebed to the surface might prove to be the last mistake of her life.

CHAPTER 40

Scott Katzer was surprised how easy it was to kidnap the woman who had been following the man he saw kick in Ashley Regan's front door in Charleston. If it hadn't been for her, he wouldn't be here now.

And he wouldn't have the book.

It almost felt like the book had been handed to him. It was like child's play.

When he first spotted her at the marina, he thought she was drunk by the way she staggered toward her car, her faculties definitely impaired. She didn't resist when he grabbed her and threw her in the back of the van. Almost like she wanted to lie down. She didn't attempt to yell or struggle while he bound her arms and legs. It was a disappointment, anticlimactic. He was looking forward to a struggle with the woman. He craved the feeling of dominance. He wrapped duct tape over her mouth in case she sobered up and then he drove off.

Within minutes, she became nauseated. He heard her retching behind the tape. Fearing asphyxiation on her vomit, he pulled the van to the side of the road and removed the tape. That's when he noticed splotches on her skin and wondered if her rash, nausea, and malaise were due to some sort of allergic reaction. He lifted her up, one arm under her legs the other under her back, and hoisted her into a casket in the back of the van. The same casket he'd used to transport

Samantha Connors. He closed the lid to the casket but left her mouth uncovered.

He got back in the driver's seat, pulled back onto the highway, and headed toward Nashville.

Years in the funeral home business might have dulled his olfactory senses but an hour into the journey he thought he smelled urine and he flipped on the rear compartment light. Urine leaked through the air vents and was dripping from the base of his specially designed casket. *Son of a bitch*. When he thought about it he realized he smelled the urine soon after she had, what he thought was, a mild seizure. It should have been his first clue to her health. Now, instead of her constant moaning and writhing, she was still and quiet, but breathing.

He had what his mother feared would end up in the wrong hands. She longed for the journal. That was all that mattered. His aging mother could have peace. The thing she said would lead them to a staggering amount of wealth or make them loath its existence, was now lying on the seat beside him.

A chronicle of her past and her evil deeds.

And the key to his own history.

† † †

Abigail Love had never felt this ill in her entire life. Every joint in her body throbbed with pain and stiffness. Her head pounded and she was sick to her stomach. She opened her eyes, darkness swallowed her. Every breath was labored.

She raised her head but it slammed into something above her—something padded. *Where am I?* Her clothes were wet. The smell of her own urine flooded her nostrils.

She tried to move her arms but there was little sensation. All she could figure out was that her hands were bound behind her. Her shoulders ached. She tried to move her legs without success. Bound at the ankles.

What had happened to her? One minute she was walking to her car, the next she was restrained inside this box, soaked in her own urine. It was all a blur.

A wave of nausea caused her to double over. Her head and feet smashed into the walls of her prison. Then a tremor rolled through her body. It started at her feet, moving toward her head until she shook violently and uncontrollably. *What was happening?* Her head jerked back and forth, slamming into the padded walls. Pain racked her body and she couldn't stop the spasms.

White spots floated in front of her eyes.

Again, she felt warm and wet.

The convulsions eased, spots faded, welcome sleep enveloped her.

† † †

Jake slipped the bass boat into the boathouse behind the cabin and tied it off. He had a lot of things to haul the one hundred feet or so from the dock to the cabin and he knew it would take several trips. Without hesitation he grabbed the three utility bags containing the contents of the casket, hoisted them over his shoulder, and carried them up the steps to the cabin. The leather pouches inside still saturated from decades underwater. Three bags totaling 75 pounds of gold and silver plus the weight of the plumber's wrench, the crowbar, and the mallet—roughly a hundred pounds...give or take a few, two bags over one shoulder, one over the other.

Once inside the cabin, he dropped the heavy bags on the floor, removed the tools, and tossed them aside. His first order of business was to secure the gold and silver.

Thirty minutes later, Jake had sanitized the cabin, concealed the casket's treasure in the Tahoe, changed into street clothes, and was already two miles down the highway leaving the cabin, Watauga Lake, and the town of Butler, Tennessee behind with no intention of ever returning.

As he drove, the afternoon sun disappeared behind a single cloud hanging low on the mountainous horizon.

One lone cloud in an otherwise cloudless September afternoon.

He checked his watch and realized he was running out of time. He needed to secure the recovered treasures. Too risky taking the treasure into a potentially hazardous situation. On his way to Interstate 81, he drove through the small town of Elizabethton, Tennessee where he stopped at Security Federal Bank and paid a year's advance rent on a safety deposit box.

After securing the gold and silver in the bank, Jake went to the local post office and mailed the safety deposit box key to himself at his parents' address in Newnan, Georgia.

Jake slipped on his headset and placed a call. Francesca, the man she was following, and Abigail Love should have made it to Nashville by now. Francesca's familiar voice answered on the second ring.

"Jake." Francesca's voice sounded frantic. "Do you have any idea what I'm looking at right now?"

Jake fumbled around trying to lower the volume in his earpiece. "I have a suspicion, but tell me anyway."

"The van pulled into a funeral home under a side awning. Looks like a delivery door."

"A funeral home?" Jake asked. "I was afraid of that."

Suddenly the objective of acquiring the book got a lot more complicated. It now made sense why Wiley would go to Nashville. "Where are you?"

"Across the street is as close as I can get without the risk of being spotted. I'm using the infrared spotting scope. An old woman is helping unload a casket from the van." Francesca paused. "Jake, the sign out front reads Katzer Funeral Home. Is that who I think it is?"

Jake was quiet. He could only imagine the whirlwind of thoughts running through Francesca's head. Probably the same ones he was having.

"I'm afraid so," He finally said.

"The man and the old woman just rolled the casket inside on some kind of gurney. What should I do?"

"Stay put," he said, "if anyone comes out, let me know."

"Jake? What does this mean?"

Jake spent the next few minutes explaining to Francesca everything that had transpired and what he and Fontaine had discovered about the book. He'd suspected Wiley had held something back. Now he knew what it was.

"Have you talked to Wiley?" Jake asked.

"I've tried calling several times," she said. "But, he won't answer."

"I'll give him a try."

"What makes you think he'll talk to you when he wouldn't talk to me?"

"Because I know something he doesn't." Jake hung up. While he was talking to her he realized the stakes had escalated to dangerous proportions. For Wiley. For Rudd. For the country.

Jake gathered his thoughts and placed his call to Wiley. As expected, he didn't answer and his call was sent to voice mail. "Mr. Wiley. I know about the connection between the book and President Rudd. I know you're on your way to Nashville and I know why. Call me back…or I'll call her."

He owed a lot to Elmore Wiley. The man had taken Jake under his wing during one of the lowest points in his life. The man had trained him, taught him self-control and restored his confidence. Wiley had shown him a new world and with it, a new life. In every sense of the word, Wiley had been Jake's mentor. And more.

Through the Old Man, Jake had met Kyli.

He was happy in his new role as emissary for Elmore Wiley but he couldn't help but sense the Old Man wasn't thinking clearly when in came to Rebecca Rudd. What their relationship was, he might never know, but he also served the President. She had taken him into her confidence during their private meeting. He'd felt like he was personal emissary to the President of the United States. In a way, he was.

Jake smiled when his cell phone rang, Elmore Wiley, right on time.

"Where are you, Jake?" He could hear the strain in Wiley's voice. For the first time since they'd met, Wiley sounded like an old man. And this time, a little rattled. His cool, polished demeanor gone.

"On the way to Nashville." Jake paused. "Mr. Wiley, if this is true, you can't protect her."

"There are issues larger than this in jeopardy right now and President Rebecca Rudd is a key player. The world powers are at the precipice of a major alliance. That's what the emergency summit meeting tomorrow in Indianapolis is all about. Rudd has to be there. Without her, negotiations will likely fail and the global economy will be on the threshold of collapse." Wiley paused. Jake could hear labored breathing. "Don't you see, it doesn't matter whether it is true or not, it can never become public knowledge."

Which meant the unthinkable. Indeed, the stakes were high.

"Why didn't you wait for backup in Butler?"

"I didn't have time. Ashley Regan was on the move. If I didn't act when I did, then she would be gone and we would still be guessing her next move."

"What happened in Butler?"

Jake thought about it and gave Wiley the shortened version. "With George's help, I got there first and waited on Regan and her friend. Unfortunately, Abigail Love showed up and killed Ashley Regan."

"Is Butler secure?"

"No pun intended," Jake said, "but I literally closed the lid on that casket."

"And the book?"

"The reason I'm headed to Nashville. Abigail Love took the book from Regan. Then a man abducted Love and now he has the book. Both are in Nashville at this time. And sir, they're at the Katzer Funeral Home."

"Scott Katzer," Wiley said, "I figured as much."

"We need to get in the funeral home," Jake said. "Maybe we should storm the castle."

"You don't storm the castle until you know the lay of the land, Jake. What we need is a ruse to get us inside."

"Katzer knows what I look like," Jake said. "It'll have to be just you and Francesca. I'll be the cavalry."

Wiley was silent for a few seconds. "Then, here's what we'll do. Tell Francesca to meet me at the funeral home at eight o'clock in the morning. We'll go in under the pretense of making prearrangement for my comatose and terminally ill wife. That'll get us inside. We'll be wired so you can listen. If it goes south, come and get us."

"Not bad," Jake said. "What are you going to do when you get in there?"

"Don't know. I guess I'll figure it out as I go along." Wiley paused. "Get Francesca onboard and we'll talk again in the morning." Wiley hung up.

Jake's sixth sense told him Wiley wasn't being forthright with him. The Old man was still hiding something but Jake couldn't figure out what it was.

CHAPTER 41

President Rebecca Rudd relaxed for the first time since she'd arrived in Indianapolis, her briefcase open on the coffee table in front of her. Her suite at the JW Marriot was surrounded by Secret Service. The suites on each side, above and below, and across the hall were filled with her protection detail. Sharpshooters perched on rooftops covered every angle with an exposure to her windows.

Tomorrow's emergency meeting was scheduled to start at 10:00 a.m. in the hotel's exhibit hall. Her presence was essential to the success of the global summit meeting.

This was her first public meeting since Evan Makley's murder. Even though he'd somehow become involved with the assassin Abigail Love, she'd come to rely on his advice and his expertise in managing her schedule. His replacement was of no use to her tonight. Makley was the only one on her staff that was up to speed on this meeting.

Wiley's stern warning about Makley raised her suspicions about his untimely death. Did Elmore Wiley have Evan Makley killed to protect her? That was, after all, what precipitated their first meeting when she was Secretary of State. In the past, Wiley's organization only sanctioned a hit after the White House had *unofficially* authorized it. Had he stepped beyond his bounds this time?

She and Wiley had been friends for many years and she'd placed her faith in his wisdom on more than one occasion.

She'd considered him her guardian angel. Maybe that's the way he felt too.

Evan Makley had stepped on a few toes over the years he'd been on her staff. It was likely he had made a few enemies that might have wanted him dead. Many with powerful enough connections to make it happen. She shouldn't be too hasty to convict Wiley with the act.

The shrill ring of her cell phone startled her. With Makley dead, it usually only rang when it was her husband Kyle, or Jake Pendleton. This time it was neither.

She answered and listened to the caller. For the first time in her life she wanted to run and hide. She'd never backed down from a fight but the words the caller said threatened everything she'd accomplished. It threatened not just her reputation, one that she'd fought so hard to protect, but her Presidency and the fragile nature of the global economy. If this were true, negotiations would break down and the summit meeting would fail.

The call disconnected. Could it be the caller spoke the truth? Now was not the time to have to deal with this. Too much depended on the next few days. She had to make it go away, but whom could she trust?

She had an idea.

† † †

Scott Katzer pushed the casket through the entrance while his mother opened the receiving door. After he arrived at the funeral home and checked on the woman, he realized her condition had worsened. He checked her vital signs. She was alive, but not by much it seemed.

He wheeled the casket next to the embalming table and lifted her out of the casket onto the cold porcelain table.

Under the harsh white lights, he could tell her condition was grave. He noticed the skin on her upper chest was marbled in appearance. He unbuttoned her shirt and noticed it extended from her shoulders to her lower abdomen.

"This woman needs a doctor," he said to his mother.

Her glare removed all doubt about the woman's fate.

Many decades ago Heidi Katzer, then Scheller, had been a nurse in Germany. Growing up, Scott remembered how his mother avoided doctors, opting to treat the family's injuries and illnesses herself. She seemed so smart back then. Educated. Now he knew it was the years of deception that made her paranoid, always afraid she was going to be discovered as a fraud, a thief, and even a murderer.

At his mother's request, Scott removed the woman's urine soaked pants. "Look at the swelling and the edema here and here." She pointed to areas of the woman's arms and legs. "I've never seen anything like this before."

Both of them remained silent for a few seconds.

"You say she had a seizure?" His mother asked.

"At least one that I know of. She had two bladder releases on the drive here. One I know came right after a seizure." He looked at this mother. Her eyes never left the woman. "What do you think it means?"

"I think she's dying."

"Of what?"

"I don't know, but I need to question her." His mother looked up at him from the other side of the embalming table. "Where's the journal?"

Scott Katzer reached inside his coat and removed the book from a pocket. He extended it to his mother. "Here."

An awestruck look came over his mother's face as she gingerly reached out with both hands. "I can't believe it." She said. "After all these years. The book has finally returned home."

She removed it from his hands and slowly cradled it against her chest. She held it tight for nearly a minute. She twisted from side to side as if rocking a baby to sleep. Scott let his mother have her moment, knowing full well that her mind was temporarily in 1946 reliving a different time and place.

She pulled it away from her chest and caressed the front with her arthritic hands. He watched her fingers dance across the initials branded on the leather. "Wolfgang," she whispered, "I knew one day you would return to me."

She looked up at him. "Look, Scott. Your father has come home."

It was at that moment he knew his mother was mad. Her mind had finally snapped, he thought. And the book was the catalyst. She'd seemed obsessive about the book, but he assumed it was to get to the treasures Major Don Adams had shipped to the United States hidden away in the caskets.

"Mother?" His voice startled her. "Whatever happened to his family?"

She gave him an agitated look.

"His legitimate family, I mean."

She didn't speak. Her eyes cleared and he could tell her mind had returned to the present and the matter at hand. But for how long?

"Wolfgang's wife, Gisela Fleischer moved to German Village in Columbus, Ohio after your father was executed as a Nazi war criminal. She had a son by him, your half-brother, who is five years older than you. Gisela died a few years back. I don't know whatever became of him."

"All you've ever told me is that my father was a war criminal. You never told me what he did to deserve to be executed."

"Some things you don't need to know, Scott."

"Mother. This I need to know." He'd never used this demanding tone with his mother and he could tell it startled her. "What exactly did he do?"

"Very well." His mother cradled the book against her chest again. "Your father was Commandant of the legendary Dachau Prison and Crematory. During the reign of the Third Reich, he, as did many of Hitler's higher ranking officers, hoarded some of the plundered treasures. He stored most of his cache in the salt mines not far from Dachau."

The woman on the embalming table moaned and started shivering. Scott Katzer went into the hall and returned with a blanket. He draped it over the woman then looked at his mother. She was still holding the book against her chest.

"Continue," he said.

"When the Allied Forces moved in and it became apparent that the Third Reich would fall, Wolfgang loaded his cache on trucks and brought it to Zugspitze."

"And that's when you met him?"

"No. I met him long before then," she explained, "he'd visited Schneefernerhaus Hotel and Resort on Zugspitze numerous times while he was commandant. He was the most handsome man I had ever met. That's when we became lovers."

"Where did he hide his hoard of treasures?"

"Wolfgang loved to hike. During the summer months he'd hike Reintal Valley east of the Resort. During those hikes, he'd discovered several deep limestone caves. When he fled Germany, he hid his cache in those caves then he crossed the border into Austria. He was headed for Italy, but was caught before he got there."

"You knew about the stolen treasures all along?" Scott eyed the woman on the table. Her trembling had stopped but he could tell she was still breathing by the up and down movement of the blanket.

"I went to his trial and was allowed to speak to him alone. He whispered to me about a journal that Hitler had given him for his birthday and where he had hidden it. He said to keep it a secret, that he wanted me to have it." She held the book out in front of her. "This is that journal. I had no idea what was in it until I read it."

"Where did he hide it?"

"Behind a wall in the Reintalanger Hut. I found it right where he said it was hidden. If he hadn't told me about it, it might never have been found."

"When did you find it?"

"Fall of 1945. A week after his execution, I went down to Reintalanger Hut and found the book."

"What about Adams? How did he get involved?"

"In 1945 after bombing Zugspitze and destroying the valley station of the Tyrolean Zugspitze Railway, the United States commandeered Schneefernerhaus. That was when I met Don. He started pursuing me from the beginning but I would have nothing to do with him. I just wasn't interested...until Wolfgang told me about the journal. When I read it, I knew I couldn't retrieve the treasure and get it out of Germany by myself."

"So you slept with Adams to get him to help you?"

"It was the only way." She placed her hand on the journal and rubbed it across the cover. "You must understand we were poor. I had two children to support, there was all the treasure sitting in those limestone caves, so I did what I had to do, Scott. Adams oversaw the return of dead American soldiers to the United States. He had the means to help me accomplish what I needed done. In December, he asked me to marry him and move to the States when his tour was up. That's when I came up with the plan to ship the treasures back in the caskets. He came up with the idea of using only caskets of soldiers who were mangled so badly that a closed casket ceremony was guaranteed. That way no one would be looking around inside. He logged each shipment in the journal by town, cemetery, and soldier's name. And what we put inside the casket. He either modified the casket lid so small light objects could be sealed inside or he made a false bottom for the heavier items. It was a good plan."

Scott Katzer knew what happened next. "You had him do your dirty work, retrieve the cache from the caves, ship it to the States, and then you double-crossed him."

"No. He double-crossed me. I caught him making entries in the journal about Wolfgang and his history. And about me."

"So you went after him and tried to kill him. In a way, you did kill him."

She stared at him and he knew what she was thinking. How could he question her judgment? But he'd had enough of his mother's commands. He would take over now.

He looked at the woman on the porcelain embalming table, struggling to take each breath. The woman so sick she would probably die even if he took her to a hospital. The quest for the journal had turned him into a criminal to satisfy his mother's desires. He was already implicated in the death of Samantha Connors. Now this woman was certainly going to be another victim as well.

He looked at his mother and could tell her thoughts had drifted again to another time. "You were wise to keep this a secret."

Heidi Katzer's head snapped around. Her eyes penetrated him. "You must never breathe a word of this to anyone. Do I make myself clear?"

He never got the chance to object to her tone.

Without warning, a man walked into the embalming room. He looked vaguely familiar but Katzer couldn't place him.

"And that is something," the intruder said. "I am here to ensure."

CHAPTER 42

Francesca Catanzaro waited across the street from Katzer Funeral Home. There had been no activity since Katzer and the old woman transported the casket from the van into the building. She speculated that Abigail Love must be inside. There was no way to know if Love was dead or alive. The last time she'd seen Love was in Butler. She was alive but had trouble walking. At first she thought Love was just exhausted from her run-in with Jake in Watauga Lake until Jake told her about the possibility of Love having decompression sickness.

It had been over an hour since Jake called in with Wiley's plan. She kept surveillance over the funeral home as he instructed. He'd relieve her when he got to Nashville. In the meantime it was her job to watch the building in case Katzer decided to leave. If he did, or Abigail Love appeared, she was to call him immediately.

Earlier Jake had informed her he was on Interstate 40 passing Crossville, Tennessee and would be there in an hour and a half. She checked the time, if Jake was right, then he should be arriving within the next fifteen minutes.

She was getting antsy. She'd been staking out the funeral home for almost three hours. She was hungry, thirsty, but mostly, she needed a restroom break.

She was about to get out to relieve herself when she noticed a dark figure in the shadows walking up the driveway toward the funeral home. She pulled her compact spotting scope to her eye and toggled it to infrared. In the dark green glow the man wore light colored pants and a jacket. From the back he looked like he had light colored hair.

The man walked up to the van, opened the door, and looked inside. He pulled back and walked to the side door and stopped.

She zoomed in as far as her spotting scope would allow her. The man turned and faced her, almost as if he knew she was there. Wanting her to see his face. The man raised his chin slightly, pushed his wire-rim glasses up on his nose and ran both hands through his hair. One hand behind the other. Then he disappeared into the building.

"Oh my God."

Elmore Wiley.

✝✝✝

Jake answered his cell phone and listened to Francesca's frantic message.

"Jake. Wiley just went into the funeral home. I thought we were going in tomorrow morning. What do you want me to do?"

"I had a hunch that sneaky bastard was up to something. His plan sounded contrived from the get-go. Maybe he thinks he can handle this alone. For some reason, it's personal. I think he's too close and has lost his objectivity." Jake punched a button on the device. "According to Fontaine's GPS, I'm passing the airport now and should be there in six minutes. Stay put. If you see any movement, let me know."

"Hurry, Jake. I've got a bad feeling about this."

She wasn't the only one who had a bad feeling about it. Wiley's impromptu intrusion added an unexpected element to the scenario. "Francesca, where are you?"

"Across the street from the funeral home…in the Mt. Olivet Cemetery. There is a cul-de-sac at the mausoleum. You'll see it on the right of the entrance when you get here. I have a bird's eye view of Katzer Funeral Home. She said. "Jake, he looked right at me. Like he knew I was here."

"He did. I told him you were watching. He wanted you to see him. He knew you'd call me. He's counting on us as backup…or for the end game."

Jake turned on Lebanon Pike from Spence Lane and drove west. One minute later he turned into the entrance to Mt. Olivet Cemetery.

"Jake? Is that you in the white SUV? Or am I going to have to shoot somebody?"

"Don't shoot. It's me. I'll be there in thirty seconds."

Jake parked next to her at the top of the hill. He and Francesca waited in his Tahoe while they discussed their options and devised a plan.

"Are you ready?"

Jake looked at his watch. "Nope. Ten more minutes."

"Ten more minutes? Why ten minutes? We need to move and move now."

"No," he said. "It's not time."

"Time for what? Wiley has been in there too long. Something could have happened to him."

"Wiley knew what he was doing when he went in there. And if I'm right, I know why."

"What if you're wrong?" Francesca looked worried.

"Then Wiley's already dead."

† † †

George Fontaine spent all day in his computer complex and it looked like he might very well have to spend all night. The computer he'd been tracking had not been back online in hours and, other than the scanned journal pages he'd viewed so far; most of what he'd downloaded was incomplete and unusable. The last time the computer was online was in Charlotte, North Carolina, which he couldn't connect to any information he'd collected thus far.

He hadn't had a chance to catch the news today so he decided to take a break and use the opportunity to read the USA Today on his iPad. He opened the app and noticed President Rebecca Rudd's emergency summit meeting in Indianapolis was the fifth article in importance out of the top stories. Top billing went to another bombing by Afghan insurgents. Wildfires in the West, the reappearances of several pieces of lost art, and tropical storm flooding in Galveston, Texas rounded out the top five.

Fontaine scanned through each article in his typical manner, only absorbing the highlights. The article that intrigued him the most was the sudden reappearance of famous paintings that disappeared during World War II. All recovered artwork was believed stolen by Hitler's Third Reich.

Although the article stated two priceless paintings suddenly appeared in the Hermitage Museum in 1995, *Place De La Concorde* by Edgar Degas and *White House at Night* by Vincent Van Gogh, what Fontaine found most intriguing was the recent recovery of two new pieces by the Metropolitan Museum of Art in New York. *Painter On The Road To Tarascon* by Vincent Van Gogh was believed destroyed during World War II but had reappeared along with *Portrait Of A Young Man* by Raphael. The museum refused to disclose the manner of recovery, only that they were confident the items would be verified authentic works of art.

Fontaine thought about the timing, it was too coincidental not to be related to the casket invasions of the past few weeks. Considering what he did know, the odds were ever increasing that whoever sold the lost paintings to the museum also recovered them from the robbed graves.

He stood and stretched and then he heard the beeping of an incoming alert. The computer was back online. He started the trace as his server resumed the download. He scanned through the data as it downloaded and compared what he saw to the news article he had just read. Both art paintings from the news articles were listed in the journal. Now he had confirmation instead of theory.

Another alert sounded signaling the completion of the IP trace.

Fort Collins, Colorado.

Fontaine smiled. "Gotcha."

CHAPTER 43

The lack of windows at the Katzer Funeral Home made it impossible to locate Wiley from the outside.

After walking the perimeter with Francesca, Jake realized the only way to locate the Old Man was to enter the building. What he would give to have the RTI unit now. One of Wiley's many *toys*, using strategically placed sensors, the enhanced radio tomographic imaging unit would have allowed him to use radio waves to scan through the walls of the funeral home, locate, and track the movements of every occupant inside. He'd used it successfully a year ago in Yemen on a rescue mission and knew it would come in handy now.

Jake and Francesca met at the side door where Katzer's van was parked. Jake tried the double glass doors but they were locked. He motioned to Francesca who pulled out her lock-picking tool and unlocked the door.

"How do you think Wiley got in?" He asked.

"Same way we did, I guess," she said, "he picked the lock."

"That doesn't make sense. Why would he lock it back? He knew we were coming."

"Maybe he didn't lock it." She paused. "Maybe someone else did."

"In that case." Jake pulled out his handgun. Francesca followed suit. "They might be expecting us." He eased the door open hoping no chime would sound alerting the Katzers of their intrusion. None did. The receiving foyer was a fifteen-foot wide hallway that extended for twenty feet before it ended. Two opposing narrower halls extended perpendicular to the landing, one toward the front of the funeral home, and one toward the back.

The one to the front was dark.

"It's got to be this way." Jake motioned to the rear of the building.

Francesca nodded.

The hallway stretched all the way to the back of the building before making a ninety-degree turn. The lights were off in the hall but Jake could see the glow from an illuminated room coming from around the corner.

Two doors on the right. One on the left. All empty. The doors on the right were offices, the one on the left was the preparation room. A vast assortment of makeup and applicators lined the racks and shelves. An exit door along the rear wall of the building was labeled *Crematorium*.

Jake took a quick glance around the corner. The hallway was empty. A door at the end of the hall was open and the room occupied. He heard voices. He turned to Francesca, she was holding her finger in front of her lips. She'd heard them too.

He reached the doorway and glimpsed inside the room, almost everything was stainless steel. The room glistened under the bright overhead lights. Three white tables were pushed against a far wall with what looked like huge vents hovering over each one. On one table was a woman covered in a blanket. He assumed she was Abigail Love.

The table next to her—Elmore Wiley.

A tall thin man paced the floor muttering to himself. Had to be Scott Katzer, Jake thought. There was no sign of the old woman.

Jake signaled Francesca and they entered the room, guns drawn.

The man looked at Jake.

"You."

† † †

Scott Katzer was shocked when the man and the woman walked in the room pointing their guns at him. He didn't recognize her, but the man's face he knew. He was the man who brandished the gun in Charleston and kicked in the front door of Ashley Regan's house. The man whose presence prompted him to call 9-1-1.

"Guess I know why you're here," he said.

The man nodded at the woman. She walked over and freed the old man from the embalming table.

"Mr. Wiley, you okay?" She asked him.

"I'm fine."

"Why didn't you wait for us?" The younger man asked the older man.

"I thought I'd storm the Castle."

"What was all that talk about knowing the lay of the land first?" The younger man rebuked.

"Things didn't exactly go as planned." The old man pointed. "This woman is very sick."

"Is that Abigail Love?" The younger man asked.

"Who is Abigail Love?" Katzer asked. "All I know is this is the woman who followed you from Ashley Regan's house in Charleston to Butler, Tennessee. How she knew to go there is anyone's guess."

"She's an assassin," the young woman said. "She was paid to locate and acquire the book." She pointed to the young man. "And then kill him."

"She won't be killing anybody anytime soon," Katzer said. "I don't know what's wrong with her but whatever it is, she's getting worse."

"She has the bends," the younger man said. "Decompression sickness. If she doesn't get to a hyperbaric chamber soon, she will die. It might be too late already. She was deep underwater for too long when something startled her. She ascended too fast with no decompression stops. She has excess nitrogen bubbles in her bloodstream which have lodged throughout her body."

The younger man walked over to the embalming table where the sick woman was lying. He checked her vital signs. "Her real name was Deborah Layne." He pulled the blanket over the woman's head. "And she's dead."

"Good riddance, I say." Scott Katzer recognized his mother's voice.

She was standing in the doorway pointing a gun at the three intruders.

† † †

"Drop your weapons," the old woman shouted. She had the leather journal clutched in one hand.

Jake made a quick assessment of their predicament. He nodded and dropped his handgun to the floor. Francesca did the same.

"Now. Both of you use a foot and kick the guns to me," she ordered, "and don't try anything. I may be old but I can still pull a trigger."

Jake and Francesca did as she requested. Jake instinctively brushed his arm against his waistband. The pocketknife Wiley gave him last year was concealed there. Jake always carried his knife. Just like Francesca always had a dagger strapped on the inside of her right leg. He looked at her. Her eye blink was imperceptible to anyone but him.

"Scott, get over here and collect their guns."

Scott Katzer collected the weapons, tucked one behind his belt and held the other on Jake, Wiley, and Francesca.

"All of these women have been difficult." She pointed at a table with the barrel of the gun. The table with the dead Abigail Love lying on it. "This one always groaning and wouldn't shut up. Then there was that Ashley Regan woman who took my book," the old woman held up the journal, "and gallivanted all over the countryside stealing what was rightfully mine."

"Rightfully yours?" Jake said.

"Yes." The woman shook the gun at him. Her face flushed. "Rightfully mine." She looked at Scott. "There was also that woman you grabbed by mistake."

"Sam Connors?"

"*Samantha* Connors." The old woman corrected. "Ashley Regan's roommate."

"What did you do to her?"

Silence.

"What did you do to her?" Jake stared at the old woman. "Did you kill her too?"

"It was a simple case of mistaken identity. She is no longer a concern." The old woman said.

Jake studied Katzer's mother. She clutched the book against her chest with her free hand. She was visibly agitated. Which made her dangerous.

"How many more have to die because of that book?" Jake pointed to the journal.

"As many as it takes." Her voice trailed off. "As many as it takes to protect this family."

"Mother? Scott? What the hell is going on?"

Jake knew that voice. He looked past the old woman.

President Rebecca Rudd stood in the doorway.

CHAPTER 44

Rebecca Rudd entered the embalming room. Jake observed the distressed look on her face. Understandable, considering the bombshell just dropped in her lap.

"You heard?" Jake asked.

"I heard enough." She looked at Scott Katzer and then Heidi Katzer. "How could you?"

Neither mother nor brother said a word.

"How did you know?" Wiley asked Rudd.

"I told her," Jake said.

Wiley pointed his finger at Jake. "I'll deal with you later." He turned to Rudd. "Rebecca, you shouldn't be here. I want you to leave. Now."

"No, Elmore." Rudd looked at Wiley. Her voice changed. "This is the one place I should be. And don't blame Jake. After you called me, I called him. I put him on the spot. He couldn't say no to the President. Jake did exactly what you asked him to do."

Rudd stepped toward her mother.

The old woman was visibly shaken, her aging body trembled. It seemed the one thing she didn't want to happen just did. Her daughter, the President of the United States, had discovered the truth.

"Mother, what have you done?"

"Whatever it took to protect you." Heidi Katzer started crying. "I've spent most of my life wondering if this book would ever surface. When you first went into politics, I tried to stop you. But you were so innocent and naïve. You said you had nothing to hide, that you had never done anything wrong. But Rebecca, our closet is full of skeletons."

"What are you saying?" Rudd looked at her brother. "Scott, what have you done? What skeletons is she talking about? I thought that book only contained the locations of Nazi treasures shipped to the United States in caskets of World War II casualties." Rudd walked over to Heidi. She raised her voice and pleaded to her mother. "What else is in that book? Tell me now."

"Don't say a word." Wiley yelled at Rudd's mother.

"This book belonged to your real father."

† † †

Had she heard her mother right? Her *real* father. Matthew Katzer was the only father she'd ever known. He had been a loving father and good provider for the family. When she received word he had died in a tragic accident, she was devastated. She rushed home from college to be with her mother. She thought Matthew Katzer was the only man her mother had ever loved.

Until now.

"What do you mean my real father? I remember when Daddy died. I had to console you. You cried for two days. We cried together. I refuse to believe Matthew Katzer was not my real father." Rudd pointed to the leather journal under her mother's arm. "Let me have the book."

"No," Wiley said. "Listen to me, Rebecca. I told you before and I'll reiterate it now. It is in your best interest not to know what's in that book."

"If this book says Matthew Katzer is not my biological father, then as the President, as your daughter, I demand to know who my real father is." Rudd turned to her brother. "Scott, who is our father?"

Scott turned to their mother. "She has a right to know."

Her mother stared at the floor for a few seconds then raised her head. "Your real father is Wolfgang Fleischer."

If Rebecca Rudd had tried to think of the worst possible answer, she never could have matched that name. The name of a man reviled in history books. She felt light headed.

"Wolfgang Fleischer? The Dachau Prison Nazi war criminal?"

Her mother nodded.

Rudd collapsed to the floor.

†††

When President Rebecca Rudd fainted, Jake rushed toward her only to be forced away by Scott Katzer and the handgun he was holding. Jake's Glock. Katzer motioned for Jake to stand next to Wiley and Francesca.

Katzer walked over to a cabinet, grabbed a bottle from a shelf, and soaked a cotton ball with the liquid from the bottle. He waved it under his sister's nose and she slowly opened her eyes.

While the Katzers attended to Rudd, Jake leaned closer to Wiley. "Who the hell is Wolfgang Fleischer?"

"Ever heard of the holocaust?" Wiley asked.

Jake nodded.

"Fleischer was the commandant of the Dachau political prison and concentration camp during World War II. Under his command, over 15,000 political prisoners were executed, most in the Dachau gas chambers, and then cremated."

"Cremated?" Jake lowered his voice. "Do you see the irony in all this?"

Wiley shook his head.

"Fleischer was in the business of disposing of dead bodies...and so are the Katzers." Jake saw Wiley's lips turn up. "It's the proverbial 'apple doesn't fall far from the tree' thing."

Francesca whispered. "And she found someone to ship all Fleischer's stolen treasure in caskets."

Heidi Katzer raised her gun. "You three. Be quiet."

Scott helped his sister to her feet and walked her to a chair. She sat down and looked at her mother.

"Where was I born?" Rudd asked. "And no more lies."

"In your grandmother's house in Ehrwald, Austria."

"When?"

"March 15, 1944. You and your brother were less than ten minutes apart."

"But our birth certificates say June 6, 1946 in Nashville. How can they be wrong?"

"I was a nurse. I came here in April of 1946 and got a job at Protestant Hospital. Baptist Hospital now. I had easy access to birth certificates. It wasn't that difficult to do. That's where I met Matthew. I put you in school when you were eight years old and claimed you were six."

Rudd hung her head low. Jake could tell the President had full comprehension of the magnitude of what her mother just told her.

"I can't be President," Rudd mumbled. "I was never even eligible in the first place." She looked at her mother and yelled. "Why didn't you stop me? Do you have any idea what you have done?"

Rudd stood. "And for God's sake, put down those guns."

"No," Heidi said. "Not until there are no witnesses." She motioned with her gun. "No loose ends."

"You can not kill them." Rudd said. "Haven't you heard a word Mr. Wiley has said? He is on my side. These people," Rudd pointed to Jake and Francesca, "have been working behind the scenes to keep this from blowing up in our faces. All this time, they've been trying to protect me. It's too late for protection now. I know the truth, as ugly as it is, and there is only one thing left for me to do. Tomorrow I will step down as President of the United States. And I'll do it at the summit meeting."

Rudd stepped in front of her mother. "Now give me the gun."

"No, Rebecca. I can't let you do this."

Rudd grabbed at the gun in her mother's hands.

A single shot rang out.

CHAPTER 46

Scott Katzer watched his sister stagger backward and fall to her knees, an expression of disbelief on her face. Her hand cupped her side where the bullet passed through. Blood oozed through her slender fingers. Wiley rushed toward her. Scott raised his gun and shot the old man in the shoulder. Wiley stumbled backward, hit his head on an embalming table, fell to the floor, and didn't move.

After Wiley fell, Scott pointed the gun at Jake. "Don't move." Too much was happening too fast. Did his mother really shoot his sister? Her own daughter? He knew she had an evil, ruthless side, but he never thought she would harm her only daughter.

"Rebecca." His mother cried out. She grabbed her chest and doubled over. "Oh God, what have I done?"

He looked at his sister. The side of her white blouse covered in blood.

She outstretched her bloody hand. "Scott. Mother."

He turned around and saw his mother lying on the floor clutching her chest. His father's leather journal had fallen beside her.

The young man named Jake stepped forward.

Scott pointed the gun at him. "Stop."

"I need to help the President," he said. "Please. Let me help your sister."

He looked at his sister and then his mother. "Okay. Help her. And you." He aimed the gun at the young woman. For some reason, he was afraid of her. "Sit down against the wall. And don't move."

"No. I need to help Mr. Wiley," she yelled.

"He'll be fine." Katzer waved the barrel toward Wiley then back at her. "You, stay still."

He knelt down beside his mother. Her wrinkled face was fully red. Her hand still clutching her chest, fingers squeezed tight. "Mother. Mother. Can you hear me?"

"My journal." His mother raised her head and stretched her arm across the floor. "My journal." Her eyes momentarily opened wide then slowly closed for the last time. Her head fell to the floor.

His sister cried out. "Mother. No." She started sobbing.

† † †

Jake sat down beside the President and checked her wound. The bullet made an entrance and exit wound, a superficial injury, about two inches above her hipbone. Fortunately for the world, she was not gravely injured. He held pressure on her wound while the President watched her mother collapse to the floor and die. Tears flowed down her cheeks. She buried her head into Jake's chest. He wrapped his free arm around her.

"Mr. Katzer," Jake said. "Your sister is President of the United States and she needs your help. She needs medical attention. We must get her out of here."

Jake looked at the old woman curled in the fetal position on the floor, hand still clutching her chest. Her painful expression had turned peaceful. It would remain a mystery why she shot her own daughter. Probably a misfire when Rebecca Rudd grabbed the gun.

"Scott," Rudd called out. "Why? Why did all this happen?"

Katzer sat on the floor next to his dead mother. He let the gun rest on his leg, hand still grasping the grip, finger still on the trigger. "I don't know. You've been gone a long time. You don't know Mother like I do. She's not a good person."

"How long have you known about our father? About that book?" Rudd asked.

"A long time, Rebecca."

Francesca moved and Katzer raised the gun. "I said don't move." She raised her hands.

"Ten years? Twenty?" Rudd asked. "Why didn't she say something? Why didn't she stop me from running for President?"

"I think it all happened so fast and you were so excited and enthusiastic about helping the nation and the people. She couldn't bear to crush your dreams." Katzer let the gun rest on his leg again. "She made me do things to protect you. Horrible things."

"Horrible things? What do you mean?" Rudd groaned as she tried to move. "You mean kill people?"

"No. All I did was capture them. Mother did all the killing." Katzer's voice choked. "She tortured the first woman. Strapped her to that table and tortured her. She burned her with the heat spatula and when she found out she wasn't the woman with the book, she went crazy and killed her. She stuck a drain in her jugular and bled her out. Right here on the table." He stared into his sister's eyes. "But I would have killed to protect you...your reputation. We're family. That's what family does, protect each other."

"No. No." Rudd started weeping harder. "This is wrong. This is a nightmare."

Wiley grunted and mumbled.

Katzer turned his head to look.

Jake saw Francesca make her move and shoved Rudd to the floor, shielding her body with his. Rudd groaned in agony. He kept his hand pressed against her wound while he held her down.

The blade of Francesca's dagger struck Katzer in the chest just below his left collarbone. He yelled and fired a shot at Francesca. He missed. Francesca ran toward Katzer. Katzer raised the gun again and fired.

"Scott. No." Rudd yelled.

His second shot missed.

Francesca kept running.

Katzer's third shot struck Francesca in the upper arm. Shaken, she slowed but kept attacking. Katzer was on his feet by the time Francesca reached him. She grabbed him and their momentum carried them against an embalming table. Katzer pushed her away, grabbed the HVAC hood, and smashed it against her head. She staggered back. Blood trickled from her forehead. He kicked her in the stomach. When she doubled over, he slammed his fist into the back of her head knocking her to the floor.

Jake heard Wiley's voice.

Wiley pushed up on one elbow. "Jake, I'll take care of Rebecca."

Jake sprang to his feet and lunged at Katzer striking his arm. Katzer's gun clattered across the floor. He jabbed Katzer in the ribcage. The older man grunted and stepped back. He threw another punch at Katzer's chin but whiffed. Katzer's long arm made a roundhouse swing at Jake, landing squarely on his jaw.

Katzer was taller than Jake with a longer reach. He was also stronger than Jake had anticipated, especially for a man in his sixties. The jolt made his knees momentarily weaken.

He dove into Katzer, knocking him to the floor. He grabbed the dagger, still stuck in Katzer's chest, and wrenched it from side to side. Katzer screamed. The man's face turned blood red. During the struggle Katzer managed to grab his handgun and, before Jake knew what happened, pistol-whipped him across the side of the head. He fell flat on his back and Katzer pounced on top of him with his hand gripped around Jake's throat.

In a daze, Jake's head pounded.

"Scott. Stop!" Rudd screamed.

Katzer ignored his sister's pleas.

Jake grappled at Katzer's hands but couldn't pry the man's fingers free from the death grip around his neck. He couldn't breath. He swung at the older man, but the man's long arms kept him at bay. His breathing labored. Vision blurred.

He knew he only had seconds before he'd black out. His ears started ringing. How did this old man get the upper hand? This man was President Rebecca Rudd's brother. For her sake, he'd tried not to use lethal force on her brother, even though the man clearly didn't feel the same way. But now it was a matter of survival. All bets were off.

Katzer pointed the gun at Jake's face.

Jake stealthily slipped his right hand to his waist searching for his knife. He pulled it out and with the flick of his thumb the spring-assisted blade snapped open. As he readied his arm to plunge the blade into the man's gut, the deafening blast from a gun fired at close range pounded in his ears.

Katzer's shirt turned red. Blood splattered on Jake's face. The man fell on top of him. Jake felt the full weight from Katzer's body squeezing him next to the floor. He heaved the lifeless man, rolling him to the side, and turned to see where the shot came from.

President Rebecca Rudd's hands shook as she held the gun.

Rudd was hysterical. Her eyes streamed tears. "Is he alive?" Her fingers slowly opened and the gun dropped to the floor.

Jake leaned down and checked for a pulse. There was none. The President of the United States had witnessed her mother die of a heart attack and then killed her twin brother.

"No, ma'am. Your brother is dead."

Francesca found bandages and alcohol in a closet and brought them to Wiley.

"How's the head?" Jake asked Francesca.

"Pounding. How's yours?"

"The same."

She cleaned and dressed the wounds of the injured Rudd and Wiley.

"Elmore, what do I do now?" Rudd's voice broken between sobs.

"Rebecca, you do what you were going to do before all this happened. It's over now. Go back to being the same President you were."

"You know I can't do that. I just killed my brother. He is dead...at my hand. You heard what was said, I'm not even a natural born citizen of the United States. I took an oath to preserve, protect and defend the constitution of the United States. I'm ineligible to be President."

"You saved my life. You made a decision to sacrifice somebody you loved to do the right thing." Jake interrupted. Rudd and Wiley looked at him. "The people of the United States wanted you to be President and if you'll recall, you won by one of the largest margins in Presidential election history.

You have the summit meeting tomorrow. Your country needs you. Don't let them down."

"Jake's right," Wiley said. "You can't bail out on this meeting now."

"But Elmore. After what's happened here tonight, how do I explain it?"

"You don't." Wiley explained. "Let the news come to you and handle it accordingly."

"I can't do that, Elmore, it's wrong."

Jake hadn't noticed Francesca was gone until she walked back in with an armful of clothes, a marble-sized knot on her forehead.

"I found these in your mother's office. You'll need to change before we leave." Francesca said.

"I need to stay. I just can't do this." Rudd began to cry again.

"Madam President," Jake said softly, "you have no choice. It's your job."

"Jake's right. He will sanitize things here." Wiley said. "I'm taking you back to Indianapolis. You have the summit meeting tomorrow. Your country needs you to be strong."

CHAPTER 47

Jake pulled his seatbelt snug while the Citation readied for the 8:00 a.m. departure from the Nashville airport. He read George Fontaine's message for a second time. The subject line said it all:

It ain't over yet til the fat lady sings!

The attached file explained how Fontaine had cracked the blackmailer's computer and had discovered the next targeted cemetery, including the name on the plot. Fontaine's best guess was that the grave would be hit tonight.

Wiley and Francesca escorted President Rebecca Rudd from her family's funeral home business back to Indianapolis on Wiley's personal jet last night just after midnight. Not the same jet he used to covertly fly her to Nashville earlier in the evening. Jake made those arrangements using the Citation that flew him to the Tri-Cities airport in northeastern Tennessee the day before. Wiley had been insistent she attend the summit meeting as if nothing had happened. Jake knew Wiley was right. The news would likely reach Rudd before her summit meeting commenced and her reaction had to be convincing. The world would be watching and she'd have to make the performance of her life.

Jake hadn't slept at all. Wiley had given him specific instructions on how he wanted Jake to clean up the scene from the night's unfortunate turn of events.

Jake surfed through the media websites on his iPad. It was the top story on all the news outlets:

PRESIDENT'S FAMILY KILLED IN TRAGIC CREMATORY EXPLOSION

Every article explained it the same way, a natural gas line leading to the crematorium exploded trapping the President's mother and brother inside the funeral home. Due to the crematorium's proximity to the rear of the funeral home, Rudd's family was trapped in the inferno that engulfed the building. Fire officials indicated the Katzer Funeral Home was completely destroyed. The Press Secretary stated that President Rebecca Rudd was shaken by the news but remained focused on leading the summit leaders through to successful completion of negotiations.

According to Fontaine's message, Francesca had flown with Wiley to El Paso where he could privately seek medical attention for his gunshot wound. Last night was the second time the Old Man had been shot while he was on a mission with Jake. He handled the injury better than most men half his age. For a man in his early seventies, his stamina never ceased to amaze Jake.

After dropping Wiley off in El Paso, Francesca was taken back to Tennessee to start her search for Christa Barnett. Fontaine had gotten a hit on Regan's rental car in Knoxville. Wiley sent her there to locate and retrieve the woman for debriefing.

Wiley took the leather journal with him with the promise to President Rudd that when he returned the book to her, it would never again be a burden but a benefit. His cryptic remark left Jake puzzled.

Jake was growing weary of this mission. In the beginning he was intrigued by the prestige of becoming the personal emissary to the President of the United States but now he'd been in too many cemeteries, seen too much death, and was ready for a change of scenery.

Thankfully, he could feel the mission coming to an end. There were only two loose ends left.

The blackmailer.

And Christa Barnett.

Could it be that Barnett and the blackmailer were one and the same? Or perhaps co-conspirators? After all, she was fluent in the German language. She had translated the book. She conspired with Ashley Regan. Or maybe there was a third conspirator all along. One Regan or Barnett brought in. One that was working the other half of the list of graves. The ones containing the lost artwork. The ones belonging to black soldiers.

Jake had been dispatched to take down the blackmailer. Elmore Wiley had tasked Francesca with locating Barnett and bringing her in to Commonwealth Consultants for interrogation.

According to Fontaine's briefing he'd tracked the blackmailer's computer from the Charlotte, North Carolina airport to the Phoenix, Arizona airport to Denver. The flight times matched the air carrier schedule of U. S. Airways. After matching the stolen art listed in the journal with the blackmailer's new location, the only feasible target was the Grandview Cemetery in Fort Collins, Colorado.

Jake leaned back in his comfortable leather seat as the Citation accelerated down the runway. It was just over a thousand miles to the Fort Collins-Loveland Airport, which meant he had two hours to take a nap. Then it would be time to end Project Resurrection once and for all. He crossed his arms and rested them on his chest, took a few deeps breaths, and drifted off to sleep.

While the Citation taxied to the jet center at the small airport, Jake shook off the cobwebs from his deep sleep, pulled out his customized iPad, and checked his messages. A single message from George Fontaine. According to the message, when the computer Fontaine was tracking came back online, he ran an IP trace and verified the blackmailer's computer was in Fort Collins. Just as Fontaine had expected. And best of all, confirmation of the blackmailer's identity.

Jake smiled. He knew it was almost over.

After the pilot shut down the jet's engines, Jake grabbed his backpack and walked toward the building with the red canopy hanging over the door. He found a comfortable recliner in the pilot's lounge of the jet center and connected his iPad to the fixed base operator's wifi. Jake opened the file Fontaine attached to the email and sifted through the data accumulated thus far.

Analyzing the shipping pattern of Major Don Adams seemed simple. It was the man's rationale Jake was having trouble understanding.

The Major only shipped remains of soldiers whose bodies had been so badly mutilated that a closed casket ceremony was ensured. In some instances, as in the case of Norman Albert Reese Jr., the only personal items inside the casket were shreds of the man's tattered uniform.

Adams had shipped the famous paintings stolen by the Third Reich in sealed packaging hidden in compartments within the dome-shaped lids on the caskets. Sections of the wood strips that interior trimming was attached, was cut out to make room for the artwork. The sealed artwork was then inserted into the slot and the trimming reattached.

When Adams shipped heavier items, as in this case stolen gold, silver, and jewels, he had designed a shallow false bottom that rested on top of the casket's ribbed bottom reinforcements. The false bottom was divided in to small compartments to avoid the heavier items from shifting when the casket was lifted. The balance of weight and the lack of substantial remains created the ideal deception that a body was inside.

All in all, Adams methods and ingenuity were brilliant. His mistake was dying before he had a chance to recover the items. One thing Jake was having trouble understanding was why Major Don Adams matched the stolen artwork with the caskets of black soldiers and the gold, silver, and jewels with caskets of white soldiers?

Jake closed the flap of his iPad cover putting the display to sleep. He leaned back in the recliner and closed his eyes.

It was going to be another long night.

CHAPTER 48

Fort Collins rested near the northern end of Colorado's Front Range along the Cache La Poudre River. He parked his rental car in Old Town and walked through Old Town Square, which he thought was more a triangle than a square. At the recommendation of one of the local pilots, Jake planned to eat lunch at a sidewalk café called Austin's American Grill.

Before he ate though, he had some time to kill so he walked around the Fort Collins Historic District and spotted the downtown visitor's information center. Inside he found a brochure about the history of Fort Collins cemeteries in a slot on one wall. The brochure gave a description and address of the Grandview Cemetery. He folded the brochure and slipped it in his back pocket.

While he waited for his food at the sidewalk café, he noticed the street sign. He was at the corner of College Street and Mountain Avenue. It seemed every town with a college had a College Street. Fort Collins was no different. He remembered passing Colorado State University on his way from the airport to Old Town.

According to the brochure, Grandview Cemetery was a mile and a half west of where he sat.

The clear blue skies and low humidity were a refreshing change from the heat and humidity of Nashville. The crisp air here was exhilarating. In the shade the 74-degree temperature seemed cool, in the sun, not so much. He'd heard there were forest fires in the mountains to the west but he'd yet to see any sign of smoke in the distant sky.

After lunch he drove his rental car west on Mountain Avenue. The tree-lined historic street was straight and divided by a grassy median. A street car came from the opposite direction along rails in the median. Birney Car 21.

A city park came into view on the left as Mountain Avenue appeared to dead end. When he stopped at the dead end he saw the large stone sign in front of him.

Grandview Cemetery
Established 1887

Jake entered the cemetery and pulled forward to a small stone building covered with vines that obscured half of the facade. A clay colored chimney rose from the flat roof. The sign by the door identified it as the cemetery office.

Jake walked in and found a woman talking on the phone, her unfinished salad lunch on her L-shaped desk. Her business cards were in a plastic container in front of her chair. Her title read Administrative Aide for the City of Fort Collins Culture, Parks, Recreation & Environment department. What a long title, he thought. She propped the phone to her ear with her shoulder while she rifled through papers on her desk. From what he could gather from the one-sided conversation, she was explaining to the person on the other end about the availability of plots in the cemetery.

The woman looked up and smiled as she hung up the phone. "May I help you?"

Jake pointed to her salad. "I'm in no rush. Please, finish your lunch."

"It's been one of those days. Busy. Busy. Busy. I've been nibbling on my lunch for the past two hours. My computer went down. And the phone won't stop ringing."

"Is it like that all the time?" Jake asked.

"No, usually it's dead around here." The woman smiled. "So to speak. What can I do for you?"

"I need to find someone's plot."

"Dead or alive? There are 34,000 plots in this cemetery and 23,000 have somebody in them."

"Dead. Interred in 1946. World War II casualty."

"That eliminates everything on this side of the canal. On a normal day I would just look it up for you but, as I said, my computer is down." She handed him two pieces of paper. "Here's a map of the cemetery and instructions to access the Fort Collins website. If you have access to a computer, you can look it up yourself. The server is working, it's just my computer that's on the fritz."

Jake took the papers and thanked the woman. Her phone started ringing again.

"We have several World War II veterans and casualties scattered throughout the cemetery but the majority of them are buried in Section E." She picked up the phone. "Hold please." She placed the receiver down.

"Section E?"

"Section E was designed and plotted to commemorate how this city's forefathers traveled here, by wagon train. Section E is laid out in a circular hub and spoke pattern. Like a wagon wheel. You'll understand when you see the website."

Jake raised the papers. "Thank you." He turned and walked out of the office.

He got back in his car, pulled out his iPad, and logged in to the Fort Collins website. It was a good thing she gave him the instruction sheet because the website was not very intuitive. When he reached the Grandview Cemetery page, he used the search feature and entered the name George Fontaine had given him. After he located the gravesite he was looking for, he clicked in the checkbox by the name and hit 'Zoom to Selected.' The virtual map zoomed in and detailed the plot in the graveyard. The woman in the office was right, the plot for Section E did mimic a wagon wheel.

Jake started the car and drove into the cemetery.

He crossed a concrete bridge that spanned a small canal. Rustic stone sidewalls with built-in flower receptacles lined the bridge. He circled around Section E until he was near the location of the grave, parked his car, and walked into the cemetery scanning for the marker with the correct name. Walking through the rows of headstones, looking at the names and lifespan of the deceased, Jake thought about how many young men had lost their lives protecting this country. His father and grandfather had served in the Navy, just as he had.

In another section of the cemetery were a young woman and small child. She held the little girl with one hand and carried fresh flowers in her other. They stopped at a gravesite where the woman knelt down and placed the flowers in a metal vase.

A short distance beyond them was a maintenance man trimming grass with a hand-held trimmer. Blue smoke billowed from the machine. The hum of the gas-powered engine filled the air.

His eyes stopped at a large silver spruce tree. Beneath it was a spire shaped granite marker. The name engraved in the stone was Michael Patterson Roundtree. A 1945 casualty of World War II.

The name George Fontaine had given him.

Jake pulled out his phone, marked it with his enhanced GPS, and smiled. "I'll be back tonight, Mr. Roundtree."

CHAPTER 49

According to the Fort Collins website, Michael Patterson Roundtree was a military veteran. No other designation. According to Fontaine's research, in 1992, Roundtree was posthumously awarded the Medal of Honor for bravery in action during combat.

What Jake found most interesting was what the journal described hidden inside Roundtree's casket. In 1944, seven paintings by Peter Paul Rubens, among others, were looted from Gemäldegalerie, an art museum in Berlin. One painting by Rubens, believed stolen by the Russians, was rumored hidden somewhere in Moscow or St. Petersburg, but Adams's notations in the journal told of a different fate of the famous artwork. The entry in the journal beside the name Roundtree listed *The March of the Silenus* by Peter Paul Rubens as sealed inside his casket.

Jake checked his watch, 3:15 p.m., at least nine hours before the blackmailer would try to make a move on the Grandview Cemetery. To satisfy his curiosity, he decided to go to the Main Library to research Michael Patterson Roundtree. He parked in the lot on Remington Street where East Oak Street ends and walked the two blocks toward the library.

He liked Old Town Fort Collins. It was interesting how locals liked to brag about the history of their towns. He'd learned some of the unique architecture in Old Town served as inspiration for Disneyland's Main Street USA. He wondered if after tonight they would brag about the discovery of long lost art found in a graveyard. He smiled.

The fresh air was crisp and clean. And dry. The high humidity in the east during the summer was like living in a sauna. He liked the big trees planted decades ago throughout downtown. Colorado's Front Range was a barren high desert typically devoid of trees. Fort Collins seemed an exception.

When he walked past the St. Peters Fly Shop on East Oak Street, he had an overwhelming urge to try his hand at fly-fishing in the area. He'd heard the streams and rivers in Northern Colorado were brimming with trout. He fought off his desire to go in the shop, determined to end Project Resurrection tonight.

He passed the boarded up Fort Collins Museum. The sign in front of the closed museum indicated it had been relocated a few blocks away. Behind the museum was the Old Town branch of the Poudre River Public Library. He entered the recently remodeled library and was directed to the second floor to access the reference section and the library computers.

Within minutes of using the library's computers, he found what he was searching for, a 1992 newspaper article about Michael Patterson Roundtree's posthumous awarding of the Medal of Honor. The photo attached with the article showed a young man in uniform the day he was shipped off to Germany in 1944 to fight in World War II.

The man in the picture was black.

✝✝✝

Francesca located Ashley Regan's rental car in front of an urgent care facility in Knoxville, Tennessee. If Jake was right about decompression sickness, she was surprised Christa Barnett was able to drive this far without medical attention.

Francesca entered the urgent care's lobby and walked directly to the receptionist. She placed a photo of Barnett on the counter and pulled her counterfeit FBI credentials from her pocket. "I need to speak to the doctor in charge of this patient immediately." She demanded.

"I'm sorry, ma'am. But he's with a patient right now."

"This can't wait. Get him."

"But, ma'am."

"Get him." Francesca's tone changed to match her frustration with the receptionist.

A minute later a man with a graying mustache in a white lab coat came through the door. "I'm Dr. Miller. What's this about?"

Francesca put the picture in front of him. "It's about this woman. Is she here?"

"What's she done?" He asked.

"Dr. Miller, I'm not here to answer questions. I'm here to get my questions answered. Now, is this woman here?"

"She came in last night. I sent her to U-T Medical Center."

"U-T? What's that?"

"University of Tennessee Medical Center."

"I see." Francesca looked at the doctor. She didn't like him. He'd already copped a defensive posture. "What was wrong with her?"

"Doctor-Patient privilege."

She had had it with his insolent attitude. "Dr. Miller, every heard of the Patriot Act? This is a matter of national security so I suggest you cooperate or I'll haul your ass in for interfering with an investigation. Now this is the last time I'll ask. What was wrong with her?"

"She had fever and chills accompanied with stiffness in her arms and legs. Said she was scuba diving and surfaced too fast. I sent her to UT Medical Center for hyperbaric oxygen therapy."

"Thank you, doctor." Francesca stepped closer. "Now that wasn't so difficult was it?"

She turned and left never giving Miller a chance to respond. She called Wiley with the news.

By the time she got to the Hyperbaric Oxygen Therapy room at the University of Tennessee Medical Center, Wiley had posted armed guards at the door. Through the window she saw a small room with several machines and a clear tube in the middle. A male nurse and woman in a lab coat were inside. She assumed the treating physician was the woman standing over the clear tube talking to the woman lying inside the chamber.

After Francesca identified herself, the guards let her pass. She entered the room and got the attention of the physician. "Is this Christa Barnett?" She asked.

"That's about all I know," the doctor said. "That and she had some sort of scuba diving accident."

"Are you her treating physician?" Francesca asked.

"Yes." The woman held out her hand. "Dr. Flanagan."

Francesca shook her hand. Flanagan wasn't a tall woman, several inches shorter than she was. She had thick brown hair and a pleasing smile. "Dr. Flanagan, has Ms. Barnett indicated how the accident happened?"

"No. She hasn't said much of anything. She's traumatized and very emotional."

Francesca looked at the chamber. She could see Barnett's eyes were red and swollen from crying. "How much longer in the chamber?"

The doctor looked at her watch. "She's been in there since around nine o'clock last night so what's that, twenty hours? I should be able to release her in the morning provided she gets follow up care. She still isn't out of the woods. "

"Can she be released sooner?" Francesca asked.

"I don't want to risk it." She pointed to the door. "Is all that really necessary? Two guards? She can't even get out of the chamber unless it's opened from the outside."

"I'm afraid so, doctor. And make it three guards."

"Three?"

"I'll be staying all night as well."

† † †

Jake parked his rental behind the Fort Collins Housing Authority building on Mountain Avenue. He pulled into an empty slot between a beat up dark colored van with plastic taped over the left rear window and a flat bed truck. It was approaching midnight and he hadn't seen any cars in the past five minutes.

He slipped a silenced Glock into the holster. A throw down weapon, just in case. He grabbed his penlight and night vision spyglass from his backpack, and slipped them into pockets in his specially designed tactical wardrobe. Lastly, he pulled a black beanie cap over his head to camouflage his blond hair.

When he stepped from the vehicle he felt ready for anything.

He avoided the streetlights as he made the less than five-minute walk to the Grandview Cemetery. He passed the darkened cemetery office building. A light breeze stirred the vines draping from the roof. The sky was clear and the moon was bright. In the moonlight, the headstones struck a strong contrast against the dark green grass.

He crossed the stone bridge spanning the small canal and could see the amber glow from the forest fires behind the mountains to the west.

It had been Colorado's worst fire year on record and had been in the news for weeks. And as bad as the fires were west of Fort Collins, the fires further to the south were even worse. According to the local newspaper, this year's fires had closed Lory State Park just west of Horsetooth Reservoir. Tourists, hikers, and campers were forced to evacuate with less than a day's notice. Fire tankers were flown in from all over the United States and Canada to help but when the fires broke out to the south, many of those tankers were pulled and relocated to the more populated areas near Colorado Springs.

Jake used his phone's GPS to orient himself and followed the dirt road until he reached Section E in the Grandview Cemetery. He stepped quietly; always cognizant he might not be alone in the graveyard. His peripheral vision caught two eyes staring at him. He froze and crouched low. He pulled his weapon from the holster and retrieved his night vision spyglass, another one of Wiley's specialty gadgets. The eyes raised and ran off. A cat. Jake holstered his gun. Stupid cat almost lost all nine lives tonight.

When he was in the cemetery earlier in the day, he noticed a large monument under a low-hanging blue spruce tree with the family name Crane. The grave of Michael Patterson Roundtree was fifteen feet inside the wagon wheel design from the Crane marker. The space between the spruce tree and the Crane marker offered him an ideal location to await his prey, with a clear vantage point of anyone approaching Roundtree's grave.

By ten minutes past midnight, Jake had settled beneath the canopy of the large spruce tree. Now came the hard part—sit and wait.

CHAPTER 50

At 1:45 a.m., Jake saw headlights on Mountain Avenue coming toward the cemetery. One of the things he'd noticed about the western states was most of the roads were oriented either East-West or North-South. And they were long and straight. When the vehicle reached the entrance, it made a u-turn, headed east, and slowed. Jake pulled out his spyglass and searched for the vehicle.

It stopped in front of the Fort Collins Housing Authority. Same place he'd parked. He hoped his vehicle wouldn't raise suspicion. He readied himself. It shouldn't be long now and he would be facing Rudd's blackmailer.

Almost ten minutes passed and no sign of anybody. He remembered Wiley's advice; *Always let your quarry come to you.* He remained silent. Then he heard it. A faint sound at first, steadily growing louder. A shuffle step followed by a clank. Shuffle step. Clank.

The noise grew closer when another sound startled him. He heard a snort and then the sound of hooves pounding against the ground. It grew stronger. The ground felt like a stampede. The blackmailer had startled several deer and one of them was running straight at Jake. He pulled himself flush against the Crane grave marker. The Grandview Cemetery was a regular zoo at night, he thought.

Jake listened. Nothing.

The shuffle step had stopped. Jake knew the blackmailer must be close.

Too close for him to move.

A few moments later the blackmailer moved enabling Jake to get a better fix on the intruder's location. He eased a glance around the stone marker.

His target, shovel in hand.

The dark figure was hunched over a grave. A beam of light flashed across the marker of Michael Patterson Roundtree.

Jake silently withdrew his gun and stepped from behind the Crane monument.

"Arthur DeLoach. I've been expecting you."

The old man jumped. Even in the pale moonlight, Jake thought he could see the distress on the old man's face.

"How? Who are you?"

"I've come to put an end to your grave robbing," Jake said.

"How…how could you know?"

"Wasn't difficult. The Internet is a wonderful tool. You can research anything you want, but it leaves a trail. A cyber trail. And that's what you did. You left a trail. And the breadcrumbs led me here."

"What are you talking about?"

"You never should have tried to blackmail the President."

"What are you talking about?" The old man truly sounded surprised. "I haven't blackmailed anyone."

"Mr. DeLoach, We know about everything. We know you either copied or scanned Ashley Regan's journal when she brought it to you for restoration. We know you've been selectively digging up graves with stolen artwork in the caskets. What you didn't keep in your Charleston home, you sold."

"Sold? I have sold nothing." The old man sounded indignant. "You have made presumptuous accusations. The Nazis were the thieves who stole those art pieces. All I wanted to do is return them to their rightful place, the museums."

"Everything in your home has been seized," Jake said. "All of the art confiscated. Everything you have done has been for naught."

"You've been in my home?"

Jake nodded.

"You don't understand. When Ashley Regan brought me the book, I knew its value. I speak German. I knew what was in that journal. If I hadn't done it, she would have." DeLoach said. "She is the one who would have sold them. I have an appreciation and understanding of great art. These pieces need to be displayed where art lovers can go and enjoy them. If she had taken them then there is no telling where they would have ended up. These pieces don't belong in someone's private collection. They belong to the people. They should be in a museum. Ashley Regan is an idiot."

"Ashley Regan is dead."

"Dead?" DeLoach wobbled on shaky legs. "Oh my. No one was supposed to get hurt. I didn't want anything like that to happen."

"You should have turned this over to the authorities. People have died. And now, you're going to jail."

"I don't understand. I was so careful. How did you know? How did you find me?"

"Like I said, you can't blackmail the President of the United States and expect to get away with it. Those emails you sent were traced back to your computer. A tracker virus was uploaded and we followed you from cemetery to cemetery. Your computer led me here."

"My computer is at home." DeLoach's voice had become somber. "I never sent any emails."

"No, but I did."

The voice came from behind him. Before Jake could turn around, a blunt metal object slammed into his back. He fell to his knees. Pain radiated across his upper back.

"Zula Mae. No." DeLoach yelled.

CHAPTER 51

The last thing he remembered was the old man yelling somebody's name. As he regained consciousness he heard two people talking. Arthur DeLoach and a woman. She must have been the one who hit him from behind. Jake's head throbbed after she hit him with something and knocked him unconscious. His back hurt. His neck hurt. He lay face down on the ground and listened, trying to recap in his mind what had just happened and plan his next move.

He'd never considered DeLoach might not be working alone. In retrospect, he should have. The man was old, very old, and probably incapable of digging up the graves himself. It stood to reason he needed an accomplice with a strong back.

Jake tried to move. The groan was involuntary.

"Should I hit him again, Mr. Arthur?" The woman asked.

"No, Zula Mae. He's had enough." DeLoach responded.

"But, Mr. Arthur. You heard him. He knows everything. We have to kill him."

"Nobody dies tonight, Zula Mae." DeLoach paused. "Are you responsible for sending that email? Did you really try to blackmail the President of the United States?"

"Yes sir, Mr. Arthur," Zula Mae said. "You said those paintings were worth millions of dollars but you're giving them away. I do all the digging and you get all the credit. I want something too. I read your translation of the journal and your genealogy study of the President. If you won't use it against her, I will. If I can't get anything from these paintings, then I can get something from her. She'll pay to keep me from telling the truth."

Jake felt his holster between his chest and the ground. It was empty. Then he remembered, his gun was in his hand when she struck him. He looked up at the woman. She was standing over him holding a shovel like a baseball bat ready to take another swing. Judging by her silhouette in the moonlight she was a few inches shorter than DeLoach but considerably thicker. There was something about their verbal exchanges that sounded intimate. Not like lovers, but companions. A familiarity with each other that led Jake to believe they'd known each other for years.

DeLoach stood next to her holding his gun.

"Put down the shovel, Zula Mae." DeLoach pointed the gun at Jake. "He won't be any trouble."

Zula Mae lowered the shovel.

DeLoach backhanded her across the face.

She let go of the shovel and fell to the ground.

"You idiot," DeLoach said. "I told you I had ensured we could never be caught. If you needed money, you should have spoken up."

"I'm sorry, Mr. Arthur." Zula Mae pleaded. "You're an old man and won't live many more years. What happens when you die? What will I do when you're gone? How will I survive? I'm too old to look for another job. I was only looking out for myself."

"You should have brought your concerns to me," DeLoach said. "Now look what you have done."

Jake started to get up. DeLoach was fast with the gun.

He turned the gun back at Jake. "Stay on the ground and keep your hands where I can see them," He said. "Now, who are you?"

"I work for President Rebecca Rudd. She knows I'm here, as do several others. There is nowhere for either of you to go. If you turn yourselves over to me now, I will help you work out a deal with the President."

From the corner of his eyes he saw Zula Mae move. She grabbed the shovel and swung it at DeLoach. The tool struck him in the back of his knees. The old man collapsed to the ground. Jake's gun tumbled behind a gravestone covered in darkness.

"You will never hit me again, old man," she yelled. Zula Mae slammed the back of the shovel across the old man's forehead then jammed the blade into his throat.

In the darkness, the moonlight shimmered off the blood gushing from the man's neck.

Jake wobbled when he tried to stand. The woman raised the shovel above her head and charged at him. The blade of the tool came crashing down toward him. He rolled sideways as the shovel blade smashed within inches of his face.

He kicked the shovel from her hands, bounded to his feet, and lunged at the woman's midsection tackling her to the ground. She landed against a stone marker with a grunt and fell to the grass.

Jake landed on top of her pinning her to the ground. Her arms swung wildly at his face. He blocked her swings with his arms and yelled, "Lady, stop fighting."

"Okay." She was winded and spoke in choppy words. "Just get off of me."

Jake pulled himself off of her and took a step back. He moved toward DeLoach when Zula Mae kicked out and made a leg sweep, knocking his feet out from under him. He fell to the ground and the woman pounced on him.

They rolled on the grass grappling to gain the advantage. She kicked at his crotch and missed. She turned her fingernails into weapons and scratched his face. He pushed her away with his left arm and landed a punch with his right fist across her jaw. "I said stop fighting. I don't want to hurt you."

She didn't listen and started swinging her fists at him. He dodged the first jab but her second attempt landed a blow to the side of his head. His already throbbing head pounded harder. Every heartbeat felt like a drum beating against the side of his brain.

He'd had enough. He realized he would have to end this with brute force.

He knocked her away with a heavy push, sprang to his feet, and stepped away from the woman.

She pulled herself to her feet still full of rage. Apparently unwilling to stop, she lowered her head and charged him like a bull ready to gore its victims. He sidestepped her approach and with both hands together, fingers interlocked, he clubbed her in the back of the neck sending her crashing headfirst into a monument. Her head thudded against the stone. She fell to the ground and didn't move.

"Damn, you're one crazy-ass bitch." He looked down at her then pulled out his penlight and searched behind the stone marker where his gun fell. After he found it, he tucked it back in his holster. He walked toward DeLoach's body and flashed the beam from his penlight onto DeLoach's face. He saw the old man's throat gaped open from the blade of the shovel. A pool of blood soaked into the grass under the man's head.

Jake leaned over and checked the old man for a pulse.

Arthur DeLoach was dead.

Jake didn't hear as much as felt her vibration through the ground. The same vibration he felt when the deer charged only softer. He turned and the woman was rushing at him with a knife in her hands. The moment called for a split second decision. No more fighting.

He stepped behind the stone marker of Michael Patterson Roundtree, withdrew his handgun, and leveled it at her charging silhouette.

He fired two shots into the center of the target.

Zula Mae staggered and fell to her knees. She sat on her heels. He remembered the Special Forces mantra his old friend Gregg Kaplan always recited—*Two in the chest, one in the head works 100% of the time.*

He took aim at the woman's head.

His finger tightened on the trigger.

He stopped, then relaxed his grip and lowered his gun.

Overkill, he thought.

The woman fell over.

Zula Mae, President Rebecca Rudd's blackmailer, was dead.

EPILOGUE

Jake Pendleton, Francesca Catanzaro, and Elmore Wiley sat in the Executive Conference Room located inside the Situation Room in the West Wing of the White House. Francesca had a bandage on her forehead and, since the last time he'd seen her in Nashville, had dyed her hair black. Wiley's arm was in a sling from the injury to his shoulder.

Rudd came in, sat down, and scanned through the documents in the folder. She didn't speak, not even a cordial greeting, just read in silence.

Tonight, the dark circles beneath her eyes were her most prominent feature. A lot had transpired over the past three days. The summit meeting was hailed a historic success. The resultant agreement considered a major step forward in the peace process by world leaders and a needed shot in the arm for the global economy. Rudd's public approval rating rose another ten points overnight. This first woman President now held the highest approval rating any President had ever received.

"Elmore," Rudd finally spoke, "I've always trusted your judgment. You've never steered me wrong. I did what you asked of me in Nashville." Rudd paused. "But now I've had time to consider the recent events and its impact on my Presidency. I have always held this job to the highest standards of honesty and dignity. To remain in office would be tantamount to a gross breach of power."

"Breach of power?" Wiley said. "Ms President, you need to look at the big picture. This country needs you. Right now, the world needs you. You are, hands down, the most influential person in the world. Even our enemies respect you and all that you've accomplished. To give up now would be to betray the trust every American has placed in you."

"Trust I do not deserve," Rudd said.

"Not true, ma'am." Jake spoke up. "Trust you have earned. You are the same woman you were one week ago. You still have the same passion and leadership that put you in this office."

"Under false pretenses, I'm afraid."

"How do you figure, ma'am?" Francesca said. "When you ran for office, were you aware of anything that would disqualify you as a candidate?"

"No, but I have that knowledge now, and it makes me ineligible to be President. And that's all that matters...*I know*. That's what I have to live with. If I don't step down, I would be in violation of my oath."

"With all due respect, Ms President, you're wrong." Wiley's voice sounded angry. "Why is *that* Constitutional requirement for presidency bothering you after three years in office? After everything you've accomplished, it doesn't make sense."

"You wouldn't understand," Rudd hesitated, and then continued. "I am no longer who I thought I was. I love this country and have always been proud to be an American...and now I've found out that it was all just a lie. Not only am I *not* a citizen of the country I love, my biological father was one of the worst murderers in history."

"Are you seriously going to contend that the natural-born citizen clause, something many feel is outdated, is so important that it trumps all the good you've done? Stepping down now is the wrong decision. Nothing good would come from it, only harm. Ms President, this is one of those times where you need to mindfully consider what is best for the country you serve. Put away your personal feelings of recent discoveries and focus on the positive things you have accomplished…and those you have yet to accomplish."

"I think it serves the country's best interest if I'm honest and forthright with what I know." Rudd said.

"Madam President," Jake looked at Wiley then back to Rudd, "then if that's the case I would assume it's in the country's best interest to also disclose that you had Senator Richard Boden executed."

The room went silent. Rudd glared at him. He could tell his statement took her aback.

Wiley pushed his chair away from the table and stood. "Jake is absolutely right. Almost every President in history has crossed the line at some point. And, just like you, they've had to deal with their own moral dilemmas. Many, to the detriment of this country. Just glance back in history at how many Presidents have crossed the line or as you put it, a breach of power, and most without any real consequences. Remember George W. Bush and the Iraq WMD debacle? How about Truman and the IRS corruption charges or Warren Harding and the Ohio Gang? Iran-Contra. Watergate. The list is long, and in most cases, trumps the out-dated natural-born citizen clause. In each incidence, the line was crossed because they believed it served the nation's best interest."

"But, I killed my own brother." Tears welled up in Rudd's eyes.

"And saved my life doing so," Jake interrupted.

Wiley looked at Jake and then turned back to Rudd. "Your brother, whom you loved, was about to kill an innocent man and you made the moral decision not to let that happen. You could've let him shoot Jake, but you chose to do what was right. *That's* what makes you a great leader." Wiley paused. "Besides, there was no bullet found in your brother's body."

"What?" Rudd's mouth gaped open. "But you all saw me shoot him."

"Rebecca," the informal nature of Wiley addressing the President by her first name caught Jake off guard, "the *official* autopsy report stated he died from blunt force trauma from the explosion. There is no mention of a gun shot wound at all."

Rudd was silent for a few seconds. Jake could tell she understood the true meaning of Wiley's last remark. "What about the fire?"

"According to the fire marshal's report," Wiley continued, "the explosion was the result of a faulty natural gas valve on the crematorium. Unfortunately your brother and mother were inside embalming a female corpse."

"Abigail Love?"

"Fled the country," Jake said. "She's on the lam and Interpol has already been advised."

"What about the journal? That's what started this in the first place. Where is the book, Elmore?"

"Nothing in it is incriminating." Wiley reached into his briefcase and pulled out the leather journal. He placed it on the table and slid it toward President Rebecca Rudd. "See for yourself."

Rudd opened the book and flipped through the pages. "Why are so many pages faded and illegible? And why is there is no mention of my mother? Why are some of the other entries missing as well?"

"Madam President, there is nothing missing." Jake said. "Everything in the journal was written in pencil and much of it had faded beyond the ability to restore. The book was inside a glacier for over 65 years. What did you expect?"

"And Ashley Regan?"

"Still missing along with her partner Samantha Connors." Jake said. "Apparent boating accident in Butler, Tennessee. Authorities have been searching the area where she was last seen and have found nothing. The sheriff sent dive teams into the lake but nothing will turn up."

"Christa Barnett?"

Francesca spoke. "Ms. Barnett had a regulator malfunction while quarry diving near Athens, Tennessee and was forced to surface without a decompression stop. She drove to Knoxville to seek medical attention. After a few days in a hyperbaric chamber at the University of Tennessee Medical Center, she made a full recovery. She believes that after she translated the journal for Regan and Samantha Connors, they doubled crossed her, took the loot for themselves, and staged the boating accident. She was very upset her lifelong friend betrayed her. Her only crime was translating the book for Regan."

"And the translation," Rudd asked, "what happened to it?"

"Still missing with Regan and Connors." Francesca replied.

"I notice there is no entry for Butler, Tennessee." Rudd said. "What happened to that?"

"Apparently, there never was one." Wiley pushed his glasses up and made a one-handed hair swipe. "Part of the ruse to set up the boating accident scenario."

"What about the emails from the blackmailer?"

Wiley sat back in his chair.

Jake shrugged his shoulders. "What emails?"

Rudd shook her head. "Arthur DeLoach and his 60 year old house keeper?"

"Sad case of double cross." Jake smiled. "DeLoach only wanted to return the art works to the museums but his housekeeper got greedy and tried to cut him out of it. She attacked him with a shovel during a grave robbery in Colorado. He apparently shot her twice during the attack. They both died on the scene." Jake looked at Wiley then Francesca. "There were no emails that I'm aware of. Do you know of any?"

The two shook their heads.

President Rebecca Rudd was silent for several seconds. Finally, "Elmore looks like you've wrapped everything up in a nice clean package." Rudd looked at Wiley. "But I still have to do this."

"Rebecca, if you do this, then you will certainly be removed from office, but not for the reasons you think." Wiley's voice changed. Jake noticed calmness in his tone. "Every piece of evidence pointing to your past says one thing, you were born in Nashville, Tennessee in 1946 to Matthew and Heidi Katzer. There is no evidence to suggest you are not a natural born citizen. If you try to refute it, you'll create chaos for the government and your party. People will lose confidence in, not just you, but the system as a whole. And after you fought so hard to gain that confidence. Your mental competence will also come into question."

The four sat silent for several minutes. Jake could tell President Rebecca Rudd faced a moral dilemma of great magnitude. But this wasn't her first. After the success of the summit meeting, she was a shoe-in for a second term, which meant this wouldn't be her last dilemma either. Wiley had anticipated that Rudd would have a change of heart and gave

Jake, Francesca, and George Fontaine meticulous instructions for sanitizing every aspect of Project Resurrection.

President Rebecca Rudd stood and walked across the room with the journal in her hands. She stood with her back to the table and tilted her head down. Jake could feel the tension in the room, not just from Rudd, but from Elmore Wiley as well.

Rudd took a deep breath. She raised her head, and with her back to them, finally spoke. "I guess we can't have the citizens of the United States believing their President has lost her ever-loving mind, now can we?" She turned around and faced them.

"No, ma'am." Francesca said. "This country is fortunate to have a leader like you."

Rudd held up the journal. "Any ideas how I should handle this?"

"I have one." Jake said. "You have a golden opportunity to turn Project Resurrection into a positive."

"I'm listening," the President said.

"Commission a military task force to exhume every casket listed in the journal that hasn't already been robbed. Have them remove the items, catalog and store what they find, then reinter the soldiers' remains. After all the stolen treasures have been recovered, announce to the world what you have found and return the recovered items to the country of origin. It's a win-win. The world recovers what the Nazi's stole from it in World War II and you can clear your conscience by righting the wrongs of Wolfgang Fleischer."

Rudd looked at him without speaking then she faced Elmore Wiley. "What do you think?"

Wiley looked at Jake. "I think Mr. Pendleton has offered you wise counsel."

"I think so too." Rudd walked over to her chair and picked up a portfolio. She looked at Jake and Francesca. "I can't thank you enough for your discretion and dedication. I owe you a debt of gratitude the likes of which I can never repay." She handed the portfolio to Elmore Wiley and turned to Jake and Francesca. "We'll be talking soon."

Wiley opened the portfolio and pulled out a document and a letter sized manila envelope. He held up the document. "I forgot to mention, the President and I have worked out a deal. From now on, your assignments will originate from here, the White House." Wiley handed Jake the envelope. "Here's your next assignment, I'll meet you back at Commonwealth in an hour."

Jake and Francesca left President Rebecca Rudd and Elmore Wiley alone in the Situation Room and were escorted out of the White House.

Jake opened the envelope in the backseat of one of Wiley's Black Crown Victoria limos.

"Well?" Francesca said. "Where are we going?"

Jake handed her the letter. "See for yourself."

"Interesting," she said, "this doesn't sound easy."

Jake looked at Francesca and smiled. "When I was in the Navy they used to say, *the only easy day was yesterday.*" Jake pointed to the letter. "We have to make a detour on the way, though."

"A detour? Where are we going this time?"

"Georgia."

"What for?" She asked.

"I need to get my mail."

"For real? What could possibly be in your mail that's so important we have to detour from our mission?"

"A key."

ACKNOWLEDGMENTS

First things first, to my wife Debi, who always gets first read, who sits in the shadows while I revel in the limelight, and who didn't complain when I dragged her with me from cemetery to cemetery during the research phase of *Breach of Power*. Thanks for keeping me in line, on track, and for reeling me in when I needed it. Thank you for your ideas, your suggestions, and your criticism. Without your valued input, these books would always be lacking. Lastly, thank you for your patience and support, as the arduous task of cranking out stories must seem like a never-ending process. I love you with all my heart and soul.

With each new book I write, the list of acknowledgements grows. I am indebted to those who have graciously volunteered their time and energy to steer this author in the right direction. Perhaps it's their occupational expertise or a past experience that has provided me, through our interviews and discussions, a rudimentary foundation to write about things I know nothing about. To each of those listed below, you have my sincerest gratitude. Thank you for making *Breach of Power* my best book yet.

Special thanks to Mary Fisher for the best book cover yet!

Thank you to the following for providing me with the good *stuff* to include in this story: G. J. (Cos) Cosgrove, Tim Eyerman, Jack Heard, Sgt. Jon Hepler, Alan Marsh at the Andersonville National Historic Site, and Alyce Nierman.

Thank you to Tom Colgan for his editorial advice and to Cheryl Duttweiler for providing *shrink* services to my characters along with her proofreading skills.

Some authors call them *test-readers*. Others call them *beta-readers*. Whatever the title, every author understands the value of extra eyes reading their material. Thanks to Bruce Evors, Scott Katzer, and Terrence Traut, along with authors Richard C. Hale and Dean K. Miller for your honest and unbiased, and unabashed input.

Whenever real people get their names in fiction stories, they run the risk of being cast as good, bad, and sometimes downright evil. Thank you to the *real* mother and son team of Heidi and Scott Katzer for making such evil antagonists. I hope your characters met your expectations.

Lastly I want to thank you, the reader, for buying this book. It is my genuine hope that you found this story entertaining and that those unexpected twists and turns left you smiling...or perhaps cussing...either way, it works for me.

WRITER'S NOTE

Research for *Breach of Power* took me from cemeteries in Nashville, Tennessee to glaciers in Alaska. From Fort Collins, Colorado to the Andersonville National Historic Site in Georgia. And from rural cemeteries in the North Georgia Mountains to Fernandina Beach, Florida. This story culminated from news articles that sparked my imagination to ask two simple questions: why & why not?

The first idea came from a news clip I read from Austria where two hikers found the remains of a man who was believed to have fallen in a crevasse in a glacier over 55 years prior. That got me thinking, why? Was it an accident? Suicide? Stupidity? Was he thrown into the crevasse? Was he running from someone? Why not?

Then one morning, my wife handed me a newspaper article about the mission called *Task Force Christman* and said, "This is pretty cool, maybe you can use it." A day or so later I read another article about stolen Nazi treasures that had recently been recovered. Why couldn't I draw a nexus between them all and call it fiction? Why not?

Now to separate fact from fiction—Zugspitze is the highest peak in Germany and sits on the German/Austrian border. The Schneefernerhaus Hotel and Resort and all the details about it are real. The climb from Garmisch to the summit of Zugspitze via the Höllentalferner glacier was taken from several actual accounts from hikers who have made this trek. It is as accurate as I could make it without taking the journey myself.

Within months after the release of *The Toymaker*, I was made aware of further spy drone enhancements with nanotechnology. The details about the miniature mosquito spy drone, nicknamed *Skeeter* in the book, are correct. Actually obtaining *official* specifications about the drone and its capabilities ventured into the "I can neither confirm nor deny" realm. So draw your own conclusions. It's a good bet the description is closer to accurate than anyone is officially willing to admit.

Mount Olivet and Calgary cemeteries in Nashville, as well as all the cemeteries mentioned in *Breach of Power* are real and accurately depicted. That's where the facts end. The events that took place in the cemeteries are fictional. There is no *Katzer Funeral Home*, and certainly not one across the street from Mount Olivet, so don't try to Google it, nothing will show up.

As I briefly mentioned above, *Task Force Christman* is a real mission mandated by Congress. I encourage you to look it up and read more about it as I just lightly touched on its details. Our soldiers did indeed work long midnight hours cataloging the entire Arlington National Cemetery.

Anderson National Historic Site: This place is amazing. I encourage each and every one of my readers to learn more about it. It is a part of this country's history that everyone should know existed. If you ever find yourself in West-Central Georgia, I strongly encourage you to take a day and explore the site.

The underwater town of Butler, Tennessee is real. The facts about it are accurate. The town was relocated to higher ground by the Tennessee Valley Authority as mentioned in the book. Although nearly all of Old Butler was moved to the ridge where New Butler now sits, some structures were left behind and not destroyed. The two buildings mentioned in *Breach of Power*, including the old jail, and the bridge are still at the bottom of Watauga Lake. The proximity of the bridge to the buildings was adjusted for the purposes of the story. Scuba divers occasionally dive to the bottom of the lake and the water is indeed cold and murky.

Grandview Cemetery in Fort Collins, Colorado is as depicted, and yes, deer nestle in the cemetery all year long. On my first visit, my son spotted several deer that had sought out the warm, dry ground beneath a large blue spruce tree where the February snowfall couldn't reach. During a separate visit, the mountains to the west of Fort Collins were under siege by raging wild fires. At night, if you looked to the west, you could see the amber glow of the flames as they consumed the forests. It was sad to see this devastation in such a beautiful part of our country.

We've all heard of lost Nazi treasures. Hitler's Third Reich plundered banks and museums stealing anything they thought of value. Several priceless art pieces remain missing today, several of which were believed destroyed by the Nazis. Along with art, the Nazis stole large amounts of gold and silver. Some of these treasures were stored in salt mines. When it became evident the Third Reich was about to fall, many Nazi commanders fled Germany with their caches. Some of these officers even stored treasures in chests and sunk them to the bottom of some of Germany and Austria's mountain lakes with intentions of later returning to recover their cache. Others tried moving their hoards to Italy only to be captured in Austria. Much of this stolen Nazi treasure remains unaccounted for today.

CPSIA information can be obtained at www.ICGtesting.com
Printed in the USA
BVOW03s0204041113

335410BV00002B/66/P